LOVE REDEEMED
LOVE'S IMPROBABLE POSSIBILITY
BOOK FOUR

LOVE BELVIN

MKT PUBLISHING, LLC

LOVE REDEEMED

from the *Love's Improbable Possibility* series

Book 4

by Love Belvin

Published by MKT Publishing, LLC

Copyright © 2014 by Love Belvin

All rights reserved. This book may not be reproduced, scanned, or distributed in any printed or electronic form without written permission from the author. Please do not participate in or encourage piracy of copyrighted materials in violation of the author's rights. This book is a work of fiction. Names, characters, places, and incidences are fictitious and the product of the author's imagination.

ISBN: 978-1-950014-68-2 (Hardcover)
ISBN: 978-1-950014-17-0 (Paperback)
ISBN: 978-1-950014-13-2 (eBook)

MKT Publishing, LLC
First print edition 2014 in U.S.A.

Cover design by Marcus Broom of DPI Design

"May these words of my mouth and this meditation of my heart
be pleasing in your sight,
Lord, my Rock and my **_Redeemer_**."

(Psalm 19:14 New International Version)

CHAPTER 1

Rayna

I jump right into work with an interview for an assistant. The candidate is the last of many screenings over the past two weeks. Sarah-Megan Shepller is a promising twenty-three-year-old student, studying to be a licensed physical therapist. Secretly, her name tickles me. I have to call her Sarah-Megan as she has two first names like the actress, Lisa-Raye McCoy. She's sharp and extremely knowledgeable about techniques and treatment plans. She seems to say all the right things and projects the confidence needed to command my attention. Sarah-Megan is the only qualified candidate who's available to start right away, which furthers my intrigue. According to her renowned affiliations, she's committed to the profession. We even know a few people in common, professionally.

Ahhh! So there is a bit of sunlight after yesterday's bitter storm.

Yesterday was god-awful. Learning the paternity of Tara's baby not only sheds light on my future with Azmir, but it also brings with it increasing doubts about being able to fully trust him. He has so many layers, countless secrets. It makes me wonder what other pieces of him are floating around, hiding themselves from me, the woman who's agreed to be his wife. The prospect is frightening. These discoveries: learning of his pseudo affair with Dawn Taylor, him withholding the paternity results, his lying about his knowledge of it just before proposing—they counteract my efforts to settle my heart and find security in my relationship with him. All day, these dubious thoughts loom despite my efforts to push them into the recesses of my overactive mind.

After the interview, I attend to two patients who actually followed their treatment plans. I can tell their rehabilitation is progressive and can give approximations for complete repairs and healings. A busy workday is providing the best short-term remedy to my wrestled mind. My morning is going well until Sharon pages me, informing me of a visitor. She knows to have them wait until I instruct her otherwise. Since Harrison's visit and our current A.D. Jacobs' imposed security, there is now a stricter protocol to follow.

"Who is it, Sharon?"

"Ms. Tara Harrison."

My heart skips a beat and I let out a deep sigh. *I knew this morning was going too well to be true!* I don't want a show and feel I could handle Tara *physically* if she has plans to become recklessness.

"Show her to my office, please."

"Okay," Sharon agrees.

Moments later, there's a knock at the door, and I know it's Sharon showing Tara in.

Tara is always flawless, well-poised, with no detail out of place. She's wearing fitted indigo blue jeans, a black sheer shirt, and an off-white blazer with black booties. It's clear she's fashion forward. Every time I see her she dons something impressive. I wonder how much of her style is attributed to Azmir. *How much of my style is accredited to Azmir?* Her large hoop rhinestone earrings level her high and very long ponytail. She looks great. I'm relieved to see she doesn't have her baby with her.

She was entirely out of line for that last night.

"Tara." I stand and greet her, trying to sound as if I'm raising the white flag, though deep inside I'm trying to command the wherewithal to battle another round with her. This will be difficult because I'm still fatigued from the events of last night.

Sharon turns on her heels, leaving the door slightly ajar.

"Rayna...or is it Dr. Brimm?" she asks with a hidden sneer.

"Rayna Brimm will work just fine. How may I help you?" *Seeing as you are in the stalkerish habit of visiting me at my most intimate places. What's next—church?*

"I need to talk to you. I think I have a handle on you now." She walks the short walls of my small office, observing my accolades.

"A handle. *Oh?*" My favorite line used to bait people.

When she makes her way to my desk Tara takes a seat, slowly depositing herself into the chair across from my desk. After a beat, I follow suit.

"Yes. I really didn't like you—well actually I hated you—when I heard about you and...it's clear why. I have to admit I was clearly knocked off my feet yesterday when you told me you lived with Azmir. I had no idea." Tara issues a penetrative glare. I'm curious as to why she's here. She snorts, "Imagine my surprise when I learned he no longer lived in the same place where I last visited him for the past four years or so." Then her gaze travels into the distance as she murmurs, much to herself, "I can't believe how much our worlds have drifted. Then there's you," her contemptuous glower returns to me. "...the new girl, who has all of this..." She waves at the office.

Oh, how much the fruit does not fall far from the tree. She's sounding like her father.

"I swear I paid no attention to the potential seriousness of it until yesterday, when I saw you two...*together*."

Hmmmm...

I stand to go and close the door just in case she tries to get slick. "Tara, seeing Azmir and me attempt to settle in after a day's work hardly qualifies as seeing us "*together*."

I return to my seat only to meet her contemplative gaze again.

"Oh," Tara's brow rises up her forehead. "I saw you two... together." She lowers her head at the word.

With my eyebrows narrowed, my head tilts, and I ask, "What exactly do you mean, Tara?"

"Let's not be coy, Rayna." Tara sighs long and hard, seemingly forcing out her next round of words. "I heard Azmir yelling when I was waiting on the elevator, and I went back to the door to try to hear what was going on. I couldn't, so I tried my luck at opening the door, and to my surprise it opened." A sinister smile etches her beautiful face. "We came back inside, and I tried to listen more, but couldn't hear anything from the foyer. You know how large that place is." She scoffs before continuing. "So, I went down the hall to *your* bedroom. I could hear mumbling, but could hardly make out the words, so I left Azina at the door and tiptoed into the walkway of the room. I guess you guys were in the closet, but I could finally make out your words and I listened."

She pauses to read my reaction. I'm floored at the thought of our privacy being impeded upon.

"Okay," I urge her with squinted eyes. I want to make sure she's saying what I'm afraid she's saying. I silently pray she isn't prepared to tell me what seems to be, in slow motion, her direction.

She groans as though she's wounded. "When I heard him beg you not to leave him, my chest caved in. I couldn't believe my ears." Tara's eye slowly seals. "Never in a million years would I have ever thought I would hear Azmir so vulnerable, so...needy. I've known him for quite some time and a part of my issue with him was he was very reserved and not emotionally expressive." There's a pregnant pause as we both measure her last revelation. "Anyway, I thought I was caught when I saw him carry you out of the closet. I had gotten so caught up in your fight I lost all senses." Tara shakes her head and places a shaky hand on the side of her nose as she collapses her face into her hand. "I knew I was crossing boundaries—legal ones, but I couldn't leave."

My heart's pounding in my chest and I catch my head falling back from my neck giving out on me. I can't believe what I'm hearing.

"Tara, what are you saying?" The world stops spinning on its axis and my bottom lip hit the floor.

Tara scoots up in her chair, with her voice cracking as though she's trying to keep from breaking down and says, "I saw the two of you *together*."

I feel a gut blow.

"Tara. Are. You. Saying. You. Watched. A. Very. Private. And. Intimate. Moment. Between. My. Fiancé. And. Me?" I speak slowly to be clear. I cannot believe this is happening to me.

She exhales before answering. "Yes." Her shoulders go limp and her eyes dance on the floor below. "I saw him go down on you...like his life depended on it, begging you to stay with him. He told you he *needed* you. *Wow!*" She snorts in disbelief. "I saw how naturally and...quickly you responded to him." Her voice croaks. She isn't able to control her emotions any longer. My head drops to my chest. I feel violated and exposed. I can hear no more.

"The way he made love to you..." Another pause. I close my eyes, shaking my head at her audacity.

What has become of my life?

Her voice becomes more projected, causing my gaze to rise to meet hers. Her beautiful chestnut eyes are brimming. Tara's losing control. "It was as if you were his lifeline. I can't stop wondering if he'd ever had those feelings...or that need for me." She wipes the increasing flow of tears from her eyes and takes a deep breath. "I remember when things were good, and I swear I *still* can't recall that type of passion from him." She pauses. And I can't breathe. Steeling in my seat, can't move if I willed myself to. "I can also remember so many times when he asked me to prepare myself for better because he was working for a better life. I didn't get it. I just thought he didn't get me. *He wants to change me* is what I would tell my mom." At this point, she isn't giving me eye contact. I can tell she's rooted in thought.

Is this a *come to Jesus* meeting?

"When he was with you, he was so desperate." Shaking her head, she seems broken.

"What is the point of telling me all of this, Tara? You were wrong for coming back into the apartment unannounced!" I furrow my brows and ask through gritted teeth, "Why are you even here?"

Tara's unmoved by my animated terse. She doesn't flinch or grimace. But she does answer. "Because I now realize how much I've lost. I never knew Azmir could be so...emotionally available. He had always seemed to be above me and dissatisfied." She pauses again, this time giving me room to consider her words.

The Azmir she's been describing is not the man I encountered in the cafeteria of his recreation center last January. He's not the man I lie down with each night. Not the sensitive man who employs patience and a soft hand in his approach to me.

"*I don't know...*" Tara exhales, snapping me from my musing. "If you decide to stay, then I'll have to live with my transgressions. I'm sure you've heard about my relationship with D-Struct and considering the way he was with you last night, possibly by Azmir—though he never confided *shit* in me. It was stupid, but I refuse to be judged because no one knew what it was like constantly feeling like I wasn't good enough for Azmir. I mean, damn, I knew he was older, but I wasn't ready for rocking chairs. He wanted me to be something I wasn't. I hated his hood ass friends." Her curious eyes wander over to me. "I don't know how you're doing with them, but felt if Azmir was on the come up, *why in the hell would he still hang out with the likes of Petey and Kid?* And that Wop... Ugh!" She grimaces as she shakes her head resolutely. "I wanted no part of them."

Hearing her assessment of Petey and Kid is like a blow to the gut. They were Azmir's inner circle, my friends. None of them deserving of the disdain she's expressed. I recall Chanell, Liz, and Tionne's description of her, and can now confirm they were on par with their depiction of Tara. For a minute, I consider asking for her take on Mark and Eric to confirm her sense of superiority, but I can't formulate the words, so I remain quiet, afraid of the next discovery or confirmation of just how snobbish and selfish Tara indeed is.

"Then he had the nerve to close up on me," she continues her forlorn invective rant. "It was like we were in the same space, but he was eons away. I couldn't take that shit anymore, so I started hanging out more and...I guess I got caught up. There were a lot of perks with being his girl. I got a lot of attention," she confesses with a shrug. "I slipped up." Tara shakes her head again, trying to snap out of her trance.

"I fucked up and got pregnant in the meantime. I wanted so badly for my baby to be Azmir's, but I knew it wasn't and decided to try my luck. Azmir's no dummy, so it was no surprise when he asked for a DNA test and kept pressing the issue." Her eyes rise to mine and in no time slant. Mine narrow.

Where is she going with all of this?

"If you fuck up, I will be waiting in the wings. And so help me god, I will push, crawl, beg, and fight for another chance with him. I will come with full force and with no thoughts of you or your marriage *if* you make it to that point." Tara speaks each word through clenched teeth and with conviction.

"*If?*"

"Yeah." The sinister smile resurges. Something is brewing in her brain. "I saw the video. This morning, after trying to fall asleep with a broken heart and having another sleepless night with a newborn, I got an e-mail from a good friend of mine of you deep throating some random island guy. I thought to myself *she's no different from me...just a fuck-up away*," she giggles.

I stare at her in sheer disbelief of her boldness. She returns the gaze, telling me she's most sincere with her threats of watching my throne of Azmir's heart. *Should I take this seriously or is this simply a desperate attempt at her trying to get into my head?* She doesn't falter in her gape and neither do I. Tara has presented a challenge to me I can't refuse. She doesn't deserve Azmir. More than that, he's mine. She blew it, not me.

My heart nearly leaps from my chest when I hear the door burst open. Two large figures fly in, flared and brewing. Instinctively, my back flies into my chair and my mouth swings open. Azmir looks at me with examining eyes and then at Tara with a derisive glower.

His head cocks to the sides as he calmly utters in between a flexing jaw, "You are really testing the bounds of my patience, Tara." I hear the air roughly sloughing from his flared nostrils. "Have you any idea just how much in violation you are?"

Without a tremble, she comments back, "We're just having a civil conversation...like old buddies."

I watch as she tries to conceal her mirth. Does she like seeing him worked up like this? *Does she enjoy his attention, no matter the cost?*

John, my assigned security detail, is standing guard by the door. My eyes bounce back and forth between Tara and Azmir. I idly wonder where he's come from. He said he had a meeting in Culver City, which was nearly an hour away *without* traffic. *And how did he know she was here in my office?*

Trivia aside, he looks overwhelmingly dapper in his trousers, matching vest, crisp white dress shirt, and brilliant blue tie, once again stretching the bounds of virile sophistication. I suppose he left his suit jacket wherever he's just flown from. I rarely see him in three-piece suits. Perhaps that's the etiquette when meeting with a bank. His height and confident poise all work together, giving him the classic authoritative and commanding appearance he radiates. I notice the slight swelling in his bottom lip that must have come from our altercation last night.

Jesus, Rayna! I internally berate myself.

"I've been patient, I've been generous, *and* I've recently learned I've even taken risks I wasn't aware of, trying to soften the blow of our separation." Azmir inches nearer to her and bends his lengthy frame to get close to her face. "If I have to tell you to stay the fuck away from her once more, I swear on my life, you will see a cold and unrelenting side of me that will haunt you until your fucking death."

His Brooklyn tongue and tone is chilling, similar to his warning to me earlier in his car, but this time more vile. A chill runs through me.

Tara gasps and I can see her cringe in her seat. I doubt she was expecting this type of response from him. She isn't alone.

"I was about to leave, Azmir," Tara shrieks.

Just that quickly, her demeanor changes, like it did last night when she learned I didn't know Azmir was not her child's father. She's now afraid; no more cockiness coming from her direction as she shakily stands, gathering her purse. Tara heads for the door as John's opening it, and in true melodramatic fashion, like her father, she leaves me with parting words.

"Rayna," she calls out to me, causing me to rise in a knee-jerk reaction. My nerves are likely just as frayed as hers now. *So, I'd assume.* With my full attention, she warns, "The wings can be lonely, but it's only temporary...until *you* leave the stage."

In the next beat, "Tara," I call out, "...my wing days are over. I'm in the starring role now. Have a nice life." I offer a soft smile. "I plan to."

Tara wears her smuggish smirk as she leaves. Azmir's on her heels after looking over to me with his nose still flared and jaw still flexing. "I'll be outside at five, waiting to go to your session."

Awww...great! Just what I needed.

I had hoped he would grant me time alone this afternoon.

It would take days, if not weeks, to process all that has gone down over these past few days. The blows just keep coming, relentlessly.

I try to continue my day without breaking down, and I hope and pray for no more unexpected visits or revelations. Azmir sends lunch over, as usual, eliminating the need for me to go out, no doubt. I haven't heard from him since he left my office with Tara, and I'm mortified at the prospect of telling him we had a peeper in our bedroom last night during one of our most sacred times together.

How could she watch two people have sex—her ex no less?! Is she psycho?

I have to tell him. No matter how hard it will be, he has a right to know. I mean, I would want to know. I'm still pissed with him, but that doesn't counteract his need to be made aware of Tara's major breach of our privacy.

The afternoon runs through much less eventful. I meet with the other therapists to confer my candidate recommendations and am surprised I'm not alone in my selection. During my final patients, anxiety collects in my belly about my looming conversation with Azmir. I've thought of several ways to break it to him; some elaborate and others more concise. It really doesn't matter. It simply has to be done.

At five minutes after five, I walk out of the office and to Azmir's car where Ray is waiting for me with the door open. I slide in to find Azmir finishing a call.

"I'll have to take a look at my schedule to see if I can fit the trip in." He sighs, appearing exhausted, yet deliciously handsome in his three-piece suit. His compelling fragrance appeals to my libido. "I know, Kyle; I am fully aware of this. Yeah. No, I'm not saying that at all. What I am saying is I will not make an unnecessary trip out there if you're not ready to play ball. Unlike you, I don't like being a bachelor; I have an all-consuming personal life I'd like to maintain." He gives a sexy chortle, I assume, in concert with Kyle on the other side of the phone. "Gotta go, Kyle." He ends the call.

Azmir turns to me with a hint of a smile. I'm not sure what, if anything, he's going to say.

Five-four-three-two-one...

"Azmir, Tara saw us last night," I let the words spill from my mouth, giving him no eye contact. Instead, I fix my gaze on the back of Ray's headrest. "All of it."

Wheeeeeeew! I did it. I can now look at him.

"All of what?" he mutters, his chin is tilted and there's shocking humor in his eyes. I'm not sure if he's caught on to the seriousness of what I've said. So, I shuffle my body to face him, lean in and qualify, "She watched us...have sexual...relations in your bedroom." My face is now slanted toward my lap, making my words clear so he can get the complete picture.

"She was in our bedroom last night...after I told her to leave?" Humor disappears from his eyes upon the revelation.

I nod my head as my eyes stay glued to his, happy he's gotten the message.

He turns his head to the window and slowly brushes his lower face with his hand, clearly exasperated. With a mirthless chuckle, he mutters, "Ain't that some shit."

I exhale and turn to face my own window, retreating to my haunted thoughts. *We have so much we need to work out in order for us to work, MirMir.* I sulk internally at the overall state of our relationship.

"How do you feel about that?" His voice is low, empathetic.

I don't want Ray to hear, so I whisper. "I don't know," I shrug. "I was more concerned about how you'd feel."

He slants his head slightly. "Why?"

"Because you were...*raw*...and emotional, which is *very* unlike you. Even *I* was surprised to see you open up the way you did last night." I shook my head at the realization of Azmir's stripped state being bared to Tara. "To hear you speak the words you spoke. It was an extremely personal moment you wouldn't want exposed to anyone, much less your ex."

I can't believe he's asking for an explanation!

He takes a minute to absorb my words, even adds a nod of assent to my sentiment. Within a few beats, he speaks again, gazing deep into my eyes, "I couldn't give a damn about anybody knowing how I feel about you." Azmir pauses, using his penetrative eyes to bear into my soul, beckoning my full understanding. "No, I'd never be so exposed to anyone else, but I have no problem expressing myself to you. I need you to know this, Rayna. You will be my wife. There is no emotion or act I will conceal."

I bite back a cry. His words sear me. I don't want to break down; it isn't the right time. "As far as Tara, I'll take care of her." He shrugs. "Who knows. Maybe now she understands our new reality. After learning this I'm still baffled at why she showed up to your job." Azmir goes back to the window, reflectively massaging his chin.

"That brings up a good question: Where were you this morning and how did you know she was there? You told me you were due in Culver City."

Azmir takes his time providing an answer. He's still window watching, contemplating from that view. Without looking at me, he murmurs so low I can barely hear him, "I changed the meeting place. I didn't want to leave you in LBC without transportation. Your security detail called me about Tara when he realized she wasn't a patient."

And I see why he's merely audible, it's all bull! He didn't want to leave me without transportation? *No! You didn't want me to have a good excuse to leave the premises without your permission!* This is crazy. To keep from having another blow up, I sit in silence the rest of the trip to the church.

Inside the administration building sitting behind the main church, Azmir walks me in and is standing, viewing the artwork on the walls while I sit, waiting pensively for Pastor Edmondson. I feel like a kid observing Azmir's tall frame in his three-piece suit, no doubt appraising the spot from inch to inch. Even on God's property I'm aroused by his physique.

Flashes of the night before pop in mind. *He was so passionate and desperate for me.* Tara wasn't alone in her shock of his behavior. Azmir has always exuded coolness and composure. *What came over him?* Was it something I gave off, or what he wants me to be? At the risk of sounding like Tara, *I* don't know if I'm on his level. I don't know if I'm enough for Azmir. I think in due time these insecurities would egress, but now I've accepted his marriage proposal and wonder if we were moving too fast.

The door to the back offices opens and the clicking sound snaps me from my absorbed thoughts. Pastor Edmondson's eyes go straight to Azmir, unavoidably, due to his undeniable magnetic presence.

Azmir turns to him as Pastor Edmondson intuitively extends his arm, "Azmir! To what do I owe this surprise? I saw you in service the other day and was saddened Rayna didn't bring you around back so I could meet you." Pastor Edmondson is so excited and clearly expresses it. "But you're here today in the flesh. I'm John Edmondson, the senior pastor here at *Holy Deliverance Tabernacle Church*." He's sporting a genuine and eager smile as he greets Azmir. "I've heard so much about you. It is a true pleasure to meet you."

"Azmir Jacobs," Azmir gives a gentle smile. "Rayna has had great things to say about you, and I am indebted to your work with her." My breath hitches. "Under your counsel, I've witnessed great changes. The pleasure is all mine."

"Oh, I would say much of her transformation has been inspired by a man who cares deeply for her and has motivated her change," Pastor Edmondson replies while still shaking Azmir's hand as I hold my breath. "Congratulations on the engagement. You've chosen well."

My heart fills with elation. Pastor Edmondson has never doted on me this way during our sessions. He's always been encouraging and attentive, but to hear him speak *of* me is overwhelming.

Azmir turns to me tentatively and murmurs, "I am truly a blessed man, Pastor. Thank you very much." And then returns his attention to Pastor Edmondson.

"Why don't we head on back to my office?" Pastor Edmondson opens the door and gestures for Azmir to step in first.

I stand and dart my eyes to Azmir. *What? Is this why he came?*

With a soft chuckle he says, "Oh, no, Pastor. Rayna and I are down to one car today. I only rode in with her. I'll wait out here until she's done."

"Certainly, you didn't come all this way to sit in the waiting room. Please join us—that's if Rayna doesn't mind." He glances my way, asking my permission. My mouth is wide open, but nothing comes out. This is all so unexpected.

I carry my gaze up to Azmir who speaks up, "I actually have a few calls and e-mails to return. I'll be more than occupied out here," he urges in his CEO mien.

Pastor Edmondson releases an exhale and admonishes me through his eyes before saying, "We won't discuss anything betraying your confidence in our private sessions." He looks over to Azmir, "Come on. This is as good a time as any." Pastor Edmondson's impelled urging doesn't go unnoticed. Either I blatantly say no and risk offending them both or I bite the bullet and grant Azmir's attendance in my counseling session. That latter option feels less confrontational.

Azmir catches on to my assent and extends his arm, motioning for me to go ahead of him.

Inside of Pastor Edmondson's spacious office, he asks us to take a seat before him and brings a chair over to complete our newly formed triangle. He sits with his pad and pencil as always and begins with, "Azmir, I just want you to know I am a licensed psychologist as well as the pastor of *Holy Deliverance Tabernacle Church*. My wife is a licensed marriage and family therapist. We've combined our spiritual callings with our professional passions, making this assembly a fully encompassed community. With that being said, all things discussed today will be held in strict confidence, in compliance with my professional oath."

Azmir nods firmly in agreement. Then Pastor Edmondson turns to me, "So, Rayna, how would you like to handle this session. We can pick up from last week...or perhaps free-style to include Azmir?"

"I don't know. Whatever you prefer." I'm out of my usual bounds.

He smiles kindly. "Okay... Well, why don't we start with the Proverbs thirty-one passage Twanece had you read. What are your thoughts on the virtuous woman?"

Twanece Edmondson is his wife and the first lady of *Holy Deliverance Tabernacle Church*. When I told them about my engagement, they were both beside themselves in cheer. She quickly instructed I read Proverbs thirty-one to get an idea of what type of woman God is calling all women to be. It also encompasses the role of the wife.

"She's impossible," I express, adamantly. "And quite frankly, encourages my anxiety about this whole marriage thing." I can see Azmir shifting in his seat from my peripheral view.

"She is quite the consummate woman, isn't she?" Pastor Edmondson chuckles.

I shake my head, "My goodness... I don't know how one person can possess so much confidence, wisdom, and faith. I mean, I'm overwhelmed just trying to find where I fit into his universe," I trill, referring to Azmir. "I've been focused on building a small space in the corner of it so I don't interrupt anything else. But even that doesn't seem to be working for me."

"A small space?" Pastor Edmondson echoes.

I speak with caution, realizing I may have loosened my filter with that previous statement. Then I acquiesced to the moment and put it all out there. "Yeah, when I decided to move in with Azmir, I told myself I wouldn't nag him...I wouldn't be the type of woman who wants to take over. I knew he was an extremely busy and successful man. I felt if luck would have it, he would want more with me, and then I would take the very little I could and run with it. Then we started the **Purpose Driven Life** journey last summer and I learned it wasn't luck, but a blessing to be with someone and not alone because God didn't create us to isolate us...and I deserve to be loved. I welcomed the opportunity Azmir was giving me but..." I caution my flow of emotions.

"Take your time," Pastor Edmondson soothes.

I steal a glance over to Azmir, who sits, watching intently with his legs crossed and chin resting on the palm of his hand, fingers splayed long and elegantly about the side of his face. It's hard to think in his titillating presence. He's just...*beautiful*. He narrows his eyes, confused by my gaze, causing me to self-consciously look over to Pastor Edmondson, who sits patiently.

Oh!

"Well, lately there has been a crazy turn of events that's caused me to wonder if I'm enough for him." I turn to see Azmir's grimace. *Crap!* "I've had recent discussions with people from Azmir's past and in these exchanges it became clear there is so much that makes up this great man, and I'd have a lot of catching up to do in order to be an appropriate life partner to him."

"Why do you think you're insufficient as you are?" I can sense Pastor Edmondson getting edgy. I hate having to express myself, and this is why. It takes too much effort and pressure!

"It's not what you think. I'm done with thinking I somehow don't deserve a relationship or love. Neither do I question his attraction to me." Pastor Edmondson exhales in relief. Something he never does. I need to reassure my development of my self-image. "I know...I know!" I raise both hands in defense. "I'm a good-hearted, educated, and independent woman. Any man would want, at least, those qualities. Yeah...I'm beautiful and attractive...blah-blah-blah!" I wave off. "We're past those discoveries. Besides, even Azmir has assisted in *that* department."

I look over to Azmir, who gives a mirthful snicker through hooded eyes. I have to quickly shift my focus from him. I then notice Pastor Edmondson blushing in embarrassment.

I recline in my chair. "I don't know... Azmir has money, and that provides *much* of what I think a wife can bring to the table. He has a cook, cleaners, several assistants, a wealth of businesses, narrowing his chances of ever going broke. He has people vying for his attention and friendship. He can have any woman he wants. Look at him!" I swing my arm loosely in Azmir's direction. "A lack in any of those areas I've mentioned is where a wife—a suitable partner could pick up. At least the role of a wife I'd seen coming up and what the Proverbs thirty-one passage describes. I don't know where to pick up and be needed in his life." I raise my brows, indicating my need of a break in speaking.

"Azmir, would you like to add something here?" Pastor Edmondson invites him into the conversation.

Huhn?

Things just got real. This is no longer a monologue. Now it's a discussion; something I'm not sure I'm up for.

Azmir sits up and rests his elbows on his knees, in a defenseless posture. With an expectant pause he utters, "I don't know what to say, because I'd never thought of my life being so full and complete until you moved in." He exhales, appearing to be very contemplative. I want to throw him a lifeline by telling him he doesn't have to feel obligated to speak. But before I can formulate the words, he continues, "When I met you, I thought you were *extremely*...attractive—putting it mildly in front of the pastor." Azmir throws a glance over to Pastor Edmondson.

"And when I got the opportunity to get to know you, for the first time in a long time, I felt an overwhelming sense of rejuvenation—and the first time I'd felt it from a person. I wanted to be in your world...hell—*excuse me Pastor Edmondson*—I feel like I'm still trying to claw my way into your heart." Azmir sits back in his seat and silence coats the room for a moment or two. I'm now steeled in my chair, considering his words.

Before I know it, Azmir speaks again. "When you smile my heart flutters, when you're indifferent my mind churns, when you cry my stomach twists, and when you run my chest tightens. I know my world is complicated, but it's by no means full without you." He turns his penetrative gaze upon me. "I just ask that you work *with* me to find our way."

I can't believe his affirmation and in front of a total stranger. I'm speechless.

"Azmir here seems to be firm in his take on your relationship," Pastor Edmondson surmises, speaking to me. Then he turns to Azmir and offers, "But separate of your relationship with Rayna, I hear uncertainty in your position on your own life. I'd like to sit down and help you sort through them as well as take on premarital counseling sessions with you."

"I don't know about that." Azmir stretches his lids and his brows lifts. "I'd have to take some time to consider it." His words are even, but firm.

"Do you mind if I ask why?"

"I'll be completely honest with you, Pastor. I'm sure much of your guidance will include elucidating all the wrongs in my life and practices, and quite frankly, I'm not so inclined to subject myself to that scrutiny. I'm a decent man, trying to marry an extraordinary woman. Not trying to get converted."

Pastor Edmondson gives a full compassionate smile reaching his eyes. It's as if Azmir's blunt rejection somehow bounces off him.

"I can totally understand your apprehensions and can validate them as well. Historically, so much of Christian-dome included condemning people to hell and ostracizing the wounded." I muzzle my *amen*. Pastor Edmondson sits up in his chair, "But Azmir, all I want to do is tell you about a friend name Jesus, Who loves you and wants to meet you where you are to demonstrate His love, grace, and power. It is not my concern what you used to do; neither do I want to measure your imperfections. That isn't necessary for this type of introduction."

Azmir shoots him a look of disbelief. "Pastor, with all due respect, I'm sure one of the first things that will come up is our sexual practices and how we should handle them moving forward. It's not something I'm willing to discuss or debate. Ever."

I'm beginning to get nervous. Azmir is a man of strong authority; an alpha male and I don't like his resolute tone with my pastor. And I know he's most rigid in his stance about sex with me. *I mean, look at how he reacted when I suggested we go without in Tahiti.*

Pastor Edmondson chuckles, "Azmir, I am very clear on the Bible's stance on fornication. I fully agree with it and can give you countless reasons why it is a solid edict, but I'd much rather discuss where your heart is now and condition that first, to make room for God's will for your life. Rayna can tell you that it is not mine or my wife's practice to condemn, but to nurture and prepare hearts for God's love and instruction. I'm fully aware you live together and am overjoyed you've asked for her hand in marriage. I would like to prepare you for a lifelong, sustainable, and flourishing marriage using godly principles. That is all."

Pastor Edmondson rises from his chair, and we follow suit, preparing to end the session. He walks to Azmir and me without his previous warm smile. And with a proffered hand to Azmir he says, "You're a good man, a true leader. Very few warriors of your caliber are made anymore, Azmir. You will be of great help to the kingdom. I would like for you to consider this."

Azmir stiffens as he gives Pastor Edmondson a contemplative gaze. I can tell he's trying to gauge Pastor Edmondson's motives and authenticity.

Within seconds, Azmir takes his hand and says, "I'll certainly consider it, Pastor Edmondson. This has been very enlightening. Thank you for having me."

Pastor Edmondson humbly nods, "The pleasure was all mine

and gratitude should be given to Rayna for providing this connection. Good evening, folks." His smile returns.

I say my goodbyes and we leave, heading to the marina. The drive is quiet as I'm sure Azmir wrestles with recounts of the session just as I am. Only my thoughts are rushing in and the phenomenon of zapping neurotransmitters is rapid in my brain. All evening, things about my ambiguous relationship with Azmir keep replaying but coming now with more clarity. This man loves me. For months, I've confused his offerings of a commitment for strong attraction or the traditional chase he and I agreed to last January in the cafeteria of his recreation center.

All this time I've misunderstood what he's been offering, what's been taking place between us. Being with Azmir has conjured deficiencies that scared me once I recognized them. I realized a while back that I couldn't recognize the essence of his desire for me because I didn't love myself enough to feel worthy of it. I'd always thought when people who professed to love me were done, they simply moved on from my life, even my mother. She had escaped the world of parenting when she found something more compelling to occupy her time. No one other than Michelle stayed past my insecurities, my fears. Even her force of love I'd grown comfortable with was snatched away from me.

Azmir has kept pushing, has kept fighting, kept holding the mirror to my marred soul. He's chipped at the ice surrounding my heart. I've been undoubtedly drawn to him, which gives him access. I've tried running. God, how many times have I run from this man who's chased me down countless times! He'd always been clear about what he wanted, never asking for anything unreasonable. He's only wanted the assurance of my commitment to protect his heart. To be a stable being in life. When I thought it was him trying to impress me with luxury gifts, trips, and a car, it had been about him trying to gain my attention. When I thought it was about sex, it had really been about him wanting a connection.

When I'd thought it had been about control or possession, it was really about him fighting for permanency in my heart.

My god, he's been clear all this time.

Yeah, he's thrown me by not telling me loves me and giving me the coveted title of his girlfriend, but hell—when had I earned his trust to be given such a title? And with all the frantic running I've done; how could he have trusted me with the depths of his feelings? The revelations don't end. They follow me to the marina, through dinner, into the shower and to bed.

And before closing my eyes to slumber, I make a decree within my heart. No more running. I will love Azmir the way he deserves. I'll give him the devotion and staying power I've never been granted. He's mine—something he demonstrated when he asked me to move into a home he'd never even had his best friends in. And from here on out, I will certainly be his.

CHAPTER 2

Rayna

"Are you nervous?" Ray asks from the front seat of the Bentley.

I'm toying with the massage controls of the console, discerning the various settings. *Who needs this in a car?* Just a minute ago I was exploring the television, flipping through the available channels.

I can't understand for the life of me why Azmir would purchase a new *Bentley*. What's the difference between this one and the last? Yeah, he's gone from some variation of brown to a classic black shade called black crystal, according to him. And he's explained the new sharp edges to the body, the oval exhaust pipe, and the jeweled front headlamps, but who cares about those insignificant details. The last car was perfectly functional under the hood, sleek in appearance, and came with the same pretentious accessory of a chauffeur. It wasn't enough, so he had to upgrade an already luxuriant car.

"*Just ride in it. You'll appreciate the indulgence during the experience,*" is what he offered as an answer when I'd asked him the reason for the new purchase this morning as we dressed for work.

He'd packed his clothes for his overnight stay in Seattle, where he has a series of meetings running late into the evening.

"You know what? I'll have Ray drive you today. This way you'll get the experience right away. Trust, you'll understand," he insisted.

"Azmir, don't forget, I have that thing," I reminded him. "I'd like to go alone."

"Ray understands discretion, Brimm. How many times must we visit this topic of privacy and professionalism? And besides, Ray is more like family. He'll look out for you. I won't even send John along," he covertly issued an edict. And of course, he employed his coochie-creaming smile. The one that had us both late for the start of our day.

Now, I'm checking out the features, trying to circumvent my anxiety.

"No," I answer Ray.

I'm not sure if he believes me or not. I don't even care. I'm upset at having to be babysat once again and during such a personal time. A desperate plea.

"Is this them?" Ray calls out, causing my head to sprout from the middle console.

My mouth dries and a spike of bitter film coats my tongue as I see Amber's weathered turquoise Accord pull into the driveway. When the brake lights appear just before she turns the engine off, I see a little head bounce up and down from the rear seats.

It's now or never, Rayna.

On tenterhooks, I grab the bag to the left of me on the floorboard and use my other shaky and suddenly moist hand to grab the chrome handle of the right side door. Blowing out a cool breath, I step outside onto the curb. I pinch the plastic mailbox posted across from the lawn between my index finger and thumb in dither as I stride past it. I don't realize I'm doing it until I feel the clench of my fingers. In fact, I don't process walking; it feels more like I'm floating. With all of my nervousness, I can't cognitively coordinate body functions. I feel like Spike Lee's distinguished camera shots when the characters are gliding to their destination instead of actually walking.

When I arrive just feet away, in the driveway, Amber notices me just as she's opening the back door directly behind the driver's seat. Her mouth drops slightly, and I use the tip of my tongue to wet my lips. I'm sure my expression mirrors hers, but for different reasons.

Being jarred by my presence, she doesn't notice right away when the little head full of sandy blonde curls comes bouncing out of the car. When the little person turns to me, my breath catches at the sharpness of her brilliant hazel eyes. The eyes widening in wonderment at recognizing me.

"Auntie Na-Na!" She jumps in place and begins running in my direction.

Erin.

I bite back a cry. I won't cry today. Not *here*. I told myself it would be counterproductive.

She's slightly taller than I'd last seen, not too much. But what's clear is the baby fat in her face has ebbed a little. She's growing into a school-aged doll. Features stolen from her mother I can easily recognize. And some not so familiar I can assume are from her father, were sharper. Her voice is the same, but her words are spoken with more clarity. My little girl is becoming a big girl.

I fall on my haunches, and we embrace for what feels like hours, but in reality, it is just for seconds. Her hair smells of strawberries, her favorite fruit.

I pull back so I can get wrapped up in those hazel irises again, she murmurs, "I thought you forgot all about me."

My brows rise and trying to measure my reaction, I allow my smile to expand with it. Rushing out on a breath, I respond, "Never. Auntie will never forget her favorite little girl."

I notice in my peripheral, Amber making her way towards us as Erin retorts, "Well, where you been? I was missing you."

It takes every fiber of my being to not break down. I keep

reminding myself crying would only scare and confuse Erin. She'd never understand. I give a cursory glance towards Amber, who wears a discerning scowl.

"Honey, Auntie's moved. I don't live by the beach anymore. And now that you've moved, too, it's hard to see you like I used to. But I miss you every day, ladybug. Every day."

Erin's eyes light up at that name. It was what Michelle would call her.

Michelle.

Ughhhh! Next thought, brain!

"I had a birthday!" she gleams.

A birthday I had all planned out, but never saw to fruition. It felt like yesterday when I'd taken Michelle out for a spin in the new car Azmir had just given me—or let me "borrow"—and detailed the vision of a ballerina's ball party I'd thought up. When I could get her to focus more on the specs of the party rather than the features of the Benz, she excitedly approved. I wish I could go back to that very day and say so much I'd deferred to time. Like making sure she'd made it known I would be a part of Erin's life upon Michelle's departure from this side.

"I know. And that's why Auntie's here." I pivot to find the large gift bag. I then move it towards her. "I have a few things for you. I think you'll find them cool. At least I hope you do."

"Ooooh! I will! Promise!" she assures as she goes for the bag. It's almost as tall as she stands and far wider.

"Don't forget your book bag, Erin," Amber softly chides as she hands it to her.

I take the double shoulder strap bag and appropriately place it onto her little shoulders, so her hands are free to handle the gift bag. Just then, I see the front door open and a brunette woman with a bob cut, warmly calls for Erin.

Erin yells to the woman she'll be right there then turns to me solemnly and mumbles, "If I eat all my veggies and make my bed the right way would you come back, Auntie Na-Na?"

I choke out, "Baby, I'd love to see you no matter what you do or don't. I love you, Lil E."

Her face lights up one thousand kilowatts, which tells me I'm not getting choked up too much.

"Thanks! See you later." She hugs me tightly. My eyes flutter during the embrace.

Cue Regina Belle's "If I Could."

Amber and I watch as Erin tows the oversized gift bag behind her, up the driveway and into the house with gingered efforts.

Before I break my doting gaze, Amber turns to face me again. Her honey blonde hair draping her shoulders. "So, it's true," she tilts her chin, gesturing towards the *Bentley*.

I pivot to follow her line of sight, then turn back towards her. "What?"

"You have a Sugar Daddy," she replies noncommittally.

That quickly, I am offended. So soon has she come from her corner swinging.

"Look, Amber. I didn't come here to—"

"You didn't have to come. You were not invited."

"How long are you going to play this game? I'm only asking for one weekend a month. More if you need me. I just want to help."

"Help who? Help me? Or help settle your conscience for my cousin taking you in? Well, lucky for you, Rayna, she's dead. All debt has been cleared...null and void." Amber spews her words evenly. I guess as to not alert Erin or anyone else in the house.

"Looks to me, you've moved on to your next benefactor?" She motions towards the *Bentley* again. I can't help but feel that word *benefactor*, in its context, rings familiar. That aside, right now I can visualize kicking Azmir in the shin for forcing me to take his car. Not that mine would have been any better; Amber was only familiar with my old *Cavalier*. "I heard he's pretty well off. You always luck up."

I don't know if she's goading me for a fight to prove I'm as classless as she's always asserted, or if her ire for me soars that high. I also don't know how long, at this rate, it will be before I finally break. Break down and break her nose...or her face.

Five-four-three-two-one...

"For me," I mutter.

"What?" Her brows narrow in confusion.

"I need to do this for me. I need Erin in my life for me. Yes, I'd owed Michelle a debt of gratitude for the multitude of things she did for me. But this goes far beyond obligation for me. I've bonded with that little girl in there," I motion behind her, toward the house Erin had run into. "I'm no stranger to her you saw that."

"I'm going to tell you just like I told Uncle Dave: Erin is being taken care of by her *family*. She's loved and is thriving. You will not use her as a reason to further nip off this family. You have a new conquest." She motions again toward the *Bentley*, and absentmindedly, I turn to find Ray has come out and is standing next to the car, possibly sensing our heated conversation. I exhale, frustrated for just breathing at the moment.

"You have a new life now and thank God. For years you leached from Michelle. She moved you out here, gave you a place to live, got you a dream job—"

"You can have the position!" flew from my mouth, unexpectedly by my brain. I'm desperate to wager a deal now that we're face-to-face. I want that much to be a part of Erin's life. "Is that what this is about? I swear you can have the role. I'll go back to central as an attending PT. Or I can float...I don't care; just give me some time with her."

Amber chuckles, "Rayna, don't be foolish. I will have that position just as soon as I'm done with my internship. I've been assigned to Adams." She gives a menacing smile. "I'll complete my hours and put in a request to manage the Long Beach City office. Then, you will be completely abdicated of my family; all of us."

"Is that what you really want?"

She chuckles sinisterly, "Of course! I never liked you from the first time I saw you, Rayna. This we know. And at first it was simple jealousy from my big cousin, who I looked up to, bonding with someone else." I'm glad she can admit how insular her grievances were. Michelle and I had known it from day one but viewed it as insignificant. How wrong we were. Amber now holds all the cards.

"But then I learned my instincts weren't as off as I thought, and certainly sharper than my cousin's. You use people, Rayna, all the time. And I now suspect your manipulation from the start of your relationship with Michelle."

"Excuse me?" I don't understand this new revelation. Amber wasn't around when I met Michelle.

"How ironic was it that you met a fellow undergrad whose family owned a physical therapy firm, especially when you wanted to study it in school?"

"I didn't exactly arrive at Duke with an occupation in mind," I argue.

"Which then narrows it down to something less strategic. You took on a field she could help advance you in when you were done!"

My mouth collapses at her most absurd theory.

"Amber, Michelle invited me out here just days before my graduation. I had no plans after graduating. She did what a real friend does; she helped me navigate when my ambition was stifled."

Amber laughs again. "*Ambition was stifled.* Big concept for a girl from the hood. More evidence of my cousin's influence. Influence I'm proud of because, similar to her mother, she was notorious for being influenced by others instead of being proud of who she was."

"Whoa!" I shoot back cautiously. "I can't speak for her mother, but Michelle was African American, too. She was true to who she was. She was a black woman, Amber—"

"Half black!" she corrects archly before waving her hand in the air dismissively as she pinches the bridge of her nose.

I couldn't believe she was making this about race. Although I'd made baseless accusations in the past, Michelle's family has never displayed an ounce of racism—blatantly—towards me. In my younger years of knowing them, and because of their history with Michelle's mother and her inclination to date black and Hispanic men, I held myself protectively against them. However, when I sit back and evaluate things, Michelle's family—those I'd been exposed to—had been nothing but generous to me, on the surface.

My better judgment is telling me Amber's using all the ammunition she can conjure because she's that livid. It doesn't make sense. You can't admire and look up to your big cousin, and yet hate her ethnicity at the same time. That is the trickery of racism; it is always easy to resort to—to incite hatred, pain, and anger. It's always easy for folks to find themselves accused of it because they unknowingly fall into the bowels of ire with a party of another race and use the most convenient and absolutely wrong weapon to fight with.

"...it doesn't matter. My point is you've moved on to another victim; one we've clearly assisted with seeing he owns the property the LBC branch is on. Yeah, I heard about the nice piece of change he donated at the charity. And let's not mention the debt he paid off to Sebastian Adams."

This clears up how she's learned of Azmir. She wasn't at the annual fundraising ball, so she didn't learn about his donation firsthand. It also clears up her familiar usage of the word *benefactor*. She did mention Adams was her field supervisor—George Adams, Sebastian's father.

"I'm still waiting to see how you're going to get out of this viral pornography of you on your knees. You may have sicced your Sugar Daddy's lawyers on the firm, but as soon as it's proven you are the classless woman on the tape, your tenure with *Smith, Katz, and Adams* will disintegrate." Amber cocks her head to the side, "That tape only further demonstrates your trashiness...your low class, 'round the way girl essence. Yeah, Michelle got hooked by your *woe is me act,* but here's where the buck stops." She points behind her to the house. "She's where the gravy train ends for my family!" A fling of saliva hits the tip of my nose as she edges closer and closer to me in her tirade.

I feel hands gripping my arms and I defensively snatch away, then wildly peer over my shoulder to find Ray.

"I think it's time to leave, Ms. Brimm."

In the midst of my escalating feelings of deprecation sponsored by Amber, I jerk my head towards him. Without words, I ask him to back off. Ray's eyes pointedly divert to my hands. I glance down to see they're balled into clinched fists, and I mean rock-hard coiled bunches. I haven't felt this familiar fight or flight phenomenon in so long. I'm perhaps seconds away from hauling off and clocking Amber clear across her face. I'm suddenly aware of my heavy breathing, and I'm sure it hasn't just started. I've been so wrapped up in being the catchment of her venomous words, I haven't been aware of my instinctual reaction to them.

Apparently, neither is Amber, who's catching her breath as she brings her fist to her mouth, realizing her state of fury. This little tête-à-tête has grown into a near physical bout, at least for me it has.

"Look...just get the hell out of here!" Amber hisses. "And I don't care if you come with gifts instead of empty-handed or in a chariot instead of clunker, you're not invited here. Stay the hell away from my family. With time, she'll forget about you. She's still young; by this time next year she'll pass you up on the streets you'll eventually be begging from." She then steps closer. "I don't care how dressed up and polished you appear, you're nothing more than a ghetto, trashy, manipulative, conning, leaching whore. Erin deserves better than your kind."

"I will—" I jump, but don't advance forward.

"Ms. Brimm, it's time to leave," Ray calmly and firmly murmurs as he holds me from behind by my upper arms. He pulls me around to walk to the car. After he closes the door, I watch Amber give me a bidding shaking of the head before turning for the house.

I arrive at the marina wounded beyond repair. I don't

remember much, as I'm still floating, nerves atwitter. Time eludes me. I have a strong recollection of crying at some point. And not just any crying; bawling my eyes out, sputtering out breaths, boo-hooing, gulping in air—completely sobbing. I vaguely recall pouring myself a glass of *Mauve*—now that it's hit the home-shelf of A.D.—perhaps two. There is a little memory of me grabbing a box of tissues as the salty streams of self-pity came running down my face. Yes, I'm upset by how my visit to Erin had turned out, yet, in all honesty, I'd experienced a huge degree of disappointment in myself for being so affected by it.

I've been making great strides with my newfound resolve of inner-strength. And still my adapted mission of *Regaining the old Rayna Resolve* has been a monumental failure. How could I have allowed myself to get so upset by the words of someone who thinks so little of me is beyond me. Still, when I think of her logic, the way she gave her distorted estimation of me, it makes sense. I made a horrible decision to accept that money from Sebastian. And it's still haunting me. But I didn't use Michelle. I was not leaching off her family. I haven't acquired a Sugar Daddy. I did not influence Michelle to behave the way she did on that video—*God, I could kick her for that!* I am not wrong for Erin.

Not that I need affirmation of any of this, but it would be nice to talk with someone about this. Someone who knows me. Clearly and painfully, Michelle is not an option. I no longer have my *go-to* person, my sounding board.

My body shivers.

Out of nowhere, I feel a sense of comfort. This perceptiveness stems from an abrupt reminder of *his* essence. It's so potent, I can swear to smelling *his* enthralling and all-consuming fragrance. It permeates even my subconscious.

He's my sanctuary, my home-base. He's my duvet against the cold world, a soother. Azmir is my lover, my partner. He is my friend. My home. He's enduring and compassionate. Loving beyond what I deserve. He's understanding and keen to my temperaments, my needs. He's my enforcer for whatever obstacles presenting since I've known him.

He's fallible. He's beautiful. He's infuriating. He's mine.

Mine.

He's betrayed me with Dawn. Lied to me about Tara's baby. But he's still with me, sticking it out. *Yes...* He's caused me to hurt, but isn't that the cycle of love? The hazard of love? Loved ones will hurt you and disappoint you. However, it is not reflective of their commitment to you. People fail and fall. But the best way to demonstrate love is to return it unconditionally, and that's what I've purposed in my heart to do with Azmir. For Azmir. For me.

My love for him is so palpable, I can feel him in his absence. I can smell his natural fragrance, the very one secreting from his pores although he's miles away. My connection to him is that electrifying.

So cogent, I can even hear his voice, "Awwww...Rayna," in almost a distant whisper.

I can feel the electric pulses from his touch...from so far away. My skin prickles all over.

"Baby..." His velvety voice causes those trustee currents to course through me.

Then, I can feel the heat of his hard body as though it was next to me, emanating comfort and solace.

Being raised in the air jolts my subconsciousness, impelling me to an awakening. My eyes open but marginally; they won't widen for me at all. I feel the swelling in my face just above my cheeks. But what I can't miss is the blinding beauty of his face. His classical features are like a light blazing into my corneas, dilating my pupils. Am I dreaming, or is Azmir really here, at the marina?

I gaze motionless into his brown orbs. I don't know what signs I need, but I wait to learn if I'm still vacillating or if Azmir has really returned from Seattle.

He doesn't speak as he moves me from the sitting area of the master suite to the bed. It takes a few seconds to discard the decorative pillows. And when he's done, he gently settles me into the bedding like precious porcelain. Any other time I would scorn him for being so delicate with me. I would spew viciousness to disturb his mood. But not today. Today I will receive his comfort.

Once I'm adjusted in bed, Azmir scoots back on his haunches from the floor. "Have you eaten? Are you hungry?"

I shake my head.

"Do you wanna talk about it?"

I shake my head again.

At a loss, Azmir stands directly at the side of the bed with his fists resting on his hips. He's wearing a black suit, tailored to his glorious frame. Even clad in dress pants, his thighs present muscular. Here, in this moment, for more reasons than one, Azmir is divine. Even his voice lulls me.

"How can I help, baby? Well, what can I do for you?" he asks regretfully.

I want to tell him how much of a sedative his presence alone is. I want to jump up, kiss him on the lips, and ask about his day and if I can warm his dinner. I want to ask why the change in schedule and is *he* okay. I want to lose myself in his arms and tell him how horrible my day had ended. Share with him Amber's wrath and cruel summary of my existence. But I'm depleted of energy, even of my appetite. So empty I can't speak, though I need him to know what I'm in *need of*.

My spinning brain commands my languid arm and trembling hand as I extend my index finger to him, indicating what I need. And it doesn't take him long to understand the gesture. Azmir strips down to his boxers within seconds, adjusts his solid frame behind me in bed, and holds me until I succumb to siesta yet again.

The last thing I remember is internally asking: *Is this love?*

I think it is.

love ∞ believe

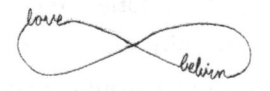

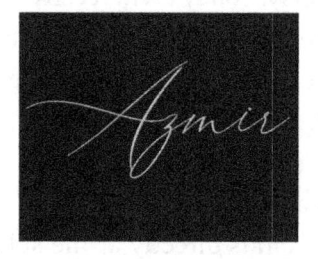

Azmir

"Yeah, Jackson, it'll be great getting together with cats from back home. Yeah...cool," I agree, speaking on the phone to a friend of mine from the East Coast.

"That sounds cool to me, too. I'm looking forward to the distraction, Divine," Jackson sighs.

"I know it's rough, man. There are some days I swear if my Pops were still here, my life would make more sense, you know?"

There's a tentative pause. I know Jackson is still in a heavy mourning period. If only words could heal the wounds of death. Rayna is still grieving Michelle. As much as she tries to hide it, occasionally I'm awakened at night by her mumbling of words to her dearly departed. And on worse nights, she calls out *J-Boog*. I never ask questions. Instead, I pull her into my arms and whisper affirmations of my love and commitment softly into her ear, telling her I'm here and will always comfort her. Some nights take long minutes for her to transition from a body-tensing nightmare to her melting into me, falling into a peaceful sleep. Most of the time I'm positive my method of comfort is working. I do my best to protect her, even from her nightmares.

"Yeah, man," Jackson mutters, breaking me from my reverie. "I'm good. I'll get through this."

"Yes, you will," I affirm. "Jackson, you're a strong man. You can do this. I'm sure your father—"

"Mr. Jacobs, Sergeant Lombardi has arrived," I'm interrupted by Tracy, my assistant manager, here at *Cobalt*.

"Send him in," I request.

Returning to my call, I announce, "Jackson, that's my one o'clock. I have to go."

"Okay, man. It was great talking to you, as usual. I appreciate your friendship, Divine," Jackson proclaims. This young dude has always been wise beyond his years. I guess being his father's best friend since he's been out of diapers did that.

"That means a lot. We may have lost Quincy, but I'd like to think we've gained a solid friendship as a result." I watch as Sergeant Lombardi scrolls into my office, observing every fucking thing, from the windows to the walls, after assessing my person. Goddamn *One-Time* tries to be so intimidating they're actually comical. "Listen," I call out to Jackson. "Why don't I host a dinner at my house? This way, you knuckleheads can meet my fiancée."

"That's what's up. I've heard she's brought your Hugh Heffner ass to your knees," Jackson jeers. I won't deny any rumor of how Rayna's captured my heart. There's no sense in it.

"So they say. So they say," I murmur with mirth. "We'll be in touch, Jax."

"I'll text you next week."

"Indeed."

As I place the phone back on its cradle, I turn to my midday visitor. I watch as he takes his time examining my office. I feel no concerns or anxiety of having *One-Time* in my space. I need him to know this as well. I remain silent ambling over to the conference table near the panoramic window I see he's so fascinated with.

Within seconds, he turns to acknowledge me. I extend my hand for him to take a seat across from me. With a moment of hesitation, he complies. Here is a battle of authority at its best. This is my fucking court, there's no way he's leading this assembly. I'm sure to take my seat after his descent.

"So, Sergeant Lombardi, how can I be of service to you?" I

initiate—and very politely as I pull my pocket watch from the breast pocket of my shirt.

Lombardi's eyelids rise. "Service? I'm not sure that's the appropriate term for the purpose of this visit." He lets a small snort slip.

Here we go with the bullshit. And so soon. I extend my arms and rest my elbows on the table.

"Sergeant, it is the middle of my workday. I have countless tasks to take on before I close my eyes this evening. I cleared a few minutes to extend an invitation to one of L.A.'s finest who's been inquiring about me for months. I think the least you can do is grant me the courtesy of cutting the bullshit and getting straight to the point." I issue him a tentative glare. I can quickly assess he doesn't appreciate my tone, but wisely decides his next move.

"Well, Mr. Jacobs," Lombardi stretches his eyelids again and brings his intertwined fists to his mouth as he speaks, "Since May of this year, the *Special Investigations Unit* has been investigating a Detective Darryl Harrison and his alleged involvement in distributing and trafficking illegal substances. Your name has surfaced in the investigation as a partner in one of the largest drug rings in Southern California. I've been simply doing my due diligence of ruling you out as an accomplice or adding you as a target of possibly one of the most prevalent drug operations in recent years." Lombardi pauses to read my reaction to his answer.

I take a moment to retort. "Distributing and trafficking illegal substances...with Detective Harrison," I repeat for clarification. "Sergeant, serious allegations such as this one couldn't possibly have you sniffing around in some of the most undesirable neighborhoods, asking about my activities, or a lack thereof, for a possible co-conspirator conviction," I inform with incredulity in my tone. It sounds so ridiculous.

"I think you diminish the seriousness of it, Jacobs."

"I'm simply regurgitating what my mind has processed."

"Well, chew on this while you're at it: if I learn you do have any involvement with Darryl Harrison—which I'm certain you do—I will prosecute you along with that sorry ass excuse of a man wearing the badge I honor and protect every day of my life." Lombardi gives me a warning glare.

I nod my head tentatively. "Sounds like you've marked me a suspect already." I'm now confident he has no case against me.

"I'm good at what I do, Mr. Jacobs. I've been in investigations for nearly twenty years. It's only a matter of putting the pieces together. If you don't believe me, you can ask your buddy, Harrison, when he calls you collect to inform you of his recent arrest, happening..." Lombardi glances down at his watch. "...right now." His gaze returns to me, sans a smile or cocky grin. He's trying to play hardball.

Do they really have Big D?

"Sergeant Lombardi, I've invited you to my place of work—without my attorney. This seems like a witch-hunt I will not engage in without my legal team." I'm sure to give him a strong regard so he can see how firm I am on his attempt to shake me like some street-level runner. If he's out to get me on anything, he'll have to come better than this. I know the game. My black ass would be down at the station in cuffs if Lombardi's assumptions were solid. "Quite frankly, I don't believe you have the shit you need to throw against the wall to watch and see if it sticks. Detective Harrison is a former friend of my father—"

"The man he murdered," Lombardi interrupts. I pause at his words. I quickly decide I won't crack underneath his allegation. If he can prove it, then that would be the doom of Darryl Harrison. Lombardi's inquisitive stare hooks into me, awaiting my reaction.

With lifted brows, I snort, "Shit just got more interesting. So, to be sure I have this correct: you're investigating a fellow decorated officer, who may possibly be trafficking and distributing illegal substances I may be a party to. And said officer allegedly murdered my father?"

Lombardi doesn't provide a response. He sits with his gaze keenly fixed on me.

I continue with, "Well, this has been a well-informed meeting, Sergeant Lombardi." I rise from the table. "I'll leave you to continue to waste taxpayers' money. Me, on the other hand, I have far more valuable things to do with my extremely limited time." I extend my hand to close this conversation.

Lombardi glances at my proffered hand for countless seconds before rising from his seat. I can tell he feels it. He knows I can see the frailty of his case. I mean, for fuck's sake, he's fishing for evidence in the hood. That's bold...and desperate at best. Never again will he get penciled in my appointment book.

"Introduction," he utters.

"Pardon..."

"This has only been an introduction," Lombardi states resolutely, ignoring my hand. "See, you may not be a low-level management hustler, but you are a scum peddler, no less. You may have the benefit of hiding behind your millions in legal armor, but crack crumbs will always trail back to the pusher. You, Azmir Jacobs, are the pusher of dope to the masses." Lombardi finally takes my hand in a firm shake, one I am prepared for in power. "Mr. Jacobs, I don't know how I'm going to get you, but you will fall...and crumble. Darryl Harrison is en route to his knees as we speak. You'll meet him there. I'm sure of it."

With a smug grin etched to my amused face I murmur, "Good luck with that, Sergeant."

Lombardi walks over to the door and inches away he turns to me. "Your fiancée you mentioned earlier while on the phone?" His face wrinkles and head angles, "How much are you willing to lose the possibility of a future with her? How important is that happily-ever-after with her?" If he thinks I'll flinch, Lombardi is more deluded than I thought.

"Just as much as I am willing to bet your far-reaching case against me is just as defective as your imagination. Good luck, Jimmy."

I know I'm pushing pretty hard with that reference. But I need him to know I am a discerning man. I know my opponents, even before they realize. *Fucking respect me.*

Lombardi chuckles as he makes his way out of my office. After closing my door, I pay a few pensive moments to our exchange. I have to recount his offerings of information to contemplate how I will respond to them. I'm at the end of my reign in the drug world. I'll be damned if I get hung on charges at this stage of the game. Fuck that. I have a real future now. I have Rayna. She's my now and my forever. I get chills just acknowledging this. No matter what obstacles lay ahead, I swear they'll be overcome because I am just that determined to make this woman as happy as she deserves to be. She's given me reasons to look beyond money and power. She's the reason I'm looking forward to living with no guards. No limits. Just Rayna.

I've made it my mission to be a constant in her world. She needs that. Consistency. She's spoken about that and security. She's told me those two phenomena have come up in her counseling sessions. And secretly, I've jumped to the challenge. She's going to be my wife soon; I have work to do and with great enthusiastic pleasure.

With great trepidation, I pick up the phone to initiate the next demonstration of my attempts at restoring her world.

CHAPTER 3

Rayna

It's Friday night, a week after Azmir's proposal. I'm still reeling at the idea of being someone's fiancée. *'Azmir proposed. Azmir loves me.'* resounds repetitively in my mind from the moment I see the gorgeous ring on my left hand. Doubt, which is always accompanied by fear, appears in succession. I fight, each time, the dark clouds of pessimism. *I can do this.* And almost without fail, Michelle's comforting voice echoes through my head—my heart, *"You alone are worthy."*

It's been a battle, but I'm determined to win and to learn to love this man and trust him freely. Azmir deserves that. He's been my rock in such a short period of time. He deserves my determination. In the moments I don't want to fight for myself, I will fight for Azmir. Always.

It's been a long day already. I've spent the entire morning and afternoon with Yazmine at a flower show in Pasadena. Even though I have *big brother*, also known as John, shadowing, I thought it would be nice to take her out there to get an idea of the type of garden she's preparing to grow in the backyard. I don't have a whole lot of space back there, but it would certainly be nice to see beautiful flowerbeds in the yard. She needs something to keep her occupied and collectively, we thought this would be nice. Sharon told me about the flower show a while back, and I figured today was a great opportunity to experience it with Azmir's mother. I even bought her a few things to help get her started. She was so anxious to begin when I left her to it.

I then rushed to the marina to shower and change for this evening. Azmir is sponsoring a skate-a-thon for the youth in the Watts. He chartered buses and paid for drivers to escort those without transportation to the skating rink. He invited me down, though he knew we wouldn't be able to travel together. He has a meeting but insisted I take Chanell and have Ray drive us in the Range Rover. Because of the element of people, Azmir insisted I coordinate my arrival with Petey, so I'd have security. I don't understand why muscle is necessary, but don't challenge him. He knows these people better than I do. Also, from my experience with them down at the club in Compton, I think it's best not to argue.

Chanell and I walk through the rear entrance where Petey's at the center of command. He assigns another guard to me. *Sheesh! Seriously?* I'm so happy to be out with Chanell, I don't resist anything. Besides, I know these are Azmir's orders. Chanell and I hit the small wet bar and order a couple of drinks. She, of course, knows everyone in the building and hit all of them with, "Yo, 'dis Divine fiancée!" I don't know if my buddy is that happy for me or if she scores points by being tight with Divine's woman. I take it all in stride because of my affinity for Chanell.

After twenty minutes or so of people watching—or should I say, having people watch me as if I were Michelle Obama—I nudge Chanell, "Let's hit the rink."

Chanell's eyes light up like a Christmas tree. "You wanna hit the rink, Ray?"

I wrinkle my face. "Why wouldn't I? Let's go, girl," I issue with a hint of attitude.

She informs her girls standing next to her. I pat John on the shoulder, telling him we're going to rent skates. Before I know it, we're on the floor gliding. I haven't skated in about ten years or so and I'm a bit rusty. Chanell is far worse off. She's trying to hold onto others for support. She knows full well her amazon frame can bring the both of us down as she tries using me to stay afloat.

"Chanell, you better let it go. I'm still trying to regain my memory, girl!" I playfully scold her.

"Wait the fuck up, Ray! Im'ma get it. I just need a minute!" she cries desperately. It's hilarious to watch.

"Okay. I'll slow it down." And I do. It takes her several rounds to get the right coordination, but she eventually gets it.

Skating turns out to be a blast! I'm sure the alcohol helps. The music is off the chain. The D.J.'s on fire. He plays party records like Frankie Beverly & Maze's *Before I Let Go*, CeCe Peniston's *Finally*, Beyonce's *We Like to Party*, and Jeff Red's *You Called and Told Me*. I'm in a nice groove on the rink. I take note of the many times the D.J. shouts out Azmir in his absence. He's showing love to the man who made it all possible. My heart's elated. Azmir is a man of many layers. Just a few weeks ago, I had accompanied him to a charity function at a mansion in Beverly Hills and tonight we're with the folks of the Watts. To say my life has been whimsical since encountering Azmir is saying very little.

I'm jamming to the New Jack Swing era when someone skates up so close to me they're on my backside. *What the...!* I jerk my head around to see Azmir flashing his coochie-creaming smile. It's warm and well received by my heart. He's such a gorgeous man. He's wearing a black fitted long-sleeve knitted shirt with dark indigo denim jeans. His hair is freshly cut into a Caesar and his fast growing goatee is such a turn on. I could get used to it. He gives me swift kiss on the temple. I guess he wants to keep it simple in public. Or is it that we're skating and there isn't much fondling we can do without falling? Either way, I'm smitten by his presence.

Wait. Is he skating? And effortlessly?

"I didn't know you could skate," I yell over the music.

"Ms. Brimm, you have no idea the extent of my talents."

I blush. With his long arm, he grabs me by the waist, and we glide together to the music. The D.J. blasts over the speakers, "Ayo, e'rbody! We got royalty in the building. Divine, the god, just hit the door and now he on the rink with his fiancée. Let's show my man some love, y'all. He 'bout to get hitched. Congrats to him and 'da future Missus. One love, yo." The crowd goes up in applause and whistles.

I'm so embarrassed, I try to hide under Azmir's long arms while keeping my stride. I'm not used to fanfare. I don't think Azmir likes it either, but he's been floating on cloud nine since I said yes. He gives the crowd a wave. They love it.

And as we brisk past a young guy watching the rink from the floor, I hear him yell, "Yo, man! I always looked up to you like a father, man. Much respect, homie!" Azmir raises his hand to the kid in acknowledgement of the endearing statement as we skate past.

That's a rather warm response to the announcement, opposed to the chicks giving the nastiest gawks. I've grown accustomed to those and the other type of women who point and whisper.

"What are you drinking?" Azmir asks while taking my drink from my hand and sipping my cocktail before I can answer.

"Ilk! This is disgusting. What is this shit?"

I shrug. "Some sort of martini." I giggle.

"All right. That's it. Time to go," he commands, pointing to an opening where we can exit.

"Already? You just got here," I protest.

And so did I for that matter.

He nods his head in resolute stubbornness. "I have something I need to show you. We have to go." He grabs me by the waist to guide me over to exit the rink. My stop is barely smooth. Azmir's is more so. I see the guards making room for us so we can get to the counter to return our skates. I had one of the security guards hold my *Tom Ford* pumps while I was on the rink. The last thing I needed is to have them five-fingered by the staff and have ruined a good night for Azmir. As I'm slipping on my shoes, my attention draws to Petey approaching us.

"Y'all out, Duke?"

"Yup. Got some plans for shorty," Azmir says, pulling me close to him. The onlookers seem so amazed by our presence. "You good, right?"

"Yeah, man. Ronnie holding shit down," assures Petey.

"Be sure to tell 'em I said he did a good job on the planning this year. This is a neutral location."

"Yeah, so far no drama," Petey informs. Azmir extends his hand to Petey in an upright position and leans into him to give him some dap. Petey follows suit and then turns to kiss me on the cheek. He's been greeting me this way since Vegas. It shocked me at first because he doesn't come off as an expressive man. Petey reserves his smiles. But he's warmed up to me without effort on my part. I soak it all up. It's nice and I know Azmir approves.

"Soon ta' be 'da Missus! I like that!" Petey gushes. I'm once again embarrassed by the attention but flattered to receive it from Petey. I give a bashful smile and ask him to give Chanell my regards. I lost her when Azmir whisked me off the rink.

The bodyguards navigate us through the crowds to the back door where we jump into the *Range Rover*.

"How did you get here?" I ask Azmir. I know he wouldn't leave his car behind and seeing Ray brought me leads me to wonder.

As he plays around on his phone, he murmurs, "Oh, errr...Kid dropped me off. I had him pick me up from my meeting."

"Oh, okay." I sit and wonder, *'Where are we going at this hour?'*

Seconds later, he maneuvers in his seat to face me and says, "Listen, where I'm taking you to...where we're going is to meet with someone." His face is preoccupied as he's trying to process his thoughts and spoon-feed them to me at the same time. I know Azmir; he's struggling with something.

"Jacobs, you're scaring me," I say with a soft smile because the truth is he's giving a disclaimer. And disclaimers are typically preceded by bad news. "It's not befitting of a confident and powerful man such as yourself to appear so...anxious." I continue to smile softly.

With distress and doubt in his eyes he snorts, "Trying to walk the straight and narrow with you makes a man second guess himself quite often."

In this moment, I want to straddle him and reassure my feelings for him, but I don't want to overdo it. I *woman up* and use my words instead.

"Azmir, I trust you. You have to know this," I chuckle. "For crying out loud, I've agreed to be your wife. And after hearing Pastor Edmondson explain the role of a husband in a household how God sees it, I realize it's a *huge* commitment." I gleam up at his beautiful face. I was going for humor, but Azmir doesn't follow suit. I pause and search his eyes but can't pick up the nature of his apprehension.

As the truck comes to a stop, he gives a sharp exhale and bows his head, embattled. It tears my heart, so I do the only thing I can think of doing. I pull him up by the chin and lay the warmest and most impassioned kiss on his lips. Once over the shock, he returns the sentiment and grabs me by the waist. Azmir's strong arms pull me into him, but not trying to go beyond the kiss. He wants me to know he's here in the moment with me.

I withdraw. "Better?" I ask with a faux pout mixed with a smile. Azmir's eyes dance around my face as if he wants to share so much but relents.

"Come on. We're here," he says before sliding out of the truck and grabbing my hand to take me with him.

We walk into a boutique hotel where Azmir asks the concierge at the front desk to direct us to the conference room. The young man instructs us where to go. Azmir doesn't let go of my hand and I grow anxious by the second. As we approach the conference room door, he abruptly turns to me and pauses. He doesn't say anything, but as I give a soft reassuring smile, he plants a light kiss on my lips and then turns to open the door.

The room is long and partially lit. In the center of it is a long conference table with space for over a dozen. As my gaze makes its way around the empty room, I take notice of the frame of a small woman at the other end. She seems similar to the size of Yazmine, but I know it can't possibly be her. It makes no sense. I just left her contented with gardening tools to plant to her heart's delight. She never mentioned seeing me again today.

I look up to question our whereabouts. Azmir says nothing and eventually the shadow of the woman strolls towards us. My eyes are glued to her. As she walks into the light, her silhouette disappears, and her image comes into color. Once my brain registers the encounter, I lose my breath, something that has never happened to me. Air completely abandons my lungs. My body freezes instantaneously and chills.

Azmir catches on right away because he tightens his grip on my hand and steps close, so he uses his body to hold me up. My mouth is suspended in the air and my eyes wide open. It's as if I'm seeing a ghost...because I am. It's Samantha, my mother. I'm reminded yet once again she slightly resembles the woman I knew a little more than ten years ago but has aged tremendously from her hard run with the streets. Oddly enough, she doesn't seem as desolate and malnourished as she did back in the summer when I saw her last.

Her eyes sparkle as she regards me expectantly. Her gaze says so much before she speaks. She appears meek, nervous, and proud —all at the same time.

The room is silent. All that can be heard are extraneous noises in the walls. I can't move. My breath is the first to return. But my breathing is exasperated because of the long delay. My eyes loosen and begin to blink rapidly; I'm sure because they're so dry from being opened for so long. But my mouth won't close, nor does my body move.

"Hi, baby girl," she greets humbly. My breathing is still erratic though I am trying with all my might to slow it down. Azmir reaches down to grab my shoulders as another sign of support.

"Can I hug her?" she asks Azmir first then me. "Can I hug you?" I guess that's her nervousness showing.

I believe Azmir tells her it's okay because I still can't speak. She comes into me and wraps her arms around my numb body. Azmir scoots back just a bit as to give her room to embrace me. He doesn't go too far to show he's still here for support. His hand is still laced with mine and his leg is still firm against my leg. My body still can't move. Samantha moves back into her original position.

With my eyes still flickering I exhale the word, "Hi." I've been working on it from the moment I recognized her.

"Hi, baby," she returns with an even wider smile.

"Let's sit down and talk. I'm sure Rayna has lots of questions. Can I get you ladies something to drink?" Azmir asks, preparing to leave the room. I pull hard, yet discreetly at his hand, letting him know he isn't to leave my side. I turn to him with eyes still wide, though no words come. He confirms he understands what I'm saying with a gentle nod. His eyes are wide and lost, too. We're all in a precarious place.

The three of us sit and initially no one says anything. Samantha is looking to Azmir and me to take the lead. I'm still coming down from my shell shock and can't give much at all until I've landed.

"Ummmm..." Azmir attempts. *Good because I can't do this!*

"Rayna, your mom called me a few months back saying she was ready to get clean. I didn't want to notify you because honestly, I didn't know how you'd react." He uses his hand to gesture, something he never does. His hand keeps going from his chin down toward the table—up and down. It quickly becomes a predictable pattern.

Crap. He's nervous!

He continues, speaking slowly. "I knew this was a personal matter and how uhhh...selective an individual you are, but I felt after having lost Michelle, you could use another familiar figure out here."

Is he saying he isn't enough? Am I overbearing? What in the world is going on? I begin panicking.

"Uhhhh...so I made a few calls and got her into a reputable rehab in Huntington Beach. I've heard great assessments from trusting sources," he mutters nervously as he caresses my knuckles while still holding my hands.

I don't like seeing him like this, but I have nothing to say. I now understand his hesitance in the truck. I try desperately to search for suitable words.

"Well, anyway...she's completed her program and has been successfully discharged." Azmir continues, "She's been staying here for the past few days until she gets on her feet."

"Yeah, I ain't never stay in a fancy hotel before. Years ago, when you and Keeme was babies, we stayed in a *Super 8*. That wasn't nuttin' like this. Thank you, sir." Samantha's dim smile was genuine in expressing her gratitude for Azmir's apparent benevolence.

"Azmir," he corrects.

"My bad," Samantha retracts. "Azmir. I know you don't want me to be too...formal, but I gotta give you yo' props, baby. You looking out and all."

"How do you two know each other?" I ask, suddenly finding my voice. They both shoot each other a look, I guess asking who would explain.

Azmir lost. "Well, back in Jersey, over summer...the morning we checked out, I ran into Samantha in the lobby."

"And you didn't tell me?"

Azmir stills. He cautiously proceeds.

He slowly shakes his head. "Nah. There was so much going on with you at the time. You'd never spoken much about your mother, so I didn't think she was an open topic," Azmir's deep voice reduces to a grovel. It's cautioned, humbled, and apologetic. "I wasn't being underhanded—"

"No. He saved my life," Samantha interrupts him, speaking matter of factly. "He gave me a second chance. If he never gave me his business card 'dat day, only gawd know where I be today." She shrugs her frail shoulders. "Could be dead."

Although I have more questions, the picture is becoming clearer to me. Azmir secretly assisted my mother into sobriety. I'm not immediately sure how I feel about it, but what I do know is I need to get out of here before my emotions take over. I'm not prepared to become undone in front of them. So I offer, "Is there anything I can do for you? Have you gotten any doctors out here?" I can't help my professional tone. I'm not familiar with mother/daughter etiquette.

Samantha cracks a toothless grin, "Nah, baby. Azmir here done set me up real nice. I got doctors and a dentist. I'm going to get my teef on Monday," she says directly to Azmir who nods, still in fear of me feeling he's intruded.

"I got me a job interview at the grocery store on Tuesday. He got me some nice clothes, so I'll look halfway decent," she giggles.

Azmir gives her a soft, polite smile. I can't help but feel a little jealous. Azmir has technically set me up in a new life myself. He's given me a car, bought me new clothes, helped me '*keep*' my job, and gave me a nice place to stay, too. My thoughts are running wild. This is too much for me.

Clearly, I'm visibly uncomfortable. Azmir tightens his warm hand on me and at the same time Samantha utters, "Now I ain't mean to upset you. Your boyfriend here thought it could be nice if we talked," she pauses. "I can go back if you want me to, but I wanna stay and start all over with you. I done missed out on so much," her voice chokes more at each word.

I gasp and grab my mouth. Azmir lunges slightly, grabbing my one shoulder while still gripping my hand.

I take a moment to consider her offer, but there's no time to evaluate what having her here would mean to me. The last thing I expected when I awakened this morning was to see my mother here in L.A.

"No. I don't want you to go back. If you want change, I can certainly understand. I got it out here, too," I murmur, looking over to Azmir as I use my left hand to caress his hand that has been attached to my right since we've left the truck.

Samantha must catch a glimpse of my ring. I notice as she sits, fixated on it for a few seconds. It gives me the same self-consciousness I've come to develop when it draws attention from others. I shift it with my thumb and slowly withdraw my arm from the table.

But before I'm done, she gestures to the ring with her head and asks, "Is 'dat a..."

I don't know why, but I look down at the ring. "Ummm...yes," I glance over to Azmir, who's wearing an impassive expression. "An engagement ring," I answer, a little embarrassed—more or less uncomfortable. I don't know how I feel discussing this with my *mother* after the fact.

She tears up again. "Oooooh! Y'all getting married?" she cries, slowly trying to mask her emotions. I nod my head. With her eyes to the table, she whispers, "I'm gon' have some grandbabies."

My body freezes. *Grandbabies? Let's just take it one step at a time. I'm still adjusting to living with a man and then consenting to be his wife!* The thought of so much responsibility is overwhelming.

Azmir breaks the awkward moment and seemingly on cue. I've needed to go for a while already. This is all too much. "It's getting late. I think this was a nice...icebreaker. Maybe you two can arrange to become reacquainted...in the near future?" he poses more as a question than a suggestion.

"Okay. I'll be here. Ain't got much to do, but wait on you," Samantha supplies with a forced smile.

"Are you going to be okay alone?" I ask, not wanting to be rude.

No matter my total disarray from the shock of learning she's here, I can register she's absolutely alone with no one...but Azmir to call on.

"Oh, I got mo' time to do in prayer and meditation. I done spent too much time running from Gawd. I gots lots a makin' up ta do. But when you up to it, you can call or come by to see me here. As soon as I can get a job and a place, Im'ma be out 'dis young man hair. I'm getting there," she stands.

We follow suit. "Don't rush. You can stay here until I—" Azmir stops as he steps closer to me and places his hands on arms. "...*we* find something more comfortable for you. Call if you need anything," Azmir insists.

Samantha bows her head in humility. We say our odd and brief goodbyes and leave. As soon as we hit the cool air outside of the hotel, I give the biggest exhale. It feels like I've been holding on to it since walking in.

love ∞ believe

Azmir

The ride home is bleak for me. Rayna rides in silence, gazing out the window. I wonder what was going through her mind. More specifically, I wonder if she's upset with me. I can't help but feel like I've crossed the line...like I've overstepped. Rayna can be so fucking solitary that it drives me crazy. I did it with the best intentions. Honestly, since she'd championed my reunion with my moms so well, I thought this was along the same lines. Harmless even. *So why in the hell am I feeling so nervous about this?*

"I made reservations at *DiFillippo's*. I figured you'd be hungry," I murmur over to Rayna as she sits glumly, gazing out of her window. I actually had Brett make the reservation there to buffer the blow of the meeting with Samantha. She loves their dessert selection. Frankly, it was a preemptive measure.

"I'm not very hungry," she mumbles, not even looking at me. She keeps her regards outside of the window.

Damn.

"Do you want me to call and order the crème brûlée to go?" That's her favorite. It's that time of the month for her and she loves having it during times like this.

She turns to me, "I'm actually just drained. It's been a long day. I would rather take a hot shower and go to bed." She flashes a forced smile.

Yeah, I'm in the fucking doghouse.

Once we arrive to the apartment, Rayna stops into the office to grab her laptop and then makes her way into the master suite to charge it up. I wonder what she's doing on there at this hour, but I know it's work related if she's on there. I go into the office to return a few calls and emails.

Ten minutes later, I find my eyes numbing. It's only eleven thirty, but I'm exhausted. I head back to the bedroom where she's still laid across the chaise on the laptop.

"You mind if I jump the line and hit the shower before you?" I ask fucking pathetically. I just want some type of interaction with her.

Barely looking at me, she answers, just audibly, "No. Not all. I'm just editing my quarterly reports. I'll be another twenty minutes or so."

I stalk into the bathroom, undress, and shower. Once I'm done, I come back out into the bedroom to find her exactly where I left her, even in the exact same sitting position. I decide to go out into the great room to hit up my sports channels until I doze.

Just under an hour later, my eyes are fixed to the television. The lights are off, but my peripheral picks up a nearing object on the floor. I turn my head to get a full view and see Rayna coming closer. She's on her hands and knees, crawling over to me like a cat.

The fuck?

I don't say anything. I just watch her. She wears her knee-length Japanese wrap. Once she arrives, she grabs onto my legs and raises her upper body to my kneecaps. When she rises to her knees, I notice her wrap is open and she has nothing on beneath. Her beautifully coiled breasts sit nice and naturally, without the restraints of a bra. I'm able to get a peek of her neatly manicured pubic area. I'm really enjoying the new and groomed look to it. She started getting waxed down there after my dentist found evidence of my frequent dining on her during my last checkup.

Rayna doesn't say anything but wears an intense expression. I feel her pulling at the drawstrings of my pajama pants. Once the tie is undone, she grabs the elastic top of my boxers and pants and pulls them down. *Damn.* I think I know where this is going. *Shit—I hope I know where this is going.* But I don't get why. I resigned to her being upset with me for overstepping with her mom. In the car she didn't say it, but her actions were cold and didn't give very much other than reproach. She's on her period, so I know she's not trying to smash.

My dick bucks out and she kisses him as if *he's* welcome. I watch as Rayna plants small kisses all around then starts to mildly stroke me with one hand before applying soft nibbling and masterful scrapings. I'm losing my fucking mind by the second. Eventually she works herself up to taking the head into her mouth. It's a nice, warm, soft sensation. I sharply inhale and relax my neck, laying the back of my head in the couch while she takes me in inch by inch. Once all of my cock is wet, she uses both hands to massage me. Ms. Brimm never fails to blow my mind while blowing my rod. She starts to pick up speed while concentrating on the tip of my penis. Her delicious acts scream inspiration.

Wow. Just an hour ago she was giving me the cold shoulder, now she's giving me warm head. What happened in between?

Damn. That's what it is. Rayna's done accessing my actions with her mother. *So finally she sees I did nothing malicious?* She's doing better at verbally expressing herself, but this is the works of her body. I guess a man can't complain.

This shit is getting heated, and I'm caught up already. I grab her by the head and flex my hips. Her grip is perfect. I hear the smacking sounds of her oral lovemaking. That shit drives me wild. With her lips wrapped around her teeth, she takes me deeper. My breathing accelerates and I can swear I feel her uvula.

"*Shiiiiiiit!*" I whisper, feeling my orgasm stirring.

I have to give her the warning.

"Brimm, baby... *Goddamn!* I'm 'bout to *cooome*..." I drawl out.

She always lets me come in her mouth, but I have to be a gentleman and continually give her the option. *Fuck.* I hope she doesn't withdraw tonight.

"Rayna!" I murmur—more or less singing because I'm coming.

I'm still holding her head while thrusting my pelvis into her face. She's looking me dead in the face like a "G." *My future wife the "G."* I can't stop shooting and my fucking toes are curling now. I don't know how she does it, but she doesn't waste a drop of my soldiers. She doesn't let up until I stop moving. Shit. I can never get used to this. The value of Rayna's mouth exceeds my fortune.

Rayna hops to her feet and scuffles out of the great room. She returns in no time with a warm washcloth to clean her saliva from me and lifts my clothes up my legs, adjusting them on my waist. I just watch in amazement.

Once she's done, she asks, very soft and lovingly, "Friends?"

Her eyes are humble and sexy as hell through those long eyelashes. I grab her by the sides of her face and lunge my tongue in her mouth. I feel savage. I want to ingest her. She can be so difficult at times, but tonight she did well. She didn't let the clouds of doubt and uncertainty of my deed gloom over our heads for too long. This is how she knows to love...to coexist. I can do this. I can meet her halfway. I can love her.

With my left hand, I hook her by the shoulders and scoop her up with the right by the ass and lay her on the couch. I maneuver enough so we're laying side-by-side with me resting on the back of the couch and our heads on the armrest. She giggles. I don't.

"I love you. You know that?" I need her to know.

"Of course I do," she smiles while flashing the engagement ring.

"Oh, yeah," I snort. "But that's for others to know. I need *you* to know in your heart."

She's still smiling contently and being entirely contrary to the woman she was earlier.

"Azmir, I told you, I just needed to process everything. That was a lot..." her voice trails off.

Shit. No. *Stay with me here.*

"I know. And I want to move at your pace and not a measure faster. With everything." She knows I'm alluding to setting a date for our wedding.

"Yeah, about that." She wrinkles her little brows pensively. "How does next spring sound...March?"

Finally—a date! My heart sighs in relief. Rayna reaches up to caress my face. "I sure wouldn't mind holding out a little longer. I would love to see how long you'll grow this." I smile.

"I told you I'm not cutting it until you're legally mine."

"I know," she whispers, still wearing a giddy smile. I lay with a full heart, drinking her in.

"What?" she asks.

"I wanna fuck you so bad right now," I growl.

Her eyes grow to the size of lemons. "I think you've caught me at a time where I'm indecent, Mr. Jacobs," she retorts, referring to her period.

I glance slyly down her body. She slaps my arm.

"What did you say to me in Puerto Vallarta?" she asks as she taps her chin with her index finger. "Hmmmm...*a haram*?" Rayna reminds me, playfully chiding.

"A haram it is," I agree. Though the level of intimacy I've come to have with Rayna defies everything previously believed as immoral. I want no barriers to her. No restrictions to her heart and/or body.

I shift to my feet and lift her from the sofa. We head back to the bedroom where I pull back the linens and gently lay her down before getting in myself. I pull Rayna into me so close. I don't want any measure of distance between us—not physically or emotionally. Having Rayna in my world has taught me just how fragile life is, how vulnerable I am. My world is complicated, extremely sensitive. So far, I've managed to rope her in with blinders. But how long they'd be effective, I don't know. *And when they come off...*

A shiver runs through me at the prospect.

"Hey..." Rayna calls out, turning to face me. Her soft hands cup my face as she examines my eyes intently, searching for something. "What was that about? You were trembling. What's wrong?"

If only I could be transparent, baby...

In this moment, I hate my existence. I detest the life I've built over the years. It's too convoluted, very much alloyed for Rayna's innocence. *For fuck's sakes, she said she vowed to never date a drug dealer when we were in NYC, last summer!*

And I'm beyond that: I manufacture drug dealers! I develop them under my careful tillage. Though I'm at the end of my reign, a month seems decades away. I wish I could keep her here, in my bed, wrapped in my arms until I'm no longer responsible for organizing a multi-million-dollar drug trade.

How can I make this plausible: Rayna, here, in my bed, until the New Year? Hmmmmm...

"Azmir," Rayna calls again, pulling me from my sick thoughts.

I push her soft frame further into me, needing her warmth. Her inquisitive gaze doesn't waver, though I'm damn near smothering her. *Shit!*

"I'm just thinking about what we'll be like as senior citizens. Would we eat *Jell-O*, pudding, and shit like that—that old people like?" I lie. "Will our arguments go from the amounts of money I spend on you to who used the last of the denture adhesive?"

Rayna belts out a gut-wrenching laugh. It causes my heart to leap in my chest. I enjoy seeing her light-hearted.

Now, in a more sober place, I murmur, "You know life won't become magically problem-free once you take on my name, don't you?"

Nestled under my shoulder, Rayna nods her head with her eyes suddenly humor-free and mouth slightly ajar.

"I mean, Brimm, things may become a little more intensified if only because of my career trajectory," I warn with a pleading tone. "There will be lots of...*outside forces*," I quickly think to use a term she'll understand. It's the one she used to describe that asshole, Thompson, the night after her firm's charity ball. I need her to get this.

Her eyes race in their sockets, assessing my face as she muses over my words. Rayna nods her head as she murmurs, "Okay. I know...I get it."

"Well then, why the pensive face?"

There's a tentative pause before she answers, "It's just things you keep from me...ways you extend yourself to people. When you do, it brings them into our bubble."

I exhale deeply. I know what she's hinting at. That fucking Tara. I know it was wrong to keep that information from her. I knew the moment she discovered my helping out Tara and her baby, she'd go ballistic. Rayna can't begin to understand the weight of responsibility that's always been placed on my shoulders by those less fortunate. I've always had the burden of providing for others.

Although her father betrayed me, I couldn't ignore Tara

having no income and apparently, neither did her father. It didn't matter how she, too, had betrayed me. I'd gotten over that shit the minute I learned of it. Sadly, I felt relieved I'd finally gotten my "out." I was happy as hell to walk away from the relationship.

Tara's a brat. She was raised as a trophy child. She was privileged, trained to be delicate and high maintenance. She'd never even gone to school after I met her. I'd always believed it was because her parents never pushed it once my relationship with her became official. She didn't have to do shit but create expectations for me to live up to. My decision to help her and her baby out financially was wrong. Though before Rayna's blow up over it, I didn't understand just how fucked up it was.

"I have a secret to share," Rayna's timid voice breaks my attention.

I turn to her, "Spill it."

"It's a little embarrassing," she whispers as her cheeks heated up. I don't know if I should be concerned or not, but my patience is already wearing.

"Brimm, I can see you want to tell me. Go on," I command a little harsher than the mood calls for.

"Okaaaay..." she sings, unable to wipe the burning grin from her face. I wait, something I've vowed to do for Rayna when she needs it. But she finally speaks.

"Wait. This is top secret—extremely sensitive information I've only shared with one person!"

I'm stumped. I have no damn clue what's going on in that busy, incommunicado mind of hers.

"Okay, now it will be two people." I raise my eyebrows to show she needs to get on with it already.

"You gave me my first vaginal orgasm." Rayna's widened eyes reach mine. She can't gain a hold of the grin that's plastered her face.

"Why are you so embarrassed by that?"

"What? Why wouldn't I be?" Her goofy smile dissipates slowly as her brows fold together. "Wait...did you know already?"

I don't want to answer that. I don't want to fuck up the moment. This trivial fact is a lot for my lady to share. But I don't want to lie either. "Of course, I did." I plant a kiss on her forehead to keep with the pillow talk mode we've just found our way to and to soften the blow.

"Huhn?" her big eyes tell me she won't drop the subject.

"Yes, Brimm, I knew—well, I knew you hadn't been touched in the ways I had touched you—"

"What! What's that supposed to mean?" Rayna jumps from my enfold and into the air. She's now sitting up, peering down on me for an explanation.

"What are you doing? I'm cold now." I try hiding the humor in my voice.

"Explain, Jacobs!"

I rise to rest my weight on my elbow. "Okay...okay. Just come back down here. I was comfortable." I fail at hiding my humor.

She doesn't move. "Tell me, how could you possibly know?" Rayna is not dropping this. The answer is not a topic a man wants to take on with his woman. It can get very hairy.

"Brimm, baby, you do know I'm damn near forty years old, right?"

"What does your age have to do with how you knew that before you, I'd never had a vaginal orgasm?"

Damn.

"Because I'd been with enough women to know the depth of their sexual experience—"

"And?" she spits, interrupting me.

"...and I knew what your walls were telling me, which was you were in need of a deeper release. An internal release, not topical."

Rayna's head dips back in a hard laugh, exposing her beautiful neck. Her laugh has always been infectious to me. I watch raptly as it takes some time to slow her mirth.

After some time, with glazed eyes, she gazes over to me, "Azmir, are you serious?"

"I'm serious as hell. You like to keep contained, but your body withholds nothing. I could tell you were afraid at first, but you'd never tell, which was cool. You didn't know me very well back then."

As I speak, Rayna lowers herself back to the bed, taking to her pillow. "Yeah, that feels like years ago. I can't believe we've only known each other less than a year...and we're getting married—"

"...first week in March. Yup," I conclude the thought. She doesn't need to focus on how little time we've known each other. Just on our forever.

Rayna's hooded eyes curiously rise to meet mine, "Okay...now you tell me a secret. I wanna learn something new about you, too."

"Uhhhh...let's see," I quickly think of how I can play along with her *moment of truth* game. "I don't think you shared anything new; just confirmed what I'd already known," I admit.

"Well, was there anything *impressive* about me...since you've brought up my inadequacies?"

"Of course, there were many impressive things about you, sexually. It's clearly the reason I've had more sex with you in the past few months than I have with any one woman."

"Huhn?" Rayna's eyebrows narrow. "This can't be true. You were with Tara for what...six years?"

"I know," I nod. "It doesn't seem plausible, but by the time we hit the ninth month mark, where you and I are now, I hadn't had as much sex with Tara. That novelty had run its course long before then."

Rayna looks even more confused. And per usual, I don't want to explore this conversation. It could reveal more than I ever want her to know about me.

"So, does that mean our time is coming? The time when sex isn't as interesting as it's been? It's the same question I asked while we were in the shower, the night I officially moved in with you." Rayna's eyes dance in their sockets. "Oh, my god, Azmir, I can't even imagine life without sex with you. Sex with you is like—"

"Fucking amazing," I chime in with a definitive tone.

She turns to me with squinted eyes, but a full on blushing face, "Well, yeah, but you didn't have to be so conceited about it."

"There's nothing wrong with great sexual chemistry. That's what we have, Brimm," I say as she burrows into my arms, finding her place of comfort.

"Yeah...*great* is an understatement," she whispers, much to herself. If I know my lady, she's horny as fuck right now just thinking about how I smash her. But there's nothing I can do about it. She's bleeding.

"If it makes you feel any better, I have a secret as well," I murmur.

Rayna's head shoots in the air and eyes light up like a Christmas tree. Unable to hide her curiosity, she sputters, "Pray tell."

My gaze makes its way to the wall ahead, in the distance. "I was nervous as hell the first time we smashed." Now I'm looking for her reaction.

Rayna shakes her head as her eyes roll to the back of her head. She tries like hell to conceal her smile.

"What? I was," I argue.

"But why must you use the word *smash*? Seemed like more than that to me at the time."

"Well, we both know it was very special, but I wasn't my best. I was nervous." I can't believe I'm admitting this shit.

Her eyes shoot up to me. "Why?"

"I don't know," I shrug over a sigh. "It took so damn long...and so many near-incidences that when it was finally time, I wasn't on my A-game." I get caught up in those historical feelings from the night at the *Four Seasons*. "At some point after tasting you that first time, I decided to over-perform. I mean, I knew I had to impress you, but I also knew moving forward, I wanted to be sure to please you."

Rayna's soft hand brushes against my chest. "But you did...the very first night."

"I know, but it wasn't with my preferred comfort level. I've never been intimidated by sex. With you everything's...new." My gaze finds its way to her.

She swallows hard, "It was beautiful. And so was the second and each time there on out."

"Oh, I know the second time was remarkable. Once I realized I had another opportunity and you'd stay with me in Phoenix, I quickly decided to get my shit together and show you I'm the fucking man. I made sure you wouldn't forget me anytime soon."

Rayna howls like she's being tickled. I watch her, completely content by her joyful state. Though I added the comic relief, I'm serious as hell.

"I'd like to have a dinner party," I announce, attempting to remove us from the previous topic.

Rayna shifts in the bed to face me. "Really? Where?"

"Here."

"Really?"

I laugh. "Yes, here. In our home."

"Who would you invite?"

"I have a few of my east coast buddies I'd like you to meet."

Rayna's penetrative gaze is into my chest as she's processing this.

"Do I have to invite people?" she asks as her brown irises reach mine.

"No, baby. Just show up in all your sexy grandeur. I want to show you off to my friends."

Rayna exhales as a gorgeous smile cracks on her face. "I want to host it."

"You don't have to worry about cooking for so many. I can set it up with Chef Boyd."

"No, I want to host your friends. I think it'll be good for me... something new, you know?"

She's really serious about this. I smile at her determination.

"I'll need Boyd's help, but I want to spearhead it," she mutters while her eyes bounce back and forth between mine, tentatively awaiting my reaction.

"Go for it." I kiss her forehead.

"Really?" Rayna's eyes grow wide in excitement.

"Of course. I actually like the idea of you in my kitchen cooking, preferably naked...in heels."

Rayna's head tilts back on a hearty laugh, and per usual, my heart inflates.

I wait until she's done before I take on a sobering topic.

"Rayna, about your moms—"

"It's fine," she intercepts my attempt to clear the air. "Really. I need some time to adjust, but *we're* fine."

I nod as I study her expression. I really don't know where to go from here. Rayna can be very difficult with things like this. Less than an hour ago, I just knew this was going to be a "silent" night.

"Okay... But you know I love you, right?" I don't like feeling like a broken record; I desperately need her to know I'd had her best interest in mind.

Rayna once again raises her left hand, displaying the symbol of my pledge of forever. She's barely able to hide her roguish grin.

I think she gets it...

CHAPTER 4

Rayna

A couple of weeks after learning Azmir invited my mother to town found me still adjusting to the idea. I'm not angry, but I feel a part of my privacy had been breached when he invited her into my world. It's been easy being in a new state, with no one who has a true reference of you and your past. My bones have been closeted. Outside of my nightmares, I've been able to escape that old world. The pain. My mother being here can be a liability to that locked closet.

What if she slips up and mentions the shooting? The murder.

I try to be mindful of calling to check on her a few times. She's been receptive to it. She's also been busy, trying to rebuild her own life; interviewing for jobs, keeping up with her doctor's appointments. There's been very little asked of me, and I'm relieved. Ironically, I can now appreciate Azmir's apprehensions and mixed feelings of developing a relationship with Yazmine after so many years of being separated.

Azmir shocks me and attends another counseling session with me this week. Last week I'd gone alone, minus the shadow of John, my security escort, who of course stayed out in the waiting area.

And this week Mr. Jacobs himself is tagging along. He hasn't said why, just that he wants to come again.

He remains quiet for the most part. So quiet I'm able to forget his presence for much of it and speak freely with Pastor Edmondson about my fears of never seeing Erin again, and my guilt of having my brother incarcerated while I'm away, flourishing, and free from the perils of home. Though I don't elaborate on the extent of my onus, the fact that he would never be in that cell had I not been involved with O. I'm not ready to go there yet, and Azmir's quietness isn't so great that I've forgotten he's here entirely. However, I'm able to be open about my brother's absence from my life contributing to my loneliness. Pastor Edmondson and I are able to agree on that being one of the reasons I've been consistent with his visits and maintaining his commissary.

Speaking about Akeem is very emotional. It takes immense resolve for me not to break the levy of tears growing behind the pain of it all. I manage to remain tear-free throughout the entire session. Before I know it, Pastor Edmondson is announcing the end of the session. We stand for our goodbyes, and I feel Azmir's warm hand on the curve of my back. It doesn't feel sexual, perhaps for comfort. I'm not quite sure and begin to get nervous about the backlash of what I've shared over the past hour. Other than saying he feels privileged to attend the session and he would like to appear at more, Azmir doesn't say much at all.

En route, while gazing unseen out of the window, Azmir mutters, "I've got something to talk with you about."

My belly toils in the worst way as Ray, behind the wheel, drives us in his customary silence. This won't be good. I knew it was a horrible idea having him sit in on my counseling session. I knew it would be a matter of time before he either threw something in my face or confronts me about something I'd shared, hence yet another reason why I hate expressing my feelings.

I roll my eyes as I exhale and wryly caution, "Yeah? Bring it."

My body goes rigid as I prepare myself for the blow. This time I will not consider Ray when I respond. I won't give a second thought to having another showdown with Azmir.

"I spoke with your mother today." He then turns to look at me. I don't know what's coming next, but I do suddenly feel like an ass for assuming the worst with Azmir. And I suddenly realize Azmir never throws things in my face, neither does he hold on to much. *Nice, Rayna!* I turn to him sheepishly and nod, asking him to continue. "She didn't complain, but I can't help but think she's run her course at the hotel she's been staying in."

My eyes retreat beyond Azmir and into his window as my mind churns. This is truly a dilemma because I have no solution. My mother knows no one out here; she has no support. She's mentioned joining a church, but it wasn't very long ago: too recent to have close acquaintances.

I swallow hard before uttering, "I don't know how to remedy that. I'm sure the same rules established for Yazmine apply to my mother with regard to living with us at the marina." I turn to Azmir for his reaction.

He gives a slow, but affirmative nod. "Yeah, I didn't think you'd be receptive to your moms living with you—"

"It's just that...Azmir...it's going to take time for me to adjust is all. I'm trying...I really am..." I try to explain.

"Rayna, I am not judging you. Trust me, I have no room to." His voice was even yet firm. "If you're not ready for a traditional relationship with your moms, it is not my job to force you. I'll support and protect you. I just want to help. Okay, baby?" His eyes are filled with genuine concern. I feel guilty for bringing this to him. Although he's brought Samantha out here, he did so as a means of supporting me.

"Okay, so what do you suggest? I don't want you buying her a mansion on the hill. You're doing far more than I expect with her medical care."

"Nah, I don't think it's best for her to be alone considering her health. She needs companionship. I was thinking of having her stay in Redondo Beach with Yazmine. She could use some company herself."

"Would they be compatible? They don't even know each other. That could be disastrous." I cringe.

"I don't know, but I'll take care of it. I'm sure they'll have something in common. Worse comes to worse, they can decide it isn't working and one could leave. It wouldn't be a big deal. I'll speak with them both."

The sad reality is I know Azmir is the best person to handle this and alone. I've easily warmed up to Yazmine and have even hung out with her a few times since she's been in town. My mother is a separate issue. I need time to adjust to her being around after so many years. Although so many things about her is familiar—her voice, her scent, her style—so much has changed—her appearance, her complexion, her aura, her grace, her confidence. It's going to be a huge adjustment. One I have yet to settle on.

"Okay," I cowardly assent to.

A couple of weeks later I'm at work, finishing up on a patient when I get a text from Azmir, saying he's arrived next door to work. Apparently, he left his pocket watch at home in a rush out the door this morning.

I left extra early to get to my doctor's appointment before work but returned home to shower and dress for work. For some strange reason, I always feel like I need a shower after seeing my GYN. That gooey lubricant used to probe my private has always made me feel yucky. When I was dressing to leave for work Azmir, who had left out before I'd returned from the doctor, asked me to grab his pocket watch and said he'd be at the rec today and could get it from me then.

I quickly decide I can use some fresh air before my next patient, so without replying to his text, I hop next door to take it myself. When I get to his office reception area, I come upon Old Lady Peg. I grunt inwardly. Azmir doesn't spend as much time at the rec center as he did when we'd started dating. Therefore, I don't have to see Peg as much and endure her arctic regard toward me.

As I near her desk after entering the doorway of the area, I apply a practiced smile, "Morning, Peg. I hope all is well. Is Azmir available?"

Peggy lowers her chin to see over the frames of her glasses. She gives me a once over before her eyes roll from me, back to the file before her.

"Afternoon. It is three minutes *after* noon, Ms. Brimm. So, good afternoon to you," she pauses, seemingly taking her attention back to what she was doing before I arrived. "And Mr. Jacobs is in a meeting now. You can have a seat until it's concluded," she murmurs, never looking up for a response or a reaction.

My eyes spring erratically as I process her crudeness. I don't know what to do. Ice Queen Peg is an employee of my, now, fiancé. Why do I feel like the adolescent crusher of her child? I honestly don't know what to say to this woman who, at every opportunity, thickens the barrier between us.

My eyebrows furrow as my lips pout, "Ummmm...Peg?" She slowly peers up at me. "You do know I woke up this morning to this man we speak of, don't you?"

Arctic Peg's nose swings in the air at that comment, affronted. "Yes...yes, darling. I do have knowledge of you living with Mr. Jacobs. And of your recent engagement. I am his legal secretary, Ms. Brimm. How could that piece of knowledge escape me?" She won't stop with her venom.

I've had enough with Cold Cruel Pegster! I've never been anything but warm and respectful to her, only to have her zap me with sheets of ice. There's no way I can continue with Azmir and have his *staff* regard me so rudely.

"Peg, I'm not sure where we went askew when we met. I have no idea what I've said or done to make our exchanges so...glacial. But I don't want to do it anymore. Tell me what I've done so I can apologize and make amends. This needs to end here." I pluck a brow. "Today."

Frosty Peg appears unmoved, but I definitely have her attention. She sits back in her chair and removes her glasses, placing them on the desk. Straightening her shoulders, she utters, "You lied to me the first time I encountered you. You presented yourself no differently than the droves of women who vie for his attention daily. Only, he was pursuing you as well." Her head goes toward the right as her sight sets out to the distance, recalling months ago when I'd lied to get a couple of minutes with Azmir to thank him for the *iPhone* he'd surprised me with.

"I've worked under wealthy businessmen for decades. I know the life of a man with many resources. I was the second student enrolled in the fine *Long Beach City School of Legal Assistants*. I'm very proud of what I do and have been doing it since your grandmother was doing *The Frug*. I've seen the dark underworld of rich men. The dives in morality they take because of their privileged statues. I've worked for men who would only let my Mr. Jacobs in their offices to clean their shoes." She lets out a huff after. I guess at the idea of someone thinking so little of Azmir.

"When I met him," Peg refers to Azmir. She's suddenly gained an arch in her cheeks— *is that a...smile?* "I'd been laid off from a job I trained my successor to do. I had no idea they were using me only to fire me and after twenty-six years of service." She snaps her tongue on the roof of her mouth.

"When I walked into that warehouse...into that small hole in the wall, I was broke and broken. I made my way into an even smaller room where I laid eyes on his dark skin, dressed in a button up, jeans, and construction boots while sitting over a mountain of paperwork. I knew right away this brown boy was going to turn me away. I didn't even know if I wanted to work for him—the place was horrendous." Peg chuckles at the memory of it. I'm standing awkwardly, envisioning the Azmir from back when.

"He looked so disorganized, in such disarray!" She cups her mouth to muffle her mirth. I can't believe she has a functioning sense of humor. "He was on the phone, and when he spoke, I could close my eyes and not know what his ethnicity was. He was the brightest man I'd met his age. Almost instantly, I'd decided I wanted the job. I didn't have the description of the company, but I didn't care. This young man was promising," Peg's mirth falls into a warm smile. But then her eyes find mine and her cheeks drop into a scowl.

"And I later learned he was loyal. I got the job and started the same day. And despite my age, and the color of my skin, a few months later, I moved into an office park he rented out to run the company. Then he brought me here when he purchased this massive lot and built this beautiful architecture." Her eyes gleam with pride. "He spends more time working than any of those rich bastards I'd worked decades for. He helps people, puts their needs in front of his own. He's a workaholic, which is why it didn't surprise me when his relationship with Ms. Harrison failed. I wasn't happy to believe he'd be alone. A dark, handsome man with his brilliance, charm, wealth, and resources, but no wife or children?" Peg snaps her tongue again and visibly trembles at the thought. I remain silent, trying to process her perspective.

"Anyway, along with wealth and power, comes fanfare of the female persuasion." She goes back to her paperwork, there on her desk. "You lied when I first met you. To me, you were no different. He's a good man. One who needs an honest and pure woman on his side. Someone who will fiercely protect him—"

"And I won't?" I sputter. I can't believe she's alluding to the fight between Azmir and Brian Thompson. "I was trying to surprise him romantically that first day. I think I've proven I'm not like the others. And the fight was...a mess, but we've worked through that mishap. We've moved on—together." I square my shoulders, feeling a burst of confidence. "I may not have been perfect while dating, but I will be the best wife I can to him. I will work damn hard to give him the partnership he deserves." Peg's eyes ascend to meet my determined gaze. "I love him. I can love him. I will love him."

We engage in a stare down. I will not waver. I'm sick of doubting myself and I certainly won't tolerate being doubted by others. If Azmir wants me after all of my running, second-guessing, and mistrusting, then damn it, no one else can judge me!

"Understood, Ms. Brimm. I guess time will determine all." With a slight nod, she continues, "My best to you and your nuptials."

I know that's as close as I'll get to her approval. So I accept it, hoping it will begin a course to a warmer exchange between the two of us. I give Peg a firm nod and proceed to Azmir's office door instead of waiting as she asked, feeling good about myself for finally standing up to Old Lady Peg. I, in fact, feel like I have a better understanding of her. Whether or not the feeling is mutual remains to be seen.

I enter the office with my eyes in search of A.D. in the massive room. I immediately recognize the voice of a woman—actually two. My gaze finally lands in the conference area where Azmir is seated with Shayna and Dawn. My first inclination is panic, but considering my conversation with Peg and my new resolve of who I am in Azmir's life, I refuse to coil.

I can tell the moment Azmir has processed my presence. His eyes slowly go into a priapic slant, and he whispers my name, *"Brimm..."*

Azmir rises from the table and meets me in the middle where he takes me at the small of my back and plants the most passionate kiss. It isn't the most indecent; I know Azmir's oral embraces now. There is one where he needs me, another where he misses me, and one where wants to *smash* and my clothes will be torn off momentarily. And then, there's this one when he's just...*happy* to see me.

Not too long ago, I would've folded under the presence of Dawn Taylor. But today, I fold into his lush stature and let him smudge my lip-gloss.

"You're a sight for sore eyes," he murmurs lazily. Then with his eyes squinted, he asks, "You okay?"

"Yes, of course I am," I answer with light incredulity. I don't like to see him all worked up over me. I've caused enough trouble. "I'm bringing your pocket watch," I murmur as I pull it from my white coat pocket. "I still can't believe you left it behind. That's not like you at all," I admonish as I study the pocket watch while handing it over to him. "You're known for this timepiece."

Azmir takes the watch and lets out a bellied chuckle, "Only by you, Brimm...only you," he scoffs.

He looks adorable in his plaid business shirt, wondrously fitted dress pants and matching tie. Without his suit jacket, his Prada belt—my favorite belt—is displayed. Azmir looks delicious as he always does, no matter what he's wearing. My hands itch to caress the stubble on his beautiful face. He looks just edible, which brings me to the reality of our surroundings. Our mixed company.

I crane my neck to see beyond Azmir. "Hello, Shayna. Hi, Dawn," I greet the ladies who are still sitting with dozens of papers, folders, and pictures in front of them, on the small conference table.

"Hi, Rayna! How are ya?" Shayna returns.

I give her a courteous nod and notice Dawn on her phone. She gives me a brief wave, which lets me know she is aware of my presence.

I tentatively turn my gaze back to my handsome man in front of me. He's too good to be true...and he's mine. I feel my cheeks heating up and my face cracks into a full-on smile.

"I should go. I need to grab a bite before my one thirty arrives," I mutter.

"Wait," he pulls me into him more snug. "How was your doctor's appointment?"

I didn't expect Azmir to want to make small talk while he's in the middle of a business meeting, but there's this austere look in his eyes I can't reject. I quickly decide to entertain him. "It was, for the most part, routine. I'm still healthy after your excessive usage," I whisper in jest.

Azmir laughs again. My smile widens as a result. I'm experiencing his laugh more and more lately after all of these months of knowing him.

"So that's it? She just examines you and that's it?"

"Pretty much. We did chat about new..." I take a minute to readjust the volume of my voice. "...methods of birth control. She's sent me away with a bunch of brochures to help me decide."

"Why would you need a new method? What's wrong with *Yasmin*?" The concern in Azmir's brown irises is palpable. What's even more alarming is his knowledge of the brand of pills I take. I swear I have no privacy of person where this man is concerned. Now I'm clamming up. This is a personal topic, and his associates are mere feet away.

"Nothing other than the burden of remembering to take them every day," I say quietly. His inquisitive gaze doesn't falter. My eyes shoot over his company to find Dawn stealing glances our way. I know Azmir won't drop this topic right now if I ask him to. I have to give him an answer, but it will be brief. "It's just that I'm considering something a bit more long-term. I don't wanna give us any surprises so soon into our nuptials." I smile cautiously, trying to soften the tone of this conversation.

"You were a *surprise*. Running into you at the perfect time of my life was a great *surprise*," Azmir murmurs as he pulls me into his tall frame, using both arms with mine caught between us. "A baby would be a welcomed *surprise*—hell, addition, just like you are."

What in the hell?

Aghast, my eyes peer over to his waiting party to assess how much attention we're drawing and if they'd in fact, heard Azmir's crazy decree. *We are not having this conversation. He has not just spoken those words.*

"A-Azmir..." I'm at a loss for words. I'm waiting for him to throw me a bone by saying his comment was timed wrong or just plain ol' crazy. But no. He stands there, waiting on me to continue. I sigh, resting my forehead on his chest.

"My, my, my! What are the lovebirds up to that have them whispering over there?" Dawn calls over, thankfully shifting Azmir's determined gaze from me.

That catches both our attention and Azmir and I move our sights to Dawn at the table. Her crimson lips bear their usual smirk. I don't know specifically what it is, but I'm sure she's playing at something in that sinister head of hers.

Azmir doesn't speak, but needing a cue, I do. "I was just letting Mr. Jacobs know I'm preparing for the *Mauve* event. I have to pull together a glam squad to assist." That wasn't premeditated, but it sounds decent and right on time. My eyes go back to Azmir whose face is now fixed in a scowl, and I'm sure it's because I've begun a new conversation with a new partner and with such ease.

I break from his embrace to end the baby addition conversation. His fixated glower doesn't waver, and I subconsciously wonder how I changed his disposition so quickly, in a matter of minutes.

Nice, Rayna!

Dawn perks up, turning her body towards us and even from a few feet away you can tell she's hit with revelation. Dawn's expressions always make you feel there are malicious thoughts or swindles regarding you going on behind her eyes.

"Well, I do have the perfect stylist for you!" Dawn announces spiritedly.

"Oh, yeah?"

I'm not short of stylist options. Being Azmir's...now fiancée comes with said perks. But this lifestyle is still new to me, so I always keep an open mind. Plus, Dawn is in PR, she likely knows the "who-to-know" of the entertainment industry.

Azmir doesn't join in on the conversation. He's pensive, I'm sure mulling over our missed conversation about a baby. His eyes go between me and the area behind me. I manage the moment by not falling under his gape. I'll easily cave in emotionally and again, we're in mixed company.

"Yeah," Dawn answers, going back to her writing pad and jotting down the contact info to the stylist she's recommending. "She would love to hear from you. I'm sure she'll work wonders with your physique, too."

I don't know how to take that comment. It's recited with a snide tone, but with Dawn you never know. Since I'm already in hot water with the big guy, I decide to let the comment slide and take the info from Dawn's proffered hand as I cross the room.

"Thanks," I offer cautiously.

Although we've made a conjunct, yet silent agreement to be cordial, I don't trust Dawn. I've only transferred her formidable presence in my mind, from *threat of losing Azmir to his Plan B* to *annoying lurking of my Clean-up Woman*. Either way, she isn't to be ignored because she isn't extraneous energy like Tara and her father. She's a powerful ember force, just waiting to be reignited.

My eyes slowly leave Dawn and return to an anxious A.D., still reeling from our previous conversation. I walk into him and rest my hands on his chest messaging the desire to soothe his concernment. However, my resolve, my actions are timid. As I tilt my head back to look him in the face, I mouth, "I love you."

I don't believe the women behind me have any idea of what I just messaged him, but I know he feels my words by the way his eyes soften and he takes me at the small of my back again. He doesn't reply to what I said, but exhales strongly, making it clear my words have affected him.

"I have to go," I murmur.

Azmir nods in assent, but in a flash, his face turns tight as his brows wrinkle. "I need to talk to you about something. Think we can chat after counseling on Wednesday, over dinner?"

I don't know what to think about the impending topic, but quickly decide not to panic. That quickly, I choose peace over angst. I shake my head then realize a nod is more appropriate. "No problem. Any time you want. Sure."

Azmir plants a gentle kiss on my forehead causing those trustee zaps to shoot through my body. I turn to walk away to ensure he doesn't pick up on it. As I approach the door, I hear him call out, "Dinner in Redondo Beach with YS."

That stops me in my tracks. I know immediately he's referring to Thanksgiving dinner with Yazmine and Samantha. Azmir and I discussed a few days ago where we would spend our first Thanksgiving together. I'm perfectly content having dinner alone at the marina and covertly expressed it. He mentioned Yazmine's desire to have us over along with Samantha, but it didn't sound definitive. *I guess it now is. Ughhhhhh!*

"Perfect," I muster an ominous grin as I watch Azmir take his seat. "I'll make the biggest and sweetest ham you've ever tasted!"

Azmir spits out the heartiest chuckle I have ever seen in public. I mean he's tossing his head back and grabbing his abdomen in an all out laughter. My face cracks a mirthful smile.

I made the great A.D. laugh? Wow!

"Yeah, right! Yazmine would have you and your swine out on the curb before you could say, '*But my name is on the deed*,'" he belts out, as he's unable to slow his humor.

At that, *I* laugh as I make my way out of the door.

These darn black Muslims. Ain't no pork ever hurt nobody! I joke to myself, leaving Mr. Jacobs and his associates to their business.

Azmir

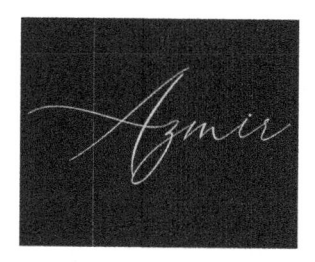

I've just left a meeting with Petey, Kid, Santiaga, and Paulito, who both seemed impressed with Kid's knowledge of the trade. Santiaga and Paulito were of Mexican and Italian heritage, respectively, and were of a different breed than us. They weren't ecstatic about my departure—hell, they were competitors in many markets and never met together. But I'd always been a unique individual. It had taken three years for me to get into the same room as Santiaga, and five for Paulito. They don't meet low-level pushers. I had to prove myself and establish my reputation in the streets before they'd even acknowledged me. Sure, they'd known exactly who I was. They'd supplied to me for years. But it wasn't until I annihilated my competition and started to request more stock, they'd considered breathing the same air as me in a room.

They understood taking over my competitors was no easy feat. There were men in the game longer than I'd been out of training shoes, but I was hungry...and clever. I knew how to steal their most valued soldiers right from underneath my competitors. And the ones I couldn't weren't strong enough in numbers to go to war with my newly constructed militia. For two years, there was a blood bath in South Central L.A., some of which I organized, orchestrated, and eventually triumphed from.

I had to earn their respect and I did, which is the only reason why they agreed to this sit-down and transition to Kid and Wop. They didn't like it because they didn't understand. In their world, businesses were of heritage and arrangements were not temporal. They were lifetime commitments passed down from generation to generation. You didn't make it to the levels I have and just walked away from it as if it no longer satisfied your passion. Again, because I've been so loyal and lucrative to them for so long, they respected my decision and even agreed to transition their transactions to Kid, with provision. That meant if Kid fucked up, it was his own ass.

The meeting was intense and draining. I knew Kid was nervous out his ass but forged ahead. We concluded on a handshake and agreed to never keep in touch. Ever. They can't risk me flipping. Paulito specifically said he wouldn't tolerate indecisiveness. That's fine with me. It's taken me years to withdraw from this business. I'm sure I won't regret it tomorrow, the next day, or the next year.

After that meeting, Kid and I met up with Petey and Wop to finalize our plan regarding D-Struct. It's been confirmed he spearheaded the arson of my property in Pasadena. It's also been established how Big D gave him the instruction to do so. My plans for Big D are awry because of his arrest, but D-Struct has to be handled. Once that meeting had been concluded I met up with Rayna.

Rayna and I finished her counseling session. It's more or less turned into our sessions. That wasn't my original plan, but it's somehow evolved to such. Initially, I just wanted to be a part of something causing Rayna to open up. Something she's been so committed to. And obviously because it gives greater insight to the enigma of this embattled woman. My embattled woman. But before I knew it, Pastor Edmondson began asking me questions, ushering me into their conversations. Then his wife began attending some of the sessions and I noticed those were more marital themed. There were lots of biblical references, something I went from reluctant to, to indifferent, to curious about.

Pastor Edmondson and I even had lunch together last week to discuss philosophy, something I find fascinating. We debate, but his aura always remains calm and inviting. He isn't at all judgmental and doesn't push me on my opposing views. Of course, Rayna doesn't know this. We agreed to keep it between the two of us until we establish an official relationship, if that were to happen at all.

There are questions and revelations derived from our conversations I haven't resolved internally, so I don't want to share my meeting him with Rayna. I don't want to confuse her if suddenly I come to no longer wanting to have these conversations with her pastor or attend her sessions.

While we're at *Hakassan* in Beverly Hills having dinner, I prepare myself to break some news to Rayna. Information that's sensitive and just as convoluted.

"How's the duck?" I ask.

Just before taking in another mouthful, and with a placid expression, she quickly returns, "It doesn't beat the hazelnut-crusted one in sun-dried cherry sauce in Phoenix, but it'll do." She then she supplies a charming wink and a sexy soft smirk while chewing her food.

She often references Phoenix with an affinity, making it clear that particular time together holds significance to her. I share the sentiment.

"The food's great...like always with you," Rayna murmurs after swallowing the contents of her mouth and going for her glass of wine.

I know she's enjoying it. The food here is superb. I've been several times. It's one of Tara's favorite restaurants. She loves the Beverly Hills stature and the possibility of running into celebrities here. And that's the sheer difference between the two women. Rayna couldn't care less about the ambiance or location. She'd been just as content eating in at the marina.

This place is out of the way of the church and marina, but I had my assistant make a reservation when I'd gotten a call from a boutique here in Beverly Hills. My order is available. I insisted on picking it up instead of them shipping it.

"I'm glad you like it," I say. "Listen, Brimm." I watch as she takes another sip of her wine and reclines in her seat, opening herself up for conversation. I requested a private table because of the nature of this dinner. "I want to share some recent events that may or may not concern you."

She slowly swallows her pinot noir and nods.

"Samantha will be moving in with Yazmine."

"What?" Through my peripheral, I can see Rayna's mouth hanging. "Really? When and how were you able to pull that off?" fumbles from her mouth.

I shrug. "I told you they've both expressed loneliness. I've gotten them together for lunch and they've been out without me." I hear Rayna gasp. "They get along. I don't see either of them finding it difficult to cohabitate with someone. My mother has had cellmates to acclimate to. And Samantha has had similar conditions with her rehab stays. It should work."

Rayna nods tentatively. I know Samantha is still a weak spot for her. She's not yet embraced her being back in her life. I quickly decide to move on to more pressing news I must share with my lady. I don't want to further delay this information. I take a swig of my brandy.

"It's recently come to my attention Daryl Harrison, Tara's father, has been arrested for murder. I believe you should know this for several reasons—"

"Oh, my god. Azmir, are you okay? I know he's no longer in your life, but he used to be your mentor. I don't know why you two ended your relationship, but this has to be killing you inside." Rayna speaks low, and with wide eyes filled with great concern.

If only she knew how arrogant his ass was when he'd met with Yazmine for the first time after her release from prison. She said pompousness dripped from him as he all but told her my father was a distant memory, and the details of his death were no more important than his nineteen-eighty-six income tax filings. Yazmine was really shaken up about it. I'd never asked her about her agreement with the *FBI* because I wanted no parts of them. So, Big D's arrest came as a surprise to me. I'd had another way of dealing with him about his order to burn my place in Pasadena, but the *FEDs* had caught up to him before I'd been able to confront him.

"I'm fine with it." I give an expectant pause to prepare myself for the next detail I need to share with her. "I'm fine with it because it's my father he's been accused of murdering," Her beautiful lips parts. "He arranged to have him murdered."

Rayna then cups her mouth. She looks as though she's sick. After a moment, she whispers, "This is crazy! Azmir, I'm so sorry." She then takes one hand and goes for mine.

"It was a shocking discovery, but after some time...I'm dealing with it." Morally, that's the best answer I can give. I observe her eyebrows narrowing under the dim lights of the room. "Before you ask, I first heard about the alleged murder a few months back, just after my birthday. I didn't want to believe it at first—shit, I didn't believe it at first." I swallow back the memory of the sensation I felt when I learned of it. "But since then, the evidence has mounted."

Rayna gasps, "Azmir!" she whispers. "What does Yazmine have to say about all of this? I'm sure she's sick all over again from losing her husband."

"She knows. Her early release from prison was contingent on helping with his arrest, though I'm not sure how much she has. She's how I found out." Rayna's eyes grow bigger. "Listen, baby, I really hate hitting you with this shit. And in all honesty, I've waited to tell you, not wanting to worry you. But I had to make you aware because of the level of complexity of my relationship with Daryl."

"What does that mean?" she asks, aghast.

"It means although he committed the most reprehensible

offense against me, there is still this debris of obligation I have to him."

"And what is that?"

"His estate," is the easiest way I can term this. "There is money left aside, privately for his...family in the event of an untimely death or, in this case, an emergency. This is something he's shared with only me or I'd fucking walk away without giving two shits about anything concerning him."

I fucking hate having to explain this shit to my lady on behalf of D's fucked up ass, but there's a degree of loyalty I have to keep with. Something that will be the last act of devotion I'll give to this depraved fucker. Something I know will not sit well with Rayna, which is why I've been mindful of what I share with her.

Rayna's eyelashes flutter. I can tell she's uncomfortable, anticipating what's coming next. "What do you have to do?" She clears her throat nervously. "What's your obligation to him...to them?"

"It's just instructions and distribution, something I've been dragging my feet on and will continue to do until—"

"Until?" she asks anxiously. I know this pushes her to the edge. But she's asked that I not keep things from her, especially regarding Tara.

"Until his family makes it clear the money is needed. At that time, I will instruct, distribute, and say goodbye...forever." I watch raptly as Rayna processes my words. She understands this ultimately means Tara.

Her eyelids clad in gold and bronze eye shadow slowly close and her luscious nude lips collapse. I grow gravely concerned. Rayna, historically, hasn't done very well with adversity in our relationship—or outsiders to our bubble, as she's termed it. I want to know what she's thinking. I wish I had a mole inside that incommunicado mind of hers. The one constantly overworked where I'm concerned. She's always doubted me. Questioned my devotion to her. Challenged my exclusive commitment to her. I don't want another flight attempt. I need her flexibility on this. Her lips make infinitesimal movements as if she's already firing off her opposition of what I'm presenting.

My anxiety begins to skyrocket. I have to say something; I need to intercept her dissension. To offset her rebellion. I know it's coming, I just hope I can effectively block it. *Shit! This is going to be a long night.* A cold and lonely night for me. My mouth opens to speak, only I have no fucking clue what I'm going to say.

But before I can align my brain with my voice, she blurts, "Okay."

"Okay?" I breathe out, asking in disbelief.

With her eyes trained to the table, still fluttering, she eventually moves them to meet mine and murmurs, "No more running. No more *operation shutdown in self-protection* mode to protect something you already have." I look at her, not exactly following. "You have my heart, Azmir. I didn't give it voluntarily. I even hated you at times for conquering it, but I no longer have it to protect. It's yours."

Baby...

I can't speak to affirm. I'm in total shock.

She whispers with determined eyes, "I told you, Azmir, no more running. I may have been knocked clearly off kilter by your... forceful...all-consuming presence in my life, but I'm no weakling. I'm yours. To love, honor, respect, and protect, but not to coddle." Her resolute eyes dance in mine. She wants me to understand her message. "I'm here for you. We'll get through this."

There's a long pause between our words. A cloud-exchange is taking place over our table. She has just pledged her devotion, denouncing ever doubting me again. Now it's my turn to take her at word. She said *we'd* get through this.

"Azmir, baby, say something," she whispers on an insecure cry. I know she needs my assurance. She's just taken a huge leap of faith, something typically terrifying her. I try to fight my incredulous state.

"I wanna fuck you so bad right now," I murmur, not entirely in jest. I also want to scoop her into my arms and shower her with declarations of eternal love and protection.

Rayna's eyes illustrate the speed of her mind, processing my words. Her head falls back as a shriek of laughter erupts from her belly. She laughs so hard and long, tears pour from her eyes. I let go of a chuckle myself, at her hearty merriment. I don't know how to express how much I love this moment between us. It's pivotal and delights me.

After finishing dessert, we make our way to the art boutique where we pick up a *Francesco Basso* painting, capturing Rayna at her last showcase. The one I missed. I'd scored expensive ass *Franco Basso* to seize an image of her in action so Rayna can see the fire in her eyes when she dances. She maintains she only does it for recreation, but the emotion she puts forth while dancing is something I've longed for since I saw her dance at my birthday party. Because I'd taken so long to be intimate with Rayna, I grew attached to her and wanted that same passion applied towards me. As much as it makes me sound like a little bitch, it's the truth and took some time for me to cop to.

We're standing in the middle of a private showing room in the back of the popular boutique. Rayna's mouth is cupped by her shaking hands and her breathing is erratic.

"Oh, my god, Azmir!" I hear mumbled beneath her hands.

Franco is standing next to the easel boasting the painting, wearing a measured smile. *Smug ass.* When I came to him with the idea, he tossed his fucking nose in the air, saying he'd had a waitlist for some king in a third world country as if I gave a fuck. I'd been one of the few who helped his soft ass out of a financial bind a few years back. And while he's paid me back, he wouldn't come off his six-thousand-dollar price tag...needing to be paid in advance.

Goddamn prick!

A sales rep peeks through the black curtain closing off the room in search of him.

"Ah! Ah!" he sucks the roof of his mouth with his tongue. "I with a customer!" Franco's Italian accent is brutally thick, until he talks money. Then he seems second generation American. *He's so fucking melodramatic.* The rep scurries out of the doorway and his eyes arrive back to my beautiful fiancée who's still awestruck.

"Are you going to say something, Brimm?" I urge as softly as I can muster. I'm anxious.

She slowly turns to me, finally releasing her mouth. "Jimmie is on a four-year waitlist for his. And when he signed up *with a deposit*, it was six. That's how I know his work...from Jimmie," she whispers forcefully. "Did you know Mr. Basso came to the U.S. with nothing and is now one of the most sought after artists? Michelle Obama has two of his paintings and is waiting on her third!"

"I sent it to her just last week," Franco hisses while rolling his eyes.

Rayna jumps at a one hundred-eighty-degree angle. "No!" she gasps. "You can't be..." She then looks back over to me.

Franco has a contented smile plastered on his face. *Cocky bastard!* He knew my lady didn't recognize him.

"Let's go, Brimm. We need to discuss where we'll hang this *Basso*," I speak softly as I wrap my arm around her waist.

Her body is rigid; she's really in shock. And I'm growing annoyed by the second from simply breathing the same air as this asshole. I want my lady alone, in my bed, beneath me, shaking from the art of what's hanging between my legs.

We give our goodbyes to Franco and make our way home.

CHAPTER 5

Azmir

Thanksgiving has rolled around and is met with mixed feelings. I know it will be strange for, at least me, to be spending a family holiday with my Earth. It's been damn near twenty years since I've spent a holiday with her. I don't know what the atmosphere will be like. Coincidentally, this will be my first major holiday with Rayna as well.

I've been accustomed to holiday dinners with Tara and her family. Patricia would make a big to do over the linens, silverware, and even her apron, attempting the ideal family meal. Big D would entertain her pretentious antics the way he'd always placate her idealisms. Tara would be shooting off at the mouth with either a complaint or a request for some astronomical wish list item. And I would, I guess humor her as well, just to get through the damn meal. After dinner, I'd cop a spot in front of the television for the game. After a few years, I'd watch television until I could no longer take the mundane of it all and would leave to get some work done. Big D and I never discussed business during family events, so he wasn't much company.

This year, I have a new family and a new lady. And the new

family is my mother and Samantha. My mother invited her girlfriend, Pam, from Chi-town out. I think it's nice that my mom is reconnecting with her old buddies. With Rayna's mom being in attendance I don't know what to expect. Samantha has been trying to move at Rayna's pace with reuniting. And if I know my Rayna, she's giving her mother a hard way. I will not involve myself in their affairs. So long as Rayna isn't hurt, I have no problems with stepping aside and allowing them to work through this alone. I have my own adjustment issues with Yazmine. We're good, finding our way amenably.

On our way over to Redondo Beach, Rayna doesn't talk much. I don't know if it's her nerves or she just enjoys the peaceful quiet, but when I shut off the engine, she doesn't budge.

I turn to her. "Are we good, little girl?"

Rayna's eyes rise to mine and I can see her pupils flip. She goes from introspection to company that quickly.

"Y-yeah...I'm good. Are you ready?"

Her eyes dance between mine. I can now tell she's pensive. *But what can I do?*

"Are you going to be okay in there? I don't know about you, but this is the first holiday meal I'm having with my Earth in two decades. My head's a little fucked up right now." I try warming to her.

She turns her gaze to the house, considering what I've said. After a few beats, she sighs, "Yeah, this is quite unusual, isn't it?" Her tone is just as forlorn as her words. She then turns back to me. "But we'll be fine." Then she cracks a beautiful smile. "Let's go. I'm starving." She kisses me, hungrily sucking my bottom lip before slipping out of the *Wrangler*.

I go to the rear cargo area to grab the turkey. Rayna spent the entire morning in the kitchen, preparing a maple-pear glazed bird. The damn thing is big enough to feed at least my *Cobalt* staff. We climb the steps to the porch, and she rings the doorbell. Her eyes are everywhere below her neckline. I can swear she's nervous. Before I can ask, the door swings open.

Yazmine throws her hands in the air. "Beloved, y'all here!" she shrieks as she engulfs Rayna in the biggest embrace.

Rayna reciprocates, "Mrs. Jacobs! I'm starving."

"We ready for ya, baby. C'mon in!"

Rayna makes her way inside and Yazmine turns to me. "Mir-Mir, you got a big ass bird there. Come, put it down. Is it cold?" she reaches up as I stoop down to allow her to kiss my cheek. "You so damn tall, beloved. Just like your uncle." She always said that when I was a kid coming up. My uncle was her brother, whom I've never met. He was killed in war before I was born.

"No, it's straight from the oven."

I walk into the house and head straight to the kitchen. It's funny, each time I'm here, I never feel familiar with the place. Rayna hadn't lived here long enough for me to acclimate myself to it. I find my way to the kitchen where I see Samantha, over the stove, stirring gravy.

"Happy Thanksgiving, Mrs. Brimm," I greet while holding the turkey in the large broiler pan Rayna's transported it in.

She turns, and with eyes as big as saucers filled with excitement, trills, "Azmir! You guys made it. Let me clear 'da counter for the turkey—wait, is it warm already?" The same question Yazmine had.

"No, it's hot...been cooking all day."

"Oh, good. Use them muscles and bring it into 'da dining room." She waves me on, and I follow her into the dining room where she has me lay the bird in the center of the table.

I see they set the table with five settings, reminding me of Pam's arrival to the West Coast. The table isn't mounted with *Mikasa* and crystal glasses like Patricia's but is built with great expectation of enjoying the holiday. I watch Samantha quickly remove the lid and foil from the turkey. It looks great. I often forget that my lady can cook. She only does it on the weekends when we're not traveling, which isn't often because I'm always whisking her off for a short stay somewhere. So, when I get her cooking, I'm amazed.

Samantha turns to me with a wide smile resembling mine. "She did good." Her cheeks are high with pride.

"Yes, she did," I nod. Speaking of which, "I'm going to put my jacket away and find Rayna," I murmur before heading out.

"Okay. We should be ready ta' eat in like ten minutes," Samantha calls out behind me.

I find Rayna in the living room with Pam. Yazmine is hanging her coat and yells out for me to bring her mine. As I stroll over to drop my jacket, I see Pam is holding up two bottles of cheap wines to Rayna, I guess offering them to her. Yazmine and Samantha don't drink, so Pam must be holding her favorite two.

I sidle up behind Rayna and pull her into me. "Pam, how are you...and what do we have here?" I feel my nose wrinkling.

"Divine!" Pam greets excitedly and I see the twinkle in her eyes.

She knows me as Divine because when my mom disappeared back in Chicago, though I tried walking the straight and narrow, I still had my hand in the streets. Pam was a closeted coke lover. I wouldn't call her an addict, but she definitely had her get-high preference. She liked to lace her weed with it on occasion. I used to fuck with her niece, Tonda, when I had initially moved to L.A.

"How are you?" I ask again.

"I'm good. I have my old buddy back. I'm just so happy y'all back together." Pam holds the bottles of wine under her wing as she speaks animatedly. "This is a real nice spot you put them up in."

"Thanks, but I can't take credit for that." I gaze down at Rayna who's beneath me as my hands are splayed on her shoulders. Rayna glances up at me and shoos my graciousness. "I take it you've met my beautiful fiancée, Rayna."

"Oh, yeah! She pretty as hell, Divine. Real pretty. Wait 'til I tell Tonda. She missed out on a good thing. I hear you the man out here!"

Rayna's cranes her neck up to look at me at the mention of Tonda's name. I'm sure Pam isn't attempting to be rude. She just lacks etiquette and doesn't know you're not supposed to reference a former lover in the presence of a current lover—or in my case, a fiancée.

"That won't be necessary. Tonda is a grown woman now, who I'm sure has gone on to better options."

Before Pam can put her other foot in her mouth again, Yazmine yells out, "Dinner is ready, y'all."

We all turn in the direction of the small dining room where Yazmine has summons us to. When I turn back, I comment, "I'm a whiskey man." I nod towards the bottles Pam is cradling. "And Rayna was just complaining of a headache on the way in." I pull Rayna farther into me, garnering her attention as I continue, "I don't think a drink right now would help with it."

Rayna's big eyes slowly shrink as she processes my request of her not drinking that cheap ass wine Pam's offering.

She looks over to Pam, "Maybe later, huhn?"

Before Pam can reply, I order, "C'mon, let's go wash up for dinner." And we take off to the powder room.

In there, Rayna hisses, "What's the deal, Jacobs?" while washing her hands.

I furrow my eyebrows, initially confused. "What...that cheap ass wine she was trying to give you?" I scoff, "That shit'll have you sick after one glass."

Rayna shakes her head as she dries her hands. "Well, to help me get through this, I may need three glasses and if the only thing available is *Alizé*, then I look forward to recovering into tomorrow."

She leaves out of the powder room with a playful scowl on her face. This isn't looking good already. I follow seconds later after drying my hands.

At the table, we all feast well on the spread the ladies prepared. Rayna's turkey is off the fucking chain and is centered by mashed potatoes, Yazmine's famous candied yams, collard greens Samantha made sure to cook with smoked turkey, mac-n-cheese, Yazmine's cabbage, stuffing, ziti, roast beef, and rolls. Rayna was quiet, yet polite. Samantha isn't much talkative either, but courteous.

"So, Divine getting married. Ain't that something. I remember when you was damn near a baby," Pam giggles, clearly set nice by her candy wine.

"Yup. My boy is now a man and marrying a beautiful young lady. I can't be happier," Yazmine interjects. "I could remember when he came home from the hospital. Mmm...mmm...mmm!" she shakes her head. "Seem like yesterday."

"I can only imagine what he was like as a boy. He definitely a fine young man now. You did good, Yaz," Samantha speaks up. She's never short of a compliment for me.

"Azmir was smart, reserved—very observant. Couldn't get nothing over on him. But when he wasn't into something, you would lose him. If it wasn't for him, he wasn't with it," Yazmine pipes out.

"Reserved...hmmmm..." Rayna whispers while eyeing me suspiciously. I know she's teasing me. Her smile brightens my world. I wrinkle my nose to her.

"Oh, yeah. His daddy taught him ta' be 'dat way."

Pam almost interrupts her, "I bet he was a lady's man, too, huhn? 'Cause them girls in the Chi was wild over him—young and old."

Yazmine swings her head so her ears move vertically, indicating a convoluted answer. "Not so much when he was small. Dasu trained him good and...hard."

I observe how raptly Rayna and Samantha watch my mother tell a story I've heard a million and two times as a kid coming up. It's not something I've sat through recently and I'm not exactly sure if I'm emotionally prepared for it today in front of mixed company, but Yazmine continues.

"Dasu would tell 'dat boy all the time 'dat he wasn't built like the rest of 'em. He would say 'dat my Azmir is a warrior, a leader. He drilled into 'dat there boy 'dat he needed to know how to govern people and he must start with observing them because 'dat was the only way he could conquer them." Yazmine's eyes turn haunted. I know those were my father's words verbatim. I have vague recollection of them, but she uses the same phrases each time she speaks of my father's legacy to me.

Yazmine pauses, clearly becoming emotional by her trip down memory lane. I don't know how to respond to it. She snorts, "After all these years, I still miss my Dasu. There ain't no man like 'em. Ain't gon' ever be." She offers a forlorn smile.

I don't notice Rayna's gaze upon me until I feel her grab my thigh underneath the table. I turn to her to find sentimental eyes. It's clear she's affected by Yazmine's pining. Or at least that's what I originally assume until she mouths, "I told you they knew."

I narrow my eyebrows, not understanding her reference. She then whispers, "The lion...your reflection," before cutting her eyes to my mother.

"I can tell he's done his father proud. I'm still getting to know him as a man, but I can see he did it. He made Dasu's dreams come true."

That comment from my mother makes me wonder if my dark world had been a part of his dream. Yazmine never speaks of my father's hustling and neither do I. Nevertheless, the fact that he and Big D had a side hustle always causes me to wonder just who my father was. There's one thing for sure and that's the apple didn't fall too far from the tree when you consider me living a double life.

"Dasu ain't want no other kids after Mir. He said he got his boy 'da first go round and ain't no need to try no more. I was good with 'dat, too." She smiles affectionately and so does Rayna. Too much mush for me, but that's women.

"That's sweet," Samantha murmurs in wonderment.

"What type of girl was she?" Pam tosses her hand toward Rayna as she stuffs her mouth with a roll.

Naturally, all eyes land on Samantha. I don't know if this is a good conversation to take on. Rayna has already been anxious. That's the strange thing about Rayna; she enjoyed hearing my mother's stroll down memory lane, but I can tell right away she doesn't relish the attention of her memories. This is *complex Rayna*.

After a long pause, Samantha perks up, "She was bright...real bright. And she was a helper." Samantha's gaze rises to Rayna, whose eyes stay trained to the table. "She helped the other kids in her class who weren't getting their studies like her. She talked a lot. The teachers always said 'dat she was gonna be one of 'dem."

Samantha's smile can't be ignored. She's proud...a proud mother. I sit and try to imagine my Rayna as a beautiful school-aged girl. I bet she had long ponytails twisted into barrettes at the end. I wonder if I could've bagged her had we grown up together. *Would we be together today?* Nah, I ran the streets too fucking hard back in the day. I wasn't checking for a real relationship. I just wanted ass and never found a shortage there. I would've broken her heart. Hell—I feel like I've been doing that since I've met her, and no one has ever meant so much to me in my life. *Nope*. It's good we didn't cross paths before I was ready to give her the world and she deserves nothing less.

"So, she was a good student? Mir was, too, before 'dem hormones got 'da best of him," Yazmine jeers, referring to the streets. They begged for me...still do, but I'm done. As I turn my gaze to Rayna, I realize I've taken on a new addiction, a healthier one.

"Oh, yeah, before my days turned...dark all of my kids made good marks, but Rayna..." Samantha's eyes go adrift again, only this time it's obvious there's guilt behind them. "...she was special. My little fighter. She was strong and bold. Never took no mess off'a nobody. Not even her daddy..."

The table goes quiet, and I become uncomfortable and can imagine what my girl is feeling. It's my turn to grab her underneath the table. Her hand is cold. *What the fuck?* I slowly bring my eyes over to her to find her staring straight ahead as she scrapes her bottom lip against her teeth.

Samantha's abrupt croaky voice tears my attention from Rayna. "I 'memba one night I was tryna' talk her daddy into moving us out the projects and he shot my idea down. It was sad...I didn't understand why he said no. I had a good plan. We coulda been outta there in no time. But more than I was mad at Eric for saying no, I was hurt for my baby girl. See, everything is in her eyes."

Samantha's eyes lock with mine, as she speaks to me directly. "I'm sure you know 'dat 'bout her by now." Her eyes grow big, "She wasn't always like 'dat. Before 'dat night, she let everything come from her mouth. Rayna always told you like it was. Memba, she was bold." Samantha lets out a chuckle that quickly dissipates. "Until 'dat night. Since then, I had to find a new way to find out what was going on inside. I saw everything in her eyes," she nods. "But then I fell off. Traded my pain for numbing—that crack demon. I decided and faced 'da consequences. I would wake up from time to time, though ...outta the fog."

The table is eerily quiet. Rayna's eyes will not find their way to her mother. She continues eating her food as she has been since Samantha started speaking. I don't know how to respond to this emotional stirring. I will protect my girl at all costs, but I can sense no malicious intent coming from Samantha whose eyes are now in her plate.

"The first time I stayed in it for months. I fell in there hard...real hard. When I woke up, my baby boy was in county." Samantha's eyes rise to Rayna. "And my big girl was gone."

Rayna coughs and grabs her throat. It isn't loud, but definitely concerning for me. I hand her a glass of water, which she takes. She gulps it down, but then sharply rises from the table and heads out of the small dining room. I follow on her heels. When we reach the powder room, her glazed eyes tell it all.

"Azmir—" she whispers, fighting a cry.

"It's been a long day for you. I'll go say our goodnights and get our coats."

"I don't want to do this to Yazmine," she implores, straining the tears within.

"Don't sweat it. She knows what time it is," I retort, knowing how perceptive my mother is. I'm not about to risk Rayna having a meltdown just to save face. I want to get her to bed and resting if that's what she wants.

After leaving the dining room, explaining Rayna isn't feeling well to the women, I make my way to the closet to retrieve our coats. I feel a timid hand on my shoulder and turn to find Samantha.

Damn. What do I say if she asks for more of an explanation?

Samantha appears humble and warm when she whispers, "Don't give up on her."

"I would hope you wouldn't either," I offer. "She just needs time, I'm sure." I know that's what upset Rayna.

"She ain't always been so...fragile. She changed, but I saw when it started...know it's my fault. But I thank gawd she got you. 'Dat help me close my eyes at night." Samantha chokes back on her tears. "I don't think I be alive today if you ain't help me out. When I wake up in the morning, I still can't believe I live in my child's house." Samantha waves her arm randomly behind her, towards the living room.

I stand silently, not having anything more to offer. All of a sudden, I see Samantha's face warp into an expression I'm extremely aware of, considering she's given Rayna so many of her distinctive features, many of them cause my chest to tighten. It's pensive and I know she's stewing on her next comment.

As she's passed down to her daughter, Samantha has caramel skin. Only while Rayna's skin glows in its radiance, Samantha's is dim, likely due to her chronic addiction. She's an inch or two shorter than her daughter, and although her hair doesn't reach the length of Rayna's before she cut it, I can tell by the roots, Samantha has the same texture and ability to grow it in the mass and volume Rayna does. Her shoulders aren't as poised and don't hold the air of femininity Rayna's does. In fact, Samantha holds no feminine grace at all, similar to Yazmine. It's as if at some point during their days in the wilderness, they ceded refinement for survival; Yazmine from her years in prison and Samantha, from her forfeiture to heroine.

In our private conversations over the past few weeks, Rayna and I concluded both Samantha and Yazmine are just a fraction of the women—the beings—they were when we were children. The most obvious indicators were their postures and poor dialect. We both agreed to being aware of their broken argot. It was a sad fact, but common when you assent to the dark world. The streets. I know this.

"Azmir, you can't give something you don't have," Samantha mutters, calling me back to her presence before me. I wrinkle my eyebrows.

She shakily wets her lips to try again. "I watched her the few times we been together since I been here. She got a lot of layers around her. She protected. Guarded."

Now Samantha's speaking terms and facts I *do* recognize about Rayna. Things that are to my detriment.

"Rayna lost a lot when she was so young. Stuff 'dat you don't get from nobody but ya' momma and daddy. We took 'dat from her, being selfish and weak. Call it unconditional love. 'Dat child missed out on so much when we took it back. She was almost still a baby. She still messed up in here..." Samantha points to her head.

"...and in here." She then pats her chest; I'm sure, referencing her heart. "When you don't know unconditional love, you can't receive no love from nobody. I seen it before in my programs. Heard counselors talk about it. Never thought it applied to me." Samantha's eyes squint in pain. "Never thought it would apply to my kids. Make sense now, ya' know?"

I swallow hard before giving an emphatic nod. Slowly, I'm understanding Samantha's argument. Her plea.

"Sometimes people look past it...sometimes people run away at the sight of love." *She knows?* I wonder if she's aware of Rayna's infamous response to my fuck ups. She squeezes her eyes shut, seemingly painfully and whispers, "I don't know what her thing is, but I know she got one. And you..." She places her hand on my upper arm affectionately. "...you gotta understand she can't give what she don't have...she don't know."

We lock eyes in rapid transmittal of something I cannot explain. Something that happens when two desperate people with similar motives make a connection. When they silently decide on the same agenda. Samantha wants a piece of Rayna's heart, too. A piece she forfeited years ago. A place I want to be a part of like the need of my next heartbeat.

Rayna opening the powder room door breaks our exchange. Samantha clears her throat as she removes her hand. But before Rayna's within earshot, she whispers, "Be patient. Don't give up on her."

Rayna hesitantly approaches us, not understanding our convening. Quite honestly, until a few seconds ago, neither did I. But I do now. I've also grown more tenacious.

"Let's go, Brimm," I murmur.

She supplies her mother a diffident smile as she passes her to get to me. I hold out her blazer to assist with putting it on, only to have Rayna take it from my grasp and bundle it in her chest, not breaking her stride to the door. I don't know what that means, but I offer Samantha a cool nod before turning on my heels to join

Rayna's treads. Samantha returns a tight smile while her eyes face the floor and then closes the door behind me.

Several steps behind Rayna, I click the key fob to unlock the door so when she arrives at the truck, she doesn't have to wait for me if she chooses not to. She chooses not to. Before I can grab my seatbelt, once I'm inside the truck, Rayna leaps in my lap and closes in on my face. Her lips move with wild abandon. She's swift as her hands rove over my head and neck. Her hips rock in my lap as her ragged breath hits my face. She sucks on my tongue, not sparing a moment to breathe. Her tugs at my neck and shoulder are boorish and her kiss is so savage, her teeth hits mine in a cling. I can taste the desperation on her tongue. And can feel the slough of despondence in the tremble of her thighs clinging to my waist.

"C'mon," she rags out without a breath to spare, her voice husky. I've never seen her like this. She reaches for the buckle of my belt; I know to unleash me. And as ready as I am for her—because no matter the circumstance, my body always responds to Brimm—I cannot do it.

"No," I grunt as I pull from her mouth, trying to fight for lucidness while my girl gyrates like a motor on my cock, pussy humming in a way I intuitively know how to respond to. How to tame. "No..." I attempt again.

"Yes." She retrieves my bottom lip, making it hard for me to resist the waft of *Cool Water* hitting my olfactory.

"Rayna," I force out, trying to capture her wild hands, roughly caressing my chest, arms and neck. "We can't do this," I whisper forcefully, feeling her tongue. Fuck! *That tongue*—makes its way down my neck via my ear. My breathing is out of control as she grinds so determinedly on my lap. This is hard—real hard. It's my job to satisfy her—to extinguish her when she's in heat. To put her ass to sleep when her pussy purrs like a starved cat. I have to regain my fleeting control.

"I want you in my mouth," she pants, bringing those lush lips back up to my mouth as her soft hands aggressively go down to my pants, scooting her pelvis back to give herself room. *Shit!* If Rayna's mouth—or hands—get near my strongman this resistance shit will be over and I'll be face fucking *and* pinning her ass up against the dashboard in front of our mothers' home. *Fuck!* I can feel my dick swelling even more at the thought.

Wait… Is that a tear I taste?

"Goddamn, Rayna! Stop!"

She's crying. Growing desperate my damn self, I grab the door handle, opening up the truck. I use my right arm to cross her back, pinning her against my chest, remove the key, and carefully leave the vehicle. I know I've fucked her under emotional circumstances, believing to be teaching her a lesson, but I can't have her believe sex is a way to communicate her pain or cure frayed emotions. We have to handle this differently.

Feeling the change in climate, on a panicked breath, Rayna shrieks, "Where are we going? I can't go back in there!"

"Relax," I bite out as I adjust to secure her on my waist.

Not wanting to cross the house and risk being seen by Yazmine or Samantha, I go in the opposite direction. Rayna begins crying into my shoulder, clawing my upper torso. I carry her like a toddler, feeling her need for comfort and soothing. I march down to the beach. Ironically, this was the way I walked after hours of sitting in the car, staking out Rayna's house during, what she assumed was, our breakup. When I was on "duty," I'd wait until I knew she was asleep and take this route to the beach sometimes for a run, making sure not to be seen. It seems appropriate at this time.

I walk and walk and walk. Rayna cries and sobs and weeps. I hold her close, protectively, needing her to get it all out. The front of my shirt is stained with tears. And when I feel a new tremor, one coming from her body temperature lowering, I finagle my way out of my jacket and swath her chilled back like a baby.

I walk the beach with her in my arms for over an hour. There are times when my arms go numb, but I still clutch my lady, sensing her need for this, lulling her restless heart, calming her tortured spirit by way of the water. Water that, at this time of the year, supersedes the billowing of her troubled soul.

She cries for about thirty minutes and after she's done and there's nothing left but the hyper-activity of her diaphragm from the strong sobs she's endured, I walk for an additional thirty minutes before returning a zombie Rayna to the *Wrangler*, strapping her in with the seatbelt, and covering her with my jacket before getting in and heading home. I don't understand what freaked her out over dinner but decide not to pry it out of her tonight night. Whatever it was spooked her. And I just want her past it.

Once at the marina, I run her a bath, sit and soak with her, and meditate on her breathing. After that, I put her to bed, and she drifts off almost immediately. I lay and watch her sleep for a while. So many questions running through my mind about this woman who holds a part of me I didn't know was available, leaving me so fucking vulnerable. I take some time to consider Samantha's words of being patient with Rayna. I've asked her to spend the rest of her life with me; I'll be nothing short of patient. She's a rare treasure and I know this is a fragment of what completes the woman I've fallen in love with.

Ha! Listen to me, all sentimental and shit! That's what love does to even a G.

The next morning, I awake to lugging, licking, and warm breaths hitting my chest, down to my abdomen. Then I feel tempered chomping on the shaft of my cock. Initially, it feels like a dream—a wet dream, but within seconds, I know it's my girl, with a warrant for my arousal. Once I'm able to grasp consciousness, I rise from my pillow, flip her onto her back, and make way to the junction of her twiddling thighs. Rarely does she initiate morning love. This is my thing, but I'm prepared for this. I dip between her swollen lips, coating my tongue with her nectar. I drive into her canal, bringing her sweet lubrication onto her folds. I suck and spar until her legs judder.

I know this isn't the way she wants to ascend. I know she needs to be rocked...and hard. My girl desires to be fucked; and that's what I do well. I fuck Rayna until she loses consciousness. I don't want her taking flight this morning; I just want to push her to the edge to help her remember. Remember I am here and will provide for her. For whatever her needs are. That her emotional breakdown last night does not deter me.

"Turn over and grip the top of the mattress," I instruct.

Rayna skitters onto her knees with anxious anticipation. I hear her hum with pleasure before I shift behind her. She's ready. I smack her right cheek and pop my hand back.

"*Uhhhhh...*" she moans.

I smack the left cheek, but my palm remains to grip this one.

"*Ahhhhh!*" she yelps a little louder.

Removing my left hand, I wait a few seconds before making my next move. It's apparent I'm taken too long for Rayna when she rears into me, wiggling her ass. My lady is begging for it. I have to fight for control after seeing her mounds in the air, wagging for my cock. Damn it if she hasn't come a long way from that cool, take-charge lover I encountered on my birthday, when we first fucked. Now she understands who controls her pleasure. She needs me. And this is how she knows how to express herself. To love. She's come a long way. She'll probably talk about her ails later, but right now she wants to be fucked.

Rayna joggles her ass again, but I don't touch her.

"Wait for it!" I bite out.

She whines her impatience. I don't want to exasperate her, but

I enjoy seeing her in this position. I can smell her arousal. I want to feel it now.

"Open your legs," I growl.

Instantly, she spreads her knees, and her hips open up.

Without warning, I gingerly smack her pussy with my left hand, being careful not to use too much force, but applying the perfect speed, angle, and impact. It feels like slapping into a puddle of gel.

"Ah... DIVINE!" Rayna cries out as her shoulders shutter her head leaps ahead and left cheek slams against the headboard.

I know she hasn't climaxed, and I don't want her to. I just want to get her off the ground. Rayna shoulders and back heaves over heavy breaths. I give her a minute to collect herself as I examine her trembling caramel torso. *Goddamn.* Once she's able to gather herself, she wiggles her ass again, trying to reach me, but I back away.

"Do it! Now!" she demands through gritted teeth. And I know, that quickly, I've taken her as far as I can.

I pull her hips back to me. "Hang on, okay?" I growl.

She nods her head with gusto. My lady's fucking ready.

I bring the head of my cock to her slickened folds and once I assess her entryway, I slam into her.

"*Uhhhhhhh!*" she cries and I feel myself pulsating inside of her. Fuck! She's fucking dripping wet. So warm. And so damn snug.

After calming myself, I start to move at a steady pace. I take my time stretching her, filling her to capacity.

"Harder! Faster!" she croaks on a cry.

Prepared for this, I deliver.

I move swiftly and with urgency, slamming into her soft ass. I know what she needs. I understand she's telling me she no longer needs kiddie glove handling. She doesn't want me to regard her with the level of compassion she required last night. Today's a new day for her. And today she wants her femininity affirmed. She doesn't want to be nurtured. She needs to be fucked. And I will do for her whenever and wherever she needs it.

I stroke her long and strong. Grind hard and fast. I plummet with power and purpose. Grip her hips with might and fervor. Taking my body into a zone to be sure to handle her before I explode, I thrust into her until her body quakes violently, and she sings my name with so much force, I'm sure in this moment she can't remember hers. When her face slams into headboard and shoulders collapse in the same manner, my mission is accomplished, and her frenzied tremors causes a vibration in my groin as her walls grip my cock. I explode inside of her and watch my sweat drip onto her curved back while shivering above her.

"Azmir, I'm sure you've guessed I'm not out here with you just for golf," Terry notes as he attempts a bunker. The ball is hit high and travels over the lip, staying in the green. He glances over to me. "I know you better than that."

"Yeah, I figured what was afoot when I got your text a few days ago," I answer, admiring his swing. Terry's had practice in his leisure.

Terry's posture straightens and his face tightens against the blaring sun. We've been out here for about a half an hour. "He's not doing well, Azmir."

I raise my soft wedge club and swing. "I wouldn't guess so," I murmur as I watch my ball not fly as high as his. "He's facing hefty time."

"I don't believe a word of what he's accused of." He shifts to his hip.

"I don't think you do, hence the sole reason I've met with you today, T." Terry has always been extremely naïve, in my opinion. Never the baleful speed as Big D.

"Then you can appreciate his circumstances."

"Fuck him."

Terry regards me closely as I hand the caddy my club and begin to the next hole. "Azmir, you hardly mean that."

"I do," I say after a beat. "Whole heartedly."

"Azmir, you and Darryl have had a long standing relationship. That has to account for something." I can hear the pleading in his voice.

"This I know."

"Well, then you can appreciate the bind his family is in financially. Hell, my income isn't as fluid, but I've given Tara a few bucks to keep the creditors off their backs. They need you, young brother."

I turn to face him. "Terry, I've always respected you as a man… even when I questioned your affiliation with Big D. But right now, I doubt your morality. That fucker had my father killed, had my mother sent to prison, and if that wasn't enough, he's used me to make him millions without that disclosure. That's diabolical in my book." I find myself out of breath.

I'm under enough stress with finding this motherfucker who is capable of hurting my fiancée and family. I don't need any pushback from excluding Big D from my life from his right hand man.

Terry gazes at me with what appears to be sincere empathy. "I understand your position, Azmir, I do. I'm just hoping to have cooler heads prevail here."

"I only invited you up here out of respect for the level-headedness you've always shown, Terry. You've always pulled me to the side to express your concern about my desolate lifestyle. You used to say you were concerned about me disposing of my potential."

"Yes, Azmir, you know me." His large frame, just about an inch shorter than me, but more than twice my width with flabby muscle faced me with persistence. "You know I've always pulled you to the side with discretion and told you there was more to your mastermind than the streets. I'd always been concerned about your wellbeing. You've always been alone regardless of what Darryl, Patricia, or Tara perceived. You know me, Azmir."

"Yes, I do. Remember how you cautioned me when I dropped out of Stanford? Huhn? Remember when you all but begged me to reconsider that shit, saying that was my way out of the game. You said you wanted more for me, that you saw more in me. You've played the background since I've known you, but I knew you didn't approve of Big D's guidance," I recap, losing my patience.

He scratches his head then softly mutters, "But that didn't influence you, son. You still remained with Darryl and cultivated some semblance of a bond. You and Tara remained together for around...what...six years? Time does something to bond people."

"My time with them was spent being used, Terry." I shake my head at his persistence.

I need to go, but respect Terry enough to entertain his ignorance. He's Big D's one good-hearted friend, a retired attorney. Terry had been the only one asking me *about me*. I'm not in touch with him, per se, though I'd see him sporadically at Big D's crib and other family events. He'd whisper words of caution and wisdom in passing. He's had to have known about Big D's mask. I wonder if he's ever expressed them to his friend.

"I hear you're engaged now." Terry's mouth, surrounded with salt and pepper stubble, curls into a genuine smile. "I know if you've given a woman a ring, you've found happiness. I'm happy for you, son. That alone should motivate you to be the bigger person and lift the burden off his family. You've won already."

"Yeah, I am engaged," I snort. "Did he tell you he visited my girl's job and attempted to blackmail her to get her out of the state?" I observe Terry's grimace. "And did he tell you he...commissioned..." I'm careful of my words in this public place. "...Tara's alleged baby's father to burn down my home, creating street cred for his punk ass? Huhn? Oh, the bloggers are whispering it, and the streets are screaming it. I'm paying for fulltime security for my lady and our mothers."

Terry's head drops. I may have just given news, but he should know how sick of a tyrant his boy is. "Yeah, Terry. It's good D's on the inside. It's *almost* a safe place from my wrath. But be sure to tell him, one more act of treason and I'll make sure the last time he closes his eyes will be in that same cell he's fucking stewing in."

I give Terry a final parting glance, to which he nods his head solemnly and I leave for a meeting.

CHAPTER 6

Azmir

A few hours later, while sitting in bed, Rayna enters the master suite.

"You know..." she mumbles with a mouthful, reading a message on her cell phone in one hand. Her expression is of disgust.

She's gloriously naked, exposing her smooth caramel skin that's become my favorite delicatessen as of late. Her nipples are perked, skin is flushed, and hair is in sweaty disarray. She's holding a dessert saucer with some concoction she's trying out for the dinner party with a few of my boys from New York City in the other hand. Rayna looks good as fuck in nothing. It doesn't matter she just fucked me in several ways—even in the face—I could easily devour her ass again.

"Why are you regarding your phone like it's pissed you off?" I ask as she types away before placing it on the nightstand.

"It's that designer Dawn Taylor recommended." I flinch at the cordial mention of Dawn's name by Rayna. She's been doing well at accepting Dawn as a business associate of mine, but I'll never forget the hurt I caused with my selfishness and recklessness in kissing ol' girl, some shit that will never happen again. "She's sending me awful pieces to gauge my taste." Rayna shrugs, "I just told her to bring them to my office tomorrow, I'd rather see them up close."

As she mounts the elevated bed, I can't help but ogle her lush breasts. Her round mounds are beautiful with nipples the shade of milk chocolate. And what I love most is she doesn't try to cover herself up, being self-conscious. She's just as comfortable as if she were completely sheathed in clothes.

"Here. Try..." she offers me a forkful of some unfamiliar custard. I mask my awkwardness and let her put it my mouth.

"Not bad," I nod. "And it would be better if I knew what it was."

She perks up, happy about the circular compliment. "Have you not been listening all night? It's a mini custard fruit tart Boyd has been distantly coaching me on preparing. And I think I've got it!"

"Sorry to be the bearer of bad news, but it was hard to concentrate on custard or crust when you were stripping me and pulling my cock in your mouth before I was able to cross the frame of the front door," I explain wryly.

Not that I'm complaining. Rayna's menstrual ended a couple of days ago and she is a nympho on methamphetamines the first few days after her last spotting. When she left the room for the kitchen after our last romp, I decided I was worn out. Now that she's returned wondrously naked, I'm not too sure.

While I'm expecting a punch in the arm or an aghast expression, I'm met with mild chiding of, "Azmir," she warns. Her voice husky and riddled with desire.

Goddamm, Brimm!

"So," I say, needing to change the subject before we end up at it again. "...do you like it? Has the recipe been perfected enough to replicate this weekend?"

Her eyes abstractedly scan the room as she considers her

answer. "I think so, but Boyd will sample it in the morning for a final assessment."

"When did you have time to make this?" I ask with my forehead wrinkled. I'm curious. I'm sure it took hours.

"I took a half day today," she answers before placing the last piece into her luscious little mouth.

"You? Took time off work?" I ask in mocking incredulity. "Anytime I ask you to, you always decline, saying it's not feasible."

Rayna sighs, relaxing her head on her shoulder as she lay on her side facing me. "I know. It's just that I need to make a few changes in my *operandi modus*," she giggles. More soberly, she murmurs, "I feel like I've been in a shell, a weakened state over the past few months. I need to get back to me." She takes a pregnant pause before continuing, "I feel like since being knocked on the ass —pardon my expression—by meeting you, I've been operating with kryptonite. You know?"

"So, I've weakened you?" I have to get this straight.

"In a roundabout way, yes. But in a suppressing manner, no. I guess that's what happens when you..."

"Fall in love?"

Her chestnut irises shoot up to meet mine as though I've helped complete her thought. "Yes," she breathes.

"Indeed," I express softly with a nod because I know this more than I care to admit. Rayna has fucked up my world and made it beautiful just the same. I can't imagine breathing without her sharing it with me.

"So, what about these wedding plans did you want to discuss? Or did you bring me here under false pretenses, Ms. Brimm?" I ask in jest.

She wanted to talk wedding plans, which was news to me. I'd begun to worry about her lack-luster enthusiasm over planning her big day. I mean, isn't that what women did from the time they were able to cognize the concept of prince charming?

Rayna gasps, "You would have been here at this hour anyway," then delivers the shove of my arm.

I scoff, "No, I would not have. I have far more important things to do with my evenings than having you sitting on my face."

"Azmiiiiiiiir," she groans sheepishly, burrowing her face into my arm.

"Rayna, if you want to smash again tonight, I'm gonna have to start charging you for my stamina." We both laugh at that. I love teasing her about sex. She still seems to be shy about discussing it for some strange reason. She's an easy target for embarrassment. Once we're able to slow our laughter, I continue, "About the wedding, little girl."

"Oh, yeah," she rebounds, bringing her head from my side, exposing her heavily blushed face. "About that...I've met with the wedding planner you passed to me a few weeks ago." I make a quick reference of who she's referring to before recalling. I don't want to mention this planner is someone Dawn threw to me in passing and I'd, on a half a mind, tossed to Rayna, figuring she'd appreciate a reference. "Just like the two before him, I became overwhelmed with all the options and trying to figure out my "wedding personality" as *Geraldo* phrased it."

She exhales. "I don't think I have a wedding personality. I sure as heck don't have enough people to invite to fill a church. I'm not even sure I'm a *wedding in a chapel* type of girl." Rayna waves her hand in gesture. "I don't know how or where I want to express my nuptials or take my vows." Her eyes slowly dance up to me. And just when I thought she's going to deliver a hard blow she mutters, "I only know who I want to take those vows with."

My heart races in my chest and I hope like fuck she can't sense it. I quietly expel the air holding in my lungs. This conversation could have gone either way with her. I'm still building my faith in Rayna wanting this *forever* thing with me.

Rayna sighs as she takes to her pillow. "I just don't know, you know? And I don't have girlfriends to help decide." With her eyes adrift, she murmurs, "I mean, it can just be you, me, and the officiate out it the middle of the Pacific for all I care. We can exchange our vows, let him or her off, and sail to the middle of nowhere—alone." After a beat, her eyes make their way up to me. "You know?"

Slowly nodding my head as the visual builds in my mind, I mutter, "Indeed." Whatever Rayna wants for the day she becomes mine will be exactly what I'll push for, because joining lives with her, for me, is the ultimate goal. "Now put your plate away so we can go to bed...unless you're calling out in the morning," I speak tentatively.

Rayna shakes her head. "No. I'll be in the office for my regular hours."

"Good and so will I, if you don't force me to smash you once again."

The heartiest laughter belts from Rayna's vocal cords. "Azmir, shut up!" she shouts in between her giggles. "My god! You miss your insanely sexy fiancé throughout your busy day, express it when he comes home, and you're accused of being a nymphomaniac!"

"Well..." I say, pleased with her mirth as she's still laughing.

"Well, let's see what your complaint is when I stop expressing." Rayna shuffles underneath the blanket.

"I wouldn't go that far. We saw how well that went over when you attempted that shit in Tahiti."

As Rayna finds her comfort in the bed, she sucks her teeth, "All right, Mr. Jacobs. Whatever!" and then issues me a warning glare.

The following morning, I'm in a meeting with a long-term friend of mine who, today, is serving in the capacity of a business associate. We're going over the fine print of the *Mauve* contract, the company I've agreed to partner with on their brandy line. Although the signing party is being planned, there's an amendment Steve has suggested I include in the final contract. I'll have my attorney, Chesney, go over the changes Steve and I have agreed on today. *Bacote & Taylor's Planning and Public Relations Corp.* worked their asses off, packaging the deal and seeing it to fruition, however, Steve is the mastermind behind the arrangement. He's the person responsible for bringing our names together in concept only, then proposing the idea to me and the Moreau Brothers, separately.

"You're a genius at this, you know that Stoute," I say as I proffer my hand, preparing to see him out.

"Nah, man. You know I'd do anything for you, Divine," Steve returns the love. "Few know you were the one who got me from *Sony* to *Interscope*. I'll never forget that man."

"Yeah, but your ingenuity is what got you to your mogul status. Proud of you, duke."

"Same here, man. You're making big moves, D. I don't know why you didn't just come over to us for PR services period." With his smile in place, I see as his brows narrow.

"Double S, you know me. I march to the beat of my own drum. I wanted to try this firm out, seeing they were fresh and innovative, but..." I find myself scratching my chin.

"But what?" he asks and before he can finish, my phone beeps and Peg's announcing Tara's visit. I can't say I'm surprised, but I wasn't exactly expecting her today.

"Hold on one sec," I call out as I cross the office to my desk and ask Peg to not only have Tara wait, but to call over to *Smith, Katz & Adams Sports Medicine Center* and see if Rayna can meet me in my office right away.

When I return, Steve, being the scout he is, picks right up where we left off.

"But...?" he asks expectantly.

"*Ehhhh...* Let's just say I am fielding for standby public relations services," I admit.

"Really?" The sleek grin forming on Steve's face can't be ignored. "I mean, I hate to say I told your ass so, but I told your black ass so!" he trills. "What's going on? Lackluster connections? Mediocre attendance—that's, by the way, the piss poor excuse you gave us when we first approached you years ago about taking you on."

I exhale deeply, "Nah, the girls are grinding. Let's just say the attention has been too...especial."

Steve's face deforms into an expression of disgust. "Ah, man! Don't tell me you smashed one of them—or both...I know how trifling you can get."

"*N-no*...no. No, man," I sputter, taken by his accusation. "My cock runs up in just one set of lips now a day. It's just one of the ladies—"

"Dawn!"

W-what?

"Yeah. If you're talking about one of the two humping your leg, in heat, it's Dawn." Steve is clearly picking up my bewilderment. He's always had a knack at reading nonverbal cues, which is likely why he's soared in his craft. "Let's just put it like this: she's said some things that read a little outside of her contract with you. Just be careful, man."

Strongly considering his words and with my forehead creased with concern, I nod. After bidding him a good day, I take the contract to my desk and start looking over the notes Steve and I agreed on. When I'm done, I ask Peg to have the latest intern come to my office to courier the edited contract over to Chesney.

Chris, the intern from *CSLBU* retrieves the documents and is just leaving when Rayna appears at my door knocking, though it was open. Her brows are pinched and understandably so. I reach for the phone and asked Peg to send Tara in. Then I rise from my seat and cross the room for Rayna. When I reach her, I scoop her in my arms and inhale her neck. Though she's still beyond sexy, I miss her long and wild hair. Sometimes I want to tug on it, like today, to loosen her up.

"Hey, baby," I murmur as I observe her elongated neck, stretching to gaze into my eyes.

"Hey, to you," she whispers, jarred by my affection. Not even I'm accustomed to being so touchy feely with a woman in public. But with Rayna it's different. I always want to feel on her, caress her. Shit—sometimes I can't help groping her. "Everything all right?"

It's then that I see Tara moseying into the office, wearing the same bemused expression as Rayna a few seconds before.

"Yes," I respond to Rayna, regretting having to let go. "I hope I didn't disrupt you from tending to a patient."

"Not exactly," she murmurs. I can tell she's still curious as to why I've asked her over.

Not seeing a reason to delay it, I break our embrace and lead her around to one of the chairs facing my desk. Smoothing my tie as I take my seat behind it, I ask Tara, "A seat please, Tara." Dubiously, she acquiesces.

I don't want to give drama an opportunity to erupt, so I kick off the assembly, "So, Tara, what brings you to *Optimal Health Recreation Center*?"

With strained narrowed eyes, Tara turns to Rayna, who throws a *don't look at me* glance her way.

"Time, Tara. Neither I nor Ms. Brimm here have a lot of time. We're in the middle of a workday." I minimize the curt in my tone. "Please...your reason for being here."

I can see Tara swallow as her bewildered eyes bounce between Rayna and me before she speaks. "My father." Her eyes flutter. "I'm sure you've heard he's been arrested on fabricated charges." She wets her lips, a fortifying move. "Listen, Azmir, I don't know what's gotten into you...why you no longer speak with him. I mean, I know what's happened between us, but my god, we've lost my mom, then you, and now my dad..." She was willing herself not to cry.

I glance over to Rayna, my eyes only, to see her captivated by Tara's emotional state, and likely curious as to what is going on here. I give Tara a minute to continue, but when she doesn't, I break the silence.

"And what brought you here today is...?" I speak as evenly as I can.

"I moved out of my apartment, just before having the—I mean, my baby. Daddy said he needed to cut back on expenses, and we agreed I'd need help with the baby. So, now with him being inconvenienced with these trumped up charges, I'm having trouble maintaining the bills along with my hospital bills and Azina's doctor bills."

Rayna clears her throat at the mention of Tara's daughter's name. I still don't know what inspired the audacity of her to name her child after me when she knew it would eventually be proven the baby isn't mine. What also strikes me is the mention of her hospital bills. I know the total cost of them. Big D could have easily paid off each one without sneezing, but he's blown all of his money gambling over the years. I know they've been waiting on the payout from Patricia's various policies, which I find pathetic considering Big D has made millions over the past twenty years.

I agreed to assist until some money came through and D would keep his law enforcement relationships in place until the end of the year when I'd retire from the drug game. I didn't trust him or Tara when we agreed I'd help until some monies became available to Big D, then he'd take over. So, I only paid a little at a time, refusing to get her totally out of that debt. My gut never led me wrong. Her bills were her burden alone.

Most people wouldn't understand my grievances with Big D aren't so much about him killing my father; I dealt with not having a father long ago. These new revelations haven't changed my resolve. Maybe one day I'll get the full spectrum of what my father's murder at the hands of Big D means, but right now it hasn't formulated in my mind. My betrayal is conceptualizing the grand scheme of D's mastermind. He's been a menacing son of bitch. He took out his partner who was in the way, and then used the dead man's son to build an empire. The empire his partner no longer wanted to pursue.

I can understand ruthlessness, I've been bedfellows with the means to conquering more times than I'd like to recount. But I've always been loyal, never crossing those who work with me. Never directly involving children to further my illegal ambition. Big D's ultimate perfidy of my father is one thing; his manipulation of me is something entirely different. Anyone outside of the game would think I'm still being manipulated by this final act of obligation, but even D himself knows we were done. Yeah, I have a conscience and don't wish to see Tara impoverished. But I also have a heart that has been misled by the Harrisons. And this is where it ends.

"Tara, I have access to monies your father has laid aside for emergencies such as this one. It's three hundred-fifty thousand dollars and will be available to you by the end of the workday tomorrow." I pull out a sheet of paper and push it along with a pen across my desk to her. "Please supply me with an account to have it deposited into or where you'd like the cash to be delivered to."

Tara pushes up from her seat to retrieve the paper and pen. And Rayna sits quietly with a stoic expression. I try not to read into it, so it won't take my attention from what's happening.

"Now, Tara, I must inform you I'm not in the knowledge of how your father earned this money or where it came from. Also, I'm not at liberty to discuss the details of the arrangement he and I made for such a time as this. Any questions you may have should be addressed to him." I pause to gauge her state.

She appears just as nonplussed as Rayna, who I'll deal with later. Right now, I just need her to perceive this as me being open with her on my dealings with the Harrisons.

Once Tara finishes with the paper, she returns it to my desk, and I can see the brewing in her eyes. I was with Tara long enough to know when her emotions are tumbling forward. And within seconds she mutters, "I thought I knew you. I thought by being with you for more than five years and knowing you nearly all my life, I knew you inside and out." Tara then cuts her eyes to Rayna. Rayna straightens and cocks her head to the side, preparing for whatever Tara was going to bring. Tara continues with, "The Azmir I thought I knew would have never abandoned the only family he's known when my mother was killed in an automobile accident. The one I knew wouldn't have left me during the loneliest period of my life, even if we had unanswered questions about the paternity of my child, especially because I was mourning."

She turns to me to finish her tirade. "She was the only mother you've ever known. She treated you well, although my father brought you to her as nothing more than an orphan of a former colleague. You ate at her table, spent family holidays with her." Tara exhales in disgust. "And my father. He took you under his wing even though we all knew you were trapped in that street mentality. My father risked his professional, law enforcement career and reputation to take you in and provide you with some semblance of family.

"He's given you the money from my grandfather's will to use as capital for your business. You were only twenty-five years old—a kid! And look at you now, Mr. Multi-Millionaire." She uses air quotations. "Yeah, I read that fluffed piece in *Vibe*. Cute. Too bad it was greatly fabricated. What would have been fact is you telling them that before you were even old enough to drink, my father made sure you had a roof over your head and food to eat..."

Tara pauses, overcome with grief and under false pretenses. She has no idea Big D has never put a roof over my head. I hustled to earn the pennies I garnered in my early years of slinging to pay my rent. She has no idea that when D would drop by my crib on their way to dinner at a four-star restaurant, that I would be covertly passing him off his cut. He's been able to keep the essence of our relationship from Tara and her mother. I was able to do the same once Tara and I began to see each other. And him giving me startup money was just a ploy just in case it was ever questioned where we'd *both* got our start from. Big D was never bestowed money from his father. He paid a lawyer to manufacture a spotty and antiquated money trail. D ain't never *give* me shit, only a world of opportunities.

"He saw you to being a man," she continues. "He let you take his daughter from him to date. My father trusted you with everything—look at what you're doing here today! You're giving me money he's only entrusted *you* with! This is evidence of his commitment to your relationship. And now, because we've hit a few hard bumps in the road, you up and pass us off like a business transaction? As if we didn't give you the privilege of entering our circle. Like we've given you no loyalty."

Tara brushes frustration from her face, her emotional control quickly abating. As I sit back cupping my chin, giving her time, she arches her neck, so her face is toward the ceiling. I can tell her father's arrest has taken its toll on her. After some time, her glower goes to Rayna, who watches her closely.

"And what's she doing here? What's the purpose of her having to be in the same room when we talk? Do we not have history, Azmir? The type of history we could speak about family matters alone? Has it come to this? Has she brainwashed you?" Tara's wild eyes settle on me, summoning answers. Answers that would never come. "Azmir, do you not have an ounce of loyalty?

I don't move from my position across from her but can see Rayna's face contorting in frustration. She starts shifting in her seat, attempting to stifle an outburst. I didn't invite her in here for that, and I've also had enough with Tara and her petulance. I decide to reel this conversation back in.

"Has he made you aware of his charges?"

Tara's eyes, enlarge again, shooting up to meet my gaze. "N-no...well, I've heard talks of—"

"First degree murder. Do you know who the victim is?"

Tara narrows her eyes and bites out, "No."

"My father."

Tara's almond skin pales, in total shock. "Your...your father? This can't be true. My father isn't a murderer—you know this, Azmir!"

"I know the evidence against him is stacked high. I know your father has done nothing but manipulate me over the years. I know by him allowing me to fuck you all those years, he was ensuring a future for you, not letting me into this mystical circle of trust you have flights of fancy of. He's always had ulterior motives, Tara."

I fight to remain calm. In a flash, I think about Big D visiting Rayna, scaring the shit out of her with lies and propaganda.

"Seems you're not the only Harrison with an issue of loyalty. You've no idea of the offenses of your father. I do, and yet I'm here, carrying out wishes he made when our relationship was still intact. Implementing the plan created when I believed...I was his... son." Tara sits stiff in her seat; I'm sure, trying to process my words. "The money will be made available to you by five p.m. tomorrow. Have a wonderful life."

"It will be...It has been since you've been out of it," Tara snarls. "No more of your arrogance and mystique. No more having to guess what you're thinking and how you feel about me. And no more of silently seeking your approval," she swears before turning to Rayna. "The looks, I get it. The bad boy persona, I understand. How well he can put together his million-dollar words, I've fallen for, too. His money is a universal draw to all women. The package is unbelievable, but not having all of him will drain you. There will always be secrets of his essence he will keep. And you will be standing outside of him, just like the rest of us." Tara blinks back the tears and Rayna studies her features. "No one gets inside of Azmir Divine Jacobs' head. Remember that."

Tara then rises from her seat and makes her way to the door.

Before I know it, Rayna calls out to her as she stands herself. Tara turns to answer without thought.

"I'm in his heart. I'm not sure what the crux of your issues with him was when you were together, but perhaps if you had focused on that...his heart..." Rayna's voice trails off. "That's what I've attained and where I believe is a good start at being *inside*."

After a couple of seconds of measuring Rayna's words, Tara leaves the office, slamming the door behind her. Rayna's chestnut irises meet mine and we gaze at one another, silently posing questions that somehow decidedly won't pour from our mouths. It's okay, because oddly, we both express acceptance. Hers of me asking her to come over to witness me saying my final goodbyes to a former life. And mine of her affirming her position in my world. Words aren't adequate for this moment; only the exchange of kindred energies is.

And before I know it, Rayna reaches over, caresses the side of my face covered with hair and whispers, "I have to get back to work."

I nod my head, understanding she has patients to see. Rayna bends over and across my desk, covers her lips with mine, giving me the most impassioned kiss. Her tongue tastes of fierce commitment as it moves forcefully, and her hand continues to stroke my cheek. The next thing I know, she's gone. But a piece of her lingers and far beyond her scent alone. I feel a slither of hope for this thing we are building.

Just hang on in there with me, Brimm...

Azmir

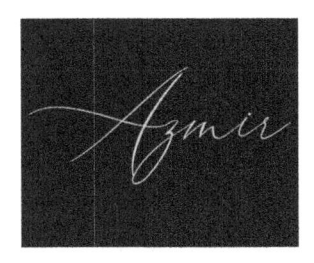

My morning is moving along well. I just walked out from giving Mrs. Ginn a clean bill of health. Though her constant complaints of who *irked her nerve* won't be missed, I know I'll miss her warm and jovial energy. En route to my office from the exam room, I meet Sharon in the hall as she appears to be directing an olive-toned gentleman in a sloppy suit, dragging a carrycase on wheels.

Sharon's eyes widen when they land on me as though she had hoped to run into me. "Ms. Brimm, Bertha McDowell is in your office, waiting on you. I escorted her in there just as I'm taking Mr. Miller here to our records room," she finishes as they approach me in the hall.

"Okay on Bertha. Who's Mr. Miller?" I ask with my brows furrowed. I'm not aware of anybody being granted access to the records room.

The older man moves forward with his hand extended, "Ms. Brimm, I'm Paul Miller, the interim counselor for *Smith, Katz & Adams Sports Medicine Center*. I know it may come as some surprise to you. I was just given the contract less than forty-eight hours ago."

With palpable hesitance, I take his hand on a firm shake. "Then you should expect my shock and slight annoyance at learning about it in this moment," I try controlling my tone.

"I got the call less than an hour ago from Wilma that Mr. Miller would be here to look into a handful of pertinent files Mr. Thompson and his team were in the middle of before his departure from the practice," Sharon attempts to explain. Wilma is Dan

Smith's executive secretary, one of very few who could authorize access outside of the partners. Sharon understands that would have been my next question.

"Okay..." I give myself a minute to recall his name as I'm still jarred from the news and even more bemused by Brian Thompson's unexpected exodus. *What in the...!* "Mr. Miller, Sharon here will give you the access authorized by the partners. I'm sure I will be contacted by someone today about the switch in law firms. In fact, I'll initiate it myself."

He gives me a courteous nod before I continue my way to my office, reeling from this bizarre piece of news. As I enter my office, I see a tall and robust woman, sporting a long denim skirt opening in the front on a high split. Her wool overcoat provides too many layers for December in Southern California. She dons a denim fisherman's hat, oversized glasses and plastic rain boots, odd for a dry day. I can now, after speaking to her over the past few days on the phone, confirm Bertha is a middle-aged woman with a fashion crisis of her own.

She turns in my direction and immediately makes her way over to me. "Ms. Brimm!" she speaks excitedly. "It's such a pleasure to meet you, officially."

Snapping out of my stupor, I accept her enthusiastic handshake, which nearly yanks my arm off.

"I'm so excited about this opportunity! I haven't styled in nearly fifteen years. I was over the moon when I got the referral!"

Really?

I point to the vacant seat as I glance over the clothing occupying the other chair across from my desk. I don't want to be rude, so I attempt to maintain a conversation with her as I inspect the god-awful pieces she's brought.

"So, how did you get my referral?" I ask as I hold up a long, royal blue mother-of-the-bride gown. It's heavy with petals around the waist.

"Well, my nephew called me up, saying his friend, Dawn, had a client for me—"

"Potential," I cut her off to clarify this extremely important fact.

"Well, of course. No contracts have been signed yet." Bertha lets out a nervous chuckle.

I go back to scanning the pieces. The next is a sleeveless, maroon, sequined gown. I can swear to seeing my grandmother in decades ago.

"What details did Dawn give, Bertha?" I have to keep her talking because I quickly pick up how when she speaks, she looks away from me. I don't want her reading my reactions—that I may not be controlling very well while inspecting the pieces.

"Well, she said though you are young, your elegance is well pronounced...more traditional than trendy," Bertha explains with her hands clasped together at her chest.

"*Hmmmm*... That Dawn knows me well. *Huhn?*" I mutter as I go to the next piece, a brown polyester pantsuit with off-white stitching at the cuffs of the jacket. "Did she tell you about the event?"

"Yes," Bertha's head pops back over to me. "She said you're the escort of a friend of hers...a client, I believe."

"Ah-huhn," I murmur as I decide I've had enough. I don't believe even Yazmine would wear any of these antiquated pieces.

She smiles politely and I watch as her eyes drift down to my hand. "Oh! You're engaged? The impression I got was you escorted, as an occupation perhaps?"

Is she serious?

Or Dawn is that damn conniving!

"Yes...happily. In fact, it's my fiancé's event I'm being outfitted for." I don't want to be offended by this woman's oblivion. It's perfectly clear to me she's been sent here as a ruse and not in genuine intent to assist. "Well, thanks for your time. I have another designer to screen, but will get back to you with my conclusion," I explain as I go for my phone in my top desk drawer and bring it back out to the chairs. "If you don't mind, I'll just take a few flicks of these to keep all ideas in mind."

On a shaky breath, Bertha concedes, "Sure. I'll look forward to your call."

I'm sure I knocked out the little confidence she's been able to summon after being out of the "business" for so long. After taking the pictures, just in case I need evidence of Dawn's tomfoolery, I see Bertha out the door. I then cross my office with my mind racing.

So, Dawn's still vying for Azmir's attention—or bed, huhn? The next contemplation is, *'Do I tell Azmir or don't I?'* I don't want any more secrets between us than what's been kept, but I have to be careful of my grievances regarding the woman who almost broke us. *The one he's decided to keep around.*

Sprawled out on one of the guest chairs facing my desk, I take a deep breath and blow it out, finally deciding to eat this one. I need to be strategic with my handling of Ms. Taylor, calculating, even. I need to think and respond as Azmir would.

However, what needs to be handled is the sudden disappearance of Brian Thompson. I recall seeing him at the meeting Chesney and his team called with *Smith, Katz & Adams Sports Medicine Center* after the fellatio tape everyone believes is starring me—or more appropriately, Divine's girl—went viral. He didn't seem himself there. I remember how his face was still healing and he barely gave me a glance. I was so stressed that day, I was more concerned with the meeting concluding than clearing the air with Thompson. But something isn't right; I feel it in my gut.

I walk over to my desk and open my center drawer. Flipping through *While You Were Away* slips, receipts, and non-pertinent business cards for one in particular. Brian Thompson's isn't the easiest to find, but it's the most distinctive, as it's a metallic blue stationery with a velvety texture in the front. Using the information on there, I try his office first just to be told by his secretary he's been on leave and isn't due to return for a few weeks. She offers to put me through to his second in command. I have to think and think fast.

"*Ummmmm*... This is more of a personal call—well, kind of. See, he inquired about enrollment for his niece, Brandy, at dance school last summer, and I told him I'd contact him if there were any openings. The slots fill up quickly." I quickly realize as my lie is growing, so is the volume of my voice. I take it down a notch, not wanting any ear hustlers to pick up on my charade. "...and I remember how disappointed she was when we told them we were booked. He left his card, but—"

"Oh, I'm sure his work cell hasn't been tended to," she quickly offers. "This sounds timely, though he never approved your access to his other mobile line. I'll give it to you anyway, seeing all his niece seemed to talk about when she was here was dancing and some show Mr. Thompson took her." I wonder if she's referring to my show. "You got a pen and paper handy?"

She gives me Thompson's personal cell and I call immediately from my office phone. His voice mail picks up after three rings and I leave a message after the beep.

"Hi...Brian," I clear my throat in a fortifying move. "It's Rayna. Rayna Brimm." Pause. "Look, Brian, I know I'm the last person you'd expect to hear from, and I'm not entirely sure you'd want to hear from me at all. It's just that I was just told you were no longer representing the firm and we never got a chance to talk." Another pause. "I'd like to meet...maybe just for coffee...no pressure. I'll be at the *Starbucks* at the Marina Pacifica mall." I scramble to search my desk calendar for availability. "...next Tuesday around noon. If you're up to it, we can meet for coffee." I sigh inaudibly and say goodbye.

I know this won't fly well with Azmir, which is why he won't know. I would have to somehow ditch John, my security. I still can't believe how easily it rolls off my tongue. Never in a million years did I think I'd need, much less have, a bodyguard. I don't know how it'll be done, but I'm going to Marina Pacifica, alone. I want to feel bad for making the decision, but my life does not belong to Azmir. It's easy for him to have me in on a meeting with his ex; I haven't beat the crap out of her as Azmir has done to Brian. He'll just have to allow me the opportunity to say my goodbye and offer my apologies for making myself seem available to him when I knew I was tied to another man.

And besides, as Tara warned, there are lots of things I don't know about my fiancé. One thing coming quickly to mind is *why in the hell do I need a bodyguard in the first place?*

CHAPTER 7

Rayna

The next evening I'm in full swing, orchestrating this soirée for Azmir and his friends. Chef Boyd has assisted as best as he can, considering he can't be with me. I've contracted several of his wait staff at the insistence of A.D., who doesn't want me overwhelmed. I relented because I have a few tricks up my sleeve and don't want him believing I need his assistance.

I'm dressed in a *Tom Ford* ivory sheath, long sleeve dress opening up in the back, fully exposing my skin, all the way down to the top of my bottom. The back is accentuated with a gold zipper curving around my derriere and into a lip at the small of my back. It's risqué at best, and I fought my resistance when Azmir asked me to wear it tonight. I contemplated it for two days before relinquishing to his will—once again. I settled on him knowing his friends and the atmosphere he wants to create this evening. That won out against my own ignorance of not knowing how to present myself for a house party with Azmir and his friends whom I've never met. And in true A.D. fashion, he included a pair of gold *Celine* sandals.

I'm in the kitchen with the wait staff, Karl and LaSean, setting the appetizer trays when I hear Azmir yell from the foyer, "Yo, Brimm, I'm home!"

Wanting him to head straight to the back and not discover one of my surprises for the evening, I return, "Okay...almost ready. Just go get dressed!"

"A'ight," he calls out, letting me know he won't go beyond the vestibule.

Next, I go into the dining room where an impeccably gorgeous tabletop is set. I chose a rich green, ivory, and gold as my colors. The China pieces are square and ivory and the cutlery is gold. Azmir has no idea he has some of this stuff—elegant dinnerware. Others I purchased as I planned this. I watched loads of *HGTV* and clipped many pictures out of magazine piecing together the motif I've had in mind for this party.

"Napkins!" I whisper to myself, remembering to get them from the kitchen counter. I washed them to release the wrinkles from the packaging. I make my way into the busy kitchen to grab them. As I'm placing them at each setting, I hear the doorbell ring. Nervousness sets in as I become aware that it's show time.

I know Azmir is likely still dressing, so I travel from the dining room, through the great room and to the door, hearing the bell sound again before I make it there. I quickly pull the door open to find a handsome couple, both dressed well. The man is tall, cinnamon, and with a close Caesar cut like Azmir's. He's nicely dressed in dark blue slacks and a black dress shirt opened at the top with a matching jacket and oxfords. The woman is wearing a fitted red midi dress underneath a brown fur shawl. She's much shorter than he is—and remarkably older. I can't help my eyes getting caught in her red-stained lips as she chumps down on gum, smacking with each chew.

Finding my voice and deciding to stop gawking at Azmir's guests, I greet, "Hi...and welcome."

A handsome smile slowly curves onto the man's face, causing

him to instantly appear much younger than his former placid expression did. He extends his hand. "You must be Rayna," he murmurs.

"Yes," I answer as I shake his hand. "Please...come in," I offer as I withdraw my arm behind me, following it up with a gesture.

The couple saunters in. I can't ignore the popping of the gum the woman does though I tell myself to ignore the discomfort of the sounds. They stop midway of the foyer to allow me to gain a lead. I do and walk them to the great room.

Offering them to have a seat, the doorbell rings again, alerting me of the next set of guests. *Boy, are they prompt!*

"Excuse me... I've gotta grab that. Make yourselves comfortable," I bid before leaving for the front door. I notice both of their nods as I turn on my heel.

On my way there, I notice my heart rate increasing. For the life of me, I can't pinpoint the reason for my nervousness. I must calm down. A part of the new Rayna is confidence in this man's world. I belong here, there's no need to feel out of place or like the novice I am. *He loves me* I quote to myself before opening the door.

This time, what awaits me is an intriguing man with chestnut skin who immediately leans into the frame of the door, resting his shoulder there. There are two things I pick up right away, one being he's alone. I'm expecting another couple. The second thing is his squinty eyes underneath his thick eyebrows. They're somewhat bushy, but not unkempt. In fact, though he isn't drop dead gorgeous, in my opinion, I can see what his female admirers find attractive in him are those eyes narrowing in a way creating a lure to him.

As he ogles me, I take inventory of him as well, only I'm not checking for goods, just his angle. His coquetry is well practiced and emits into the atmosphere, strangling me. I don't know what to do.

Great! Azmir's friend is flirting with me without opening his mouth! *How do I respond to that? This is why I'm nervous!*

"Damn, Divine," the guy groans.

Whether I like it or not, I have to repel his lascivious vibes. I can't kick the soiree off this way. How would I get through the evening? Trying to call on my brain frozen by his audacity, I feel my back warm up at a speed causing me to shiver. Then I smell him.

"I know. Right?" Azmir hums into my ear. I can't decipher if that response is directed at me or his buddy. "And that's what I'm saying to myself in the rear view."

I gaze up at my handsome, big guy who smells just as good as he looks in his all black. He's wearing a cashmere sweater rolled up at the sleeves, dress pants and leather dress shoes. I could lick him. Abruptly, I become aware of my mouth opening.

I close it quickly when I hear, "Well, damn! I ain't know you were working with all this, D."

That's his friend who's still standing outside of the threshold, gawking at me in the most inappropriate way.

"And trust me when I say, you will never know," Azmir growls in my ear, but is loud enough to be heard by his friend.

I swear I can feel the priapic heat radiating from Azmir's friend in front of me and that of Azmir's behind me; it's *that* palpable. Only, I respond to one man's scent. One man's heat. And this is proven by the trembling of my spine underneath him. Having my back bare also doesn't help.

Azmir brushes against me as he rounds me to greet the man who's *still* standing in the doorframe. "Get yo' ass in here, man!" He jostles as he goes to give him dap. The guy laughs as he reciprocates.

"Glad to see you, D," the friend returns. "Your digs is fancy as shit! My man!" I can hear the compliment in his words. He has a strong Brooklyn twang as well, provoking Azmir's.

"Yeah...well..." Azmir humbly replies. The place really *is* immaculate. Even I haven't gotten used to the immensity of it after living here for nearly four months. "Where's your date? I thought you were bringing your ol' lady?"

"I had a meeting with *Def Jam* before coming here, so she's headed from home."

"Cool," Azmir mutters. "Glad you could make it."

We move from the door, and I instinctively start my way back into living room, but I can still hear their banter from behind me. I want to get to the other guests so as to not be rude.

"So, how long have you been here, D? I thought you were still at the ranch out in Pasad—" is all I heard from his friend before he squeals, "Daaaaaaamn!" At a pitch sounding as if he's in pain.

Thinking something has happened to him, I turn to see what's going on and then notice him hunched over, using the wall table to hold himself up. *Has he hurt himself?* I turn to Azmir who gives it away as he stands, holding the bridge of his nose with his eyes closed and shaking his head.

"C'mon, man. Is it gonna be that type of evening?" Azmir lightly chides.

The guy peers up to me, still appearing injured. "I'm sorry, ma'am, but my man right here didn't forewarn me about your beauty...your package!"

My eyebrows quickly furrowed but smooth out as I'm able to muster a polite smile. These are some dynamics between Azmir and his friend. I don't know if I can endure an evening of his overt ogling. My eyes dart over to Azmir for help.

"This is her home, too, man. Seriously? Are we going to do this?" Azmir growls protectively like a lion, though his equanimity still seems to be intact. I don't know what to say.

His friend recoils. Attempting poise, he turns to me, "No disrespect, ma'am. I'll get myself together before the big guy throws me out."

I nod, and then continue my gait into the great room.

As we all gather in there, the first guests to arrive stands. I can tell the guys are all intimately familiar with each other. They greet one another with broad smiles and lingering hugs.

The first guy to arrive initiates the introductions. I purposely didn't do it at the door, wanting Azmir to do the honors. It's his party after all.

"Divine, Lenny, you all remember Evelyn," the guy first to arrive says before turning to his date, Evelyn. "Eve, as you recall, these are my uncles slash brothers. When they're behaved, they can be more like uncles. But when they wild out, it's brothers they become." Everyone laughs in unison. The bell rings and Azmir taps me dulcetly at the small of my back, saying he'll get it.

As I turn my attention back to the cypher, I consider how there's something strange in the pairing of this guy who's with Evelyn. He's fairly tall, just a few inches shorter than Azmir, but taller than the second guy who arrived. He has a sophomoric air to his appearance even with his composed and mature presentation, unlike Evelyn who can easily be assumed to be as old as my mother —too old for her date tonight; he could be my age. I'm interested to learn more about these two.

Within a beat, Azmir resumes our circle with a tall, café au lait beauty with dark brown curls, nearly down to her back. She wears a wide and bright smile as she holds up two bottles of champagne festively. Her excitable energy is infectious.

"Heeeeeey, everybody!" she sings. I can't help but return her warm smile. "I brought *Ace of Spades*. I know that's what Divine likes!" I then pick up on her rich accent. *She's a gorgeous Latina!*

From behind me—or more descriptively, over me—Azmir replies, "Thanks, Mia. That's very thoughtful of you."

"Man, fuck that! Divine and Jay can hate on *Cristal* all they want to now, because ol' dude was hatin' on blacks sippin' it, but y'all ran through cases of that shit back in the day!" Azmir's ogling friend hisses.

In true A.D. fashion, he equably replies, "Times have certainly changed." Not giving in to the fight his friend is trying to ensue.

"What the fuck ever," his friend snort in response.

"Anyway," Azmir swiftly changes the subject. "I have to introduce my lady to you knuckleheads. You..." he looks at his ogling friend now and says, "...coming into her home, fuckin' acting like you just came home from a ten year bid, threw me." He turns me towards the first guy to arrive.

He then takes me at the back, affectionately again, "Brimm, this fine young man here is a long-term friend of mine, Jackson. He can call me brother or uncle, just as long as his elusive ass calls," Azmir conspicuously chastens in his introduction while giving Jackson a tentative gaze.

Then he turns me and announces, "And this prick right here, Lenny, is like a brother to me." I give Lenny a nod, still feeling uneasy about him. He returns it, but in a much more graceful manner than earlier.

Azmir shifts to the Latina, "And this is Lenny's saving grace, Mia. I've known Mia for...has it been three years?" Azmir asks Mia with furrowed brows.

"Hmmmm," Mia contemplates on a heavy tongue. "Try four and a half," she answers with a blushing smile.

"Wow! It's been that long, huhn?" Azmir poses to Lenny. "I'm surprised little Liz isn't planning your wedding yet," he teases, and seemingly to Lenny's dismay because his face dwarfs into a grimace. It's comical. I try to stifle my laughter.

"And everyone, this is the fierce Rayna Brimm—soon to be Jacobs, as she will be my wife in about..." Azmir glances down at his watch. "...two months and three weeks?" He glances over to me with glint in his eyes for an answer. And with a heavy blush, I nod in assent. I guess I'm a nodder so far this evening because I've done more of that than speaking.

I hear the ladies *awwwww* under Azmir's announcement. Not liking much attention, I announce, "Food's ready. I hope you all are hungry." I extend my hand toward the dining room, hoping Azmir is too distracted to see the addition to his great room. "This way."

At the table, conversations flow. I can tell these guys enjoy getting together. Once again, Azmir displays a different persona with this crew. It isn't as guarded as with *The Clan* and not as poised as with Mark and Eric. With Jackson and Lenny, he's more talkative while holding court. It never matters to me who Azmir is; I enjoy all facets of him. They all rev up something deep within that can't be matched by anyone else.

"I thought you were going over to *Atlantic* with Mike Kyser, Len?" Azmir poses to Lenny.

"I've thought about it, but I don't know, man. Still weighing my options, you know?" Lenny replies as he stretches his arm to the back of Mia's chair. She smiles contently and I can tell she's deeply in love with this man. "The industry has changed in the short time since you ran the halls. Jay'll tell you."

That comment causes me to question once again: *Who was Azmir in the music industry?*

"Yeah, I saw it coming. Money's drying up," Azmir replies.

"Yeah, dudes switching up their hustle, but still in the industry in some way. I'm sure you see this every day, Jax," Lenny throws to Jackson, who's being served his second course.

"Not really," Jackson responds.

"What? You ain't pick up Quincy's portfolio yet?" Lenny asks aghast.

Jackson takes a long sip of his tea before answering, "Still weighing my options," with a tight jaw, indicating he doesn't want to discuss it.

Lenny's dubious eyes shoot over to Azmir who smoothly shakes his head, communicating for him to drop it.

"Jax will decide what he wants to do when he's ready. I have every confidence he'll make his decision based on what's best for him," Azmir informs.

Jackson doesn't reply, just takes another gulp of his drink, training his eyes in the distance on a squint. It makes me take notice of his handsome features. He's about a shade darker than my complexion with a narrow masculine face. Jackson's eyes are some exotic shade, just darker than hazel. His long nose works well with his high cheekbones and long lashes. His shoulders are broad, and he appears to be fit. Jackson's a good looking man, but too young for his friend, Evelyn. She's impeccably fit herself, but clearly will be applying for social security any day now.

Karl brings in bread and sets two bowls of it on both sides of the table. I try to think of something to say to change the course of the conversation. The tension is now thick.

"So, Mia, I've caught your remarkable accent. And your gorgeous features are just as striking. Where are you from, *if you don't mind me asking*?" I note as Mia's taking a sip of her drink.

She smiles excitedly as she tries swallowing the contents of her mouth. She's nice, and busty with bountiful curves in all the right places. She appears to be beautiful inside and out. I decide right away I like her.

"Santo Domingo," she smiles graciously. "Thank you. And I can see Divine has excellent taste and loves clase de culo!" She stretches her arms wide then pats the rear of her hips for emphasis. I know the comment of me having a big butt is made with endearment, so I stifle my giggle. I can't believe a woman has me blushing.

"Shiiiiit..." Lenny mutters beneath his breath.

I turn to Azmir who shakes his head while wearing a smug grin. I guess it's a man thing, but it makes me feel uneasy considering his lady is sitting right here with us now. I quickly get the impression his antics are not only familiar to her but tolerated as well.

Lenny goes to his phone that apparently has alerted him of a text because I then hear him call out, "This Jay, yo. He said you ain't have to invite him." He chuckles.

"I told his ass about it right after I proposed it to Jax a while back. He said he'd be out the country," Azmir explains, somewhat annoyed, somewhat lighthearted as Lenny types away.

"He said he'll be in town next week and to clear your schedule for him. He knows he gotta wait weeks to get on your books now that you're a corporate CEO and all!" Lenny croaks out on a laugh, finding their exchange beyond funny.

Azmir waves him off with his hand. You can tell this is their relationship. I'm getting to know Azmir more and more. And I'm enjoying it.

"You two must be really close," I observe aloud and find my gaze decidedly on Lenny.

"Yeah...D and I grew up together in Bedstuy and been tight ever since," Lenny explains as he finishes his texting conversation. "And when he made his way out here to L.A., my brother and I came out, too. He set me up with a job at *RCA* records when they were running things. And it just went from there." He shrugs, and for the first time, not giving me hooded eyes.

I take this opportunity to ask about his history in the music industry. It's been killing me to learn why he's so revered there.

"So, you were acquainted in the record industry?" I pose as a question to Azmir.

As much as I try to conceal it, Azmir can pick up my true inquiry. "When you grow up with well-known hip-hop artists, you kind of get to know their circle. Me, with my hustler's spirit, I made friends with every mover and shaker I could." Azmir raises my hand and kisses the back of it. I'm glad he didn't follow my seating arrangement and sat at the other end as the head. He even insisted I kept my seat at the head. "It was fun...a good waste of time while I was trying to find myself."

"And not just rappers, there's lots of talent out of the BK," Lenny corrects. "Remember when Spike was shooting *Do the Right Thing,* back in eighty-eight - eighty-nine, on Quincy and Lex?" Azmir nods. "Yo', that shit was mad fun! They tried to keep us out the area, but we snuck in the warehouse and hid out for hours just to see what was going on." I notice the nostalgic smile cresting Azmir's face. "Brooklyn was fun back then." That last comment is made dolefully. Azmir's eyes collapse into his lap, clearly in the moment with Lenny.

I have so many follow up questions to that, but settle on, "So, where's your brother, Lenny?"

"He's in ATL," Lenny answers with a mouthful.

Oh! "Is Liz your sister?" I ask, recalling my easily-made-friends with the woman with spiked hair from the party in New York last summer. The one who informed me of Tara's cheating on Azmir.

"Yeah," Lenny confirms. "I forgot...she told me she met you."

Okay...now I'm making connections. It's good to see Azmir has a structure other than the Harrisons. *What a bunch they are.*

"So, Evelyn, do you still have your dance schools in Long Island?" Azmir asks Jackson's guest—because it's hard to reference her as his date when likely she's old enough to be his mother and mine.

"Yes. We just closed on a new property near the water. Membership has been expanding leaps and bounds," Evelyn smiles.

So she's a dancer?

I notice how Jackson doesn't even acknowledge her statement as he delves into his food.

"Rayna dances. She belongs to a school herself," Azmir beams.

"Really?" Evelyn's eyes light up. "What type of dance do you do?"

"Well, it's more like what I'm into," I offer a disclaimer. "I've not been formally trained, but I'm instructed by a well-trained dancer. And I do a little bit of everything, from hip-hop, jazz, ballroom, salsa, and even a little tap."

Evelyn's brows arch like a grandmother waiting to be impressed. She isn't rude, just...mature.

"Oh, was she..." Jackson asks, clearly just hit with revelation. "...the dancer at your birthday party?"

I chuckle and Azmir nods his head proudly. I feel giddy all over again and have only had about two sips of my pinot noir.

"Ooooooh!" Lenny cries. "I missed that one, yo."

"That was a great performance," Jackson comments in a way that isn't suggestive.

"Thanks, Jackson," I nod graciously.

"I wish I were there to see it," Evelyn murmurs, wearing a moue as she peers over to Jackson.

He ignores it and continues, "I remember the look on D's face when you hit the stage. I thought we were gonna have to end the party right then and there!" We laugh.

I turn to Azmir who, in his own way, is blushing at the memory.

"Oh, shit! Are these..." Lenny says before biting into the cornbread. "...Momma Dee's?" he exclaims.

I smile haughtily at Azmir who is now looking to me for an answer. He goes for one himself and bites into it. I find myself envying the bread.

Down, girl!

"Damn. And they taste fresh out the oven," Azmir murmurs. After clearing his mouth, he moves closer to me and whispers with furrowed eyebrows, "How were you able to pull this off?"

Giddy, I shrug and whisper in return, "I'm *that* chick," then employ the smug grin I've picked up from him.

"I see," He chuckles. "Indeed."

The rest of the dinner is great. My menu of seafood and chicken goes over well, and Momma D's cornbread was the icing on the cake. I'll have to thank her again for agreeing to ship them out here. Now, it's time for my next surprise. As if on cue, LaSean enters the dining room to inform me the great room is now ready.

"All right, everyone. Let's move this party to the living room," I call out to the group.

Oblivious and tranquil, Azmir takes me by the hand and leads the way. Those trustee electrical currents hit my spine. I thought they'd get old someday soon. I was clearly wrong.

What Azmir isn't expecting is our musical guest, seated behind the baby grand piano, starting a jazzy tune. Before we're deep into the room, Azmir turns his tall frame towards me with wrinkled brows. But it's the wonderment in his eyes that takes my breath away. He's pleasantly surprised and I'm thrilled by that. I bite my bottom lip, slightly embarrassed all of a sudden. My heart's elated. Thankfully, I don't have to speak, as our entertainer kicks the show off.

"Good evening, folks. I'm here to serenade you tonight, hopefully, to add to the romantic holiday ambiance." The keys from the piano bellow melodiously. "I'll be your entertainer for the next few hours. I go by the name of Ragee, and I'm honored to play my chords at the," he cranes his neck, stretching his eyes over the great room. "...massive home of one Azmir Jacobs," he transitions into a mellow version of *Winter Wonderland*.

After experiencing his awesome talent last summer at his listening party, I had to throw him a bone and hire him for tonight. Azmir's budget for this event was astronomical in true A.D. fashion, so there was plenty of room for his fee.

Ragee goes on to introduce his two background singers who are all dressed in black, just as he is. When he belts out, *I'll Be Home for Christmas* I know I've made a great decision in including him to entertain our first "official" guests.

Not even midway into the song, Azmir turns me around and takes me into a dancing stance as he leans down and buries his face in my neck, inhaling deeply. I melt into his lanky frame instinctively, wondering how I could ever leave his enfold, even to pee. His delicious cologne does things to me, prompting me to want to do things to him. Indecent things.

During our circular movements, I can see Lenny and Mia in an embrace. He's whispering—apparently—salaciously in her ear as she quietly giggles. It's hard not to get caught up in romantic realms with the sparkling, white clustered lights I had hung throughout the great room and terrace.

Well, at least that's what I'm thinking until I see Jackson and Evelyn, sitting apart, but certainly engaged in the performance.

There's a strange set of dynamics between those two. Jackson seems sad. Like the weight of the world is on his shoulders. He's articulate, extremely handsome, polite, and...dejected. I can't wait to ask Azmir about him *and* Lenny.

My attention is taken when Azmir swipes his long pinky finger in the crack of my cheeks and wiggles it. My eyes flutter and my spine shivers. I moan into his chest. Then slowly, I peer up into his eyes and immediately note they're smoldered.

"I love having your back exposed. I can pull you against me and still get my fill of your skin in front of mixed company." His brandy-hinted breath turns my nipples taut. I want to suck his tongue right from his face.

"I was wondering what was up with the partial nudity of this dress," I tease.

"I love your skin. In fact, if you hadn't contracted with a stylist already, I would put you in a stunning gown for the *Mauve* signing exposing this silken casing again," he rubs my back chastely, using his entire palm. I close my eyes to try to focus on quieting the moans escaping my mouth.

Hearing the staccato sounds of Ragee transitioning from *Let it Snow*, the Boyz II Men rendition, to Donny Hathaway's *This Christmas* brings me back to the here and now. And *now* I'm faced with the decision of sharing with Azmir that his deputy PR guru shot me a botched designer for kicks. I'm still committed to decision of accepting her presence in Azmir's life, only because I believe it's limited to business only.

"Ummm...actually I haven't contracted with a stylist yet," I murmur, then meet Azmir's bemused gaze. "The one Dawn recommended didn't possess the...avant-garde quality I'm hoping for." My eyes bounce nervously in his gaze, praying for acceptance of my bland answer. Azmir's no fool, but I'm also not prepared to play the whiney girlfriend who cries wolf.

After a tentative pause, he nods, "Okay, I'll make a call in the morning. I already have the perfect gown in mind. The only thing that'll be left to do is me determining just how I'll keep my hands off you until I have you back home in our bed."

I can't hide my split face grin. I warm in Azmir's decision to take care of the matter. I'm getting better at accepting him and his lofty lifestyle.

I can do this.

"You've done well this evening, Brimm," he appraises, breaking me from my contemplation.

"I tried," I purr sensually. "Is there a reward for my efforts?"

"Sure, there is. What would you prefer?" he breathes into my neck, and I generously inhale the aromatic brandy blending with his cologne and natural body odors so well.

"You pounding me into the mattress until I lose consciousness."

Pushing warm air into my neck, Azmir chuckles, "Your nasty ass," in his Brooklyn brogue as he reproaches in jest into my neck on sharp intake of breath. I've caught him off guard with that request. I laugh in his capable arms without conscience. "Indeed. I think that can be arranged."

This evening, Ragee sings the most romantic Christmas songs. His voice is stellar, and I can't be more assured of my idea to invite him to this event. We all express our appreciation of his musical gifts at some point throughout his performance. We dance, sing along, drink, and laugh for a couple of hours. Even Jackson and Evelyn, in their own way, gives into the idealistic air Ragee's successful at conjuring.

The wait staff continue to bring fresh drinks throughout the evening after cleaning the kitchen and dining room. They're my lifesavers for the evening. I soon learned there was no way I could pull off hosting and waiting on guests all in one night. Also, everyone seems to love my miniature custard pies. All wins for Rayna!

It's nearly three in the morning before I feel slumber pulling at me. We're sitting on the terrace, against the backdrop of the marina, long after Ragee and friends, and LaSean and Karl, were dismissed and tipped generously. I sit and listen as Azmir reminisces and jostles with his friends about things of the past as well as current. Most of the conversation is without the women's contribution, as we don't hold that piece of their history. We women seem amenable to it as we sit and listen. Azmir capes my relaxed frame as I burrow into his with my feet underneath me. We're gathered around the mosaic patio fire pit that I question if it goes against Azmir's residency policy. If it does, he never whispers a suggestion of it.

It's nice. I'm at peace in his arms, feeling the reverberations of his laughter against me. Everyone seems to be enjoying themselves.

I don't know how long I was out before I feel the awkward movements from being suspended in the air. It takes me a few moments to realize I'm in Azmir's arms, being transported to the back of the apartment. I stir against his hard chest.

"Where are we going?" I utter incoherently.

"To get cleaned up, then to bed," Azmir murmurs and I feel the rumbling of his peak baritone voice from his chest against my arm. I love that morning grovel in his tone. It reminds me of our plans for when our guests have left.

"What time is it?" I manage, still trying to fully awake.

"A quarter of five," he answers as we enter the master suite.

He lowers me to the floor in the bathroom of master suite and unzips my dress. It falls to my feet. I step out of it to have him drop to his haunches and remove my sandals. I didn't wear a bra or panties; I couldn't fit them underneath this number. He points to the toilet, and I meander over to it. When I turn to catch a glimpse of him, I notice how quickly he discards his clothes and gaits into the shower. Once I join him, he immediately goes for my scrub and liquid soap to wash me. When he's done, I'm sitting on the bench as he cleans himself, feeling loopy, part from heavy drinking and the other half from pure exhaustion.

"What's up with Lenny? Is he always that creepy?" I ask as I wait, well entertained by the sight of his wiry frame flexing as he washes.

His hearty laughter rumbles off the shower walls. Intuitively, my lips twitch into a smile. His laughter does this to me. I love seeing Azmir light-hearted. It means I'm not screwing things up.

"Lenny is Lenny. He's been a wag since he was in diaper. He means no harm. I told him to lighten up," Azmir replies. "He was amped up tonight because he wasn't expecting to see what he saw." He then turns to me. "We used to place bets as to who had the hottest girl when we'd introduce our ladies to one another. If we still wagered such bets, I would've walked away with extra lunch money tonight according to him." He flashes his coochie-creaming smirk. "He just needed a minute to adjust to your undeniable beauty.

I sit and contemplate his words. "How does Mia deal with that?" I ask over a stifled yawn.

"As best as she can. She knows how Lenny is. I'm sure she has her way of managing him." Azmir moves from underneath the large faucet to turn the water off.

He pulls me into a standing position from the bench and walks me over to the sink to dry us both off. I wash off my makeup and brush my teeth as he dresses then brushes his teeth.

As I shrug on my housecoat I ask, "Why does Jackson seem so gloomy?"

"He's in mourning. His father, one of my good friends, passed away recently. He's still dealing with it...expectantly. They were very close."

"I guess Evelyn is helping?" I ask wryly. I still can't get over the mismatch.

"You're very inquisitive, little girl," Azmir notes.

I yawned again; this time really big. "It's just that I'm trying to get to know more about the great A.D. and these friends aren't around like Petey, Kid, Mark, and Eric. I want to know all about those connected to my man," I whine.

Azmir chuckles. "All right," his throaty vocal cords pour out, reminding me of the early hour. He's inviting me in to ask my questions.

"Well...how old is he for starters? Evelyn looks old enough to be *your* grandmother!"

He chuckles again. "Jax is about..." he squints his eyes in search for an answer. "...I would say...twenty-five—twenty-six. I'm not quite sure which of the two."

Wow! "And Evelyn will soon be applying for her pension." I rub my heavy eyes.

Another chuckle from A.D. With squinted eyes and a lazy grin, he asks, "You're quite the observer, huhn, Brimm?"

"I'm just saying, what is a guy my age doing with a great-grandma? Grant it, Evelyn's just as in shape as I am, if not more, but the aging in her face doesn't lie. That has to be..." I yawn. "...immoral on some level."

We head out to the bedroom where Azmir undresses the bed. I stand, completely fatigued, watching like a four-year-old, waiting for their bed to be turned down.

"As it seems, you're not totally averse to dating older men—"

"Older men," I interrupt him. "...not old men." I climb onto the bed when he gives my cue. "And why are you acting as if this is so normal for a guy Jackson's age? Were you into old—I mean, older women at some point in your youth?"

"I was into all types of women in my youth. Literally and figuratively speaking," he calls out as he returns to the bathroom. When he makes his way back out to me, he's holding a jar of cream.

"Hold up! What happened to my...reward? You didn't think I'd forget about it, did you?" I raise a brow, awaiting an answer. I catch his panty-snatching smirk.

"Little girl, giving you what you've requested right now would be an act of debauchery...taking advantage of a young lassie."

I giggle at his formality, though I know he's being comical. I melt as a smile slowly crests upon his beautiful face. Although the tightness around his eyes remains and redness is prominent from exhaustion, Azmir is still an incredibly beautiful creature.

"A deal is a deal," I yawn, continuing with my protests as he sits on my side of the bed.

"No, Brimm," he mutters as he pulls my right leg into his lap. He unscrews the cap of the jar and scoops cream into his large hands. When he lifts my foot and starts rubbing firmly into the core, my back arches over the bed. "You've been in those heels, entertaining my friends and me, all evening. I just want to relax you."

He kneads with a strong grip indiscriminately rolling over the base of my foot. And when he arrives at my toes—gently tugging at them, one-by-one—a short moan escapes my mouth. I quickly bite my bottom lip to control myself.

"If you keep that up, Brimm, I'm gonna fuck you," Azmir scolds on a throaty grovel.

I roll my eyes into the back of my head, oddly embarrassed by my lack of constraint. This man is trying to relax me and I'm belting out trills of a porn star.

Way to go, Rayna!

"Yeah...that should be enough for everybody. I'll leave the door unlocked," I inform into the phone while standing in the kitchen, perusing a menu.

"Sure, Mr. Jacobs, sir. I'll place that order right away," Manny assures.

"Indeed," I reply before hanging up.

When I turn from the wall phone, I'm slightly startled by her presence. I thought she'd be sleeping for at least another hour. Her short hair is tousled—sexily—as she stands in one of the kitchen entryways with her Japanese wrap housecoat generously agape for me to gain an inciting vertical view of her cleavage; belly button, well-manicured pelvis and the seam of her thighs as one crosses over the other. I swallow hard, realizing I'm salivating immediately by her sensuous company. Even her damn bare toes against the Italian marble floor look delectable.

"Mr. Jacobs," she annunciates with a throaty tenor. "Not only have I missed morning worship because you failed to set my alarm before bed..." She rakes back loose strands of hair falling into her face. "...but you also failed to act on our agreed upon recompense of my services for last evening."

Damn. I know what she's referring to. And while I know she's into "character," I also realize she's serious as hell. I can't speak, yet my johnson jerks at the gruff in her voice. We stand mere feet from each other, eye-fucking, neither one making a move. I don't know which one would be best. But one thing is for damn sure, and that's Brimm's gonna get what she came for this morning.

Attempting the first move, she slowly removes her raised arms from the entryway frame and starts her sexy strut towards me. My mind starts racing. I know that smoldering look in my lady's eyes. I understand what she's in need of. What she's channeling from me.

Timing is a muthafucka!

Rayna stops in front of me, placing her little hands on my chest then rub my pecs. "You don't have an answer for your breaches, Mr. Jacobs?" she purrs. I don't speak, still not able to formulate appropriate responses, being stuck between a rock and a fucking hard place indeed. "Fine," she lifts an eyebrow and sighs. "You don't want to use your mouth..." She lifts my shirt, scraping her nails against my abs. "I guess I'll have to use mine then, aye?"

Then Rayna's hooded eyes descend along with her body.

Fuck! Ain't this some shit. I don't know if I'm more upset with myself for the reality of this situation or the fact that I can't muster the self-control to tell my girl to hold off.

I feel her tongue run slivery down my abdomen as her featherweight hands arrive at the drawstring of my basketball shorts. I dip my head back because as much as I'm dying to feel her mouth on my cock, I know I can't allow her to do it. But *DAMN*... When she presses her face against my pelvis and inhales my private hair, my chest jerks as warm air from the area hits her lungs and cool air replaces it in my boxers.

"Goddamn, Brimm," I drag out on a breath.

"*Mmmmmm...*" she moans, and I feel exhilarated and anxious out my ass at the same time. With both hands, she grabs the elastic waist of my shorts and boxers and pulls the front down, just enough to expose the base of my strongman as it's straining just below the elastic waist. Her tongue swiftly attempts to curl around the base and my right hand slams against the marble countertop in an attempt to keep my balance.

"Goddamn!" I hear belting from a distance.

Apparently, Brimm's heard it, too, because she jumps from her knees, quickly shuffling to fold her wrap over her breasts. Impulsively, I push her behind me.

Fucking timing!

Lenny stands there with his mouth agape and eyes stretched wide. Jackson's next to him, trying to fight his burning grin by ducking his head while cupping his chin. Mia walks up behind Lenny, wearing a puzzled expression, trying to figure out what the hell's going on.

Abruptly, Lenny pushes her behind him.

"Oh, hell no! Your dick looks like the size of an anaconda right now through those shorts. My girl ain't witnessing that shit!" Lenny shouts over his shoulder while covering Mia's eyes. And it's a good thing; it would only take her seconds to figure out what they've just interrupted.

I know Rayna isn't aware of our guests having stayed overnight. She also didn't provide me an opportunity to share this information either.

What a fucking inconvenient moment!

"What the fuck did you give Ray last night, man," Lenny shrieks. "Whatever the hell it was, do share so I can get down!"

"Fuck outta here, man!" I hiss then pivot my head to peek behind me and find a mortified and shaken Rayna, who pins her forehead against my shoulder blade with her eyes squeezed shut while she scrapes her top lip between her teeth. "This is why I've grown preferable to no guests." I snort as I speak specifically to her.

"I'm hungry as a motherfucker, D. I was just coming in here to see if I could snack on something before we bounce," Lenny informs as he makes his way farther into the kitchen.

I turn completely, bend down, and throw Rayna over my shoulder. She squeaks like a child, surprised by my maneuver. "Azmir!"

After making sure her ass is decently covered, I turn to face the crowd, of three now, in my kitchen and announce, "Brunch is on its way up." I move toward the kitchen doorway opposite of the one the guests came into as I hold my lady by the ass. "I'm going to put my girl back to bed and will be back out to say my goodbyes when I'm done."

I see heat rise from Mia's neck, up to her face, the embarrassment on Jax's, and amusement on Lenny's. Rayna shrills and as I make my way towards the corridor, I feel a sharp whack into my ass.

"Azmir!" Rayna chides, but I can't miss the huskiness in her voice when she speaks. My girl knows her reward is quickly approaching.

Two hours later, I'm back in the living room, kicking it with Jax. Lenny and Mia left right after brunch. I learned Evelyn left early this morning for a flight out to New Orleans. Rayna's sleeping soundly after a long night and a rough late-morning fuck. Now it's just me and my younger compadre, sipping on something wet—me on brandy, him on juice as I now realize Jackson doesn't drink. It's great having him in town. He's *almost* like his old self, but I can see the stirred melancholy in his eyes. It's almost as if his soul has been robbed.

"So, Evelyn?" I ask.

Arching his brows, Jackson exhales and returns, "Something like that."

It's now my turn to raise my brows.

"C'mon, D. You know me," he tries to explain. "You're not the only one with strategic motives."

"Oh, yeah?" I cock my head to the side, signaling the need for an explanation. "All I'm saying is you're young, fresh, and paid. I'm sure dames your age are biting at the bits for your pretty ass."

Jackson chuckles coolly and slightly rolls his eyes. "Yeah, but they're also vying for a ring. A goddamn commitment that ain't happening. My ageless queens," I know off the bat he's referring to the older women he keeps in company of. "...aren't expecting that. They just want a good time, an incredible fuck, and then to be left the hell alone."

"Not from what I saw of Evelyn. You heard the comment she made about not being your plus one at my birthday party."

He snorts, "Yeah, I did catch that, which is why I'll be putting her ass on respite for a little while."

I laugh at that one as I see Jackson rise from his seat across from me. "I'm serious, D. Don't judge me when your ass has waited until you're damn near forty to get clinks on your wrists. *If* I follow the same path, I still have plenty of time." He jeers as he starts for the door. I put my drink down and follow him.

"I'll tell you just what a wise man recently told me: Time is not your friend, neither will it ever be." I pat him on the shoulder. "So, if you're lucky enough to find that *one* who makes you think with your head, heart, and cock—and occasionally all at the same time—don't hesitate to make her your forever."

We stop at the front door and Jackson turns to me, "Is that what happened to you?" He jerks his chin towards the back of the apartment.

I pause for a second to consider my words. It's been difficult for me to articulate my feelings regarding Rayna. She's most frustrating and all-consuming. Even now, while talking to Jax, in the recesses of my conscience, I'm deciding on what I will spoon-feed her for lunch. And how if I would wake her prematurely just to spend time with her. She's my treasure.

"That woman brings me both pleasure and pain. The weird thing is feeling a rush of pleasure even in the midst of pain, because it means that no matter how fucked up I feel, or how scared I am at the prospect of losing her, there is still some pleasure in having been connected to her."

Jackson cracks a smile as he lifts his arm to give me dap. "Well, enjoy it, man. This love thing has always been mystical to me." He shakes his head. "Seeing you holding it down makes *love* an *inconvenient truth*, my brother."

"Indeed." I return the love and pull Jackson into a hug. He's a good dude and still young on years, but I've no doubt he'll get it soon.

I walk Jackson out then go and join my domesticated fiancée in bed, hoping to catch a little shuteye along with her. The anticipation building on my way to the master suite concerns the hell out of me and feels good all at the same time.

CHAPTER 8

Rayna

The night of the *Mauve* event I'm in a massive suite at the *L'Ermitage* in Beverly Hills, getting prim and proper. I have a belly full of butterflies because I've never been to a signing event before, much less not one of this variety. I mean, not only am I going as the date of the celebrant, but I also happen to be his fiancée and this is our first event under that title. Prior to our engagement, there was so much bewilderment around the status of our relationship—for me as well as others. And even though being insecure regarding Azmir is old hat, being by his side, during a monumental occasion in his life, I'm anxious with expectation.

"Chin up...just a bit, Rayna," Chantal orders as she evens out my chin with foundation...spray...or whatever it is she's applying while Adrian was working my hair from behind.

"We're almost ready, Cookie, and you're going to be beat some kinda fierce, honey!" Adrian sings in drag. We dissembled the dining room to make a makeshift glam squad headquarters for me. Sitting patiently, I'm showered and moisturized. Once they're done, all I have to do is slip on my costume.

I hear extraneous noises from out in the living room, snatching my attention.

"Is that your fine ass millionaire, Cookie?" Adrian inquires.

As I *pin my ears back*, so to speak, I hear dribs of his silken voice and eventually those sounds draw more consistent and clearer.

"How's it going in here?" His baritone vocals pour into the room, causing the hairs on my neck to erect.

"She'll be ready in twenty, Mr. Jacobs," Chantal, a French makeup artist, assures with professional ringing.

"Almost done with her mane, F.A.M.," Adrian informs. I successfully conceal my laughter.

Fine Ass Millionaire, really, Adrian?

After a pause, I hear a chirp from my phone and turn it over.

Are you wearing panties this evening?

I gasp, "Azmir!" I trill, much to myself. I'm not sure why I'm so embarrassed. *Perhaps because you have two people barely inches away who could catch a glimpse of your fiancé sexting you.*

I text back: **Why would you text me something like that?**

I shake my head and giggle quietly, not wanting Adrian's nosy butt to ask me who and what I'm texting.

"Because I asked you a question verbally and you didn't answer," Azmir's silky thick voice chides, causing a sensation of warmth to blanket me. I can tell he's feeling slighted, I just don't know how much.

Thinking quickly, I type back: **If I don't will you take advantage of it?**

"Maybe," he growls aloud, "...maybe not."

I jump up and around in my seat only to find him gone.

In the limo, en route to the venue, my nerves haven't calmed in the least. I don't know why, but I grow jittery. Azmir, on the other hand, looks mouthwatering in his dark blue *Hugo Boss* suit, black dress shirt, and matching oxfords. He's left a few buttons undone in his shirt and each time my eyes catch the view, I can swear my tongue itches. His stark beauty and virile countenance always cause my breath to falter. And when I study his physique, my heartbeat doubles. As always, Azmir radiates reckless class and elegance. It doesn't matter if he's wearing jeans, sweats, basketball shorts, or tuxedo pants; he's virile art on display. The allure is his incognizance to it.

He seems a little preoccupied himself, but far from suffering the nerve bug I've succumbed to. I don't know how he's holding it together before such a big event. He's asked if I'm okay at least a half a dozen times from his first sight of me in my gown until we arrive to the red carpet.

Red carpet.

Holy crap!

When I arrived at the hotel earlier, Shayna was there, providing the *five steps, then posing* method of walking the carpet. She forewarned about the earsplitting yells from paps, demanding eye action. My chant the entire prep time was *I can do this...for Azmir, I can do this.*

However, when Azmir pulls me from the limo with such glint in his eyes, and gives me a moment to adjust my gown, my balance sways as I gaze over Dawn Taylor. It's not her usual sinister smile, hidden behind her usual crimson lips that has always raised my guard when in her presence. It's not even how her pupils darken as she gawps Azmir's virility throwing me. It's that she's wearing a sleeveless, full-length blue satin gown, appearing more like a partner in the signing rather than the handler of one.

Azmir must notice, too, because as soon as both our feet are planted on the concrete and we stand erect, he stills once he registers her presence. It seems like minutes before anyone moves or speaks. It's suddenly crystal clear to me Dawn tried to throw me the shabby stylist to out-dress me for this event. What's even more audacious is her knowing Azmir's colors and matching with him. It all makes sense, but what am I to do; cry like a baby to Azmir and rat her out? No! I will not allow Dawn to affect me publicly.

The screeching yelps for Azmir to pose is what snatches us

from this extremely awkward moment. Azmir doesn't speak to Dawn yet, but takes me by the small of my back, guiding forward. I don't want to, but immediately tell myself *this* is one of those moments where I have to wear a mask of unyielding, unflustered confidence as it concerns her.

Dawn turns to Marcus, Azmir's muscle, and asks him to follow another gentleman who will take him to the entrance of the venue where he's to wait for Azmir to finish the carpet and then resume his duties. Marcus gives Azmir a look, asking if he's cool with it. With a soft nod and a swift blinking of the eye, Azmir consents and Marcus walks off. Dawn lifts a virtually invisible wire from her jewelry-clad neck and speaks into it as she presses her finger into her ear, apparently listening in, communicating with someone.

Then, with her usual agenda-filled leer, Dawn directs with a long arm, "Mr. Jacobs," she ducks her chin. "Rayna," she gives me fleeting eye-action. "...this way. I'm sure Shayna has gone over the step/pose method of red carpet walking with you both. I'll be here to direct you with this. Just be mindful that we must be thorough and quick. You will hear lots of demands, but please keen your ears to my calls as I will guide you through it all to maximize publicity."

Azmir nods, but immediately diverts his eyes to mine. There's something in them. I can't tell if he's nervous or livid but, simultaneously I waft a lungful of his tantalizing cologne against his classical facial features, and it brings me unmitigated comfort. One thing is for sure, and that's I have to prepare myself to walk this long red carpet in five-inch heels and alongside a man with larger than life stature on my arm. We start immediately once we make it beyond a metal barricade separating the photogs from the carpet. Dawn walks ahead of us with me following her and Azmir behind me, to my right.

The flashes and clicks begin right away. My practiced smile I've trained for over the past few days arrives, my shoulders rise and squares as Adrian advised. My mouth is filled with cotton balls and elephants dance in my belly. I try desperately to control my tremors because I want to prove to Azmir I can handle his world just as much as I want to convince myself.

"*Azmir!*"..."*Jacobs!*"..."*Mr. Jacobs' guest!*"..."*Azmir's friend!*" They all yell, demanding our attention. I notice no one addresses me directly. They don't know my name.

It's okay, Rayna. I chastise my unusually burgeoning ego.

We implement the five step/pose method for a few feet. Under Azmir's arm, experiencing his familiar scent and feeling his well-acquainted body heat against my anxious frame, the jitters start to subside. My breathing begins to even and my steps are solid, executed with confidence. And in my introspect, I'm amazed at how in tune and synced our bodies are. I move and pivot with enough men while dancing to know synchronism isn't ordinary. You must know the personal space required for your partner and the timing in which it takes them to decide the next choreographed *or* innate move. That's the challenge of dancing with a new partner. It's a needed skill for dancing.

Here, with Azmir, our moves gel as we dance the red carpet fluidly. With this revelation, I peer up to find Azmir's gleaming regard on me. There's a soft smile on his tempting lips and the area around his eyes are light—untroubled, blithely even. In this moment, I cannot question or deny this man is in absolute love with me. His adoration is palpable and here in this space in time, I'm not frightened by it. I don't want to run from it. I want to take it head on and give him any and everything needed to make him happy. Give him the contentment he deserves.

Step, step, step, step, step, and pose...

"Rayna, this way please," Dawn directs, snapping me out of my fortuitous trance. Because my guards are now down, I obey without a second thought.

We're only a quarter of the way done with the carpet, and I move to the left of her, leaving her to Azmir's side. She points to the cameras she wants him to pose for. I even notice how she speaks directly to several of them, giving them factoids about

Azmir, *Mauve, Cobalt,* and *Global Fusion*, which I now know is the mergers and acquisitions firm he owns with Richard. I notice when she splays her hand on Azmir's arm in a gentle and almost affectionate manner.

I'm proud to see Azmir display his charming, coochie-creaming smile, even if it isn't just for me. I've been so used to having him alone and experiencing the magic and wonder of his exclusivity that sharing him here with all of these eager people makes him larger than life. It's a fascinating phenomenon. It's his moment and he's owning it. The masculine nod he gives after a paparazzo expresses they've gotten enough desired shots of him and then moving on to the next, melts my core.

I cringe inwardly when I realize Dawn's in some of the shots, smiling with an air of companionship. I continue ahead of them, being sure to stay out of the way. I can't lie and say I don't eventually feel awkward and like a mismatched ornament. *She's wearing his blue!* There was a time, not too long ago, where I would haul ass from this scenario when another woman craftily, attempts her claws into Azmir. Not today. I want this moment for Azmir, and I will not waver from being by his side as he experiences it. It isn't easy, but I will not run. I smile and gracefully wait out the time until I'll be wrapped under his arm...where he wants me.

At some point, we bumped into other red carpet walkers—extremely well known ones. His old buddy, Kobe, is here with his petite wife and they are the first to pose with Azmir. They keep their banter to a minimum as Dawn guides Azmir farther down where he takes shots with Quincy Jones who appears far more geriatric than I ever imagined. He moves slow and slouches at the shoulders, but his killer smile is still in tow. Nonetheless, his presence warms me as I'm reminded of Azmir singing *and dancing* to one of his many genius hits that night at the marina. *Moody's Mood for Love* will always be etched in my heart, as the memory will be with me forever.

We bump into the rapper, Nelly, who's much taller than I realized. He has a potty mouth as he jeers familiarly with Azmir. Then we move on to Stephen Hill. He's extremely...goofy, very silly as he chats with Azmir.

The ultimate is when we meet Gayle King and when she turns to him, her eyes light up as she sings, "Divine!"

Hold up!

Did Oprah's best friend, the editor-at-large of *O* magazine, and co-host of a major morning show just refer to Azmir by his less than corporate-professional moniker? The wind has left my body as I watch them enfold one another like it's old hat. They exchange a few words in a conversant manner before we move on. I can't believe it.

Who is Azmir Jacobs?

I try to stay out of everyone's way as I realize it's all managed by folks talking into wires just like Dawn. There are dozens of celebrities Azmir poses with, reminding me of his stature—I still don't quite understand.

This goes on until Shayna Bacote takes me by the arm, which alerts me to us having arrived at the end of the carpet. As I follow her into the opulent foyer of venue, I immediately notice she's wearing a simple black sheath dress falling at her knees with black opaque hosiery and patent leather ballerina flats. I know Shayna typically wears heels and can easily surmise her desire for comfort as she works this evening—soooooo dissimilar to Dawn's. This is a different style of professionalism compared to her contemporary who's dressed to accompany the man of the hour.

That damn Dawn!

"Ms. Brimm, you'll be seated with Mr. Jacobs at the head table. After dinner, you two will be escorted to the cocktail room for the after party where the guests will be as well as journalists who will be looking for sound bites from Azmir for publication. Would you like to work the room with him or be taken to your seat where you'll be joined by him when he's done?"

I don't want to leave him all evening. Perhaps if I do the

initial walk through with him, I can give him a break during the after party. *Errrrrrrrrrr...* I wish I could ask what Azmir preferred.

Make a call, Brimm!

"Erm...I'll stick with him for now," I inform sheepishly.

Shayna smiles, "Of course. I'm sure he'd prefer that."

I idly wonder what that means.

Seconds later, Dawn and Azmir appear just inside the foyer and I can see his eyes perusing the area. I know he's looking for me, concerned with my inclination to run when faced with Dawn's conniving antics. Instinctively, he finds me amongst a herd of attendees. His eyes soften again. And like the horny teen I'm reduced to under his blazing gaze, I giggle. In a gown costing twice as much as my monthly mortgage, shoes doubling a hefty car note, and jewelry that could feed dozens of villages with malnourished dwellers—I giggle.

Way to go, Rayna.

He immediately makes his way to me. It doesn't take Dawn long to register his abrupt journey and she follows him, sans her baneful beam. When he reaches me, his big warm hand makes its way to the bare flesh of my back, and he plants a slow kiss on my forehead.

"You okay, gorgeous?" Azmir asks, and once again, I identify the gleam in his eyes.

I haven't run.

"Of course," I smile as I lean into him with both my fists between us. "You looked so dominant out there. So well-placed. I'm proud," I murmur as my head tilts back so I can gaze into his eyes.

"Yeah?" he asks with pinched eyebrows.

"Oh, yeah!" I affirm with my smile turning toothy. "And Gail King? *You know Gail King?*"

He cocks his head to the side, tentatively, "Well, that depends on what you mean by me knowing her."

I smack him in the arm. "Azmir! I'm not asking if you've been with that woman!"

"Well, good because I haven't. I don't know Gayle that well," he returns. "And before you ask, I've never met Oprah." A knowing grin crests upon his face.

He's right. That would have been a subsequent question. I laugh at myself. Azmir chuckles as well.

"Everybody thinks because you know Gayle, you must know Oprah. Gayle has her own life," Azmir informs. "We know a few of the same people—"

"Yeah...yeah...I know. The whole circle thing," I cut him off before he repeats the same line he gave at the Trey Songz after party.

He laughs this time, allowing me to smell spearmint from his mouth. "Well, yeah. Like I told you the other night at the dinner party, I came to "Hollywood..." He uses air quotations. "...at a time when it was smaller and easier to navigate. I played it hard and got to know everyone I could. It was fun while it lasted," he ends with softer tone.

Although it's not the most opportune time to have this discussion, I ask anyway. "When and why did you end it?"

His expression sobers as his gaze swallows me for what feels like minutes long. "Like I told you in Tahiti, I've made much needed adjustments. And now, all is perfect...or at least will be once I have your hand in marriage."

My heart stammers in my chest and my mouth goes dry. Hearing this beautiful, powerful, and well-suited mogul wax poetic about my ultimate commitment is heady. I don't know how to respond to that. My shoulders sag in forfeiture of his determination. He has me—all of me—but it would be a corny follow up to his smooth declaration.

"Mr. Jacobs, it's time for the actual signing in the private dining room. Dawn will take you around for greetings before you go to the head of the room with the partners for the mock signing and photo opp. After which, dinner will be served and then the after party," Shayna informs as Azmir holds me. "Ms. Brimm will be at your side, but if you..." Her eyes shift to address me directly. "...change your mind and want to wait it out during the dinner or after party portion, you can be escorted to your seat at any time until he's done." She returns her gaze to Azmir, and I notice her invariable level of professionalism, "I'm going to check on a few things for the after party, so I'll see you then." Azmir nods in approval and she walks off, leaving us to Dawn *and her blue strapless gown*. We look like a threesome.

As we make our way to the elegant dining room, we're offered tumblers of the night's purpose, *Mauve* brandy. The velvety amber liquid is no stranger to me as I've indulged in a glass or two with Azmir, sipped a few swallows from his servings, and consumed countless tastes of it from his lips. I've even had it licked from my trembling body a time or two. With familiarity, I sip my first taste of the evening, enjoying the thick trace of spice it leaves as it courses my esophagus.

Once in the room, we're stopped by several people greeting and congratulating Azmir. Of course, I know none of them, but a few Azmir introduce me to. One of those people is Steve Stoute. He's polite during our introduction, but I don't get a clear idea of who he is until I hear him speak during the opening remarks of the signing. He's an articulate and charismatic man, who apparently has a history with Azmir and brokered the *Mauve* deal. He shares stories of their relationship and why he's convinced the partnership between Azmir and the Moreau brothers will be successful.

Here I sit, again, feeling like there are aspects of this man I'm not privy to. I try to suppress the green-eyed monster in me as much as possible. As I glance around the table and see figures who previously, I've only seen in magazines, online, or on television screens, I begin to shrink. I know the man standing at the podium with other powerful beings is mine—all six feet and four inches of him, but this is all so intimidating.

Then, when my eyes go inches to the right of Azmir and land on Dawn, I feel annoyance. She's beaming too brightly considering her role in his world. She claps too hard and enthusiastically as Azmir signs the faux contract with the golden pen. Slowly, I train my eyes back to Azmir, where they need to be, and see him gazing at me with a glimmer of sheer accomplishment he wants me to take part in. Instinctively, a smile blooms over my face and my heart swells. He's sharing his moment with me—privately, which is how we do things. On our own, private terms. I don't need to be privy to his previous life. I'm his right now, and that's all that matters.

During dinner, Azmir introduces me to Jean and Jacques Moreau, the brothers who own the company making *Mauve* brandy. Azmir explains their need of international exposure, hence how this relationship came into play. Their French accents are thick, and their body language is more feminine than that of American men, but they are absolutely straight. This is made clear by the way Jacques keeps eye-sexing me and how Jean can't keep his hands off his wife. He's clearly drunk.

"Mademoiselle Brimm, it's a pleasure to meet you. I'm just sorry it wasn't sooner. We couldn't synch schedules before today," Jacques murmurs from the left of me. "Jacobs here," he gestures his chin in Azmir's direction, to the right of me. "...told us he was a lucky man. Now we get to see just how lucky. *Jolie femme*," he growls. I have no idea what he's said, but I get the gist of it. And apparently so does Azmir.

"Yo, Jack, man...you better not be flirting with my girl. I will kick your pompous frog ass," Azmir jeers—*or does he?*

Jacques snaps his tongue against the roof of his mouth on a pout as he cuts into his food. Then I hear a sharp whistle coming from Jean, followed by a gesturing sound made by his mouth that's often used to call the attention of a dog.

"You two need to stop. We're in front of company," Jean chides and then hurls out a string of expletives in French. His eyes then shift to me, "I guess we're both getting papers on him, huhn?"

My face heats up at his repartee. I'm also warmed by realizing I'm known to a select few of Azmir's circle. Maybe the press doesn't know who I am, but his business partners do. While satisfied with the sudden revelation, I glance over to the handsome man of the hour, who dubiously shuffles through his plate with his fork as he eats. His eyes find mine and obliviously, a contented smile crests upon his face. I join him. My heart swells.

Oddly, my eyes subconsciously go in search of a target and lands on Dawn who's in the corner of the room gaping directly in my direction with a scowl plastered. I have no idea what she's hitting at. No matter how much I try, I can't get used to her creepy presence. She's so entranced with Azmir she doesn't notice I'm returning her gape.

I have him, Dawn! He's mine and you see it! What's she hanging around for? *For you to fuck up.*

My subconscious can be so cruel, abasing, and counterproductive. I go for my glass and tilt the remaining amber potion.

"Can we get you another, Ms. Brimm?" Jacques keenly offers. "Or would you prefer something lighter? I understand *Mauve* is a rather robust indulgent."

I glance over to see Azmir raise his eyebrows and shrugs simultaneously, saying he approves, which is weird because I didn't know I was asking for permission. Hesitantly, I shift back to Jacques and mutter, "Yes, please. Another *Mauve* would be great... thanks."

He calls over to the waiter and orders another drink for the both of us. It takes less than thirty seconds for my drink to be set before me. I go for my first nip and swallow slowly.

"Good, aye!" Jacques trills. I smile.

Then I hear, "He may be doing a hell of a job being hospitable, but you're going home with me tonight." I glance up to find Azmir in my ear. His eyes are smoldering, and his brandy-hinted lips are glistening. With a smirk, I nod in ascension.

After dinner, we're escorted to the dining room. Dawn is front and center, directing us to the elevator so we can join the after party on the lower level. She lays her PR charm thick as she chats with the Moreau brothers about their formidable reputation. She mentions the partnership is a no brainer considering Azmir's long affinity for the liquor. Dawn shares how since working for Azmir she's developed a taste for the amber juice herself as she clasps onto his arm on a snicker. I could choke her. Azmir holds my hand the entire trip, sometimes alternating to holding me at the small of my back. I'm grateful for that seeing Dawn is wearing his color and can easily be confused as his date.

Dawn continues entertaining the small group all the way down to the ballroom. We enter the dimly lit room to find the party in full swing with energized tunes bouncing off the walls. The place is packed. Of course, I don't see any familiar faces, but per usual, people flood to A.D. They congratulate him for his latest venture. The waiters come with loaded trays, and I'm given another drink —*Mauve*—that I rip into right away.

I stay by Azmir's side as he reciprocates greetings. I'm not totally surprised by the level of celebrity in the place. I prepared myself for it understanding it comes with the A.D. parcel. Just during previous engagements, Azmir was discriminatory in choosing who he'd introduced me to. Unlike before, I'm not suspecting of it; I decide to believe he simply understands I don't like attention and would rather shadow him. Dawn never strays far. I can always count on her being near us—near him.

We eventually make it to V.I.P. where we sit and talk with more people. At some point, Shayna brings people over to pose for pictures with Azmir. It's coordinated, so I know there must be a reason, but don't quite understand it. Though I'm by his side, I make sure not to get in any flicks unless Azmir pulls me close to him. He does it when taking pictures with two women in particular, and strangely, I know he's slept with them. I can tell by the way he avoids their extended stares and lingering whispers into his ear. He also pulls me into him by the shoulders or waist during their brief stay. Both women get the hint almost right away.

Cameras are constantly flashing, but eventually they don't disturb my inebriation. I'm on my fourth tumbler of *Mauve* when I realize Dawn's sitting to the left of Azmir. It isn't strange she's there so much as how long she's there—and how she's posed with him in more pictures than I can keep count of. I study her giddy expression as she keeps chatting with him and a few people on the other side of her side of her.

"You okay, Brimm?" Azmir asks in my ear over the pounding music, reminding me Dawn has to be that close to communicate with him. *But why that much?* "You look a little tight." He wears a look of concern.

I won't crack. I won't be affected by Dawn. It doesn't matter that she's been around Azmir tonight far more than her business partner. I won't complain to him. I won't ask for her to trade responsibilities with Shayna. And I won't ask him to rescind their contract. *No!* Azmir is mine. He's coming home with me tonight and that's all that matters!

I force a seductive smile as my eyes dance in his. I lift my glass, "Of course I'm not okay. I'm out of *Mauve*, honeee," I slur in drag, sounding like Adrian.

Slowly, Azmir cracks that disarming panty-snatching smirk that gets me each time. Even through it, I can tell he's trying to scale my mood. Azmir knows something's off with me; you better believe I fight for a steely veneer. *Dawn will not win!* I hold on to my jovial mask. He doesn't even turn his gaze as he raises his hand, catching the attention of a waiter.

"More *Mauve* or do you want something else?" he asks. Just then, in my peripheral, I catch Dawn grimacing at the back of Azmir's head. I guess she wants his full attention. She looks angry that he isn't available to her. "I don't think I've ever seen you drink so much brandy. It may put hair on your chest."

Or have me put Dawn on her back!

"This is *Mauve's* night. Bring it," I challenge with a smile.

Azmir turns to the waiter dressed in all black to place the order. No sooner than the guy walks away Dawn stands and bends down to whisper to Azmir again.

When she's done, Azmir turns to me and says, "There are a few people I'm being asked to mingle with. Wanna come?"

I nod my head and he advises, "Your drink is on its way. I won't be too far. I'll move slow," before placing a warm kiss on my forehead.

"Okay," I stand because I know the drink will be here in no time.

I watch Azmir go down the steps towards the main floor. As soon as his foot hits the first step, Dawn shifts to me. Her eyes are agenda-filled, per usual. "You can sit here and relax. He's going to be a while, working the room. I'd hate to bore you."

In this moment, I have to make the decision of slapping the taste out of her mouth or remembering Azmir will be returning home with me tonight. I search every inch of Dawn's face for a reason to bash it in, right in the middle of Azmir's celebratory party. *Just one reason!* The bitch gives none.

"I'll hang out for just a little while. Be sure to make him aware of your suggestion," I say, trying to mask the venom.

I can't hear it, but I see the snort as she nods her head before turning for the steps herself. I stay in V.I.P. for what seems like an hour. At first, I'm able to follow them in sight, but that's until they make their way outside of my view. I can't just sit back and wait in my seat as though I have no interest in being here with him for such a monumental occasion. I have to do something.

So, I make my way down to the main floor and thread through the crowd in search of six feet and four inches of sheer pleasure, to no avail. I attempt to circle the first floor. When that doesn't work,

I make my way to the second floor to circle there. I see Dawn almost immediately, but Azmir isn't with her.

I don't want to, but I head straight to her and ask, "Where's the big guy?" I try to hide my disdain.

She holds up her index finger then starts typing into her phone. Seconds later she answers, "He's on the third floor with Shayna, talking to Hill Harper. Maybe you can catch him there before he heads out of here and into the private rooms up there. That's where the Moreau brothers are with their private guests."

I nod before making my way through the dancing patrons. I search the third floor twice, even knocked over someone's drink. I grow frustrated as I look over the balcony and see no signs of him. When I turn to head to the stairs, I see Shayna—alone.

I go to tap her arm and as soon as she registers my presence, her eyes enlarge. "Rayna! We've been looking all over for you. Mr. Jacobs is going crazy," she visibly sighs.

"I've been walking all over this hall, looking for you guys. Dawn said you two were here, talking to Hill Harper. Where's he?" I ask, referring to Azmir, of course.

She wrinkles her eyebrows, "Hill left hours ago. The three of us split up to look for you." If I wasn't so tipsy, I could swear to seeing her roll her eyes.

Dawn had lied. She was supposed to be searching for me and when she saw me, she lied to keep me on a wild chase. My nails dig into the skin of my fists at my hips.

"I'll find him. Thanks, Shayna," I say before walking off.

I'm so damn upset, my head is throbbing. I need to breathe...a minute to think. I recall Dawn, in one of her many fallacies, mentioning private rooms on the third floor, so I head outside of the main hall. I pluck another tumbler off the tray of a passing waitress before heading out the door.

It doesn't take me long to locate the long corridor with several doors on each side. I walk to the second one and crack the door to find it buzzing with people sloshed to the hilt. I catch a glimpse of

Jacques, grinding a woman into the wall as she giggles in drunken bliss. Other patrons are dancing, conversing, and laughing without conscience. It's the Moreau's private party.

I close the door and move a few rooms down, finding one unoccupied and slip inside. I don't bother with the lights. I plant my back against the wall and scorn myself for being so damn weak. I've never been so affected since leaving Jersey. *I was formidable and unwavering.* Resolved. A force to be reckoned with. I recall the promise I made to myself on the train ride down to North Carolina. *I'd never love a man so freely.* Is that what I've done? My yielding of my heart has somehow weakened me. It's caused me to doubt every move I make and each motive he exerts. Loving this man makes me crazy...insecure.

I take a long gulp of the amber liquid, no longer feeling the shooting burn down my chest, into my belly. I'm numb, reminding me of my existence before Azmir entered my world. *He does things to me...* makes me open my eyes to things around me I once avoided with my trained tunnel vision. There was little beauty before him. Damn it if he doesn't make me *feel*.

But why? For what? Could I trust his efforts? His guidance?

I've turned into a wimpy, whiney punk—on sensory overload since he's entered my world. I don't know what's held his interest in me. I ponder this as I lift my left hand to observe the ring. His promise of *forever*.

My chest rises and I release a hefty breath, loosening my embattled spirit. I need to regain that determined and resolute essence I used to survive since leaving home. In this moment, I'm confident it's just that drawing Azmir to me. *Or is it?* It has to be. Azmir adds to me. He pours into me. He makes me feel so damn sexy. Superior. Extremely feminine. Powerful.

No more doubting, Rayna. That's been the game plan since waking up to this ring after learning about the paternity of Tara's baby. We conquered that. Nothing else should matter.

As my brain whirs, I hear the door open, and a shriek of light enters the room as someone paces inside. It doesn't take long for me to recognize Dawn's thin frame and perfect bouncy curls, pulling out her phone.

"Shay?" she murmurs. "Yeah...I've been looking all over. I'm outside right now...I just circled the building and I'll do it once again before coming back inside. Tell Azmir we'll find her." I can hear Shayna's frantic voice on the other end of the call in the quieted room. I wonder if Shayna knows how much of a pathological liar her partner is. It shouldn't come as a surprise; Dawn's eyes alone give her away. In a more conspiratorial tone, Dawn hisses, "I hope we're not turning over this place looking for the girl, only to learn they got into a lover's quarrel, and she left. I have better ways to earn my money."

That's it! I can't stand the bitch!

"Yeah... Okay... Okay," Dawn forfeits in will, apparently in an attempt to placate Shayna. "Keep me posted and I'll do the same."

She ends the call and lets out an audible exasperated breath.

The liquor is beyond abundance in my belly and bloodstream at this point. My one hand is gripping the tumbler so hard it may crack in my palm at any moment, while my other is balled into a fist at my side. I'm battling the decision of walking over to Dawn and bashing her head into the wall or simply firing off a solid warning.

She' already won this evening. I caved. At her manipulative efforts, I got frustrated and let her keep Azmir away from me at his party, all evening—and I let her, all because I didn't want to give her the pleasure of knowing how much she's affected me. *Threatened us.* There's no way I can harm her without drawing negative attention to Azmir's well-deserved celebration. So, I decide to plead with her.

"Must be exhausting," I mutter. Even I can hear the slur in my words.

Dawn jumps and, on instinct, goes for the light switch.

Ducking behind my hand, I grunt at the bright light against my sensitive pupils.

When she recognizes me, standing with my back up against the wall—literally and figuratively—she sucks her teeth and snorts. Her frazzled stance recoils into a confident posture.

"Very grown up of you, Rayna, honey,"

I chuckle as I roll my eyes. "Honey?" I ask rhetorically. Dawn tilts her head to the side, inviting me to continue. "See, that's your problem, Dawn." My tone is soft, misgiving. "You don't respect what this woman has built."

Her head straightens. "Built?" she sputters. "Sweetheart, you're not experiencing the returns of your labor if you're in here, hiding while he's out there, hustling." It's now her turn to roll her eyes as she chuckles.

"He's mine, Dawn," I warn. "In spite of where your fantasy takes you with him, you're missing a very important element." She lowers her chin as she squints, asking me to finish with my point. "His heart, Dawn. You may experience some of that CEO mien which is irresistible. That thug passion he undoubtedly emanates. You may even speak to him several times a week—meet with him nearly as much—but you don't share intimacy with that man." I angle my head as I raise my eyebrows to emphasize, "My man."

Dawn breaks out in the most gut-wrenching laughter. I watch as her throat rumbles in mirth while her head falls back. She's either really in a laughing spell or extremely insane. After an extended period, she slows enough to inform, "I've explored every inch of his tasty mouth," she plucks a brow. "Tasted like brandy. Funny, right?" She doesn't give me a moment to answer before continuing, "If that isn't intimacy, then I don't know what is, honey." Her head tilts, exuding arrogance.

It's now my turn to belt out a hearty laugh. It's silent compared to Dawn's moments ago, but I'm sure far more gratifying. I can't believe her incredulity, and revel in her ignorance. The liquid courage from six glasses of brandy helps, too. She gives me my moment just as I had hers, though I can tell she's squirming to see how I'll get out on the other side.

"Intimacy?" I scoff. "From a kiss?" I abruptly raise my palm in the air defensively, "Granted, a kiss from Azmir Jacobs is nothing ordinary. Azmir's mouth is like cotton candy mixed with mint; sweet...and fresh." Breaking my reverie, I glance over to read her expression. She's rigid, yet I'm nowhere near done. "But dear, having him only in your mouth...via a kiss, no less, isn't even half the journey."

I push from the wall, sexily strut over to Dawn, successfully masking my incredibly imbibed state and stand directly in front of her. "You haven't even been *smashed* by A.D. That...," I chuckle sensually. "...is life altering. And do you know what it's like to have *him* in your mouth?" I exhale deeply, involuntarily retreating to the memory of it. Once my mind takes flight with memoirs of Azmir, I can't be responsible. "The fullness of his heavy appendage, coursing your mouth until it reaches down your throat? The weight of him, pushing in and pulling out against your needy tongue? How the ridges from his throbbing cock rub against the corners of your mouth, stretching it to near pain from trying to fit him all in. How your belly fills from him emptying his *soul* inside you?" I cock my head to the side. "Huhn?"

Becoming antsy and agitated, Dawn pivots a ninety-degree angle and, like partners executing the perfect cha-cha slide, I swivel along with her. She's now facing the door, debating her next move to leave. But I'm not done. *Nope!* Not by a long shot. I have a point to prove.

"How about having him between your legs—over you or behind you—plunging deeper than your depths have ever been known to exist?" I sigh after a short pause. "Do you, Dawn," I enunciate her name fully and appropriately as I softly move one of her perfect bouncy curls behind her ear. "...know what it's like to have Azmir Divine clawing at your hips, holding you to him as though he's desperate to fuse with you? Having a man of his caliber so vulnerable and needy, trembling against your pelvis from sheer bliss is...intoxicating. Have you experienced the exhilarating feeling of having him shoot his hot, virile, and powerful seeds in your provocative uterus?"

I see her chest rise and eyes slowly close as I move closer to whisper seductively in her ear, "Do you know that wielding force of having his seed implanted in your womb? The empowering sensation of carrying *him* inside of you?" I nod my head before sharing, "*Mmmhmm*, we were expecting," my whisper is softer.

Dawn audibly gasps. I lick my lips, suddenly aroused by my own torment, before whispering, "Yeah. He's that potent." She swallows hard.

I'm hardly done with her. I have so many examples of intimacy with A.D. Jacobs. I want to be soundly and thoroughly comprehensive on her need to back off. I'm standing, staring at her rigid frame, contemplating my next move. You never want to reveal too much about your lover and his skillset to *any* woman, but most certainly not to your *standby*. And if what I decreed to Tara as she left my office some time ago about my wing days being over is true, then Dawn is, in fact, my understudy.

I hear the door push open, forcefully. I know it's him, finally locating me, making my argument to her that much more credible. Azmir is good at finding me. But I don't shift in my stance. Neither does Dawn. I've enraptured her in the fantasy of intimacy with Azmir.

"Brimm, let's go," his tone is curt, commanding. If I didn't know him so well—*us so well*—I'd be embarrassed by it.

I stay in my pose with Dawn, in her personal space with my mouth to her ear, appearing very...*intimate*. "That's intimacy, Dawn. And it can only be experienced once you're in his heart, not on his payroll. See, when you obtain his heart, you influence his payroll."

"Brimm!" Azmir calls again, this time with a little more urgency to his tone.

I slowly pull back, turn, and stroll over to an impatient Azmir who's standing erect with his hands resting on his tapered waist, pushing back his suit jacket. When I reach him, he laces his hand with mine, and tows me behind his lengthy frame, out the door. I manage to keep up with his hasty strides without stumbling, giving away my blotto. I'm damn near pissy drunk, but content being back with Azmir.

We leave Dawn alone in that room, meditating on intimacy with Azmir Jacobs.

There are no goodbyes on our way out. No last minute potty breaks. No eleventh hour recollections of checking in with someone before our departure. Before I know it, we're out of the venue and at the door of Azmir's limo.

"Good evening, Mr. Jacobs," Ray greets. "...Ms. Brimm. I trust the event was successful."

The scowl on Azmir's face tells it all, but I'm confused by his annoyance. Did he hear my exchange with Dawn? *Or is he upset you left his party, Rayna?* I don't know what's incited his sour mood. My inebriated state won't allow for a sound mind to reason.

I nod to Ray, providing a polite smile, hoping to hide my drunkenness. I then duck inside the plush and spacious limousine, trying to provide a little decorum. It takes a few seconds for Azmir to join me. I can hear him murmur something to Ray. I'm sitting with my back to the partition, observing the mild sounds pouring from the speakers and smelling the fragrance of fresh leather upholstery while waiting to pull off.

From my peripheral, I can see Azmir yank off his suit jacket. He tosses it onto the bench across from me before getting in the car, planting himself center of the seat opposite mine. His penetrating gaze sears right through me. It makes my mind fight for lucidity as it floats in liquor. What's his problem? I don't want to be intimidated. I'm sick of being a coward. *I did nothing wrong!* To express this, I lift my chin in the air.

Azmir scoffs, unmoved by my assertion. "Gown. Off," he enunciates, and I struggle not to get caught up in the allure of his luscious lips stretching at each syllable.

My face morphs into a puzzled grimace. *What's he hitting at?* I'm not sharp. I've drank way too much.

"Now, Brimm. Gown off!" he growls.

I freeze...can't move at his command. We're in motion, in the back of his limo, on our way home. *Why is he asking me to take off my gown?* He hasn't moved to take off *his* clothing. *Why would he—*

My thoughts are abruptly halted by the swift movement of Azmir leaping across the car and flipping me two ways until he locates the zipper of my gown, then peels the fabric from my skin. His grip isn't delicate. He's too hurried for soft touches. Within a matter of seconds, I'm stripped down to my thong and heels as I lay awkwardly on the floorboard of the car, breathing rapidly. With incredulity, my eyes rake up to Azmir whose breathing pattern matches mine. His scowl is still in place. He *is* angry.

We stay locked in our positions, eyes warring. I don't know what it means or what his deal is, but I won't lose. I'm on a winning high from destroying *Desperate Dawn*. I have the fumes of victory to take on the great A.D., too. I don't know my next move; I also don't feel pressured to make it because I didn't start this mindless obstinacy.

From a side panel within his reach, he clicks a button, and the volume of the music increases to a near blaring level. Funny how, Raheem DeVaughn, of all artists, croons. Then, Azmir slowly lifts his hand and crooks his index finger as he beckons me to him. I take a minute to contemplate my next move. I'm naked in the back of his limo, wearing only a thong and heels!

Hesitantly, I rise to my knees and shuffle over to him. As I approach his wide stretched legs, my eyes are immediately taken by his straining arousal. He's swollen against his thigh, underneath his dress pants. My mouth collapses and I idly wonder if it pains him. My heart pounds and my belly jerks at the comprehension of his need.

With dubious eyes, I meet his glare. He bends over and whispers in my ear, "You know you want it, Brimm," he torments then sits back. I hear the smugness in his hoarse vocals. His chest rises and I can tell he's holding back. And *now* I know what's ahead, what mood he's in. What *I'm* in for.

But now what?

He cocks his head to the side and pushes his tongue into his molars contemplatively before slowly returning to my ear, "You talked your shit to Dawn about what it feels like to have me pour my soul into your mouth...down your throat."

My breath catches in my throat. He lifts a brow, knowingly.

He heard.

Returning to me, his tongue trails the curve of my ear and he whispers, "What are you waiting for...I'm loaded tonight," he sneers.

To any unknowing party, his command would have a semblance of abasement...disrespect. But to me, it's an invitation to empowerment. I know this realm of his being—his need. He's trained me and I've taken it further in gaining the mastery of pleasing Azmir. I'm supreme in satisfying him. This I know.

With athirst, I leap to undo his pants and push them down to his hard muscular thighs. The thumping from the bumps on the road makes it jerky, but we manage over it all. I'm drunk and unbothered by the disturbance. His wide-rimmed, thick, long, and glistening appendage plops up in the air. It throbs, matching the rhythm of my pulsating clitoris below. I feel nasty...dirty and ready to play lasciviously with him.

I lurch, taking him into my mouth, feeling a spike of adrenaline from the excitement of pleasing him. I wet him, using my tongue to sketch the long, thick, jagged vein that always catches my attention. Gloriously imbibed, I apply my soft chomps, fully awakening his thickness to be rewarded with Azmir, whistling air through his clenched teeth. I bob to a steady cadence in his lap, delightfully slurping him...on and on...on and on. I suck him in with gusto, relaxing the sphincter of my throat to let him in when he begins to pump into my face.

"Fuck, Brimm!" Azmir cries, untamed. Then I hear another increase of volume on the music. And now I know he's losing control.

I'm so drunk, I don't feel the discomfit of accommodating him, only the increasing desire to have him lose it...in my head. I feel the impressions from the pads of his fingers pressing into my lower skull. My fists jerk him firmly over the secretions of my mouth. His elongated thigh muscles flex against my elbows. When I finally think to peer up at him for an evaluation, I see his smoldering eyes, fighting for sobriety. My widely-respected, well-endowed, and authoritative mogul is empowering me once again.

After a while, I'm ready to unravel him. I know he's ready. I remove one hand and lower it against his sac, intermingling my fingers alongside his fullness rhythmically.

His eyes fly open. "Gahhhhhhh!" he groans without reservation. "I'm about to blow," he warns. *As if I'm going to decline the most stimulating part of pleasing him.*

I reposition myself against the floorboard, preparing to vacuum everything he shoots into me. This is where I want to be, theoretically, with Azmir. I want the ability to weather every storm that's presented. I want the resiliency of resolve to remain through dark times.

As he shoots his warm, intimate specimens into my belly, I inhale every morsel with pleasure. But before I can relish in his completion, Azmir flips me across the opposing leather bench, rips my thong off, and pushes my legs in the air as he buries his face in the apex. Azmir laps his skilled tongue over my sex as he breathes with urgency, summonsing my release. I grab his head, feeling the pricks of his hair against the pads of my fingertips. I hold him close to me, not wanting to lose a moment of his diligence.

In my alcohol-induced emboldened state, I wish Dawn were here, privy to our tryst. As his big hands are splayed over the back of my thighs, pressing them toward the leather, I wish she could observe *our* intimacy. Understand the intensity this man engages in with and for me. I so badly wish she knew how solid we are so she can stay away. *Far away.* With Tara, it freaked me out learning she watched Azmir and me have sex. But for Dawn, it would be remedial. She needs to learn. To know.

My back arches off the bench. The thought of Dawn being away and having Azmir bobbing between my thighs, sparring at my pearl, takes me over the edge and clawing up the wall adjacent to the partition. The grasp of my clammy hands slips down the window before Azmir quickly grips my hips, pulling me back down to ride out my release. And I do, with shaky extremities and air violently soughing from my lungs.

Azmir flips me so I'm upright against the back of the bench and my legs are stretched over his broad shoulders and scoots my pelvis against his. He's on his knees before me, with the wide bulb of his erection positioned at my lips. Next thing I know, he plunges forward, searing me in two with the girth of his manhood.

"*Uhhhh!*" gushes from my tried lungs at his fullness.

His eyes flutter and mouth collapses at the sensation, then within seconds, I see determination just before he rocks his pelvis into mine. He holds me at the waist first and eventually takes one of his big hands and clasps my shoulders. My diaphragm is pushed into my spine, leaving me little room to breathe. But when Azmir's inside of me, this deep, I don't want to breathe. I want to *feel*...to communicate with him on a level where words are not appropriate. He brings his mouth down to mine, and I feel the coolness of his tongue and draw my hands to his face to pull him closer to mine. A sheen of sweat layers the skin on his face and his shirt is completely sodden. I grasp he's still fully clothed other than his pants being lowered to knees.

He pulls back then he continues to pound me. His long fingers probe at my nipple, pulling it to a nearly painful length, further melting my core. I feel my belly stirring with pleasure. His left hand clutches my thighs against his chest as he moves powerfully in and out of me. Azmir then trails his luscious lips up my calf and grabs the diamond ankle bracelet he gave me in Vegas. I lose it. Unable to control my vocals, I scream insanely as I feel his sacs smack into my rear.

When he recognizes I'm done, he pulls me into his chest. Cupping me at the chin, he pulls me into an impassioned kiss that doesn't allow me to catch my breath from the earth-shattering orgasm I've just succumbed to. But again, I don't want to breathe around Azmir, I only want to *feel* him. And that's exactly what I do as he throws his tongue deep into my mouth. He doesn't do his usual butterflying effect. No, he's too caught up for that. He's pouring into me in a different way. His lips move swiftly as they turn firm against mine. I feel his heartbeat viciously through his shirt. Even in my woozy state, it isn't lost upon me how he's *still* clothed while I'm in just my stilettos.

Then I'm flipped again and bent over the couch opposite of the partition, still on my knees. He enters me with zest, and before I can catch my breath, I feel those zinging sensations of pleasure coursing through my wobbly frame. I steady myself to catch each plunge. I now feel the mist of sweat sprouting from my body against the plush leather. My moans are feral. I feel like I'm losing my mind in pleasure. His scent blankets me. His touch sets me on fire. His thrust melts my core. I bite my lip to feel pain in order to keep consciousness. It's fleeting with each delicious drive into me.

"You a'ight, Brimm?" Azmir calls out in his Brooklyn twang. "Looks like you're struggling. Stay with me!" he barks.

I can't think to speak. I can't formulate the words to tell him I'm on another planet. I don't want to talk at all; I only want to *feel*.

He lifts me upright, into a vertical position as we're still on our knees, him behind me. Azmir's hips still pump deeply and thoroughly. He lifts my upper torso, brings my arms up, and one by one, over his shoulders where my hands find their way to the back of his head. His warm hands then make busy with one thrumming my peaked nipple and the other pinching my lips from below over him firmly. As he thrusts into me, we knock against his hand, and I can feel the massage against my pearl. Ripples of pleasure undulate my core in no time. My head collapses back on his shoulder. I feel sensations from the spores of my scalp to the pads of my feet.

Before I know it, my body stiffens in orgasm-readiness at the rhythm of him plunging up and down...in and out. My body begins with low and steady trembles. The trembles turn into convulsions as I moan mindlessly from the onset of my orgasm. Azmir grips my shaky frame and continues with his masterful lunges into my core. My spine gives and my torso jerks, almost leaping forward, but he holds me until I land back on earth.

Amazing.

I'm depleted. Completely exhausted. So much so, he has to hold me up because I'm prepared to collapse on the floorboard. He pulls out of me and flips me again. This time I land on my back where he plants himself between my legs. His plunges never falter. They're still strong, resolute, and generous. I can still feel ripples of pleasure from his unrelenting horsepower. Even feeling each inch of bliss he delivers, I'm fading. In my befuddled state, I still have sense to know I'm crashing. I focus my intoxicated eyes on his beautiful face and recognize the intense zone he's in as he rocks deliciously into me.

I don't know how long or why he chose to take on this rendezvous tonight. Neither do I care. I enjoy every artful thrust and feel each droplet of sweat of his lightly splattering over my trembling body. I submit to him and ride out everything he gives, trying to remain conscious. I'm slowly fading and this time, unlike in Phoenix, I know why and where.

"Fuck her," I vaguely hear in my descent. "To you, I make love...smash...and fuck. She'll never have me. She'll never know me. She will never have my heart."

Before I can react in total shock of his admission, my consciousness wanes and I go under in complete pleasure. I don't know how long I'm out and because of my previous experience with passing out during sex with Azmir, I don't panic when I come through. In fact, when I awaken, I don't open my eyes right away, but I do notice the limo is no longer in motion. I smell sex in the car and oddly find comfort when it reminds me of how I've lost consciousness in the first place. I'm curled in Azmir's lap with his tux jacket draped over me. Then, completely fatigued, I fold into slumber.

I'm then awakened by sounds. I slowly open my lids and barely focus them to see Azmir cracking the window and pulling something white and fluffy into the cabin. I hear someone quickly greet him to have Azmir thank them before the window closes.

The next thing I'm aware of is being lifted into fresh air. I barely manage to crack my eyes and observe Azmir carrying me effortlessly into the private entrance of the building at the marina. *We're home?* I feel the plush cotton material of the oversized terrycloth robe I'm wrapped in. How Azmir fully put it on my naked frame, I don't recall. The attached hood is over my head as the side of my face rests on Azmir's strong shoulder. Down at my feet, his tux jacket covers what the housecoat can't.

I go back out.

I wake up to running water surrounding me as Azmir lowers me into the Jacuzzi. I hardly realize he's naked, too, with my heavy eyes. Although I'm awake for most of the bath and makeup removal—yes, I swear, he removes my makeup with cloths—I don't last much longer. After that, I'm awakened by Azmir demanding I take two pills and down nearly two glasses of water.

CHAPTER 9

Rayna

T he next time I rouse it's the following morning.

My eyes regretfully open to the glaring sunlight, pouring through the floor-to-ceiling windows of the master suite. I shift my head to the opposite side of the room where it's dimmer though not much. My body goes rigid, expecting symptoms of a hangover. Thankfully, my bout with dehydration is limited to my mouth and not my brain. *No hangover.* Once that assessment is out of the way, my thoughts transition to the man of the house.

Where's Azmir?

As I push myself up from the bed, using my arms and shift my legs to support me, I cry out, "Ow!"

My thighs are throbbing, and my sex is deliciously sore. Memories of copulatory activities in the back of A.D.'s limo flood the forefront of my mind. My lower back aches as well, but very dissimilar to that associated with my period. No. This is from my muscles being stretched in unfamiliar ways. Again, my thoughts race to the whereabouts of Azmir. Having the increasing urge to empty my bladder, I hop out of the bed without thought and screech from pain again. I find myself hobbling all the way to the toilet to relieve myself. I feel marginally better when I'm done.

Passing each room down the long corridor of the apartment, I search for Azmir. It isn't until I'm well into the great room that I hear him on the telephone in the kitchen. Gripping my silk robe around my delicate body, I make my way in there to find him standing over the kitchen table, searching the contents of his messenger bag. Azmir must sense my presence because in no time, he peers up from the bag and finds me at the entrance of the kitchen, off from the dining room. His eyes go from inspection, to discovery, to lackluster of the discovery. In other words, him finding me isn't welcoming.

He looks good...damn good considering our late night activities and the hour we made it in. His tall frame is wonderfully clad in a dark indigo suit, stark white dress shirt, and merlot oxfords. His hair and face are well trimmed, and he smells divine, even from a distance. I notice his tongue toying with a toothpick in his mouth, causing me to envy it *even in my aching state.*

"Yeah, Rich...I got it. I'll see you in a bit," I hear the translocation of Richard's, Azmir's business partner, voice. "Indeed."

When he's off the call, he doesn't even look back in my direction.

"You okay?" I ask timidly.

He continues organizing his bag and eventually murmurs, "I'm good." There's a brief pause before he informs, "Boyd prepared you an omelet with turkey sausage, turkey bacon, veggies and cheese, home-fried potatoes, and *uhhhh...*freshly squeezed orange juice." He still doesn't give me eye contact even through that lengthy description. "Oh, and there's a fresh pot of coffee on. I asked him to put one on for you instead of using the *Keurig*. I didn't know what kind of condition you'd be in this morning."

It was nice that he asked Chef Boyd to prepare hangover food for me, but something's strange. He's off—we're off. I start to bounce around, in my head, logical reasons why. The loudest cause can be me disappearing during his signing party last night. I have vague memories of how he burst into the private party room during my tête-à-tête with Dawn. *But I thought we'd made good on that in the limo.* It can't be because of my confrontation with Dawn, he already knows about that. I can't think much beyond that because my recollection of last night is fuzzy.

After grabbing his bag from the chair, Azmir stands to face me. He finally meets my eyes as he informs, "I have a meeting in the San Fernando area this morning. Shouldn't be all day. I'll reach out to you when I'm done. Manny's on duty today. Let him know if you need something right away." Then he turns on his heels to exit the kitchen from the other doorway leading into the great room.

"Azmir?" I ask, my mouth annoyingly dry and now my nerves are frayed. He turns to look at me. "Is there something wrong?"

I see the cogs churning in his mind when he furrows his brows rapidly. His head turns back to the doorway he was heading to before reversing back to me.

I start to grow impatient. There's something thick in the air between us and I need to know now. "Are you going to spill it, or do what you've asked me not to do, which is internalize it?" I try keeping the sarcasm from my voice. The struggle increases by the second.

Deciding whether to answer or not, he thumbs his face from his jaw to his bottom lip then cocks his head to the side before relenting, "You told Dawn about the baby..." His gaze falls to my abdomen region. "...our baby?"

This is the absolute last thing I expect to hear. My neck slightly jerks, I'm barely able to process his implication. I can recollect our heated exchange, even remember feeling victorious after leaving Dawn in the room alone and being whisked away by her favorite fixation: Azmir. However, the specifics are a blur.

"I recall being somewhat explicit with her...in a roundabout way of telling her to back off—"

"Back off of what?" he asks irritably. And before I can even answer, he bites out vexingly, "You know what...don't even answer that. I don't care to know what caused that little catfight between you two last night. Hell," he sways his neck. "I even got off on hearing you be so aggressive and staking your claim. But what I will absolutely not tolerate," he speaks vehemently as he pivots toward me, but maintains a distance causing a pang to run through my belly. "...is you brandishing our loss as a goddamn weapon to fight with someone who works for me." His eyes are sharp as his index finger points towards the floor.

I want to speak, to defend myself, but he's that quickly snatched my confidence straight from my throat as he continues, "That loss may not have weighed much for you emotionally, but your feelings of it isn't the only to be considered."

That knocks the wind from my lungs. "You don't think I was affected by losing a baby?"

"Were you?" Azmir's eyes widened. "You treated it as someone would a fuckin' cosmetic routine they didn't want anyone to know about but wanted the world to see the aftermath of. You went in for surgery, did your time recovering without telling a soul, and never gave it a second thought."

I can't believe his demeanor, his underlying accusation. My first intention is to react aggressively; to come out of my corner swinging with a nasty verbal defense that somehow would involve me asking him why he would keep a woman he clearly knows is after him as a business associate. The dirty fighter in me wants to compare that to the likes of Brian Thompson still working with me at the firm. I want to spew so much, it would make him feel as shaken as I am now. But I don't. I don't out of sheer fear. Azmir is livid. Beneath the surface, he is a boiling volcano ready to erupt.

"Losing the baby was a painful experience for me, Azmir," I grit through my teeth in an attempt to keep the tears at bay. "It wasn't an in-and-out procedure for me in spite how you may have perceived it."

He cocks he head to the side again, bringing his tongue back to his molars, contemplating my words. After an abbreviated pause he returns, "Oh, yeah?"

I can only muster one soft nod of my head.

"Karen Bridges, one of my executive admin assistants at the rec...you may or may not remember her. She was in on the leasing proposal meeting when you first visited my boardroom." I almost immediately recall her. She's the redhead with red plastic framed glasses who entered the room just before Azmir and Brett that day. "She miscarried last summer, too...was well within her first trimester. She opted to take a brief leave of absence to *mourn the loss of fetus* according to HR." Azmir squints, "If I'm not mistaken, you returned to work as soon as you were cleared from the hospital."

My mouth collapses. He's being mean, hurtful even—all unusual characteristics of my Azmir. My eyes grow to continue to absorb the tears. I feel wounded.

Azmir's eyes slowly close as he continues to fight his escalating emotions. Conspicuously absent is my aplomb mogul.

Calming his tone, he mutters, "You don't share personal information with my business affiliates—*I* don't share personal information with my business affiliates. For fuck's sake, she informed me if that type of shit got out, she'd be the person doing damage control."

Another mention of Dawn flares my anger once again. I don't want him to get the wrong impression of the cause of our fight last night. "What else specifically did she say to you when she ran back to tattletale—"

"It's not about what she says!" he roars, shaking me to the core. "It's about my feelings! I lost a fuckin' baby! And if I don't want it used as ammunition in a bout between you and a business associate I could not give two flying fucks about, it's my goddamn prerogative!"

Feeling his admonishment, my eyes fall to floor, which is symbolic of my tail flopping between my legs. I find myself, again, being seen as insensitive. It's painful. I have no rebuttal as my eyes sweep the floor. A few seconds into it, I hear Azmir's loud exhale of exasperation. Then I feel his warm lips press into my chilled forehead before he makes his way out of the kitchen.

What's most disturbing is Azmir being right; I probably didn't feel the loss the average woman would, losing a baby. I felt the inconvenience of having been told I was pregnant and being holed up in a hospital bed until it was cleansed from my body. I felt it impeded on my bereavement of my best friend. Now I'm feeling insensitive. Inhumane. Disgusting.

A few hours later, when I thought my mood had marginally improved, I'm knocked down a dozen pegs when I find myself online, searching for coverage of the *Mauve* signing. They say when you go looking for trouble, you will find just that. I start out with *SandraRose.com* when I find pictures of Azmir and other notable figures who attended; some I recall and others I don't. I only see one picture of Azmir and me on the red carpet. But what's in abundance is those of Azmir and Dawn inside the event, appearing as the couple of the year and a very handsome one at that.

Dawn's slender shoulders look companionable to Azmir's broad and square ones. Her silken ebony skin matches his dark chocolate Adonis perfectly. Her proximity to him is carefully placed. Dawn's hands doesn't grip Azmir intimately. No. Her touch doesn't mimic mine as his lover. She's too smart for that. Dawn arches her arm behind him; I'm sure just short of touching Azmir, which would have alarmed him. But when she smiles for the camera, her head inclines toward him in a familiar juxtaposition. And there are at least a dozen photos of them like this.

The caption reads well for Azmir, for which I'm grateful. But it also speaks acclaims for Dawn and her PR firm.

"Business mogul, Azmir Jacobs is still flying high in his lucrative career with yet another power move. He's recently inked a unique endorsement

deal with the French and very wealthy Moreau Brothers (they aren't reputed to do business with men of Mr. Jacobs' skin tone) for their brandy called Mauve. The event took place last night in West Hollywood.

Atlanta's very own princess, Dawn Taylor, was there coordinating one of the biggest deals of its kind in history. Dawn is a partner in Bacote & Taylor's Planning and Public Relations Corp. and looks good on Jacobs' arm. He's listed as Vibe's **Top Richest Black Eligible Bachelor.** *Dawn, we wish you the best on this one."*

I'm sure this is Dawn's doing. Everyone knows Sandra Rose is an Atlanta-based blogger, Dawn's hometown. I will bet anything that Dawn slipped her these photos. It now makes sense why she wanted to handpick my stylist for the event.

I slam the laptop shut and toss it on the other side of the couch. I need air so I go out onto the deck, off the master suite and gaze out into the water. I'm sulking internally. My fiancé is pissed with me—and with good reason. And his bitch of a PR representative, in all her creative ways, is manipulating her way into Azmir's world. I refuse to bring this to Azmir's attention. *I'm no weakling!* I'll just have to figure out a way to deal with her in his life. A method of decimating my clean up woman.

I brood over the whole ordeal for the remainder of the day. My ruminating even follows me to bed that night.

I've just dozed off when Azmir slips between the sheets and pulls me into his hard frame, snuggling me beneath him. His scent is tantalizing, his arms comforting, and his sentiment of still being committed to me in spite of my emotional deficiencies is felt in every chamber of my heart.

God, I love this man...

Over the next few weeks, time seemed to have sped by. I spend my first Christmas with Azmir, and in true A.D. fashion, he went overboard with gifts and surprises. Outside of diamond earrings and bracelets, designer shoes and clothing I opened boxes to, he also bought me a brand new *Panamera*. This car has more power than I care to have at my fingertips or beneath my foot. We agree to me keeping Azmir's *Benz* I covet because it was once his and using the sports car on special occasions—whenever they'd be.

I couldn't top him if I tried, so I kept my gifts simple and practical. After all, Azmir is Muslim and didn't grow up exchanging gifts on Christmas mornings. I didn't want to overwhelm him. After having him open up ties, socks, athletic wear, cologne, and other traditional gifts, I handed him an envelope containing the deed to my house in Redondo Beach. I explained it symbolized my conceding to his metaphoric chase. I declared no more running, and if I do freeze up, not going very far to where he can't find and reel me in. I submitted to an infinite future with him.

Azmir must have gazed at the document unseeing for at least five minutes; I nearly held my breath the entire time. Then, in an instance, he pounced on me, taking me down on the floor, aside the Christmas tree, and sucked my entire mouth into his. It was more feral than his usual style, but I felt the emotion behind the maneuver. Azmir kissed me breathlessly.

"*I swear, I'm going to work so fucking hard for your happiness, Rayna. I swear this with everything I have,*" he murmured into my mouth, his voice was strained, and I could feel his racing heart through our clothes.

I choked back on a cry, filled to the brim with emotions. I felt my bottom lip quiver when I whispered, "*You already do. Beyond anything I ever felt I deserved, you've poured so much into me. I now know love on an improbable level. I owe you so much, Mir."*

There was so much more I wanted to say, but couldn't muster the courage, like how he unknowingly was the catalyst behind me seeking help from a higher power. Azmir makes me experience emotions I'm unfamiliar with and don't know how to manage. His presence in my life has caused me to see flaws I didn't know I'd owned. After experiencing him in my world, I never want the numbness I oddly found comfort in before him. It was a pivotal moment for us. The best Christmas ever for me.

Later that evening, we had dessert with Yazmine and Samantha. I'm really trying to open up to my mother, but I need more time. She'd been in town for nearly two months, and I was still adjusting. Yazmine is great. Poor thing hinted a request for grandchildren, and I went stiff. Perceptively, Azmir redirected the conversation, and my mother backed him up. I'm improving, but not quite cured.

Azmir flew the four of us to the East Coast for the New Year. Yazmine wanted to be with family and friends for the occasion. I guess she missed the folks she left behind to start a new life near her only child. Samantha mentioned visiting Akeem and wanting to be with Chyna, needing to spend as much time as possible with her now that she has a clearer head. She and I agreed to visit Akeem together.

Azmir wanted a change of scenery for the holiday, so he arranged for us to recite the countdown in a plush suite in the Big Apple. We lay in front of a crackling blaze, wrapped in a fur throw, nuzzling and snickering. Azmir lay on top of me, my thighs clamped around him after he'd exploded from another orgasm. We were competing and he was catching up to me. I warned it was close to countdown time. He refused to move, saying he wanted to toast the New Year just as we were. And we did. When the clock struck midnight, we toasted, kissed, sipped, and eventually slipped back into another amazing lovemaking session.

What a way to start a new year with the only man I adore.

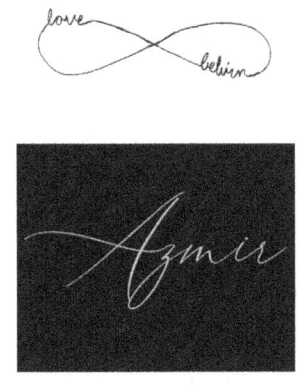

love ∞ believe

Azmir

"He's still off the fuckin' radar?" I ask with incredulity.

Kid's bouncy pupils leave me and make their way over to Petey.

"Yeah," he pushes out with trepidation.

"Kid, this dude ain't gansta. He's a college grad with a double major, from a two parent home, with a cat, a dog, and a fuckin' white picket fence. He still has an active Orange County Public Library card! How the fuck can he still be under the fuckin' radar?" I ask once again as I rise from behind the desk at Petey's *Drop It* club in the Watts. "He just had a baby. He's fuckin' traceable!"

The office is stale with papers mounting the desk in no particular organization. The walls are cold, leaving the room temperature chilled to match my mood. It's the end of January and has been two months since the fire in Pasadena. I still don't have my hooks in D-Struct's punk ass.

"I know, but, D, man," Kid argues respectably. "He got some type of money behind him."

"Could be Big D's," Petey offers.

"It would have to be," I concur. "But Big D's money ain't longer than mine, and right now his incarcerated arms ain't stronger than mine. You feel me?"

It's well after the New Year, and though my reign is over, my mission of retribution to this whimpery fuck has not been resolved.

"Perhaps I should pay one of those teens around the fuckin' block to trap his ass. Would get done faster I bet. You getting old and slow on me, Kid?" I taunt.

"Hell muthfuckin' no!" Kid grits out. "Ain't nobody round this way grimier than Ace Kid! Man, I put that on my last stack. Believe that!" he challenges.

As Petey watches perched on a stool from afar, I issue him a more challenging stare. I need to channel my sentiment precisely. I know in the past, Kid's sneaky ass could snatch anybody off the streets. He's reputed for catching dudes and chicks with their panties down—literally. But I have too much to lose. This has to be dealt with and right away.

"Kid, man," I speak soundly. "My girl is sour as a muthafucka for having muscle with her at all times, not to mention what it's costing me for the type I have assigned to her. I really don't give a fuck about the cost." My gaze intensifies. "And I can give a fuck less about his life. You want my crown? You want the rights to my throne? Get. His. Ass," I order before walking out.

That's the first challenge I issue today. The second is more like a pledge.

"Let's do it," I murmur then peer over to Rayna who's sitting next to me.

Her eyebrows narrow before she asks, "Do what?"

Pastor Edmondson's head rises from his notes; his facial expression isn't much different from Rayna's. First Lady Twanece's expression is much different. She understands somehow exactly what I'm getting at.

After my meeting with the goons, I headed straight for one of the last of Rayna and my committed premarital counseling sessions. In fact, I don't know how I'd agreed to them, not that she twisted my arm into it. I just want to do whatever I sense will make Rayna happy and ease her into the concept of being mine forever.

Over the course of the past few months since being engaged, we've been attending these sessions, sometimes weekly. Never in a million years would you have been able to tell me I'd agree to being counseled for anything, much less in a church by a reverend and his wife, but you also wouldn't have convinced me I'd meet a woman who made me do things I'd never consider doing. It's helped that I'd been able to get to know Pastor Edmondson outside of these high moral walls. We've met several times over lunch, even once in *Cobalt* on the floor.

He's been very easy to talk to. Never once have I gotten the impression he was attempting to sell me up the river with ideas of a magical being, up in the clouds, neighboring Jack and his Bean Stalk. We've talked about life, principles of being a leader on a domestic level. We've talk about sports, politics, and then Christian-dome, as he's put it. I can't lie, initially it was weird chopping it up with a white dude about the afterlife when we'd touch on that topic, over coffee. Then I told myself, it's no different than chopping it up with Richard over brews about quality strippers after a nineteen-hour day of negotiations with potential business holders. It's just that my chats with Pastor Edmondson have more substance and underneath it all, relates to Rayna.

So, when the last two sessions incorporated biblical references on abstinence and I could see Rayna visibly freeze at the topic, I started doing some thinking; some soul searching. So much of our relationship has involved inappropriate sexual communication: our anxiety of losing ourselves in each other, our apprehensions of falling in love, our expressions of anger and betrayal, and our articulation of fear.

Since our blow up after the Brian Thompson debacle, I've begun to feel a bit of guilt for having communicated my anger for her not reciting three single words to me. And what's more incredulous than my command of her speaking them is I knew she'd felt them. I knew Rayna loved me when I was manipulating her to verbalize it. At the time, I was feeling inept and not in control of a piece of my life I believed to be important to me. I desecrated her body to make me feel good about the ability to manipulate her because again, I knew Rayna loved me when I was doing it.

I also knew she ended up in Thompson's arms that evening because of my betrayal of trust when I'd kissed Dawn. A kiss I engaged in because I needed to employ the control I didn't feel I had with Rayna. From a meaningless act with Dawn, I was able to identify my desire to exert a control I wanted with Rayna, someone who is scarred from love having failed her previously.

I'm a hustler, an entrepreneur several times over, and in multiple arenas. I've been some of these things since before I was a legal adult. Control is in my blood, a keen piece of my governing and overall existence.

Love is not control. Love is willfully given and received. Love does not rush people who are broken. It's patient and kind and long suffering. I learned this through a series of premarital counseling sessions.

I've already committed to waiting for Rayna, so taking it a step further and for just a few weeks would prove challenging, but sacrificial just the same. I want to remove the physical expressions, hopefully detox her of the messages I've fed to her with my callous behaviors.

Rayna can't chew on too many things at one time. She needs space to think and deliberate, unlike me. I understand I'm dealing with an embattled woman and need to be satisfied that she comes into what I'm proposing as a lifetime offering. I'd be remiss if I don't consider the shit I've hidden from her. She's been serious and dedicated to the Christian walk, and while I'm not quite with her on it, I want to support her in whatever manner possible. That's how much I love her.

And *that* brings me here...

"Let's pledge abstinence until we're married. How long is that?" I glance over to Pastor Edmondson, though I know the answer. I've given this hours, days, and weeks of consideration.

Before he can answer I hear Rayna caution, "Azmir." She licks her lips as though she's salivating at the mention of sex. She gives cursory glances to the pastor and his wife before returning her gaze to me. "Are you... Don't you want to discuss this privately? I don't want you to feel pressure... You've already acquiesced to so much...being at the sessions."

Her eyes are wide and filled with anxiety and inquisition. I've thrown a curve ball, though it's not my intent. Shit, if she still wants to fuck up until the wedding day, I'll be down. But I know Rayna; she needs to feel she's followed every instruction to the "T" when trying to do the right thing. She's been working on herself since losing Michelle and has been pretty consistent with it.

"I've given it some thought and think more than anything, it'll be a therapeutic exercise for us," I offer.

"It would be for six weeks," Pastor Edmondson quickly adds.

The room goes quiet. Rayna's not happy. Her eyes dance into the distance as she processes all that this means. I don't want her to feel ambushed.

I'm panicking now. I don't like seeing her jarred. I've entertained this therapy shit because of my support of her, but I'm still a very introspective thinker and planner. I'm quickly deciding on just how divulging I'll be with what I'm about say.

"Rayna," I call out impatiently. Her beautiful irises shoot over to me tentatively.

I exhale deeply and find my hands on my head, rubbing profusely. I feel all eyes on me—shit, it's do or crumble.

"Sex has been a silent issue between us. From the moment I saw you at *Cobalt* at the dance-off, I wanted to *fu*—I mean..." I give

Pastor Edmondson and First Lady Twanece an apologetic nod. "...lay with you. I guess what I mean is I've always desired you. Who wouldn't? And even though we didn't jump right into a sexual relationship, I had not so virtuous motives for wanting..." I'm struggling to keep it clean. "...intimacy with you. I tried the traditional route of flaunting my money and very early on. And you made it clear that wouldn't work. So, I guess I decided on sex. When we finally did, I was curious about you...the mystique of your emotions. I wanted to unveil it, but again, not for noble reasons, only for egotistical ones. Then the more we...were intimate, my motives changed. I desired your heart. I thought sex—good sex would get me there. Yet, I didn't know what the hell to do with it once I conquered it. My ambitions didn't reach that far, only my insatiable need for you...to want me." I exhale, unable to look at her.

"I've used sex to temper you. I've withheld it to punish you. I've manipulated it even to humiliate you and make you feel as powerless as I was feeling in your world at the time. I did it because I could...because I knew no matter what my motives were, you'd enjoy it to a fair degree." Rayna shifts nervously in her seat. "But recently I've realized I don't need to use sex to win you over. You made it clear very early on I only need to give you time and stability. It may have been a late realization, but I get it now."

My gaze makes its way to her confused eyes. She's scared, I can tell.

"I just don't want that to be the theme of our relationship. While sex—*good* sex..." I chuckle and hear Pastor Edmondson snicker under his breath. "...is key in what we're about to commit to, it's been an inappropriate weapon I believe I've used against you for much of our relationship. We can hold off for the purpose of demonstrating control over ourselves in that manner."

Rayna's eyes flutter. Her mind is turning over my words and I'm sure the prospect of holding off from sex—*great* sex. I won't push her. I've put it out there, now the ball is in her court.

"We'll discuss it over dinner tonight," I murmur softly to her.

A part of me—a very rational and practical part of me—doubts my proposal. I've never denied myself much, especially sex. I didn't have to; I've always had an abundance of offerings. But this isn't about me. I've fucked around and fallen in love with a woman who's an extremist. Everything she does, she goes full steam ahead. She needs this. And I need her. I just hope I can execute my proposal with as much ease as I've offered it.

Rayna

Azmir and I do talk later in the evening over dinner and agree to "delay gratification," as he's proposed. He told me he understands I need it and he's right. I need to make sure I sacrifice something in exchange for time. I have my hidden reservations about marrying a man I'd known less than a year when I accepted his proposal. I need a bit of traction in the undercurrent I've acceded to since Azmir's entered my world.

Who cares about abstinence in the twenty-first century?

I do. I care about my being holistically. I know I've harbored a lot of junk within over the years. This is the walk I've decided on to heal myself and I will go full throttle. And when we've gone over the conduct of single men and women in previous sessions, self-consciously I've wondered would our relationship be less complicated, less intense if we didn't indulge ourselves in the haze of passion that's possibly clouded our judgment and prevented us from getting to know each other properly.

I wonder.

Maybe we've rushed into that aspect of acquainting ourselves rather than discovering pertinent details such as our family history, past hurts, and experiences that's shaped us into the individuals we are today. How did we come to be as drawn to each other the way we are? Removing sex for a pair like Azmir and me could determine a lot.

The *what ifs?*

What if Azmir and I walk into this thing knowing every secret we've guarded, every demon haunting us, every bone of the skeleton making up our pasts? There are so many things I haven't shared with him. So many details remain in my nightmares, but I dare not speak of them in the light of day. As hypercritical as it may be, I need to counterpoise those secrets with a cleansing process which can only strengthen us in this monumental commitment we've been embarking on.

I can't lie and say I don't feel a twinge of self-disappointment in Azmir having to push my hand at this decision. It's just that I could never ask him to make such a sacrifice when we aren't even of the same belief system. I couldn't have pushed his hand in this because this is personal. The renewing of my heart and mind has been my personal decision.

How lucky am I to have a man who agrees to entertain my faith. Azmir said if it would make me feel any better, instead of putting it out there officially, we can just use short-term goals to lead us up until the day. Secretly, I don't know if we'll make it a day, but I'll roll with his idea and give it a try. We've gone extended periods before, but much of that was before living together.

Ironically, work assists with our commitment. Azmir's travel picks up again. He's barely home, and sometimes I wonder if it's by design. We speak every day, most times several times a day. It's become weird, but enjoyable to experience him over the phone. It's like dating someone virtually. Because we have limited face-to-face time, the telephone and texting thing breathes new life into our communication. I'm learning more of what a day in the life of A.D. Jacobs is like far beyond what those weekly itinerary emails Brett sends over. Azmir's truly an engineer. I also learn odd intimate facts such as when Azmir experienced his first orgasm with a girl and how he learned to find a woman's G-spot. Yes, this type of conversation leaves me feverish.

The first two weeks of this commitment, Azmir stayed home about three nights and traveled the remainder. My workload changed in pace as well. In our monthly full staff meeting, Dan Smith announced his latest endeavor, which is working with scientists in creating state of the art prosthetics.

Dan believes it's time to revolutionize the world of prosthetic medicine. And he proposes going all out with his new devices, starting with looking for funders, licensing, finalizing the patent, researching more limitations in prosthetic rehabilitation, product placement, profession buy-in, and all those things one needs to bring a product to consumers. In doing this, Dan explained, he'll be pulling back from attending and his typical academic obligations such as speaking engagements. The kicker was when he assigned extended roles to the room, mine being research for this venture and most of his presentations at conferences. This sucks considering I have to pull back from attending to accommodate his request. It reminds me of that scheduling nightmare I'd undergone after taking so much time off after losing Michelle.

Dance class always relieves stress for me. Jimmie cracks the whip during rehearsals for our next dance exhibit. We've been doing a dance interpretation for the *Vagina Monologues* with a group of readers from *UCLA* in February. It's a different take on the historical production. My dance troop will do an interpretive dance to the reading which a student will recite. I'm assigned the Angry Vagina. It's fun and I learn a lot about the many plights of women and the feminine experience.

Bible study continues with my subgroup. The girls are still obnoxious and outspoken, but everyone agrees about the messages. One thing that hasn't change with this group of women is the stares and silent questions I get whenever we're dismissed and John, my muscle, is waiting on me. I hate this guard dog thing like I do maxi pads. However, Azmir isn't relenting on his decree back in the fall of me having security with me at all times. For the most part, John has faded into the back like wallpaper, like when I'm out shopping or in church where there's lots of people around anyway. But at times like this, when his massive presence can't be ignored, it's an embarrassing annoyance.

When February arrives, I still haven't decided on my wedding gown. I wake up at nearly four in the morning on a Wednesday with the revelation. I shoot right out of my bed, out of breath with *"My wedding gown!"* echoing in my brain. What woman remembers her wedding gown just three weeks before the day?

RAYNA! That's who!

I immediately grab the cordless to call Azmir, who's in Boston. It's just before seven there, but I need a sounding board. I'm halfway sure he's awake and about his day.

"Yeah, baby?" he pants, obviously out of breath.

"What are you doing?" I nearly scream into the receiver. All types of frightening images running through my head.

That's one of the many fears you suffer while on a celibacy track: your man seeking release elsewhere. During the day, when all your good senses are employed, you can convince yourself of the unlikelihood of it. But during the night, when your body craves him considerably, and all you have is his lingering fragrance from his side of the bed, making your legs quiver, your mind easily capitulates to that fear.

"I was working toward my fifth mile on the elliptical when your call came through," I can hear the veiled defensiveness in his tone. "Is everything okay? It has to be almost four over there."

Okay, now I hear alarm.

And feel guilt, you insecure girl, you!

I wet my dry lips as I squeeze my eyes in disgrace.

"Yeah... Everything's fine," I answer sheepishly.

"Well, there has to be a reason you're not soundly sleeping at this hour."

"I was awakened by a reminder."

"Reminder? What's that?"

"It's when you've forgotten a huge detail for likely the biggest day of your life," I provide.

After a few moments of contemplation, Azmir mutters, "My wedding ring? I told you I was good with the two-toned set you sent me a picture of a couple of weeks ago, and I'd take care of it."

"No. No, I know. Not that."

"Then what?" He's losing patience.

"My gown," I exhale. "Azmir, I don't have a gown." Speaking it sounds sillier than thinking it. I can't believe I've forgotten, demonstrating my non-girlie existence. He's probably going to see it as evidence of me not being one-hundred percent committed to the idea of marrying him.

"Do you have something in mind?"

Of course not. "No. I don't even know where to begin," I sulk aloud.

"I'll send you the number to the wedding planner, Tessie Bell in West Hollywood. She should be able to provide you a few references."

I exhale again. Azmir is always there to save the day. I could kiss him right now if he were here. Or drop to my knees and worship him with my mouth, something I daydream about... daily.

God, I miss this man!

Suddenly, I hear noises in the background.

"Who are those people?" I hear bursts of laughter, and someone sounding like they're firing off orders.

"Other patrons of the gym. I just told you I was on the elliptical. They don't have this type of equipment in the rooms at this hotel," he informs sardonically.

I sigh loudly at my ridiculous implication. "Yeah...you did." I'm stuck. From here there's no comeback or a turnaround. My insecurities have reared. Celibacy is hard.

"Hey," he calls out.

"Yeah?" I shriek, knowing that quickly he'll change the course of this conversation.

"When I get home, let's go out. Somewhere nice."

"*Uh*—okay," my voice is trying to settle itself. "That sounds great."

I miss him so much. I know him so well; I understand in this moment he's considering just how much he misses me. I know Azmir well enough to know he'll never fully articulate it. He isn't a man of many mushy words. They only pour when I'm way out in left field and he desperately needs to center me. I guess I'm not as bad as I thought this time.

"Call me later?"

"Yes. Of course," I promise.

"Indeed." And I know that's it.

That's the end of this conversation.

CHAPTER 10

Azmir

"So, how soon are you trying to make this transition?" I ask.

"I don't know, Divine," Michael answers before chucking a forkful into his mouth. He chews as he considers his words. "I was thinking I'd use your advice from tonight to decide that. I mean, the money is there and there are a few developers knocking, so I guess that call needs to be made now."

"Well, let me know if I can be of further assistance. I have a few people I can link you with to make sure you maximize each endeavor," I offer.

We're staying here, at the *Four Seasons* in Boston where I'm doing my last leg of the *Mauve* campaign until after my wedding. I made sure to include a friend of mine, Michael Brooks, while in town. He's a record executive, based out of New York, and in town himself. He's been trying to get up with me for a few months, so I invited him and his wife, Sherina, to dinner. Michael wants to start to engage in varied investments to expand his portfolio. I've been pretty successful over the years, and he's appreciated what I've been able to accomplish.

Earlier, I'd seen Dawn and Shayna, who are on this particular promo leg with me, en route to the restaurant. They were looking for a place to eat and asked about my plans. Since it isn't exactly a business, I invited them. We've had three events in this vicinity alone in a four-day period. It's been monumental.

"Yeah, and when you need public relations services, look no further," Dawn advises then licks her top lip, making it a seductive pitch. Her lips are a glossy red, unusual for her.

Visibly uncomfortable, Michael adjusts himself in his seat. Dawn and Shayna have been pretty much quiet throughout the meal, only making small talk with Sharina as far as pleasantries go. Shayna's eyes flick over to me then quickly to Sherina. It's clear Dawn's pitch has just made her uncomfortable as well. Michael pays Dawn a polite nod.

Sharina squares her shoulders and asks, "So, Divine, what's this I hear...you've gone and got yourself a wonderful lady? Is she the reason for the new beard?"

Sharina's obviously picking up vibes at the table because that sure sounds like a leveling question, inconspicuously directed to Dawn. I've known Sharina longer than I've known Michael. She grew up in Queens with a cousin of mine and our families are pretty close, though Sharina and I aren't exactly in touch. She used to work for *Uptown Records* back in the nineties and we knew many of the same people from the industry, including her husband, Michael, who interned there.

"Divine has had someone sink their hooks into him and has him growing hair on his face?" Michael carries the joke. They are funny as hell, acting as if Tara never existed. I wonder if word has gotten out that far.

"Something like that," I murmur as I pat my face. "It's only temporary, though. Anyway... How did you hear that?" I ask Sharina, totally ignoring Michael.

"Lenny. He was in town for Liz's graduation from cosmetology school a few weeks ago," Sharina replies. "He said he's met her and she's drop dead gorgeous. He mentioned you saying, you've *never* come across a woman who can hold a candle to this one."

Sharina throws Dawn a chasten glance when pronouncing the word *never*. *Don't start, Sharina.* This is all odd considering Sharina's never even met Rayna. I guess some women can simply smell blood in the water.

"Ms. Brimm is quite lovely," Shayna chimes in, attempting to insert some tactfulness.

The waiter comes to offer coffee, to which we all decline. I ask for the check to be charged to my account. Michael thanks me after vehemently advising it isn't necessary since this meeting was initiated by him. Even so, I've been so busy lately that it's taken months to finally sit down with him. I'm sure Sharina tagged along simply to keep in touch. I'm glad she did. They start gathering their things to leave.

"Oh, so, this means you two will be at the big day in a few weeks?" Dawn asks as she positions her wine glass to her face, drawing attention to her mouth.

"I'm sorry...what big day?" Michael asks just after standing.

"Big day?" Sharina follows with a dubious glare as she goes for her ticket for her coat that was checked.

What the fuck...

"Yeah, not everyone is invited because it's such an exclusive affair, but seeing how close the two of you seem to be to Mr. Jacobs, it's fair to say you're excited to see him get married."

"Azmir, you're getting married? Lenny didn't mention that!" Sharina gasps.

I loosen the collar of my shirt.

"Yes. I've not exactly made the date public, but the announcement went out months ago," I answer.

"We've not gotten an announcement or an invitation," Sharina croaks. I see Michael smirking behind her, I'm sure his thoughts are mirroring mine right about now.

Women and their catty ass antics.

Sharina opened the floodgates for this covert attempt at leveling Dawn. And Dawn swooped down, dropping jewels to demonstrate to Sharina, she doesn't know me as well as she's alluded to by boasting about my fiancée.

"Rina, my beloved is a very private person. She isn't familiar with the industry you and I practically devoted our adolescence to," I explain as I stand. "I'll tell you what, the next time you guys are out in L.A., look me up and we'll have dinner. And I have the perfect restaurant in mind. My lady's palate is partial to Italian just like yours. I'm sure you two will hit it off."

"Oh, yeah! She already sounds like a kindred spirit," Sharina beams. "Okay. We'll do that."

We say our goodbyes, but I don't leave the table. Michael and Sharina leave first, and Dawn and Shayna are just behind them when I say, "A moment with you two, please."

Once we're all seated at the table, the tension is so thick you can choke on it.

"What the fuck was that, Dawn?" I ask, keeping my voice low. I'm acutely aware of my sour mood over the past couple of weeks. It's precisely what happens when you go so long without ass—ass you've grown addicted to.

Dawn's brows lift innocuously. "I was simply extending the conversation. I'd easily gotten the impression they were close acquaintances to you once the business talk had ended."

"Dawn, just because I invite you out to dinner with friends of mine on a whim, it doesn't give you the liberty to discuss matters of my personal life."

"It was a personal dinner—"

"Make no mistake, Dawn, ain't shit about us personal," I interrupt her right away, still keeping my voice soft, as I am speaking to a woman. "For *Bacote & Taylor's Planning and Public Relations Corp.* this was a business casual meal. It's always business between us. If you do not subscribe to that etiquette, then there will be no more opportunities of this nature."

"You invited us to dinner, Azmir," Dawn argues.

"It's always business," I repeat. "Had you played it cool and maintained your professionalism, Michael would have inquired about your presence at this meeting during a private conversation, at which time I would have possibly plugged your services. He, being under my influence, would have considered your *professional* presence tonight and possibly called you up for a consult."

"I'm sorry, Azmir. I can understand your perspective. It won't happen again," Shayna offers.

"Excuse me?" Dawn snaps her head to Shayna. "This is the second time you've apologized for me professionally. Let's make sure you understand it will be the last. Even you admitted to feeling slighted for not being invited to Azmir's wedding. Am I lying?"

"Dawn!" Shayna calls out on a gasp. She gets up, excuses herself and then leaves the table.

I can't believe the contents of Pandora's box. Neither do I have the time to examine them. I stand from my seat.

"I'm going to forget the last minute of this conversation. I advise you to remember the first few." I slowly turn as to not attract any more attention to our table than what's been established.

"Shayna knows I'm in love with you," Dawn murmurs. "Does *she*?"

I turn back towards the table and observe Dawn twiddling her fingers, staring straight ahead.

"Pardon me?"

"Shayna knows I'm in love with a man who is about to marry another woman. Does Rayna?" Dawn's eyes then make their way to meet mine. "Shayna says it's a purely physical attraction and I shouldn't dwell on it. She's wrong. There's so much more to you than your physical features. It's everything." She exhales before returning her gaze ahead. "Rayna should be concerned. Very concerned."

"Rayna has no reason to be concerned. Ever," I state vehemently because it's true.

Dawn's head jerks over to me and her eyes fill with emotion. But she slowly nods, saying something I hope is, *I'll let it go.*

I leave her at the table and take to my suite upstairs.

Rayna

Friday, I enlist the help of the only semblance of a friend I have—Chanell—to visit a bridal boutique with me. I went to one yesterday alone with little success.

So today, we're in Beverly Hills at one of the two boutiques Tessie, our wedding coordinator, recommended. While visiting the first one yesterday, I established the style of gown I'm in the market for. The gown specialist told me I have the ideal frame for a mermaid/trumpet or column-sheath. I'm more drawn to the mermaid cut, and I want something with simple straps or strapless. I don't want a lot of fabric, just something simple and less traditional. Now that it's known I won't recite my vows within the four walls of a church, I feel free to be as eclectic as I wish.

The gown I considered at the first boutique, after three and a half painful hours of discussion, measurements, and selections was a beautiful ivory, *Chantilly* leaf lace, sweetheart gown with cascading snowflake lace. I was able to try on a sample and adored the delicacy of the fabric laying well against my skin. I was tired and hungry, and quickly decided on it until I thought to ask the price. When I asked why it was so expensive the specialist explained it was a recent *Oscar de la Renta* runway design. Although I'd fallen in love with the cathedral veil it was paired with, there is no way I'm asking Azmir to foot the bill for a gown that would only be worn once. And it's well out of *my* price to even consider.

When I told Azmir about it last night, he accused me of being scrimpy. I corrected him by saying I was economical. He may have been a millionaire for almost two decades, but I've never been even close.

So, I've come to the second boutique Tessie offered today. As I'm flipping through the catalogue the bridal specialist provided, Chanell can't hide her girlie excitement.

"Yo, 'dis shit right here proper, Rayna!" She shrills with little regard to her surroundings.

I mean, this isn't on par with the uppity boutique I visited in Beverly Hills yesterday, but this exclusive spot in Orange County is nothing to sneeze at either.

"Oh, yeah?" I push out noncommittal.

She screams that every five minutes. And I'm, of course, aggravated out of my mind with too many options to choose from. In the recesses of my mind, I chide myself for not dreaming bigger in my former years. If I'd been your typical female who had every detail of her wedding and family planning laid out in my mind at least, I wouldn't be here today, fingering through the fourth catalog in search of my *happily ever after* gown.

"Yeah, Rayna! Word bond! Just come check this shit out. It's mad cute and lacy. You know, your type," Chanell called over.

My finger stops on the bottom of the page and my eyes roll over to her across the walkway. "Really? And exactly what is my type, C? Please inform me," I challenge her.

"You know...bourgeois—but cool as shit..." she clarifies. "...but, yeah, definitely bourgeois."

I'm temperamental from this mind-numbing task already. I don't have time for Chanell's soft jabs.

"What makes me bourgeois, C? The fact that I know how to spell the word and can tell you its origin?"

"Maybe. No. I mean, I don't know." Chanell pauses before inoffensively shrugging her shoulders. "You prissy as hell, is all."

"Prissy how?"

"Rayna, man, look at where the fuck we at!" Her eyes go big as her head swings gesturing to the boutique. "This is where you prissy fucks shop. It's all good though. You still my girl, don't trip."

"C, you do know you and I come from same type of neighborhood, right?"

"*Pshhhh!*" she waves her big hand at me. "Get the fuck outta here, man! Just 'cuz you come from a city don't mean we come from the same streets, Ray." She turns back over to the wall with the gown she wants me to see.

"Chanell, where I come from, most of the kids thought if you lived in a single unit house, with no other apartments attached to it, you were rich. Where I come from, if one person in your household had a car, no matter a hooptie or not, it meant you were in a higher class than most."

"And you was probably in that high class," she guesses with her back to me.

"No. I was not. I lived in the projects, C, where rats and roaches believed they had just as much of a right to be in your apartment as you. Where I would go out on my porch at night and look for the farthest light, be it a star or streetlamp, and say, '*That's where I'm going to live when I get my first apartment.*' Where block huggers and 'bout it chicks would crack your chin if you tried to play them like a sucker. You know, for like calling them *bourgeois*?"

Chanell almost jumps out of her shoes, turning around to me. "Damn, Rayna! Chill the fuck out. I know you ain't no sucka! You proved that when them fools tried to rob Divine down in Mexico. Don't take shit so personal. You know I'm just fuckin' witchu. You my bitch: ride or die." She does some type of sacrilegious crossing of her heart and kissing up to the sky. "Yo, remember when we tore the dance floor to that B.I.G. track?"

It takes a minute to recall that night at Azmir's club in Compton. I can never forget the night I possibly met Erin's father. I never told Michelle about seeing him. I didn't want to remind her of that horrid New Year's Day.

"C, whatever happened to that Mikey dude. He was wild that night," I recollect casually, making sure not to mention where I'd recalled him from.

"I'on't know. Come to think of it, I ain't seen Mikey since that night. We used to smoke together, but he stop coming 'round the way." Chanell shrugs. "He had his ass handed to him after fuckin' wit' Divine's pussy, yo!" she jeers. "Nah, I'm fuckin' witchu. You know you my peoples, right, Ray?"

I roll my eyes back down to the catalogue, not really focusing on anything in particular.

"Rayna, you know 'dat, right?" she asks. "C'mon, Ray, you know I was just fuckin' witchu," she goes on.

I barely hear much of anything else when I shout, "Here we go!"

"No. For real! You know I fucks witchu. I been ridin' witchu since day one!" She's losing patience in her tone.

"No, C! Here's my gown! It's perfect!" I exclaim as I pound the page with my index finger.

It's a mermaid cut with a triangle neckline and corded lace. There's a scallop trim at the neckline, back, and hem of the gown. The straps are thin and the highlight of the gown is the backless design. Similar to the gowns Azmir has been selecting for me, this one is cut low, all the way down to top of my derriere. It's gorgeous. It's breathtaking. I'm in love!

"Huhn?" she asks before coming over to me. "Let me see."

I hand her the catalog as I call to Raheem, the bridal specialist.

When I return to retrieve the book from Chanell so I can inquire about the gown to Raheem, I notice Chanell's moue.

"What's that face for?" I ask. "You can't deny it's beautiful!"

"Yeah, it's dope as shit, but can you fit in something like that? It's showing a lot of skin back there," she speaks suspiciously.

I roll my eyes as I place the book on the trunk in the center of the room and point the gown out to Raheem.

"Ahhh! The *Poipu*! This is fabulous, honey!" he shrieks. I give a goofy smile and then turn to answer Chanell.

"Yeah. We bourgeois girls from the projects are smart enough to diet and exercise to keep our figures right so in the event a man asks to marry us, we can wear a revealing number like this," I shoot back at her.

I love Chanell, but I'm not about to let her believe she can categorize me like that and I'm going to roll over and take it. I'm not that removed from my roots. She's a big girl, but I won't hesitate getting as many jabs in as I can before she takes me down.

Raheem jots down the item number and then measures me. As he does, I daydream about wearing this beautiful fabric down the aisle to Azmir. When I leave the boutique, I'm in such an elated mood that I not only treat my girl, Chanell, to dinner, but I also accept her invitation to her birthday party after I declined a few days ago because of the venue. It's going to be at Petey's *Drop It* club, featuring a male review.

"Oh, shit!" she screams when I tell her.

"What type of wife will you be, Rayna?" First Lady Twanece asks.

We're sitting in her office at the church. It's vividly and femininely decorated in various shades of purple. I can't decide if it's her favorite color or holds a deeper religious meaning of royalty. The hues of purple are coordinated well to bring calm to the room. She sits behind an oak desk, but her chair is made of some white, faux feather upholstery revealing her inner diva. The lavender walls are decorated with her educational degrees and certificates. Above her head is a poster-size picture of her and Pastor Edmondson dressed in formal attire. They look good and...*together.*

"Ummmm...I don't think I follow your question," I reply.

She angles her chin in a fortifying move and says, "It's simple. What type of wifely persona will you take on when you become Mrs. Azmir Jacobs?"

"*I*...I don't know." I'm already intimidated by this conversation.

The way we have our premarital counseling sessions set up is some are done with Azmir and I together with Pastor Edmondson, some include the two of us with the pastor and First Lady Twanece and some are split with one-on-ones with the ladies and those with the men. Tonight, it's just us ladies and it's always hard for me to be confident in the same room as a woman who's mastered the balance of marital partnership. She's a wife, mother, professional, and a freaking first lady of a mega church. I often find myself trying not to shrink in her presence.

First Lady Twanece is like a jaguar. She seems beautiful, harmless, and alluring, but when the time calls for it, she will pounce and fearlessly attack. She sings in church from time to time, she's a natural soprano with her high notes, and even speaks in the same tone. But when she wants to emphasize a point or when her spirit is high and admonishing, she'll transition into an alto with natural ease.

This evening, she's an alto.

"Okay..." She clasps her hands together. "...let me ask, will you be a submissive wife; always allowing him to chart the course and only speaking up when asked to? Will you fight for equal time at the wheel, believing that navigation in a marital partnership takes two people, because one can't possibly take on the role alone? Will you be especial in watching over him, understanding he is a leader who governs lots of people and needs someone watching out for him as well?" She's rattling off these questions as she looks me square in the eyes and I know she means business.

"Will you release him to the world without much interference, avoiding being the 'overwhelming' wife? Will you stand by his side where you have equal vision? Will you stand slightly behind where you can see around him as well as what's ahead? Will you move ahead of him, on your own course, feeling the need to have a separate identity to his public one? What type of wife will you be, Rayna?"

"You just laid out so many options. I...I don't know how to choose," I fumble with my words again. "What would be the safe answer?"

First Lady Twanece cracks a smile. I'm not sure what it means. She goes to adjust herself in her seat, crossing her legs and arms before she answers, "The ideal answer is, you will be whatever he needs you to be in the moment he needs it."

"That's a tall order."

"And such is marriage," she quickly returns. "See, many women...*and men* don't understand the totality of commitment and how in marriage, it should mimic God's commitment to you. Your devotion to Azmir should not be conditional or given in portions you feel he '*deserves*.'" She uses air quotations. "It also shouldn't be based upon his commitment to you. This isn't a game of quid pro quo. Your attitude walking into this institution should be decided, firm, and maintained until either he dies, you die, or his behavior becomes so reckless, it negatively alters the core of who you are. You know...abuse of any form, a severely chronic addiction, or habitual adultery."

Is she crazy?

"Those are the only acceptable reasons for divorce?"

"Those are examples of legitimate reasons to consider terminating your commitment, but it's on a case-by-case basis. What you can tolerate from a thieving addict may fall short of the patience I'd provide one. Two affairs may ruin your confidence of his commitment to your marriage. I may be able to withstand five. It's subjective, Rayna. It is only when the essence of you changes as a result of his lack of commitment should you consider leaving."

She sits up in her chair. "The passage with Azmir won't be pretty every day. You won't be in love every day. You *will* hit rough roads ahead. And your challenges may be unique to some of your contemporaries because of Azmir's occupation and social-economic status. He's in the public eye. The role of his partner cannot be taken on by someone with jumpy shoulders. In order to increase security in a relationship, you must produce predictability. You can't up and leave. You have to know within your heart, be settled in your mind, and be anchored from your soul that you can devote your life to him."

Doubt rises from my belly. "Do you think I can do that?"

"I think you can do all things through Christ who strengthens you."

"Pretty generic," I snort. That verse is not convincing when discussing permanency.

"It is what I believe. It's what I've lived for the past twenty-eight years of marriage. I've gone through the groupie women. The mercurial shifts from him switching roles of pastor, to husband, to father, to lover, to friend, or whatever other hat the moment calls for. I've been through his identity crisis, age crisis, and every mild depression he's suffered from not being able to save the world. Our sex life has gone between incredible, fair, and lackluster…all depending on where he is—sometimes where I am.

"I cannot control John, but I can control my intent as his wife and my reactions to his behaviors. There were many days when I questioned my endurance, but far less that I wavered in my commitment. I work to be who John wants me to be, when he needs me to be it. That devotion is based on what I decided to be for my husband long ago, and not what I believe he *deserves* in that moment. Sure, there were times when I felt overwhelmed and underappreciated, however, there has never been a time when I've not been sure of my commitment. I am the wife I decided to be. So, tell me Rayna, what type of wife will *you* be?"

First Lady Twanece has given me loads to think about in this session. I don't walk out of there self-assured or with a game plan for my nuptials with Azmir. However, the session gets the cogs of my mind working overtime.

Later, as I fall into bed, heaviness in my chest has taken residence. I realize how lonely I am. There's no reason in planning my role as Mrs. Jacobs when there is no Mr. Jacobs here in his own bed to motivate my aspirations. I miss Azmir so much. So much that I let go of a few unwilled tears as I bury my face into his pillow.

We're almost there, Rayna. He's doing this for you. I chide myself before falling into slumber.

The night of Chanell's party, I arrive feeling pretty good for a woman experiencing the equivalent to blue balls for a man. I show up in distressed denim cut-offs, stopping just under my kneecaps, a black, sheer mock tank, a black and white, zebra print blazer, and red *So Kate Louboutin* pumps with a red *Prada Nappa* envelope clutch. I selected a simple look to hang out with my 'round-the-way-chicks.

Almost as soon as I walk through the door, I locate Chanell, Kim, and their girls. I inform John of where I'll be so he can make himself wallpaper. Within just feet of joining them, Kim notices me approaching and yelps my welcome. Chanell looks up, and once she recognizes me, she shrieks just the same, and I notice her call for the server who had just left their party.

"Yo! We gotta include another shot for my girl, Ray-Dizzle!" Chanell shouts.

When I approach them, I greet her first with a hug and small gift bag. I have a burst of elation at seeing her and Kim within the same group.

So I guess these two have kissed and made up.

"Bring it! Bourgeois black girls take shots, too!" I yell out, remembering her jab from the week before.

"Oh, Ray, man, drop 'dat shit! It's my born day and we 'bout to get turnt all the way up."

"Okay!" I agree, doing a little two step. "You look good, C!" I admire.

Chanell's wearing a red mini dress with a slight turtleneck-collar. She's paired it with ankle booties on a fat heel. Not my style, but I always appreciate seeing her in feminine wear. She's rocking her usual head full of micro curls. Her lips look like they were dipped in florescent honey. I don't know who applied Chanell's makeup, but they did a stellar job. She looks beautiful!

"Thanks, Ray! You stuck up ass bitches ain't the only ones wearing it proper," she crudely sticks her tongue out.

"Touché, C," I reply. "Touché."

I then turn to Kim, who was wearing all black. I can't see what she's wearing because, per usual, she's sitting down. But her hair is pulled back into a ponytail, and she has on minimal makeup which includes eyeliner, a dab of mascara and lip-gloss. In all honesty, Kim doesn't need makeup; her skin is flawless and glows naturally.

"You really got one in the oven this time, Kim," I tease. "Either that, or I gots to fight you for that radiant skin. You don't need it anymore; you're married already, I'm not."

"Girl, please! You young. I saw you up on that stage working that body. You doing it right," Kim replies, referring to the show she attended a couple of months ago.

I reach down to embrace her, and she reciprocates.

"What you wearing? Smelling good as shit!" she asks.

"*Cool Water*. Girl, I've been wearing this for six years now," I answer. "I want to try *Sean John* for women, but Azmir keeps this one supplied by the gallon, so I guess this is it for me."

"I like that. I'm gonna have to get me some," she says before something catches her attention.

I look over my shoulder to see the waitress has returned with a tray full of shots.

"Whoa!" Chanell cheers. "And another one," she quotes a famous rap intro.

We all collect our glasses and raise them in the air. "What we toasting to, Chanell?" one of the girls shouts.

"To fine ass men, shaking they asses for my twenty-fifth!" Chanell screeches. "It's a celebration, bitches!" She clanks her glass with Kim, and we all follow suit. Then we down the first glass.

I honestly can't recall the last time I've done shots. It had to have been with Michelle. But I don't care. I'm lonely and happy to be out. I told myself before leaving the marina I won't think of Azmir's absence while out tonight. I want to do and feel something different.

An alarm sounds. At that buzzard trill, the crowd goes up in yelps and shouts. I don't know what to make of it until I see men and women, dressed in no more than swimwear marching into the main room. Chanell jumps and whistles her approval of what seems to be the start of the show. The strippers aren't coordinated, but they get their start together. They quickly find subjects to grind against and start their money earning show with. I just hope they stay away from me. Man or woman, I'm not interested.

I search around the main hall and observe the character of the place. It isn't exactly a hole in the wall, but it isn't upscale either. The place is gray and smoky. I notice *Drop It* is definitely occupied by subscribers to the green leaf. I suddenly regret wearing this blazer. I hope I can get the stench out of it after tonight.

The strobe lights influence the first wave of a buzz I feel from the first round of shots I did. Then Chanell announces the second, to which I gulp down with ease. In my peripheral, I notice a group of women at a booth across the dance floor from us. After squinting my eyes through the haze, I'm able to identify Syn and a few of her cousins I saw in Vegas at Kid's party. I tap Chanell and ask why Syn isn't at the celebrant's table.

"We got into it last week. Kid done fucked up again with some bitch 'round the way and she mad I ain't snitch on him. She said we cool and shit, and that's why she came, but you can see she over there not fucking with me. So, fuck her," Chanell informs.

I can tell she's more bothered by the fight than she's letting on. I recall how at a previous engagement; she was on the outs with Kim for the same reason. It must be hard being Chanell. I guess she chose the team to bat for, which is easy considering she isn't emotionally attached to anyone. I know who she'd side with if Azmir were to creep out on me.

That thought doesn't bode well. We're celibate, and he could be out right now relieving himself of that problem. *Shut up, Rayna!* I need to deflect that pessimism and quickly. It's week four without sex with my Adonis of a mogul. I don't need to let my cynicism persevere. I turn to Kim.

"You look cheerful," I openly observe. She's been so visibly stressed the last few times I've seen her.

Of course, considering your husband, of nearly two decades, cheating on you would do the trick. But I didn't like the encumbered Kim. I like the one I can't shut up even if I tried. Well, I'm in for a treat, because tonight Kim is in an extremely chatty mood.

She scoots her chair over to me and speaks directly in my ear, "I don't know if Divine told you the latest. He don't seem like the type that carry shit around, but Im'ma tell you myself. Petey was cheating on me with this young Mexican girl."

My eyes go wide. For Kim, it appears she's dropping jewels on me I've never heard a whisper of, but in all reality, I'm surprised at her candor. Kim reaches over and grabs another shot glass and downs it before I can give away my secret of knowing.

"Yeah, girl! I couldn't believe that shit either. I mean, I know that nigga ain't no saint, but to be cheating on me like I don't give head all the time. Like I don't give up the twat whenever he brings his tired ass in the house at all hours of the morning," she snorts. "Ain't nothing that dude asked me to do in the bedroom I ain't give. I couldn't believe he tripped out on me like a starved man!"

I mask my shock by shutting my mouth. Simultaneously, Chanell shoves another shot into my face. I'm nowhere near drunk, barely tipsy, but I know I'm already over my limit. Nonetheless, the pure excitement Chanell displays when handing it to me, doesn't allow me to deny her. Plus, Kim has started on a chatter course I can't yield.

I down the third shot, and while enraptured in Kim's tale, I feel someone tap me. I immediately think it's Chanell, offering a fourth. I'm prepared to risk hurting her feelings as I turn to my left to find an anxious Petey with an antsy John right behind him. I squint my eyes, wondering where in the world Petey has come from.

He leans into my ear. "Yo, Rayna. The duke just called me all brolic and shit. He saying you can't stay. John here gonna take you home, a'ight?"

"Come again?" I can barely hear him over the loud music and quickly decide he isn't kicking me out of his club.

Petey isn't the type to play coy, even if the edict isn't coming down from his general. He stares directly into my eyes messaging his solemnity. I turn to Kim who's totally oblivious to my exchange with her *on duty* husband. I tell her I have to go as I grab my clutch.

She then looks behind me, I guess sensing my frustration. "What the hell is he doing here?" she asks, surprised by her husband's abrupt appearance.

Okay...I'm not crazy for thinking it's odd.

We make it out to the front of the club where I'm past embarrassed, I'm bordering on pissed. "Petey, what in the world is this all about?"

Petey is yelling at someone outside as John leaves for the car; he drove me here in my car. There's an insane amount of activities going on out here and my buzz is thickening. A young woman saunters past us belting, "We be all night!" Petey calls out for someone to address the ruckus she's making.

Petey draws closer to me and murmurs, "Yo, Ray, as much as I think my spot is legit and all, the homey done reached a status that he gotta protect his brand. And his fiancée being here without him ain't a good look, nah mean?"

W-what? I can't break down his many words. "No, I don't, Crack. I'm an adult and can hang out at a friend's establishment if I choose. Why is it not safe for me, because it's in the Watts? It's apparently safe for Kim." I argue.

"Nah…nah, it's different for—"

We're interrupted by bulbs flashing in our faces. They come in successions followed by clicks. Talk about buzz kill. I try covering my eyes and ducking my face.

"Rayna!" one calls.

"Ms. Brimm! Who this guy you're with?" someone else asks.

"This way, Rayna!" another yells out.

"Fuck!" That's Petey. "Where's the car, Ock?"

Petey pulls his jacket over the both of us to hide our faces. Out of nowhere, my midnight blue *Mercedes* pulls up.

"Unlock the damn door!" Petey yells after trying unsuccessfully to pull the latch, scaring the crap out of me.

He urges me inside and I quickly scoot inside the backseat to the other side. Not that it matters because paparazzi is on that side of the car, too. Petey ducks his head inside.

"Petey! What's all of this?" I ask him urgently.

His face goes from cold to apologetic. "It's the new lifestyle." he shrugs. "You gotta take it up with the duke for a real answer. Get home safely." He moves out of the doorway and shuts it. I then hear him, and a few other voices shouting at the paps to move or get run over.

My phone trills, frightening me as if that were still possible.

"Azmir!" I cry into the phone, feeling a smidge of comfort from his presence, even if telephonic. "What's going on?"

"Rayna, you cannot go out to a club in Compton without my knowledge," he advises. I can't miss the undertone of terse.

"It's not just any club! It's Petey's club," I inform him, exasperated. He knows this. He's had the owner himself drag me out.

"And you're not the fiancée of just any man. I'm sorry, honey, but apparently my status has just risen to a new plane and the media has taken an interest in me...my life. This means they are aware of my pending marriage, and it will be reported come tomorrow, on several blogs, that you are a classless bird, gallivanting in a hole-in-the-wall strip club in Compton." It doesn't take much to gather this is Azmir's CEO mien I'm on with.

My jaw drops. "But that's not true! It's Chanell's birthday party at Petey's club. They are your family!"

"The media will likely not put those details into their spin. They don't care—" he's interrupted; I can hear someone in the background. "*Yes, tell her I'll be right there, please.*" Her? "Baby, I have to go. I'll have Brett have one of my assistants contact you on Monday; you can plan something more low-key with Chanell to celebrate her birthday and apologize for your abrupt departure."

I don't respond, because I don't know how. This is absolutely insane, and I don't know where to go from here.

"Aye," Azmir barks, exposing his Brooklyn tongue, and melting my arctic resolve. "I'm sorry, Brimm. This has become old news to me since just before the *Mauve* event. I never mentioned it because you're not typically out socializing. We can talk more about it when I come home," he offers.

WHEN?

When will I have you back at the marina, in my face, in my arms, so I can feel this thing?

I want to reach through the phone and grab him into my face to scream at him...and then *feel* him. I've found myself starved of him. I'm starting to view our impending matrimonial event as a fantasy I'm chasing in the wind. Azmir has become this legend in my mind and not a living, breathing man. My man. I am losing...and fading fast.

"Goodnight, Azmir," I whisper, just perfectly concealing the cry working its way up my throat.

"Love you, Brimm."

I disconnect the call.

I hate the media!

It's my first pre-wedding session with Tyler. He termed it that to motivate me when I explained I have to be ready for this gown that will display my entire figure, even what's covered with lace. We discussed my goals and target areas to help chart our journey, coincidentally, the same thing we did when I'd first started training with him. Before I know it, an hour and a half has flown by.

Tyler has me down on my hands and one knee, pulling my right leg up to demonstrate how far I should be extending it in the air. The similarities in our professions make our jargon easy, but Tyler prefers demonstrating movements rather than just assigning them, and I appreciate that.

"You never want to lift this high," he pulls my leg up over me while I observe from the mirror straight ahead of me. "...because it can injure—"

"The erector spinae. Yeah. I can feel it," I say on a strained breath.

Azmir's abrupt presence interrupts our chase behind time. He strolls in and walks up on us while Tyler's coaching me through the technique. Suddenly Azmir's commanding frame appears in the mirror as he hovers over us.

"Divine," Tyler announces, clearly surprised by Azmir's *divine* presence. He slowly releases my leg.

Azmir's manifestation steals my breath. Every time I see his now full beard, I'm reminded of his pledge of growing it until I become his legally. He's stuck to it, and surprisingly wears it well. He's sporting a black, fitted compression shirt exposing and outlining his chiseled torso, dark grey basketball shorts and trainers. He looks fresh...no sweat, unflushed. It wouldn't have mattered if his body was misted in sweat, it's a dangerous time for me to see him in my celibate state. Although another man's hands are on me platonically, the mere sight of Azmir makes me liquidate in the most incestuous manner. He stands with his head cocked to the side, his tongue pressing back into his molars.

"I didn't think I was paying you to get that acquainted with Ms. Brimm's body, just to tone it a little to satisfy her insular grievances about her already perfect frame." His words are laced with humor, but his disposition is arctic. He can fool many of men with his stoic countenance, but not me.

Tyler's eyes momentarily widen, but then quickly relax. It's as if he has to will himself to believe Azmir is joshing. "I think you pay me to deliver results. That's my only intention here." Tyler trains his eyes to his wrist for the time and then looks to me. "It is pretty late. You've been great, Ms. Brimm. Don't forget to incorporate those new stretch techniques every night, even after dance class and you should be fine."

"Sure will. Thanks, Tyler. You're the best," I say, risking the ego of Azmir's caveman persona. I don't miss his squinted eyes. I lick my lips, suddenly my mouth is salivating. I can't believe my body still responds to Azmir this way.

"Have a good one," Tyler bodes with his arm extended towards me. I'm now sitting on my butt, facing both men. He then turns to Azmir, "Mr. Jacobs...tomorrow?" he asks tentatively.

"Tomorrow," Azmir replies, now wearing a scowl fixated on me. He doesn't even look at poor Tyler.

Seriously?

As Tyler exits the private room, Azmir's gaze deepens, and his eyes darken. As a result, my pulse quickens.

"What was that about?"

"My employees knowing their boundaries," he answers, still motionless and his face still deadpan.

"I don't think Tyler has an issue with boundaries. He's been extremely professional and is well versed with anatomy."

"Yeah, but not with yours. That's my profession and last I checked I was damn good at it."

Bravado for sure.

My eyes now match his; hooded and ready. It's been a while since I've seen him. I need to stay focused. We've vowed abstinence and have two more weeks to go. We're more than halfway there. And as much as I believe myself to be strong willed, I have little resistance to Azmir's sexual prowess. He shifts toward the door, making me wonder why he's leaving. I've enjoyed his abrupt pop-up in the middle of my day. I then realize Azmir has only gone over by the door to turn off the light. I panic.

No! Not now! We're doing so well.

"W-what are you doing?" I breathe out, attempting to mask my anxiousness.

He doesn't answer, instead he gaits back over to me, lowers himself on top of my now weakened frame and snags my bottom lip between his teeth. My body instantly shudders. My brain is gearing up to protest against my stubborn frame that will give into Azmir with ease. His eyes are open as he grazes my lip again and my gaze won't leave his if I begged it to. I'm caught in his rapture that quickly.

Next, I feel his tongue against my lip, slowly extending from one side to the next. I fight the need to moan. I feel my body jerk with my elbows against the floor. Azmir's tongue enters my mouth, sweeps against the top of my tongue and laves the roof of my mouth. His tongue sweeps wide and long, tasting every inch of my cavity until he sucks my tongue into his mouth. I'm paralyzed in pleasure, but I still have my wits even if I'm slowing losing them.

"Kiss me," he growls in my mouth.

Panting, I whisper, "But Azmir, we said we would wait. And we're in public."

"And in my place of business. Kiss me!" he barks.

Feeling his sweet breath hit my face, I break. My hands move up, gripping the sides of his face against his thick beard and I throw my tongue into his mouth, kissing hard and thoroughly. He smells so good. He feels so right. Hard, rippling muscles suspended over me, sending me into a spiral of sensations. My hands stay limited to his head and neck because I don't trust myself to go any farther. His hands stay placed on the floor beneath me, balancing himself on them, making me believe he doesn't want to tempt himself either.

His kiss is tender, sweet, unlike mine. His presence is heavy and commanding. I'm out of breath but need the continual pouring of Azmir's passion more than I need air to breathe. His kiss fades every fear. His dominating existence shields every disappointment. Azmir cures a lifetime of insecurities.

He pulls away, out of breath, panting uncontrollably like me.

"Azmir..." I cry, feeling chillingly bereft.

"Just say the word," in his deep, baritone pitch, he rumbles.

I sigh, suddenly coming back to my senses.

"You're at work. And... We said..."

"I'll take you anytime, anywhere." He staples his gaze upon me, and I believe every word of his declaration. "But my word is my bond, and my bond is my life." He lays the most gentle kiss on my forehead, earning another shiver.

So bad, I wish I'd taken him up on his offer.

CHAPTER 11

Rayna

What woman just shows up to her wedding day with no knowledge of what's coming? A date that has been settled and planned for months.

Brimm, that's who.

Yup, at the set of dawn, on the first day in March, John routes the car into the lot of the harbor and pulls where I was instructed to a few days ago via email. After pulling my duffle bag from the trunk, I say my goodbyes to him and make my way to the harbor and with awe, gaze over several impressive boats and yachts. Although I'm still curious about the agenda of the event, relief fills my lungs at my wedding not being at *Bethesda-by-the Sea*, a facility that's easily of Azmir's stature.

I've been in San Diego for the past three days, orating at a conference in Dan Smith's proxy. It's been strange being away from the office for so long, but nothing compares to being away from Azmir. I've missed him so much, I dream of him nightly. I recall Azmir using the phrase, 'two ships passing in the night' to justify our need to move in together last summer. That's exactly what we've become over the past month and a half. But with Dan

Smith's new product rolling out, I've been preoccupied with either research for the project or covering for him at conferences. His confidence in such a young colleague enthuses me and challenges me to prove myself as worthy amongst my contemporaries. This has been the only thing to distract me from Azmir's absence and leads me to this moment. *This day.*

I know where I'm headed, but don't know what to expect. Tessie, our wedding coordinator, emailed me a set of instructions a few days before, detailed with when to rise from bed to where to march down the aisle. But it's difficult for me to envision an aisle on a boat. I keep telling myself I don't care. This is what I want. I'm resolute in my decision to marry Azmir Jacobs. Even when my thoughts become dual, I fight through them. I'm finally marrying a man I've only known for just over a year. It doesn't matter that I accepted his proposal approximately nine months after meeting him. That isn't as crazy as moving in with him less than six months after our first date. *No.* What I'm prepared to do isn't crazy at all, because I love this man, I'm devoted to this man, and can't imagine waking up to a life without the company the of one A.D. Jacobs.

"Rayna?" I hear called out expectantly.

I look up to find a blushing redhead with a small frame and gorgeous emerald irises. Her smile is promising and gives away her aura.

"Tessie?" I ask, knowing I have to be correct in my assumptions. Who else would be fully dressed in formal attire at the crack of dawn...at the top of the morning...on the walkway of a marina?

"Yes," she answers with a polite nod. "I'm Tessie. It's nice to put a beautiful face with a voice." She proffers her hand and shakes mine enthusiastically. "Mr. Jacobs is a very lucky man. Not that I had any expectations of you, but I am thoroughly impressed."

I allow a pleased smile to crack upon my face. I don't know how to respond to that other than saying thanks, which I do. I guess I feel odd because all I'm wearing is a fitted sweat suit with a black *Connecticut Kings* baseball cap I borrowed from Azmir's side of the closet.

"Well, thanks for being so prompt." Tessie clasps her nicely manicured red nails together over her modestly fitted tan skirt. Her legs are clad in opaque hosiery over kitty pumps. She's the picturesque employee. "As you can imagine, we have lots to do today. We'll start with introducing you to your wedding venue and home for the next seven days."

I try to mask my staggered visage. I had no idea we'd be getting married and honeymooning on a boat. In fact, I didn't know we'd be having a honeymoon. I was told by Sharon last week that my schedule for a few days would be extended to accommodate several patients who preferred pushing up their appointments rather than deferring them to my return. I asked why and she said I'd be out of the office for a week at the request of Mr. Jacobs. I fought the annoyance rising from my belly at Azmir speaking directly to Sharon. I knew I'd be getting married this week, then eventually, on this day, but I still didn't like the feeling of being the absent bride. Sharon knew more about the details of my big day than I did. This all began the night I told Azmir I'd grown overwhelmed with the planning of the wedding and was tired of screening planners.

I told him we could get married on a boat in the middle of nowhere for all I cared! I gasp at the revelation.

"Pardon," Tessie asks, bursting my trance. I didn't realize I thought aloud.

I cup my mouth for a second, then lower my hands and murmur, "Sorry. I just thought of something I'd told...Mr. Jacobs months ago. I told him I didn't care if we got married on a boat in the middle of nowhere." I take a minute to process my running thoughts.

"Considering his plans for today, I suppose he took your wishes quite literally." Tessie winks before continuing her stride toward our destination.

Too literally.

Dumbfounded, I follow her. We walk a few feet west of where we met, and she starts with her orientation of the watercraft we begin to board. My mouth drops to my toes. It's massive!

"We're stepping onto *Princess Belle*, a one hundred forty-nine foot/forty-five meter motor yacht from the French yard of the Moreau Brothers. Mr. Jacobs not only has exquisite taste, he has friends of elite realms," Tessie notes as she peers over her shoulder momentarily. "I've done at least a dozen events on yachts, but this is by far the most impressive and elegant I've incurred," she continues with her orientation.

I'm once again caught up in reverie. Somehow, I could see the Moreau Brothers' sophistication emanating from the woodwork hailing from the railing of the walkway. We step on a red carpet as we walk onto the boat, entering from the rear. The off-white panels complement the smooth finishing of freshly polished wood. It smells of rich pine from the start of the airy foyer of the deck. It's filled with men, breaking down furniture just ahead of the built in Jacuzzi. The deck is huge, the size of a modest sized ballroom.

"The crew here is transitioning this main deck from a pool-side lounge area to your chapel. They should be done in an hour or so," Tessie informs before being interrupted by someone asking for her signature on a clipboard. "Thanks," she says as she passes it back. "Let's get out of their way and take you to your bridal salon on the lower deck. I'll take your duffle bag," she offers while removing it from my rigid shoulder. I can't believe the prestige this place holds.

My tongue skids nervously over my suddenly parched lips. I don't know where the angst has erupted from; typical wedding day jitters or feeling intimidated by all the cachet I'm surrounded by. We do an about-face and the oil painting hanging on the wall of a man who had to have been from a time I learned about in history class in high school catches my eye. The squaring of his narrow shoulders and the lifting of his chin tells me a girl from a New Jersey projects isn't whom he'd bequeathed this boat for.

We head to a room below I can tell has been strategically changed into *station glam squad*. Tessie shares Adrian will be here, along with Chantal, who I'm now learning will be doing my makeup again. But here, waiting for me, are the assistants of Reba, the stylist Azmir had contracted for me for the *Mauve* signing. We had good chemistry, so I decided to take her on for the wedding. The other set of folks here are two I don't recognize, but I'm told by Tessie they'll be doing my waxing, manicure, and pedicure.

The pine wood-laden room with a low ceiling is sectioned off. One portion is for hair and makeup. Another is for my waxing, mani, and pedi and the last, which is nearly half, is for costume. Tessie informs me I'll start with being sized—*as though I wasn't just fitted for my gown two days before*—waxing, mani, and pedi, followed by a full body massage, a facial, two-hour nap, cocktail, hair, makeup, and then suiting of my gown. It's just after six in the morning and these people are dutifully waiting for me. Butterflies invade my belly again.

"Okay, I'll leave you to it. I have to check on a few things in the kitchen…which reminds me." Tessie's finger lifts in the air. "Your concierge will be here shortly. I'm at your beck and call…and here is your Motorola radio." She hands me a walkie talkie. "Your channel is set already. Please make him aware of any needs you may have. There is a continental breakfast on the table over there, but if you want something else, Pierre will get it for you. Anything," she emphasizes. "Now, if you'll excuse me, I have loads to do before Mr. Jacobs' arrival."

"Ummm…Tessie, where *is* Mr. Jacobs and when can I expect him?" I muster all the casualness I can to belie my embarrassment of not knowing where the man *I'll be marrying in a matter of hours* is or when he will arrive.

"He's set to arrive at zero nine hundred hours. The ceremony will begin promptly at two p.m., I am sure of that." She ends with a wink.

"And paparazzi?" I ask tentatively.

The only request I had for the planning of this is no uninvited outside forces into our bubble of a wedding day. Just in months, Azmir's popularity seems to have tripled, and that's saying a lot for the man who's been a mogul for relatively four years. Going out to dinner on a Saturday night has become the hugest feat since his feature in *Vibe* and other publications. It's as if someone has turned on a switch to fame overnight. I now have Google alerts set up for my husband-to-be, and the notifications are increasing by the day. I can match the accuracy of Azmir's schedule by the candid shots found almost daily on popular blogs. I don't want to share this day with many, and certainly not with the legions of new followers Azmir has recently accumulated.

"Mr. Jacobs has made it crystal clear you don't want unauthorized pictures circulated," Tessie assures. Actually, I want no pictures circulated, but that's not an option, Azmir relayed to me regrettably. "I've been in contact with the team over at *Bacote & Taylor* regarding the monitoring of what information is out there, up to the moment, about today's event. All guests are aware of the *no pictures* policy and have been given the information as to how they will receive photographs of the event at a later date," Tessie informs and then goes to typing her perfect shade of red nails on her *iPad* as though to confirm something. "And Ms. Taylor will be here later to check on the activities herself," she ends.

Dawn?

"She's not a guest for this event," flies out of my mouth harsher than intended.

"No, she isn't," Tessie agrees. "The nature of her visit here is to verify the last guest list provided and to scout the facilities for paparazzi. She will only be on the yacht for less than ten minutes, but on the premises until we sail."

Tessie remains professional in her notification, but I'm a bit perturbed by Dawn's lurking presence.

Tessie leaves, and as advised, preparation for my big day commences immediately. I'm measured and pinched, supposedly for my undergarments. I didn't know they made undergarments for the type of gown I'll be wearing. The waxing is as distressing as it always is, and my mani and pedi is uneventful.

While on the massage table, I ponder over the oddity of not having been connected to Azmir in the past few weeks. We've spoken several times a day, most days, but would go a day or so without a sight of each other.

There's been no discord between us, just a little distance and I wonder if it's been by design. Azmir has worked like a dog, per usual, and has even traveled over the past few weeks. Though I've never shared it with him, I've been missing him like crazy. Over the past few weeks, there's been traces of him, like his soiled clothes in the hamper of the master bathroom, or paperwork left behind on the coffee table in the sitting area of the master bedroom. He'd even stopped by my office unannounced one afternoon but didn't see me because I was in with a patient.

There was one evening, a few days ago when I was plagued with period symptoms, I entered the building and Roberto handed me a single rose and card with my name printed in Azmir's calligraphy. Not being able to wait until I reached the privacy of the apartment, I ripped the envelope open on the elevator and almost immediately choked back a cry.

My dearest Ms. Brimm,

I know you're miserably plagued with symptoms related to your menstrual cycle and I am all too regretful I'm not there to help you ease them. But consider the silver lining, this will be your last cycle as a single woman. The next time you'll be my wife, my partner, my preferable obligation to soothe.

. . .

Cheer up, little girl, it'll all be over soon.

Missing you like crazy,

A.D. Jacobs

Then I entered the foyer of the apartment to find a decorative basket, filled with bath goods—salts, bubbles, powdered aromas—even candles and moisturizers. All of these small things swelling my heart in total elation.

The memory even brings a smile my face while on the massage table, here in the cabin. The last time I heard from A.D. was yesterday, during the conference I worked in Dan Smith's proxy.

I excused myself from the exam room when I heard his silky vocal cords, pouring through the phone.

"Hey to you," I returned his greeting as I watched an attendee pass me and pace down the corridor. "How are you?" I wanted to refer to him as a stranger, but that would give away my disproval of his absence.

"I'm making it. Tired...frustrated but making it." I heard him let out a long exhale from his nostrils into the phone. My eyes fluttered in comfort and exhilaration of sound of it.

How weird is that something humdrum and common as an exhale from Azmir could summon a physiological response from me? I missed him, his calming aura. His equanimity when my nerves were atwitter. His hands, causing my body to writhe. His mouth, tickling the side of my abdomen below my breast, but above my hip.

"Are you still bleeding?" Azmir asked, flaring my curiosity and confusion.

Out of all the topics of conversation or inquiries of deliveries to the marina, I wasn't expecting that question. My first inclination was to play coy and ask the nature of his inquisition, but my pining of him and his firm tone advised otherwise.

I licked my lips, all of a sudden experiencing extra moisture in my mouth as my heartbeat accelerated. "Umm...yeah," I sputtered "Yeah...a little spotting when I woke up this morning." My eyes closed on their own accord.

Something as little as my monthly period being a stark topic of conversation between me and Azmir was riddled in angst, which one would immediately think was absurd. But it wasn't. It was symbolic of the undertone of finality. We were making a huge, significant, life changing, and final decision that would reshape our lives. Lives that have already been set ablaze by secrets, betrayal, games, and even lies. In that moment, we understood what was behind us as a couple. What's absolutely vague is what waits ahead. Even with that uncertainty, we're forging ahead, almost running to the altar; only armed with a dozen and a half pre-marital counseling sessions.

"But I'm sure I'll be all cleared by tomorrow," I assured Azmir.

The phone went silent. I couldn't even hear Azmir's breathing in the quiet, but I felt his brooding. So badly, I wanted to ask about his apprehensions of the following day. I wanted to know if he'd been experiencing any grade of second thoughts. In my limited logic, it would have made him fallible—like me. It would have also provided me an opportunity to convince myself, as I attempted to convince him, why this marriage proposal was conceivable and solid. But my placid-CEO-mogul-thug-a-boo would never cop to any irresolution concerning me or anything else he's passionate about.

"I'm not worried, Brimm," he spoke softly into the phone. "I'm also not rushing mother nature. We can wait as long as we must," I could swear to hearing his voice strain at that last word. We haven't been together in weeks. For us, that is like years. But he's committed to my walk, and this was demonstrated by his proposal to discontinue sex until we're married. "I'm just checking in on you."

"I miss you, too," rushed from my mouth, unexpectedly. And before I could help myself, out came, "All of you," I whispered. My eyes closed again as my head faced the floor and I found myself gripping my neck. "Desperately."

I heard the air whistle from his teeth. I knew he was exercising restraint. This hasn't been easy for him...being away from me for so long, not having touched me intimately in so long.

Then not to mention the whispers of pessimism I've battled like hell of him seeking release elsewhere. Dawn Taylor. I've fought that fear many of nights. But the logical Rayna prevails most days. My mantra was if Azmir could propose it, he could sustain for the few weeks leading up to our big day. But the strain in his baritone, his inability to voice his need, and the palpable sense of him being like a spring coiled too tight, told secrets of his fidelity.

"Same here, baby," came out as though his voice was reduced to a tearless cry. I could barely hear him. "Until you're Mrs. Jacobs," he bade before ending the call.

And that is the summary of *the ghost that was Azmir*.

After my facial, I'm whisked off to the master suite where I engage in my assigned two-hour nap. Once again, I find myself in awe of the décor and ambiance of the yacht. In this room is a king size bed, modestly dressed in earth tone bedding. There's no headboard, the wall above it pins tan panels creating a semblance of a frame for the bed. The walls are variations of wood paneling.

There's a small Japanese style bathroom off the main room with a toilet room separate of the shower room and vanity. There's a long desk running alongside the window draped in hard plaid curtains, matching the motif of the suite. A large television faces the bed, giving the space a homely feel. It isn't half the size of the master suite of the marina, but still possesses the quality of elegance Azmir always achieves.

I notice the stationary card against the king sized pillows almost as soon as I enter the room. However, it isn't until I return from the shower, draped in a terrycloth robe that I tend to it.

Inside it reads:

Ms. Brimm,

. . .

I'm thinking about you as you prepare to become my wife. I wanted to be sure a nap was included in your itinerary. If I know my girl, she's working her brain overtime about everything unessential: anxiety over the production of today, not having seen me...or felt me...in a while, should you even be marrying someone whom you've not known for a number of years.

I don't want you at the altar exhausted from stressing over something that, in your heart, has already been settled on. Something I've known for almost as long as I've known you...and that's you being capable of being the woman I need in my crazy world. I need you by my side today...not fatigued from doubt.

Sleep and dream of me.

P.S. There is a throw blanket in the closet. Don't get between the sheets until you're with me. I don't want to have to tell my wife the woman I'd been smashing before her was in the bed we consummated our marriage.

Ending the chase,

A.D. Jacobs

    I can hardly imagine Azmir opting to consummate our marriage in a bed. That's for traditionalists and Azmir is anything but. The last thing I recall before drifting off to sleep is the smile plastering my face.

"*Brimm...breaker-breaker...Brimm,*" I hear as my consciousness oscillates. "*Brimm...breaker-breaker...Brimm,*"

I lift my neck to find the walkie-talkie Tessie gave me just inches away. I raise my arm and will it over to the radio device. I didn't realize just how exhausted I was. Seeing Azmir's encouraging words on stationery somehow put me at ease.

"*Brimm...breaker-breaker...Brimm,*" I hear again, identifying Azmir's light-heartedness.

I randomly pick a button to press, "Azmir?"

I get nothing. So, I go to another one, "Azmir..."

I hear a little static before he says, "There's my sleeping bride."

My heart skips a beat. "Where are you?" I ask.

"Down in one of the lower cabins, getting trimmed up," his Brooklyn twang is on full blast. I wonder if he's been drinking.

Does he have to drink to exchange vows with me?

"Hey, Rayna...whadup, girl!" trills from the radio, but at a distance compared to Azmir's voice.

"Is that Petey?" I return, feeling a smile break across my face in spite of myself.

"Yeah," Azmir answers.

"Hey, Petey! Glad you made it!"

"Wouldn't miss this for the world, baby girl!" Petey shouts. "My duke is finally takin' the fuckin' plunge, yo!"

I laugh—hard into the pillow. Petey's rarely so spirited.

"Yeah," I eventually return. "He better be...got me up on this boat with a white gown," I say in jest.

"Damn right. And you better bring all that sexy, too," I hear from Azmir when I'm expecting a response from Petey.

I go silent, not exactly knowing what to say.

"See you shortly, little girl...and don't be a minute late. I'm timing you," Azmir concludes, and I can hear Petey and what sounds like Kid, jeering in the background.

A regular pair of block huggers on a luxury yacht. Only the likes of Azmir Jacobs could make that happen.

At that, I hear a faint knock at the door. *If this is that Azmir, I swear I'm going to purposely be late just to spite him!*

I gather my disgruntled robe that's taken on a new form during my nap and make my way the short distance to the door. When I open it, I find myself instinctively arching my neck up, expecting to see A.D. However, when I lower my inspection, I find a frail Samantha, dressed in a pewter mother-of-the-bride gown, sheathed in sequence.

She smiles tightly. For her, addressing me isn't easy, this I know. I never make it a comfortable task for her. Even after being in L.A. for almost five months, our relationship is still unsettled.

"Can I come in, baby girl?" she murmurs with hesitation in her voice.

"Sure," I move, inviting her into the suite.

She sits on the oval chaise at the foot of the bed. She appears a little fatigued, but her condition does this on occasion. I take a seat on another square chaise next to her, tentatively. I don't know what to expect, but I've seen enough episodes of idyllic family sitcoms to know what's coming are her *before you take your vows, here are my parting words* talk. This *dialogue* has been delayed and to my gratitude.

But on my wedding day, Samantha?

Her eyes won't meet mine. Tepid anger that's been lying dormant begins to heat up, and underneath the pleasantries and faux smiles, is rising to blow the tepee. Already.

"I'm not gon' keep you long. They told me you gotta lot to do ta' get ready," she murmurs almost solemnly, and then takes a deep breath. "I know we ain't been...connected. Things between us just ain't right yet, but I wanna..." she's at a loss for words. Since being here in L.A., I can see her self-confidence still diminishes in my presence, and I've been the one to blame for that. I'm still not convinced of her presence. I haven't decided her purpose in my life now. "'Dis marriage between you and Azmir can work."

That fumbles me askew. *Why would I be marrying him if the odds weren't in my favor?* I'm steadily growing impatient.

"I say that because I see so much of Eric in you; 'dat *me against the world* stubbornness. And I know I been the cause of it—"

"Look...you don't have to open up that can of worms—"

"Eric wasn't Chyna's father."

W-what? I can't believe what I've just heard.

She shakes her head, but still rarely gives me direct eye contact. "No. Not many know." There's a slight pause. I guess she's preparing her nerves for what's to come. "He knew for years. I told him one night, feeling guilty. He stayed for a while after 'dat. I'd been out there for a while, wildin' out...getting high on the low. The saddest part of it all is we didn't know if he was Akeem's daddy when I was pregnant with him. I had a lot of church girl issues coming up. I was so restricted from life 'dat when I gotta taste, I went wild."

Another pause and I don't know who needs it more; me or my mother. I can't begin to process what she's telling me.

"I know 'dis ain't good timing, but no matter how many years you been away from me, I still know my child. You scared and I know why. It's because of what you saw. 'Da damage and confusion we caused you. You should know Eric stayed a lot of years through my addiction. I was gettin' high long before you and Akeem caught on. I was a functioning addict for a lotta years. No, it wasn't right for him to leave you kids, but I put 'dat man through so much until he...just ran." She shrugs her shoulders in defeat.

"He ran and never turned back. Nothing changes that fact," I challenge.

"Yeah, he did. And 'dat don't change, but I wanted you to know 'dat pain ain't black and white. Sometimes it comes with too many colors. I colored a lot of his anger. Pushed him to 'da point 'dat he needed a clean break."

"The break you proposed that night. I was there. You had the props and materials to back your plan," I speak forcefully with clear a memory of her making her plea to remove us from the projects all those years ago. "He shot you down and like the perfect submissive wife...like a trained dog with its tail between its legs, you didn't fight. You let him make the call to leave us in that hellhole to disintegrate!" I find myself out of breath. I know I've been holding a lot in, but not how close to the edge I've been. "And we did. As a family, we were lit aflame and chard!" My face wrinkles. "You couldn't stand up to him. Be a real woman...you just took his veto and rolled over."

Samantha quietly nods. "Because two days before 'den, Eric broke when I stole 'da rent money for 'da umpteenth time." Her regretful eyes rise to meet mine. "'Da same day, he saw me copping from O." Suddenly, I recall Akeem telling me about my ex-boyfriend being my mother's drug supplier. She's confirming that story. "He couldn't take it no more. Eric was done."

I see the tears ejecting from the ducts, being reabsorbed as she fights to control her emotions. At the same time, her attempted revelations begin to anchor in my conscience. She's presenting an argument of flexibility of perceptions. I've perceived the events of my childhood from one set of eyes all of these years. She's now giving me new lenses—another angle. She's taking responsibility for her role in our failed family unit.

Samantha is somehow able to see how those events of my troubled childhood holds bearing to my future. That with Azmir. Once again, I'm being faced with a mirror to help me view myself. I immediately identify the scars from my perception of things concerning my parents. I've been so angry with the both of them for our familial demise, but I haven't had all the facts. All of a sudden, I think about my reservations to love. My delayed acceptance of Azmir's commitment to me.

"Listen, I ain't come here to upset you or to make 'dis..." She gives a quick glance around the nautical suite. "...about me; we can discuss 'da drama of my childhood another time. But let me just say 'dat in my youth, being a Christian was lifestyle over commitment. I lost my way and—"

"Became sick. So sick, eventually you sought God like a patient in need of healing..." It's becoming clear to me.

She nods as her shoulders shudder. She's fighting for control. I, however, have a fissure in emotional rheostat. Tears pool my sockets and eventually empty from my lids. It happens so quickly, but I catch them on a rapid swipe of my hands.

After a long pause she mutters, "'Dis marriage between you and Azmir can work."

I give an emphatic nod and observe her eyes catching mine. Her hand then goes to the mattress to lift her thin frame from its sitting position. She pulls herself up shakily and stands before me for seconds long.

Then I hear a rapid, "I love you and believe in your marriage," before she turns on her heel to make her way to the door and shuts it behind her.

Time speeds up. I've had my cocktail, hair done, and face *beat to the gawds*, as Adrian puts it. I'm instructed to put on my shoes first when it's time to get dressed. A few days after purchasing the gown, I found a simple white satin, open toe, strappy *Jimmy Choo* sandal with ostrich feather covering my foot. I wonder would Azmir *have* me in these babies alone and chuckle. My gown is placed on me by more people than I need assistance from.

While eyeing my bridal attire in the mirror I hear, "Rayna, your sister is here to see you," from Tessie at the doorframe of the parlor. I can hear the distress in her voice.

She fights to be patient, but really doesn't want the last minute interruption of schedule to accommodate a guest just before my walk down the aisle. But what's more surprising is her mentioning my sister. Chanell doesn't have to pose as my—

My thoughts are halted by the passing possibility of it being Chyna. I did, after all, ask for an invitation to be extended to her and my grandparents.

"We only have four minutes before you are to be at the bottom of the steps here," Tessie warns.

With a soft nod and eventually an, "Okay..." I consent.

Tessie backs away from the doorframe and in comes a beautiful teenager in a red satin mini tube dress, exposing her smooth almond skin. Her right shoulder is inked with a red rose, marring her beauty right along with her facial piercing, in my opinion. Chyna's hair is jet black and pinned up in huge curls. Her red satin platform shoes are more appropriate for the club but are perfect for this day so long as she's here. Something deep within warms at the sight of her.

"Chyna?" I breathe.

Chyna's sucks in a breath and her eyes bulge when they arrive at me. "Oh my fuckin' gawd!"

"Chyna!" I admonish. And that's when I notice she isn't alone. There's an ebony skinned girl in a blue mini right behind her.

"My bad, big sis. It's just that...I always knew you was pretty, but...*DAMN!*" She shrieks then looks back to her friend. "Right, Tay?" Her girlfriend nods with a wide grin.

I wave her over to me suddenly feeling overwhelmed in emotions. I pull her into me. "I'm so happy you were able to make it. I didn't think you would."

"What!" Chyna trills when we release one another. "And miss a free trip to Hollywood—oh, I mean," she ducks her head. "Of course seeing my big sis get married is the biggest reason. I wouldn't miss this for the world."

"Well, I'm glad you could make it. What about Grandma and Granddad?"

"*Umm...* Granddaddy wasn't up to the long flight. You know... with the last stroke and all. He don't like to go out much. Grandma is here. She didn't want to lose her seat up on the deck, even though they told us we had assigned seats." Then Chyna backs away just a little to give me sight of her friend. "This is my home girl, Shantee. You could call her Tay for short." The two girls giggle for some unknown reason.

"Nice to meet you, Tay. I'm glad you were able to make it," I proffer my hand, to which she reciprocates on a weak shake, indicative of her age.

"We just came to show you some love before you take that leap," Chyna says then her eyes grow. "Speaking of, you ain't tell me your man was fine as fuck! I mean, damn sis!" Shantee bursts into laughter as she nods her head emphatically. "I don't mean no disrespect, but if you having any doubts about him, puleeeeze pass him over to me. I promise you, I can handle him." Chyna can't keep the humor *or lust* out of her voice, and something tells me she isn't entirely joking.

Adrian, Chantal, and the other stylists even join in on the mirth. Adrian shakes his head as he belts out laughs. I don't know if the humor is the truth in what the teens said or the fact that it came from two girls who are just out of training bras.

I've grown accustomed to women fawning over Azmir, so this isn't new. However, having your little sister who your strongest recollection of is being a toddler, do it makes it a bit awkward. The girls laugh long and hard as they hold hands with one holding her belly and the other having her hand on the wall.

I shake them off with my head and ask, "Where are you all staying?" I know unless they're crashing in my makeshift dance room at my house in Redondo Beach, there isn't much space. I also know my grandmother isn't fond of hotel rooms. She's always said they are the most impersonal and therefore nasty places to lay your head.

Hardly having caught her breath, Chyna answers, "At your place on the water." She then stands erect and sprightly asks, "Yo, who calls that place an apartment. And your bedroom...the one you share with that fine ass man! How is it that you leave the bed?"

"That place is dope as hell, Ms. Rayna! I gotta give you mad love on your world, ma!" Shantee covers her mouth with a balled fist, "You's a bad bitch—beautiful, educated, fine ass rich man, laced crib! I wanna be like you when I grow up!" She and Chyna proceed to give each other some dap.

Before I can answer, Tessie peeps her head back in the salon. "Ms. Brimm ninety seconds until your call!" I nod and she closes the door or more like slams it. I can tell her nerves are frayed.

I look at my sister and her friend, smitten by their presence, even if they're lusting over my A.D. in my face. I'm just happy to have family here. Weird for me, but true.

"I'm so glad you're here, Chyna doll," I pull her into another tight embrace, doting on her with a name I used to call her as a tot. Chyna freezes in my arms before reciprocating, wrapping her arms around me.

"Me, too," she murmurs into my shoulder. "If I could be with you every day, I would."

My eyes pop open behind her. *Chyna...I'm so sorry for leaving you behind!*

"Time!" Tessie appears again in the doorframe. Chyna and Shantee shuffle out, promising not to post pictures of me or Azmir on *IG*, *FB*, *Twitter*, or any other social networking site I'm not familiar with.

Tessie has my bouquet of pink tulips and mini calla lilies, placing them in my hand. I can't help but notice it's by design that it is the same arrangement Azmir had delivered to my office when he muscled me for our first date, after our initial encounter in his cafeteria. This time I don't need help identifying the flower type. Boy, have I been cultured to many things since then, thanks to A.D.

Minutes later, I'm at the steps of the lower deck, prepared to embark on the rose-covered runner. The runner leading to my groom. My heart thumps hard in my heaving chest. I'm presenting with all the symptoms of a nervous bride. Yet and still I'm ready.

"Rayna, I'll give you your cue. Okay?" Tessie proposes with a smile now forced and applied as an accessory rather than genuinely due to anxiety. I'm not offended by it; I can only imagine what she's being paid and what that means in terms of her reputation.

I nod in assent. Then I hear the bass drop, followed by the horn blowing, and that's just before the sextet belts out their various harmonic notes. This time, the jazzy tune rings familiar, too. I have to fight back the tears of joy. Azmir arranged for my processional song to be one holding warm memories for him.

Brian McKnight's smooth vocals sing, "*There I go...there I go...there-I-go...*" And I know in this moment it's meant for me to marry this man. My man. A.D. Jacobs.

"You can now start, Rayna," Tessie whispers while she presses a wired bud into her ear and with her other hand, holds a stopwatch of some sort.

Shelly, your mullato ass had better be with me. This is for me... and you.

I ascend the stairs and up to the rear stern of the large boat where I see two rows of people on either side. The rows of chairs are placed at a slant, creating a V as they face the small alfresco altar on the back deck. The immediate notables are Yazmine and my mother, Samantha. Then there's Petey, Kid, Chanell, Mark, Eric, Natasha, Lenny, Mia, Chyna, Shantee, my grandmother, Peg, Chef Boyd and a few others I don't recognize.

Once my eyes are done roving over the guests, I move them over to the white arch sheathed in chiffon and white calla lilies where Pastor Edmondson is with the sun shining brightly over him, and First Lady Twanece, adjacent, yet slightly behind him. Her well-poised presence demonstrates submission with underlying courage and power to assist him. Protect him. The ultimate image of marriage.

Finally, my sights land on the man of the hour—the love of my life. He stands tall with shoulders stretched wide and powerfully. His long legs are apart, giving off that virile stance. His chocolate frame is clad in a light gray three-piece suit, crisp white shirt, and matching oxfords. Azmir's refined stature and stateliness is breathtaking, beyond anything I've ever imagined walking down the aisle to—if I ever imagined walking down the aisle.

When my lustful eyes rise from his long legs, up his chest to his beautiful face, I notice him closing and tucking his pocket watch into his suit pocket as his eyes are engrossed with me. The expression on his striking face is priceless. Azmir's mouth collapses and I swallow hard. His face is full with the beard he swore to grow until I became his wife. I love the gruff edge to it and although it covers much of his beautiful face, it's an undeniably sexy alternative. He's magnificent, and apparently effortless. His boyish insouciance is on full display as his searing gaze scorches me from head to toe.

There's no bridal party. We don't need that, only each other and an officiate. I attempt a steady pace down the runner, hoping I don't give away my ogling of Azmir's chocolate Adonis. In some miraculous way, my feet guide me to him, feeling so drawn, so persuaded to be at his side. His eyes grow larger with every step I take.

Once I take my place at his side, I notice the lids of his eyes collapse and Azmir lets out a long breath. I shiver at my effect on him, though I don't understand it fully. Pastor Edmondson gives his opening prayer and asks the guests to be seated. He then goes over marriage, its creation, how it's perceived by God and should be viewed by Azmir and me, and then our witnesses.

One last wish I had for Azmir, and before Pastor Edmondson and First Lady Twanece, during one of our last premarital counseling sessions was not to have a long and drawn out ceremony. I don't need all that to take my vows before him and God. I don't want the delay, just to take my premeditated vows. I started putting them together almost immediately after leaving Tahiti. In fact, I started jotting down a few lines in my *iPhone* once Azmir had dozed off after goading me for a date of this coveted day.

What does surprise me is Azmir has written his own.

"At this time," Past Edmondson announces. "Azmir and Rayna will recite their vows. Azmir..."

"Rayna," Azmir calls out, as he grips my hand, then cocks his head to the side, and pushes his tongue into his molars, telling of exercised patience, just as he's done since our first encounter in the cafeteria of his recreation center, barely over a year ago.

"I'm going to start, of course, by telling you how beautiful you are today...on this special day...at this very moment. I can hardly believe you're mine, but this you are. It's something I've known since the fourth time I laid eyes on you. You were pensive, head buried in a leaflet. I envied that booklet...wanted the same attention...dedication. You were an unusual desire. A type of leaf never thought to turn over. I wanted you instantly. It alarmed me, the desire," Azmir peers deeper into my eyes. "I challenged myself to pursue a phenomenon holding something different—my heart at arrest. Each day after, I fought with myself until I could no longer defer my destiny. You."

My breath catches in my throat, and I'm enraptured. "Rayna, I want all of you. Before God and our witnesses, I vow to walk these dogs with you," his Brooklyn persona cannot be constrained, "...hold your hand, be your endless resource against the world, be your friend, hold you down, protect you when the world is banging at the door, declaring your guilt. I vow to be faithful to only you. To love, honor, and respect you, and only you. I vow to wake up every morning full with fidelity to you and you only. My eyes, hands, desires, and heart belong to you and will always act in accordance to your needs and preference. I want to go to battle for your love and commitment until I no longer have ammunition. I vow to be your forever until the air leaves my lungs."

CHAPTER 12

Azmir

I watch as Rayna's shoulders rise, and she holds her breath. I just hope she's absorbed my sentiment. I need her to believe in my ultimate vow to her. I feel everything I've said and more.

She chokes out, "Azmir..." and I know I've touched her. I only wish she understood how much it's felt by me. I love this woman with every fiber of my being. So much that I fear the phenomenon of what she makes me feel.

She flashes a wide smile that disappears almost as quickly as it appeared, a telling nervous move. Her lips tremble just before she proceeds, "An improbable possibility. That's the phrase I've battled with since the moment I laid eyes on you in *Cobalt*, when I was with my best friend and others. Your smile was bright, scent compelling, and eyes held possibilities that, before then, I thought of as impossible. I was eerily drawn to you from the first time I saw you...and fought tooth and nail from that moment on. I didn't know love. I knew nothing of commitment or devotion until your patience and unwavering assurance." She gives a fortifying breath and I understand her pacing; Rayna isn't keen at expressing her feelings.

"It took *you* to recognize my imperfections. It wasn't until I had a taste of your commitment that I appreciated unconditional love. Because of your assurance, I sought help with my deficits. It wasn't until running into your being that I perceived the possibility of *more*. It wasn't until I crossed paths with you that I appreciated God loving me, creating me with a purpose and illuminating love as a gift. And it is because of all this that I've come to know love's improbable possibility. You are every bit of that possibility.

"On this day, I vow to you...no more running. No more self-protection. No more feeling the need to escape what I have selected as my forever. My eyes were made to..." she coughs and fights back a blush. "...appreciate you. My arms were made to comfort you on unpleasant days and to protect you on those that are stormy. I am yours, Azmir Divine Jacobs. Forever."

That's all I hear for a while from this point in the ceremony. Each word of her vows keep echoing through my head, my heart, and my groin. Everything in me is aligned as far as Rayna is concerned. I can hardly believe she's narrated those words of commitment to me. Rayna is never good at unveiling her feelings via words. I've always had to seek alternative methods to extract them. And here, before me, she's perfectly articulated them. What's equally satisfying is I've already sensed them but needed them to be confirmed.

We exchange rings and the next thing I hear outside of my introspective thoughts is, "You can now kiss the bride."

I don't think. Never gave a conscious thought to how this would go down. I only feel what my heart and dick corroborates. I lift Rayna in my arms by gripping her ass and throw my tongue as far down her throat as I can reach.

After hearing a moan extract from her, I then feel her pull back, she groans, "Azmir."

And although I can tell she's turned on, I can hear the reprimand in her tone as well. That's when I abruptly hear the blaring applauses and pivot my neck to see Pastor Edmondson's face is red and filled with embarrassment as he laughs his ass off.

I place Rayna on her feet and when I return my eyes to hers, I can see the minx in her. She wants me. And damn if I don't need her…but I'll have to wait until a more appropriate time.

I don't get a moment alone with my new wife. We have pictures to take immediately after the ceremony, our first dance, dinner, and then guests to tend to. By the time Rayna and I come up for air, our reception is in full swing. Rayna and I split while she chops it up with her grandmother; I go to chill with Petey and Kid.

"What the fuck do a man do once he has it all, Divine?" Kid crassly asks.

"What do you mean?" I shoot back to him while observing his slightly oversized suit jacket and neatly cornrowed hair. He left Syn behind, which is to my relief. I don't want to have to choke her red ass on my wedding day.

"You got fuckin' dough, a million and two jobs, and now a bad ass broad to spoil the shit outta," he squeals, holding a *Corona*. "What's next, duke?"

I know Kid's question is loaded with more than he mentions. He's referring to my exit from the game. I'm officially out. Totally left a career I mastered for over twenty years. Most men in my former line of business don't actually stay retired. They keep dipping until they're either dead or handed down a life bid. I had been biding my time, preparing my exit strategy for almost a decade. It was just a matter of time that I'd implemented the plan.

"Fucking breathe, man," I retort. "I can now fuckin' breathe." I sigh, feeling the sentiment of that.

And I'm sure my goons do to some degree, too, particularly Petey. He'd been wanting to leave for about five years, but never trusting anyone to watch my back. He rode it out until I was done. I made sure his retirement plan was generous. He never has to work another day in his life.

We cut it up a little more and Wop joins our trio, followed by Rayna's little sister and her friend. These young girls are posting hard. It's weird having your lady's little sister throwing you fuck me eyes the first time you meet her and on your wedding day, no less. I've been avoiding them since our first encounter before the ceremony when they cornered me in the corridor.

Chyna bears a slight resemblance to Rayna, which is how I caught the relation. I kindly explained who I was, apologized for the disappointment, and invited them to tour the yacht with a crewman before walking off, shaking my head. That slowed them down but didn't stop them. Now, I'm nervous as hell, having them around my goons. Everyone has been drinking—I hope not the two youngsters.

"Yo, Divine, man!" Wop calls out excitedly. "Why you ain't tell me Rayna had a bad ass sister. We could be family." The goons burst out in laughing fits.

I watch as Chyna's friend seductively pulls her hair back as she licks her lips. And Chyna's ass is pushed out perfectly, exposing her breasts. Either she's fucking or is simply great at arching her back. *Damn, I don't want any daughters.* My baby girl would be targeted simply because of her father's past indiscretions.

"So what y'all getting into?" Chyna asks, pouting her lips pretentiously. It's all an act to me, but that shit my goons love and eats right up.

Petey shakes his head as he snickers. His ass would have probably been on it under different circumstances. He has too much respect than to fuck Rayna's little sister and her friend. Plus, Kim is around somewhere, and he's barely survived his last offense with his Mexican mami. He's been laying low; as he should.

"We going wherever y'all going," Kid asserts. "What y'all up for?" He goes for his wood. He's salivating at the mouth because Syn's ghetto ass ain't here with his leash. I have to make sure he knows Rayna's sister and her friend are off limits. I'm sure Petey is two steps ahead of me on that one.

I can't believe it when Chyna's friend winks at me and asks, "And what about you?" as she jerks her chin in my direction.

I have to put a stop to this shit. "I..." I raise my left hand displaying my wedding band, "...am about to look for my sexy ass wife in hopes of getting in trouble with *her*."

Then I feel a hand on my shoulder and turn to find Pastor Edmondson with a knowing smile. "Azmir, your guests are making their way up to the deck. It's time," he reminds me.

I nod. Everyone seems to disperse, leaving me, Kid, and Petey standing with Pastor Edmondson.

"And you," Pastor Edmondson addresses Kid. "Let's give Azmir a chance to surprise his new bride whilst you and I have a chat."

Kid's eyes shoot open in shock...or horror. Who knows considering his ass.

"Ummmm...Reverend, I was actually 'bout to get into something over there," Kid points randomly over his shoulder.

Petey and I can't help but laugh at this exchange.

"Oh, I won't take long. I just want to tell you about a friend of mine named Jesus," Pastor Edmondson informs in a humorous tone. I believe he knows more about Kid's intentions than he lets on as he places a gentle hand on his shoulder. Kid looks to me for assistance.

I shrug and say, "I have a thing over here. Holla 'atcha lata."

Petey's laughter takes on an elevating volume as he walks off in a different direction. I turn and see my special guests approaching.

Before I go to them, I glance around for Rayna. She's still conversing with her grandmother when I approach her. Rayna grabs my hand when she looks up to find me and pulls my arm around her waist as she continues to chat. I revel each show of unconscious affection Rayna gives. It reminds me of her nurturing side; the one she thought she was void of. I can stand this way forever, having her soft frame curved into mine. However, we have to move.

I offer her grandmother, Mrs. Brimm, a polite smile before I murmur in Rayna's ear, "You have a special guest here to see you."

"Oh, yeah...?" Rayna asks, not looking for any answer in particular, as she angles her head around, "Who?"

I pivot her frame beneath me in the correct direction. Our latest guests stand in the center of the galley, looking each way. It takes a few seconds before I see Rayna's hands rise to her mouth underneath me.

"Oh, my..." Rayna can't speak.

"Auntie Na-Na!" the little princess shrills and takes off running in our direction, dropping the Barbie doll she had cupped beneath her arm. She leaves her great aunt and uncle behind with pleased smiles.

Dan Smith throws me a nod and wink after I release Rayna to rekindle with Erin. When they meet, Rayna catches Erin in her arms and raises her high in the air, even while draped in her flowing wedding gown. The sight of my wife in her gown with a child gleefully in her arms on our wedding day twists something deep inside of me. I thought I had let the miscarriage go, but I see I have more work to do in that respect.

As Rayna and Erin reunite, Dan Smith strolls over to me, wearing the same pleased smile I have covering my face. I'm sure, though for different reasons; Rayna is my wife. It's my job to meet her needs. She needs this little girl in her life. For Dan, it's simply doing a good deed in the memory of his niece. Dan agreed to my surprise of waiting down in the salon with Erin until the formalities of the ceremony were out of the way. I knew Erin's presence before that would have overwhelmed Rayna.

"I'm glad I was able to do this, Mr. Jacobs," Dan offers his hand for a shake.

I oblige, "Please, Azmir will do just fine, Dan. I'm glad you agreed to this. This day can't get any better." I then turn to face him, "I hope this didn't come as too much trouble for you." I honestly could give a rat's ass if it had.

Michelle's cousin, Amber, is a bitch with a pitchfork for withholding Erin from Rayna. Keeping with my promise not to sic my legal team on this, I tried going another route. I cut a deal to donate a sizeable contribution to Smith's prosthetic endeavor. It isn't just about me keeping my word to Rayna. It also has to do with the type of fight we'd have to engage in considering Rayna has no legal right to Erin, she isn't a blood relative like Amber. If we had gone to war, it would have consisted of a dirty fight, using some immoral proclivities Amber may or *may not have* stashed away in her closet. I didn't want to do that in the wake of Michelle's memory.

"No, not much. I just had to push my familial authority in order to get Amber to reason. And now that I'm seeing these two together," he gestures over to Rayna and Erin. "I'm only sorry I didn't intervene sooner." I give Dan a final handshake and excuse myself.

The night seems to have sped by after their union. We're on the Pacific, sailing arbitrarily, under the moon. We eat, drink, and cut up in merry. Boyd and his staff are exceptional. The food is great. I've flown the biggest Big Dawg Pitbull out of New York to spin the wheels on the yacht. Flex is cutting records like nobody's business for our small crowd. Rayna owns the dance floor, even giving me a few dances after our initial dance as man and wife. At one point, there's a line of men, waiting to dance with her. It seems all but one of my friends dance with my wife. I guess Wop is too preoccupied with her little sister to care.

Later, my bride disappears down into the lower level for a while to spend alone time with Erin. I try avoiding Chyna and her girlfriend and keeping Wop's ass away from them at the same time. Kid gives up his chase of them after his words with Pastor Edmondson. I have no idea what he could have told that dude to spook him so, but I'm grateful for the halt in quest.

I find myself on the west end of the boat, in the lounge area, cutting it up with Mark and Eric, laughing endlessly at their drunk asses advising how to smash my wife for the first time. I take another flute of *Armand de Brignac* from a passing waiter as these two are in full swing.

"No...no...no, Eric," Mark blows off with his hands. "You don't want to take her missionary, you asshat! That's how you impregnate her. You don't want wedding day conception. So, you take her from the back, ease your way in there and then make her head break the headboard! Show her who's in charge, aye?" Mark proceeds to thrust his hips in the air, which to me resembles a belly dance because all I can see is his meatball of a stomach.

"Jacobs, bro," Eric calls out. "You want to pull out all of your *Romeo Romance* cards. Lick those toes, elbows—and the kneecaps is a sure way of blowing her mind! Just flutter your tongue over the cap like this," Eric flicks his nasty ass tongue in the air as his eyes close behind his lenses. I could slap the shit out of him if my disposition wasn't so elated from it being my wedding day.

"What is that Mr. Gerrity?" Rayna's face is wrinkled, and she wears a puzzled expression when she abruptly chimes in.

My eyebrows lift at the sight of her beauty, the smile clearly knocked from my face. The last time I've seen her was after saying our goodnights to the first round of departing guests. I arranged several marina pick up and drop off spots according to where our small number of guests live or are staying. The first to go was Pastor and First Lady Edmondson, Chef Boyd and his staff, Peg, Dan Smith, his wife and Erin, amongst a few others.

When we turned back into the boat to set sail again, Rayna excused herself to change out of her wedding gown against my personal preference. Her beauty stole my breath. Seeing Rayna in that gown symbolized so much making my heart race in my chest. But I know the gown is layered in fabrics, making it weighty, so I didn't fight her on it.

Now, seeing her in a white slip exposing her toned shoulders, arms, and thighs makes me shift in place. Her hair is still pushed back into a ponytail, off her face, and I find myself fantasizing about it being out and flowing, even in the new short cut I'm growing fond of. Everything about Rayna mesmerizes me, turns me the fuck on in the worst way.

"Oh, nothing to worry your gorgeous head, my Nubian queen," Eric flirts in his cornball fashion. "You are lovely in your post-nuptial guise—just stunning, your blinding glow. Your exquisite beauty raptures me, sends me a flight with desires that cannot be spoken in front of mere men. They'd never understand—"

"*Pshhhhh!*" Mark exhales.

He feels just as revolted as I do when I scoff, "Get the fuck outta here, man, with that medieval coquetry bullshit!" I'm partly annoyed and somewhat humored by that corny shit.

Rayna laughs as Eric flips me the bird while glaring at me. She grabs my hand and wraps herself underneath my arm, wearing a full on blush.

"Why thank you, Mr. Gerrity. I'm grateful for your appreciation but can't take credit for the glow." Rayna tilts her head to me and mechanically, I press my lips to it. "Some exceptional man has made me an honest woman today." I crack a smile.

"Yeah, you lucky son-of-a-bitch!" Lenny comes over, taking a seat on the bench with Mia in tow.

"Indeed," I return with a nod as I extend my arm from around Rayna to give him some dap. Rayna's burrowed into me with her back to my chest. Having her in such close proximity is dangerous in mixed company.

"So, how much did this..." Lenny waves his hand around, gesturing the boat. "...shit set you back? I'm sure a few stacks."

I know we've all been drinking heavily, and Lenny is no more sober than any of us, because he knows I never discuss money in public. Rayna goes stiff on against me. I have to quickly think of a way to divert the question.

"Don't know and ain't worried," I gently grab Rayna by the top of her head, turning it to feel her lips against mine even if briefly. "Mrs. Jacobs is paying the tab on this bitch."

Rayna gasps and her bulging eyes shoot up to me. I wink at her, and she laughs softly realizing my humor.

Eventually, our guests dwindle. Rayna's dozed off, so I leave her to see our last bit off, onto the deck. I sign off on agreements and payments with Tessie before sending her on her way. I dismiss Marcus and John who will be traveling with us this trip. They go down to the lower level for their cabins. Then I confirm over our sail plan with the head crew for our destinations.

By the time I get back to my bride, I find her sprawled out on the bench surrendered to sleep. It's extremely early, or late, depending on how you view four in the morning. The night ended earlier than I anticipated. I scheduled our sailing at six am when I thought Rayna, and I would be exhausted from lovemaking.

I lift my wife in my arms and make my way down to our cabin. She's so deep in sleep she barely stirs while I transported her. I'm relieved when I notice she's wearing nothing more than what can be perceived as a slip, I don't have to change her, just slip her sandals from her beautiful feet. I strip down to my boxers, no longer feeling intoxicated by alcohol but that of exhaustion of my wedding day. I pull a comforter from the closet and swing it open in the air for it to land on my sleeping beauty. I crawl underneath, pulling my wife so close to me there's no air between the two of us.

My wife. Shit. I can get used to this.

Hours later, my consciousness rouses. My body isn't prepared, but my mind is ready to awaken. I'm nearly delirious with fatigue. It takes me a few moments to gather myself. My eyes wearily peruse the cabin, and that's when I think of her. Her scent permeates the bedding causing me to search the room again. Rayna is nowhere to be found. Yet.

I struggle into the bathroom to shower and clean my mouth. How I was able to sleep through Rayna leaving the bed is beyond me. Excitement grows in my belly at the realization of having her with me for the next week, in the middle of nowhere, going everywhere. After slipping on a pair of *Hanro* lounge pants, I take off to the deck. I catch a deck crew-member leaving the front deck, twirling an empty tray in his hands.

"Mr. Jacobs, good afternoon," he nods, showing the deep part in his brown hair. "I just brought Mrs. Jacobs fresh fruit and coffee. What can get for you?"

Still out of it from a long night and a lack of sleep, I answer, "Just my wife for now. Perhaps something later." I still need to wake up.

"Very well, sir," he murmurs before walking off.

I head in the direction from which he came. There isn't a cloud in sight, but the sun is glaring, and the wind is peaceably forceful. I see nothing in front of the boat but open marine, the same for behind. The motors underneath create a rhythmic humming. It feels great being at sea.

After several steps, I catch my first glance of her. She's lying down on her belly, the delicate fabric of her white long peasant gown...I soon discover as I draw closer is completely sheer. I turn my head momentarily back to the direction the crewman who's just left, wondering if he got a glimpse of her lush flesh underneath the transparent fabric. Her head is facing the breeze, so the material blows down towards her feet for the most part, but underneath I can make out the contour of her curves.

"Close your mouth, Jacobs," Rayna's light-hearted reprimand jolts me from my introspect. She smiles serenely as her hand tents over her sunglasses to block the sun. My dick has no problem awakening. The image of her makes every penny I've paid for this excursion worth it.

Rayna. My wife. Goddamn.

My mouth closes mechanically, I swallow hard, and then I jerk my chin towards her, "You naked underneath?"

She takes a moment to observe her appearance, almost as though she has no clue what's jarred me. "Maybe...maybe not," she shrugs before returning to her stomach and digging into her bowl of fruit.

I join her, laying to her left to see what has her attention. She has a magazine pinned open with the bowl.

"You've left me already?" I tease.

"I was too excited to sleep restfully." She pops a blueberry in her mouth, and then offers me a strawberry, to which I oblige. "Can you believe we're married?"

While laying on my side and resting my head on my arm, I nod my head soberly. *You're damn right.* She cracks a smile as though she can read my thoughts.

Her eyes, suddenly filled with adoration, make their way to me. I can see through the tint in her sunglasses, thanks to the glaring sun. "Thanks for such an unforgettable day, Azmir. I couldn't have asked for anything better...couldn't have dreamt up anything more spectacular."

My heart expands at those words. I've only wanted to make Rayna happy. To give her *the world I've abound* is what I recall telling her in my bathroom, right after our return from Atlantic City. That's still my mission. Her intense expression tells me I'm headed in the right direction. I swipe an errant clump of hair out of her face. I can tell she's showered and washed her hair from yesterday, allowing it to air dry.

I don't speak much, content in her merriment.

"It's cool for the Moreau Brothers to lend you their boat. That's very generous of them," she appraises. "Was this a wedding gift from one set of your business partners?"

Struck with incredulity, I scoff, "*Gift...* my black ass. Try rental," I reply. Those cheap asses—well, mostly Jacques. "Jean was the one who offered it when I'd done a little idle chatting about wedding planning over lunch a few months ago, just after the holidays. It was Jacques' hating ass that brought up the payment for a rental. Not that I'd expected them to hand over the keys without me giving them something for it. Jean mentioned it being underutilized and it would be a great run for her." I shake my head recollecting the conversation.

"When the paperwork came through for my signature, Jacques made sure to include we must use their crew because they're 'most acquainted with the equipment.' And the crew had its own set of fees. I took it with his conditions," I shrug.

"This must have cost you a fortune," Rayna notes.

My brows peak to acknowledge her statement, but I'm not prepared to elaborate on an answer. I've spent double of what the average refurbished home costs in an urban city—something Rayna doesn't have to know—but every penny is worth the excitement that's vibrating off her right now. She enjoyed her wedding day, and that's all I've ever wanted.

"Hey, did you catch Boyd on the dance floor?" Rayna thankfully switches gears. "Who knew that grizzly teddy bear of a man could move so gracefully." She chuckles and I join her. Boyd thought he was on *Dance Fever* last night.

"And Kim..." Rayna's eyes grow wide. "...she was grinding on Petey like they were making their next baby!" She breaks out into a fit. I smile at her humor. The last thing Crack needs is another offspring.

"And Chanell!" Rayna's laughter explodes to a new octave. "She ate like a horse, drank like fish, danced like a *Kings*' cheerleader, and wondered why she ended her time on the boat puking her guts out!"

I shake my head at the memory. Rayna can't slow her laughing, reminiscing about it. Chanell didn't enjoy her last couple of hours on the yacht.

Rayna rides out her jollity, breathing in fresh air, taking a moment to eat more fruit.

"Chyna and her plotting-partner was a bit much, I know," she murmurs, looking out into the water. "I can't believe how much of her childhood I've missed...running."

There's a long pause, both of us relaxing peacefully with ruminative thoughts running.

"And Erin..." My chest squeezes at the lowliness in her voice awakening me from my private thoughts. "Azmir, how were you able to pull that off?" she gazes deeply into my eyes.

I reach out and pull her closer to me as I remain on my side. I know she appreciates my effort, and that's all that matters to me. We lay this way and talk for hours—well, mostly Rayna talks, and I absorb the fumes of her elation. We order a proper lunch while splayed out on our pads, chasing the waves ahead of us.

Fatigue from a lack of sleep, along with being underneath the sun wears on us. Rayna's chatter slows and her eyes start to slant. The deck crew-member brings our food out, asking where he should set it up. I tell him over on the west side of the boat, in the lounge area. He sets off to that direction.

"Let's get out of this sun," I suggest as I shift to get up and leave the stern.

"Wait," she calls out lazily. "I don't want to leave just yet. This spot is everything. I want to stay here, wrapped in your arms all day."

Little does she know; I feel precisely the same, but in my plan, we'd be more entwined. I keep the thought to myself as I reach for her hand. She takes it and lazily rises from the floorboard.

"Oooh," she cries out as she slams into my chest. "I gotta pee."

"Go handle your business," I order. "I'll wait over there for you."

I saunter over to the side deck, collapsing on the padded bench. My body is drained as fuck. I close my eyes until I hear Rayna return. We eat in companionable silence and mutual exhaustion, and afterwards she cuddles up underneath me. We watch another super yacht pass us, pointing out the luxury features we can observe from afar. Then things get quiet. Rayna's out like a light. Uncharacteristic, blissful chatter can do that to an otherwise guarded woman, I guess.

A female crew-member comes to clear breakfast and offers to bring a blanket to cover a tulle-attired Rayna. As I agree to it, I smile, ego filling my chest at her picking out this sexy nightgown to wear for me, *as my wife*. I'd love to rip it off her, but clearly, she's just as enervated as I feel. Minutes later, the crew-member returns with the blanket, collapsing it on top of us and that's the last thing I process before I go under my damn self.

A warming sensation burgeoning from my groin reaches up to my skull and stretches down to the tips of my toes. My scalp prickles and my belly jolts, stirring me from sleep. Distinctive warmth hits my face, and then I feel my bottom lip softly tugged from my face. My abdomen jerks again, this time it feels like forbidden pleasure.

A slickened muscle swipes my mouth, slowly. Then I hear, "Azmir," almost in a pleading whisper.

I can feel my toes flutter to an awakening...again spawning stirring heat from my core. It's some eerie and arousing shit. I can smell a familiar scent, feel acquainted warmth, and weight moving fluidly against my body. The pulling of my bottom lip returns and then my eyes finally flicker open.

The sun has set, illuminating the golden embers of the captain's salon right above us. *We slept the day away.* The motor still vibrates like a lullaby beneath, and water stretching miles out and seemingly above is damn near pitch black, but I soon gain perfect sight of the disturbance of my sleep.

I see an unsmiling, uncomical, and mostly staid Rayna over me. With one arm, she steadies her hovering *and humming* body over mine, and the other arm is pointing south, stroking my cock. I now realize it's what's causing my jerking. Her damp mouth is parted, and her eyes are smoldering with concentrated desire. I slant my neck to look down at exactly how she's gripping me. As I see her hand pulling and pushing me, stroking me up and down, I swear, I can blast the fuck off from the sight of it alone.

"You haven't touched me yet," she breathes into my mouth. Rayna then ducks her head and dips her wet tongue into my mouth, once again and withdraws with my lip suctioned between her lush lips. "Remember, when you showed me what sex would be like for your wife the night before you left for Atlanta?" She doesn't give me a chance to answer, but I register the occasion in my foggy brain. "Well, this is what sex is like with my husband after six weeks without," Rayna whispers before positioning herself over me. I can feel the misty heat from her sex suffusing my pelvis. My cock twitches in anticipation of her as her pussy suspends over me.

And then her pliant feminine lips slams onto me, bringing juice sputtering down my stick as she descends. I suck in a full breath.

"Ooooh!" Rayna cries out as her eyes squeeze shut as though she's in pain.

Fuck!

She's tight, only able to sluice in two-thirds of me before stopping. Her heavy eyes open and shoot to mine like daggers. She's panting, out of breath already. I'm not too far behind, reveling in her tightness. I find my back has risen inches off the padding of the bench. I can feel her inner-muscles percolating around me. She needs to move. Rayna *has* to begin her grind, or I'll go fucking crazy.

She moves her face closer to mine and murmurs, "We only have a few minutes before the captain returns." She shutters over me, gripping me like a vice. I'm hanging on by a thread, about fucking to lose it. "I need you...need you so bad. Make love to me, Azmir."

Rayna pushes down forcefully until her naked flesh slaps against my hips.

"*Baby*," I cry out, having lost all constraints. My need for her supersedes any desire for privacy at this point. I grab her by the hips and thrust upwards, eventually working my way into decisive strokes, making sure she feels me in her heights even.

And even though she's used the term making love, Rayna isn't requesting that. No. She wants to fuck and it's very clear as her soft flesh slams into me, clutching tight, jerking me to and fro. I see the sweat sprouting from her delicate pores as she gyrates wildly above me.

Our bodies join in such harmonic sequence. Physical familiarity has returned. A harmony beyond any previous plateau in our lovemaking. As Rayna claws my shoulders, I feel a zinging sensation. Fuck if it isn't a spiritual transfusion, making this experience with Rayna powerful, far more satisfying than physical sensory. It's goddamn catalytically soul-stirring. I've had my fair share of sexual encounters—some bad, some good, some horrible. And sex with Rayna has always been unparalleled, but this—this phenomenon is an experience unto itself. As our trembling bodies slam into each other, I feel whole.

There's a sheath of pleasure over the pain in her scratching my shoulders, trying to hold on to me for dear life. I'm so caught up I don't feel Rayna's orgasm eclipsing. I only realize it's upon us when she pops her torso straight into the air and grabs the front of her neck with one hand and my right knee behind her with the other. And when I see the traces of blood and small pieces of my chafed skin underneath her white coated nails, my balls tremble and my upper body and feet soar from the bench simultaneously and jerk back down in sequence, uncontrollably. I can feel the barreled loads shoot into her canal each time my body leaps.

What the...fuck!

If this physiological response happened with anyone but my wife, I'd be an insecure man. To allow my body to succumb to such emotional and physical pleasure is beyond my comprehension. I feel raw, vulnerable.

"Azmir!" Rayna cries out, while her arms encircle me.

To anyone else, that calling of my name would be perceived as panic, but to the person on the other end of what we're experiencing—what we're making together, I know she's embracing my flight, padding my landing. I shiver as unadulterated languor encloses me.

She throws her soft body onto mine, pinning me to the bench with a grip of my shoulders in an impassioned embrace. I'm assessing my body, observing my heart trying to beat out of my chest, the sweat enveloping my entire frame, and my head that's slowing its spin. *What was that?* I can't bring myself to complete comprehension. I can only *feel* the explanation of it, not verbalize it.

In the recesses of my befuddled mind, I can make out the muffled sounds from voices above us, in the captain's salon. Futilely, I wonder if they heard us. I can't feel my toes to give a fuck.

"Oh, my god, Azmir!" That cry is in alarm. Rayna lifts slightly to gain my gaze. "Your shoulders are bleeding!" she holds up her bloodstained palms. Her eyes are horror-stricken.

I look to my left and right, observing my slit shoulders. Sure enough, they're smudged in blood with fresh traces ejecting. I don't feel the stinging sensation until now. However, the smarting pain can't rival the endorphins floating through my veins or the warming balm stretching the full length of my body.

Fuck!

"I'm so sorry, baby," she grimaces. "I got carried away. I couldn't help myself. Oh, my god...I've never felt anything like that be—"

I cap her last word with a hard kiss. I unleash my tongue to wildly explore every crevice of her delectable mouth. Rayna folds into me instantly, moaning helplessly into my mouth. The kiss is so captivating, I forget to breathe.

I barely hear the captain, who obviously doesn't know we're tangled beneath him, announce the chef's call for dinner. Rayna belts out a conspirator's giggle, and then covers her mouth with the back of her hand as if that helps from tipping anyone off. In her delirium, she even has the nerve to hold the shushing finger to my face. I have no damn clue who she's quieting besides herself. I haven't whispered a word; I'm still coming down from what she put on me moments ago.

We need to get up to wash the blood off her and tend to my shoulders. It's apparent we have a dinner order to put in as well. As I lift both our bodies from the bench, making sure Rayna's ass is covered before I turn the corner for the steps to the lower deck, she tries to fight her giggling fit to examine my now brooding state. I've been perceptibly preoccupied and not with her in mirth.

"Fuck," I finally murmur over a hard exhale. "We're buying this boat."

She then breaks. Rayna can't contain her cackle...all the way to our shower.

I've arranged for us to cruise for seven days starting in Los Angeles with stops in Puerto Vallarta and Cabo San Lucas. Our next few days are filled with recreation, sunbathing, swimming on and off the yacht, island hopping, shopping, drinking, eating, hiking in the Sierra Madre Occidental Mountains, exploring, and feverish smashing. We only have a week to celebrate our union due to our demanding work schedules. I'll be heading out of town just a few days after returning from my honeymoon. Besides, Rayna was insistent on not taking too many days off work.

Nonetheless, during our week-long celebration, I bond with my wife, teaching her how to swim in the ocean amongst other things.

∞

The yacht was docked just off Baja, and we were diving off the open deck of the boat. Rayna's sun-kissed bronzed skin looked sexy as fuck in her sun yellow string bikini over her well-toned figure as she stood at the lip, prepared to jump. Her eyes were big in anticipation, though it was her third time in a row plunging into the Pacific. Each time, her contemplation was shorter than the one before. I did the countdown from below as I squinted, shielding the hard sun from my eyes.

"Five-four-three—"

Buzzing with excitement, Rayna leaped into the cool water, screaming on the way down before I was through. I heard the splash a few feet away, and when she came up, Rayna brushed her face with her hands, looking around for me. Marcus and a few other crew-members cheered her on. When she located me, she swam over, wrapped her legs around my waist as she clasped my frame.

"How was that one?" she pants in my face, covertly asking for my approval.

"Much better, Mrs. Jacobs," I reward.

Rayna then kissed me with her tongue, and I tasted the salt of the ocean. I couldn't give a fuck. My wife was happy, and nothing could please me more.

On this occasion, Rayna was a tamed learner. Another excursion brought out the Tasmanian devil in her. We were docked on Puerto Vallarta while water skiing in Cabo when Rayna became overzealous along with our boater. I guess she'd conveniently forgotten she was a novice to the sport. We were mere yards out from shore and Rayna wanted to exert bravado and hold the handlebar with just one hand while she tossed the other in the air and thrust her hips over the water. The instructor stressed to us the importance of maintaining a steady grip of the bar to avoid losing balance in the water. Well, once Rayna was skiing behind the water boat, she felt the urge to alternate swinging arms in the air. She sang to herself and even at one time, squatted.

I yelled over to her from the back of the boat to cut the shit, but drunken minds don't take too well to heeding. Rayna had downed three margaritas, well past her alcohol limit of two. I noted it, but thought *fuck it, she's on her honeymoon*. Well, during her skiing, my lady wanted to charm me with seductive moves. And while it frustrated me, it excited our boater who zig-zagged in the water to have her tits bounce in the air.

I called out to him once and he did not reply but did stop zigzagging. We were returning to shore at this point, and I'd guessed they wanted to have last minute fun. Minutes later, he did it again, encouraged by Rayna's hooting and yowling in the water.

"Hands on the bar!" I roared out to her.

She'd caught on to my rebuke, but it didn't have the correcting effect I was going for.

"Awww, c'mon, Jacobs!" she yelled out. "Lighten up!"

The boater laughed, and to add to her merriment, he zagged the boat again. This time Rayna scrambled for the handlebar, nearly losing her hold.

"*STOP THIS BITCH!*" I screamed at the top of my lungs. The guy's head jerked back to me, his eyes damn near popping out of their sockets. "*RIGHT FUCKIN' NOW!*"

The motor slowed, then sounded to a stop. I dove into the water before the boat was able to halt and swam to Rayna. I caught her just as she started to wobble from a loss of forceful wind. Maneuvering her onto my back, I swam a few feet to shore.

The instructor met us in the water, waving his hands frantically; asking in his native tongue what the hell was I doing. I made sure Rayna was on her feet when I answered him.

"Your boy on the boat is going to get his shit cracked!" I threatened.

"Azmir," Rayna called out and her little hand grabbed me at my abdomen. "It was just a little fun," she tried to mollify my brewing anger.

"Fun my ass! His bitch ass could have drowned you out there!"

Just then, the little boater waded through the water to his boss, the instructor; the instructor still questioning in a panic at the incident.

"It okay, man," the boater attempted with a balled mouth. "Just a little bump. She fine!"

The little fucker had the nerve to appear to be charging at me. When he'd made it less-than-two-feet-into-my-circumference range, all I registered was his puckered brows and his chest out.

This little dude is posting!

"Every fucking thing's okay, man! Relax—"

His wide ass head made a huge splash in the foot of water when he collapsed.

"Azmir!" Rayna yelped. "No!" She jumped in front of me.

The instructor yelled out, "What the hell you doing! I call the cops!"

"Yo, Divine!" I soon realized it was Marcus' warning.

He knew to make himself known before he touched me at the height of anger. It's actually a *Clan* rule, but especially needed to be practiced when dealing with me because of my reputable speed with the *ones*.

"Time to roll, duke," he pleaded.

I turned to Rayna whose eyes were now very much sober, lifted her over my shoulders and made our way over to the yacht.

As I marched with her draped over me, I heard the instructor yell, "Aye! You don't leave! I call cops!"

Then Marcus spoke up, "You ain't got no wins getting him back here. How much does your compadre want for the bitch slap? And don't give me nothing cray 'cuz Boss ain't even meet dude with a jab."

I was well beyond livid, I was fucking pissed. We boarded the yacht, and I took off to the shower and then to the office there on the lower deck to get a few things done. I didn't come up until dinner.

At dinner, there was absolute silence, but this wasn't peaceable. In spite of myself, I noticed Rayna looked tempting in a long, black tube dress. Her hair was all pulled back and she wore only lip-gloss. I observed how she didn't have any alcohol with her meal. She barely looked at me—not that I'd exactly gaped at her either. It was then that my anger turned into disappointment. I was ashamed of myself for fighting so quickly after reciting our vows, and on our honeymoon, no less. This isn't how we should've started, not how I planned this trip to be.

After our meal, I found myself on the rooftop patio, enjoying the night air. I sat up there reflecting. I fought with myself for being such a damn hothead. I didn't mean to lose my cool, *but dammit, it is my job to protect her*. This means if she's sloshed during our honeymoon and being careless, it was my duty to be aware of all danger. *Besides, that piece of shit was flirting with her.* That had pissed me off as well.

Regret began growing in my chest. I'd hoped I hadn't blown her honeymoon. She'd shown more merriment and had been more jovial than I'd ever seen her. Just like when water skiing, she laughed endlessly—even to a point of carelessness. But could I fault her for that? Isn't that what I'd worked so hard to knock down—her guards? Rayna was lighthearted, loving, fearless, and open to trying new things, like swimming in the ocean and horseback riding. She'd admitted to not having ever done those things and yet, she willingly gave them a try...for me.

Just when I'd decided to go find my bride and grovel my way into her good graces, she appeared at my side. I immediately noticed the somber look in Rayna's eyes. There was something brewing in the back of them. I'd soon find out just what when she kneeled before me, pulled down my lounge pants, and made love to me with her mouth. I knew right away this was her way of apologizing, something she wasn't always good at expressing. But by the way she had me clawing up the chair in almost no time, I'd gotten the sentiment. And when I'd cried out in ecstasy like a little bitch, I couldn't remember what angered me in the first place.

We sat out there, on top of the boat, staring into the obscurity of night. Rayna sat at my foot, resting her head against my leg in peaceful quiet. My chest had loosened tremendously. The silence said so much, taught me in abundance.

At some point, a deck crew-member brought out a tumbler of brandy. "Mr. Jacobs, sir," He placed the glass on a small table he'd brought out with him. "Mrs. Jacobs requested a nightcap." With curious eyes, I nodded to him. He then turned to go back down the steps.

"You didn't want one yourself?" I asked quietly.

Rayna never turned to face me. "I've had enough for today," she murmured.

I could hear the miscellany of emotions in her tenor. Guilt tumbled through my veins again. I didn't want her to carry this shit like it was all on her. I hadn't been beyond reproach earlier. I took a long swig of my drink.

"We're good," I tossed aloud, enough for her to catch my sentiment.

She didn't respond right away, but I knew she read between the lines. We were good. A minor quarrel didn't classify us as doomed. After a beat, I glanced over at the top of her head. Rayna didn't move much; she was stilled like a mannequin, gazing at the dark ocean. She didn't speak until moments later.

"I know," she sighed lowly. "This is all I've got. If I lose you, I don't know where that would put me. We *have* to be…good."

I didn't know how to respond to that, so I didn't. I did, though, meditate like hell on it up there that night. Aside from that, I took it all in. I enjoyed the moment, relished the phenomenon that was having my wife at my side as we charted unfamiliar terrain.

The following evening demonstrated a vast improvement of both our dispositions. We had a private dinner at an exclusive restaurant on the beach of Puerto Vallarta, the place where we'd taken our first vacation together. *My, how times have changed.* The architecture was splendid as it was laid out in the design of a cave. We ate by mostly candlelight and enjoyed exemplary culinary and artful spirits. *Lots of spirits.* Rayna's giggles didn't return, but her minx persona did.

After we left the restaurant, we decided to take a walk on the beach. We made it to a festival of some sort where the natives were dancing almost in a huddle, similar to when we were in The Bahamas for Rayna's birthday last year. And just like last year, eventually someone pulled Rayna into the circle centered by a firepit. Unlike last year, Rayna obliged and was mimicking the natives in no time. I'd guessed that was a part of the talent of a dancer.

Before I knew it, Rayna pulled me into a seat near the center blaze and gave me the most indecent dance in public. Her hips gyrated at varied but consistent rhythmic speeds. Her ass swayed in my crotch, my face, and at one time on my shoulder. She bent low, displaying the feminine curve of her spine leading out to the bump of a cherry that was her rear. The globes of her breasts stayed contained in the two thin pieces of detached material, deliciously displaying her neck down to her abdomen, though her pebbled nipples couldn't be concealed.

I sat and raptly watched her twirl her ass incessantly, to the beat of the live drum, to the point of sweat beads covering her perfectly bronzed skin. Her eyes stayed on me just as mine were stapled to every inch of her. I'd barely heard the roaring whoops and cheers from the crowd, especially by the head female dancer who was clearly impressed with my lady's moves. *My wife.* I could only hear the breath she extracted in my ear as she bent down at one point to lick the rim. My muscles went rigid—every tissue in my body came alive while in that chair watching my wife bring art to life with her delicious body.

At the show's end, I found her gazing down on me, intently, still in performance mode. I, myself, was still enraptured by her carnal cadence. I heard the blood rushing through my head. My heart rate peculiarly increased in excitement. My pants all of a sudden felt tight. There was only one thing to do.

Caveman is right.

I rose from the chair, dipped to toss Rayna over my shoulder, and marched to the hotel suite where we were registered to stay that night. After throwing Rayna's ass on the bed, I doffed my clothes, and watched her eyes and mouth collapse. Roaming my eyes around the room, an idea comes to the dome, and I walked to the bathroom. When I returned, I peeled her out of her long taupe dress, tie her to the bed with the belt of the hotel's bathrobe, and used Rayna's body as the instrument she presented it as on the beach. I licked her ferociously and then fucked her properly. Rayna's cries were unrestrained. Her expressions of ecstasy were a bonus because I couldn't help but plunge into her body as though it was mine to exploit. *Damn right, I'm barbaric.* She's mine and each orgasm she reached that night confirmed it.

My honeymoon was fucking great. It didn't last as long as I'd liked it to, because of Rayna's obligations at work. Nonetheless, I married the first and only woman who makes my heart leap and my toes fucking curl. I thought I'd been on top of the world before, but this feeling trumps any contentment I've ever had.

I finally have Rayna.

My life.

CHAPTER 13

Rayna

I'm exhausted. Absolutely drained as I sit at this table, entertaining my family before their flight back to Jersey in a couple of hours. Chyna and Tay are buzzing with youthful energy, Azmir is tapping away at both of his phones while we wait for dessert, and my grandmother's discomfit in a restaurant is on full blast by the way she's sitting up in her seat, posting her chin in the air. Also, her high pitched formal tone rings each time a waiter offers her more bread and to refill her drink.

Funny thing is, we strategically decided on this restaurant, *DiFillippo's*, minimizing the pretentious air the formal ones Azmir has been known to take me to hold. This one is quite modest and private, something I relish at this point in his career. There will likely be no cameras flashing or paparazzi hanging out in bushes once we exit. That would freak my grandmother out and, of course, thrill the girls.

This restaurant is nestled just outside of Santa Monica, and we're seated in a private section in the rear corner. Azmir and I are seated together on a loveseat with brocade jacquard upholstery. The girls, across from us, are sharing the same furniture, and my grandmother is in a tall chair at the head. The dim lighting plays on my mood of needing to relax...with Azmir...in the comfort of our home...alone.

The waiter comes to clear our dessert plates and offers to refill my glass of pinot noir, which I decline. Azmir ordered one of the most expensive bottles in the house for me to have consumed just a glass of it. I would've been content with just a glass and not have wasted his money. It wouldn't be a good look to increase the level of buzz I have going now.

I'm humming with desire for my husband. We returned from our honeymoon three days ago and haven't been intimate since. We've been practically separated from the moment we arrived back in Southern California outside of taking Erin on Azmir's cabin cruiser the day after we returned home. He was extremely generous in taking off a few hours to help get us reacquainted. Azmir virtually went right into work, and I acclimated myself at home, sorting laundry and mail while entertaining our houseguests. Then earlier today I concentrated on grooming by getting my hair, eyes, nails, and feet done and treated my grandmother and the girls, too.

Azmir has risen early and turned in late since our honeymoon. I have a sneaking suspicion he's trying to give me alone time with my family. Either that or he can't manage too much time with squealing young girls who clearly have crushes on him. If Chyna lived close, I'd have to get a handle on the way she melts in my husband's presence. But for now, I decide to live with it.

Azmir and I decided together to take my family out for dinner before their flight tonight as a means of sending them off properly. And outside of stomaching the frolics of teens, all I can think about is having Azmir all over me; his mouth, hands, arms, and... ummmm other extremities. I've been telling myself since we pulled off from the marina I just have to get through dinner.

My god. We've just returned from our honeymoon where we made love all but two days—and that was from Azmir's insistence of my receptacle needing a break. I don't know what the wedding vows have done to me, but my appetite for this man has increased tenfold since saying *I do*. It doesn't help that he's sitting slouched, b-boy style on the bench next to me. Azmir is clad in a hoodie, premium denims sagging just a bit—thank goodness not too much—and classic construction *Timberland* boots.

Geesh! Azmir's known to switch up his fashions, and rarely does he do the d-boy look with his work schedule. Nevertheless, other than his suits, nothing turns me on more than seeing him in a pair of jeans and classic six-inch Timbs! He's mouthwateringly delicious and I want him so badly it hurts. It also doesn't help that he's in a mood. Not one that's foul, but certainly isolated and absorbed. Oddly, the combination of it all turns me on. I need to change my focus and *no*—more alcohol won't help.

"So," I start to speak before my phone goes off. This is strange because I rarely receive any calls. I barely have friends, and I'm here with Azmir. "What have you guys done on your trip to L.A.?" I pose the question as I tap into my phone for the text app.

The girls start to giggle conspiratorially as they peer into their phones, much to my dismay. I've had enough of their childish antics and can only imagine what's on their screens.

It's from Azmir.

I know you wanna fuck.

W-what?

"I see y'all," I look up to find my grandmother's eyes pointing to Azmir and me. "...ain't no better with them phones. I see y'all just typing away, too!"

"Well?" I push them for an answer. My grandmother just smiles, I'm sure camouflaging her frustrations with their silliness herself.

Completely jolted by Azmir's text, I type back.

What makes you think that?

"We visited Ma at her place by the beach—" Chyna attempts.

"That's Rayna's place," my grandmother sharply replies.

"That's what I meant," Chyna retorts, feigning rebuke. Then comes another string of laughter from the pair.

His response comes almost instantly.

I can feel your pussy reverberating from the bench.

My eyes slowly collapse as my head tilts down towards the floor. It's the same accurate assessment he made the night at the reopening of *Mahogany*. I throw him a gaze, but Azmir completely ignores it, appearing heavily engaged in his phone.

"And what else, Chyna?" I try regaining myself.

"*Ummmm*... Went to the beach," she explains. "Went sightseeing, even though Grandma was being corny with acting all scared."

Tay chimes in, "We saw Hollywood, too. That was hyped!" The girls slap high fives with goofy smiles on their faces.

My phone tolls again.

I am going to fuck you so hard, your grandmother will hear you scream my name while she's mid-transit.

"*Ummmm*... Honey," I call out to Azmir, catching him off guard. "I think we're ready for the check now!"

Back in his *Range Rover*, Azmir drives with my grandmother in the front seat and Chyna, Tay and me in the back. The girls keep entertained by giggles and semi-verbal communications beyond my knowledge. They're whispering things I can't hear even if I care to. I look in the rearview mirror ahead to see Azmir concentrating on the road.

"Have you heard from Grandad?" I throw out to my grandmother. I serendipitously slipped her a generous check before we got back into the truck. She doesn't know the amount, I'm not sure if she even knows it's money in the envelope.

"I told you!" Chyna challenges Tay. "Ask her."

I don't give much thought to that exchange at the time, still listening out for the answer from my grandmother.

"I called him last—"

"Do it!" Chyna blurts out, cutting my grandmother off. "You want me to do it?" Chyna's eyebrows peak.

"You know, I am so sick of you two already!" My grandmother barrels out. "Ask who what?" She twists in her seat to face them. I guess she, too, has had her fill of these two.

"*Shhhhh!*" Tay hushes Chyna.

With a grimace, Chyna argues, "What, Tay? My sister is cool. She ain't gon' trip."

"Trip off what?" I ask, silently praying they aren't about to confess to going through our drawers in the master suite.

"*Shhhhhhh...*" Tay tries again, fighting back her nervous laughter.

"No," Chyna throws her outstretched hand in Tay's face to mute her. "...we was just on *IG* telling this broad those rumors about you ain't true—"

"Rumors? What rumors?" My grandmother demands before I can process the same question.

"The ones from back in the day. People was saying Rayna was a gold-diggin' hoe because she stole O's money. And him and Keeme killed that lil' girl in the shootout because O was gonna kill Rayna, but Keeme got to him first and before he could get at Rayna because O shot J-Boog. Then, they both got locked up, killing that lil' baby." Chyna didn't let up for air. "And what I'm saying on *IG* is my sister got a fat ass—*my bad Grandma*—crib out here. And even though her boss is a baller, she got her degree and a good job. She ain't never need to rob O of all that money they said she did. Right, Rayna?"

My eyes shoot up to the rearview mirror again, and this time, are met by Azmir's quizzical ones. The car is absolutely quiet. I don't know where to begin. There are so many lies interweaved with the truths of that story. Similar to the old adage: you whisper a story in the ear of the first in the circle, and by the time it gets to the last, it's a completely new fable. Matching the truths against the lies doesn't matter because now Azmir has a good perspective of what is fact. Between what I've told him previously and peppered details Chyna has just inadvertently revealed, so many of my fears are released to wreak havoc on my sound world. Under his brooding gaze, my lids collapse shut.

"First of all, young lady, Rayna ain't never been rumored to be no gold digger. She left home with barely a penny to her name and made something good of herself. And if you could stay off the Internet, you could do the same. Now shut that phone off!"

The remainder of the ride is quiet. Azmir helps the ladies with their luggage into the airport while I stay out in the waiting car, trying to keep from hyperventilating. I can't believe this is happening to me. For years, I never wanted family out here in L.A., not wanting them to tamper with what peace I had, at first, then with my happiness with Azmir once he came into my life.

About ten minutes into the drive, Azmir breaks the ice. "You wanna talk about it?" he asks expectantly.

I close my eyes to hold back the tears threatening. On an ordinary day, I would simply say no, I don't want to discuss such a personal matter. But this is no ordinary day. These aren't normal circumstances. There isn't anything typical about my being right now. Before I left for my nuptials, I could employ the word *privacy* to barricade my secrets. Today, no armor can shield what Azmir has every right to inquire of. My past.

On a shaky breath, I forge ahead. "There was so much she said that was completely off, I don't know where to begin."

"How about with what's true?"

My eyes dart over to him. He doesn't react. Azmir wears a placid expression as he navigates the *Ranger Rover*. My mind races with thoughts, trying to decide where to begin.

"O was my high school boyfriend." I shut my eyes at the rare remembrance of him. "The only boyfriend I had. He and my brother got into it one night behind rumors...about me sleeping with my brother's best friend—"

"Were you?"

"No!" I glare at him. I've never been that type of girl and I hope he isn't accusing me of it. "They were rumors made up by a so-called friend of mine. A friend that was sleeping with my *boyfriend* underneath my nose." I shift in my seat, blindly gazing ahead "Anyway, one night everything hit the fan. O went to approach my brother's best friend, J-Boog and ended up killing him. Then my brother, Akeem, got into a shootout with O...to avenge J-Boog's death. In the crossfire was a toddler who was killed."

A shiver runs through me at the memory of it. A little girl lost her life from my drama. I don't deserve to have kids. At times, I wonder if I even deserve Erin. That innocent little girl losing her life was so unfair. If I could do things different, I'd start with not giving O my attention all those years ago.

"And the money?" Azmir's baritone wakes me from my musing. "What about that is true?" I notice his brows pinch. He's growing impatient.

I exhale, hoping he'd forgotten that mention. I pinch the bridge of my nose. "I didn't steal the money...exactly. He'd been locked up for the murder when I'd decided to leave town for *Duke*. I needed money; my father had disappeared, and my mother was fighting for her life after having overdosed. My grandparents were too preoccupied with Chyna, so I didn't want to burden them with asking for money to go. Out of nowhere, I remembered an account O had opened in my name for emergencies. He said if he died, I was to keep it...to not even tell his mom about it for his funeral. I went to the bank expecting there to be a couple hundred dollars at best." I let go of another breath, feeling my heart rate increase. "I emptied the account and left home hours later."

"How much was it?"

No! Why? "Twenty-eight thousand," I murmur sheepishly.

"That's some bread for a kid. What did he do for a living?"

The first tear slips. I feel shame like never before. I'm embarrassed by my former life. *But I didn't know any better.* I was young and that was my environment. I knew nothing else.

"Sold crack," my voice trembles.

Azmir doesn't speak. He withdraws from me. Again. How can I

blame him? I've just dropped another bomb about my less than stellar past. I feel classless. Grimy. No better than the monster O was when he slung his powder to my mother behind my back. However, no amount of abasement can make me forget the promising world I've created. I took charge and changed my environment, my course. My life. For Christ's sake, I just got married. I'm no longer that misguided teen who was scared and abandoned. *I'm strong and formidable.*

"Azmir, say something," I beg, barely able to speak.

"What do you want me to say?" His voice is calm. I feel no emotion in it, and that concerns me.

I pivot in my seat towards him. "Tell me how you feel having learned something like this about your wife? What is this new piece of information going to do to us?"

He doesn't speak. He doesn't move. His eyes don't roam. Typical A.D. equanimity at play. It's long minutes before he murmurs, "It's not news, Rayna."

"*Wuh*-what?" In all honesty, I gave up on hearing back from him, so I don't trust my ears. "I didn't hear that."

He turns to me. His eyes fill with something even in the darkness of the truck, only extraneous lights glaring into his face. "The murder, O, J-Boog...not news to me."

I don't understand. I'm thrown. *He knows about my past?* How could this be possible?

"How is that possible? I've never shared this with anyone, but Michelle," I ask, feeling like the carpet is being pulled from underneath me.

We pull into the marina and Azmir still hasn't answered me.

Manny receives us in the side lobby, and I quickly wish he were a less jovial Roberto. Manny's extremely loquacious and dotes heavily on Azmir. He always has questions, forcing your attention elsewhere. Tonight, he's no different. He greets gleefully and chews on the weather, latest game scores, and his usual inquiries about

Azmir's businesses. I manage a polite smile, Azmir a tad more, though it's clear he isn't in chatty mood.

When we make it up to the apartment, Azna comes running to me. I drop to my knees to greet him. Azmir heads straight into his office with purposeful strides. I rise to my feet, prepared to continue with my query. But before I make it to his office's door, he comes back out with a file and drops it in my hands. I look up to read his expression, but he gives nothing away. Without thinking, I open the folder.

Within seconds, my back hits the wall as I cover my mouth.

"Where did you get this from?" I probe on a shaky breath.

"I have a team of investigators. A man in my line of work—"

"WHERE DID YOU GET THIS FROM?" I scream, anger bursting in my belly.

"I have a team of investigators, Rayna. You know this," his voice is even, but I know he's brewing himself.

I don't care; he's breached my privacy. I go back to the file and note pictures of Akeem and O—mug shots specifically. Police reports and news articles of the arrests, the little girl's funeral images, and statements dated that July night long ago.

"Is this even legal?" I yell. "Because it sure as hell isn't moral. Azmir, you have no right to this information. None of it concerns you."

"You concern me!" he roars. "And since you've mentioned morality, where does that put you on the curve when you can't even tell me outright about this ordeal from your past?"

"How am I supposed to tell you something horrific, huhn? When is the appropriate time to have you reply I'm not the type of baggage you want to take on?"

"You should have told me, Rayna!"

"When? On the bleachers at the *Staples Center*? Before or after I'd hung up with Michelle, letting her know I was still alive?" This is all pouring with sarcasm. I hope I won't regret using it when he claims to have fallen in love with me in a form of mockery in a fight.

"Don't give me that shit! You've had plenty of time to share this pertinent information!"

"When?" I snap. I toss the file down the hallway. "When did I have a chance? You just kept coming back...you wouldn't stop! When I ran, you kept chasing me. And then I fell into the possibility of putting all of..." I wave to the pile of disrupted papers scattered across the floor. "...that behind me. Why would I tell you? You saw the horror. You've obviously acquainted yourself with my mess—"

"Because I was marrying you!" Azmir's eyes go wild with what feels like resentment. "You think I'd walk into this shit with blinders?" his brows furrow. "It was bad enough I damn near walked into an engagement with them. You think I'd go into a life with you without knowing your ghosts?"

My breathing hitches. He's referring to my announcement of Akeem being in prison the night before we left for Tahiti.

"You wake up some nights calling some dude's name, and for months I've been too afraid to ask about it, fearing you'd hit the pavement!" He snorts, "Now I know the tale behind J-Boog!"

"I would've told you. I'm getting better at talking!" I scream into his face.

"Fuck waiting! Do I look like the type of man who waits for shit to come together, Rayna? Am I the type of man who waits for things to fall into his lap? Huhn?" I don't know if that's rhetorical, but I'm certain of the answer. "The worst part of having things kept from you is the waiting!"

"So, what... I was going to happily share I'd dated a d-boy, took his money, and skipped town? Yeah, right!" I scoff. "This would have never made it here." I lift my wedding rings to him, feeling prematurely victorious in this battle. Confident he'll see it from my perspective.

Azmir cocks his head to the side, glaring at me with incredulity, taking his time to speak. "I knew about the ten grand to Sebastian...you got the first ring," he takes a step closer to me. "I learned about the *d-boy*, the murders, the money...you got the second one with my fuckin' lifelong commitment to love, honor, respect, and protect you." He's now just inches away, bent down and over into my face, steeping anger emanating. "I'm still here!" He pushes his index finger into the floor as he howls, forceful breaths of venom hitting my face. "*I* don't fuckin' run!"

Azmir holds his scowl and proximity as I observe his erratic breathing and flared nostrils. I'm rendered speechless. I'm still angry, still feel violated, but that's pushed to the side by his expressions of being left...by me.

"But what you won't get," his voice, now terrifyingly lower, is hoarse and pouring with some strange emotion. "...is to lie, run, and keep shit else away from me." His eyebrows rise, "It's *our* fuckin' bubble now—not just yours! It's *our* lives, feelings, and privacy that get insulated, no longer yours alone."

He stands in this position for what feels like minutes long, awaiting my rebuttal, I guess, something that won't come. He's left no room for it. I stand in place, rigid with embarrassment, anger, rigged with disappointment in myself—self-debasement, shame. When he turns for his office, I almost expect to feel the door slam, but it never comes. Azmir carefully closes the door, leaving me to reconcile my demons. Alone.

For days after the fight, I'm peppered with regret. Azmir's bone-chilling homily still echoing in the darkest places of me. Though I'm still tender from his infraction, more than anything I'm feeling I let him down once again. Worst of all, I don't get the chance to properly apologize or try to explain my perspective with a cooler head.

The day after our fight Azmir leaves for New York City to attend a memorial for Christopher Wallace, something he's had regular attendance at and almost didn't make because of our honeymoon. I chose the date. It's exactly like A.D. to not make me aware of such a meaningful event to him so he could meet my request. Also in typical A.D. fashion, he invited me to attend with him weeks before our wedding. I declined, not wanting to miss too many days from work. I now challenge my decision.

It's been two days since he'd left and I'm dealing with a new type of blues: missing my husband. As cynical as this may sound, I've developed a new bond with him since exchanging vows. Perhaps it's from spending so many days with him after being apart for weeks. Maybe it's all of the picturesque scenery of the Pacific. It could be the galvanic exchange during our lovemaking sessions. *My god!* They've been powerful—from the first time I jumped him, the day after the wedding, waking him from a sleep to feel his steely girth inside of me. Each experience was just as electrifying as the last, if not more. Each day I awakened on my honeymoon, I questioned the reality of it all.

And now, I'm alone, feeling like the other half of my soul is missing. Azna aside, this apartment now feels like a massive structure of emptiness. The copious space this place provides only enlarges the void I feel from the king of the castle being gone. I feel a flicker of grief in my chest as I snuggle into bed. I seriously doubt this is what the honeymoon phase feels like.

The following day at work, my mood improves, at least. I'm in the groove of my day almost immediately, seeing patients and being wished years of wedded bliss by those Sharon manages to share my news with. Before I know it, I'm sitting behind my desk, scarfing down a tuna sandwich when my cell goes off. I don't recognize the number and therefore let it go to voicemail. I know it's not Azmir or work, so I'm fine. But then I think of Erin: *what if someone's calling with an emergency concerning her?* We're due to hang out Thursday evening and I'm greatly looking forward to that headful of sandy blonde curls to aid my blue mood.

I decide to check the message, and I'm surprised to hear April's voice on the other end.

"*Rayna, it's April. You know...April Miller from undergrad?*" her voice drips sarcasm. "*Anyway, I'm just going to get right to it. It's sad I hear about your wedding through a third party,*" Third party? "*I mean, I know we've never been besties like you and Michelle, but we're not exactly enemies either.*" My mouth forms into a moue as I hear April sigh. *Is she really angry? Why?* "*Well, so that you know, mine and Gerald's wedding date is set for June and you, and your husband are on the guest list. Contrary to what you may feel about me, I still consider you a...friend,*" she pauses, sounding to be holding back on boiling emotions. "*Look, Rayna,*" her voice is almost strained. "*I've changed. If you give me a chance to explain a few things, you'll see. I want to be friends. I hate the way we left things that day at Holy Deliverance Tabernacle. I would like an opportunity to...talk. Please call me back; I don't want to hear about the next event of your life on SandraRose.com and The YBF.*"

After she ends her rant, with my head spinning, I go straight to those sites, starting with the first she called out. I'm only recently familiar with them because of Azmir's recent rise in interest for bloggers. We've been grist for their gossip mills for months now, which is why I requested no pictures at the wedding! Sure enough, there are pictures on both sites of the boat, several cabins, the main deck as it was being broken down to suit the ceremony, and something else far more revealing and personal than all before it: my wedding gown!

My breathing increases along with my heart rate; my mouth goes dry. I can't believe anyone would go through all that trouble just to betray someone's privacy. Who would be so deceptive and guileful? I note there are no photos of the ceremony or guests, none of the cocktail hour, reception, me or Azmir, which could only mean the perpetrator didn't have the heart to sneak flicks during the event—*or they didn't have access to the festivities.*

Mechanically, I lift my office phone and dial. After two rings, he picks up. "Yeah, Jacobs?" His new moniker for me almost melts me, but his tone definitely puts me on ice. He sounds irritated. I remind myself we haven't exactly made up from our fight before he left for New York two days ago. He's now in Tennessee for business.

"I hope I'm not disturbing you." *What a thing to say to your HUSBAND, Rayna!*

"I'm in a meeting. Is everything okay?" His voice is hard, terse even.

I guess there's nothing to do but get right to it. "Azmir, do you know our wedding pictures are on the Internet?"

"What?" He grates so coldly I can't decide if he's angry at the news or annoyed with hearing from me.

I swallow hard. "Yes. I've been on *Sandra Rose* and *The YBF* but haven't made it to *Bossip* or the others yet."

"Fuck!" he whispers on an exhale.

"Someone snuck on the yacht to steal these pictures, Azmir. Someone who knew we...I didn't want them public..." I end tentatively.

"Sounds like you have someone specific in mind," he somewhat snorts.

"Azmir, Tessie told me Dawn was there. She gave Tessie some bogus excuse for arriving, flashing her PR title for entry," I speak through gritted teeth, growing angrier by the word. "She wasn't invited."

"Are you suggesting someone who's contracted with me would risk their reputation and job to get a few shots for what...a few bucks?"

My eyes fall in annoyance. Already he's ready to disprove my theory. To defend Devious Dawn. "Azmir—"

"Someone who, by the way, is paid to quell bullshit like this? C'mon, Rayna. That's like having security orchestrate an attack. It's possible, but not all that plausible for a simple businessman like me. I'm not the fucking ruler of the free world."

Him putting it that way not only reduces me to a child with a hyper-imagination, but it pisses me off, too. I don't know where to go from here. When Azmir's Brooklyn-block-boy persona is out, I don't have any wins.

"Look, I'll look into this right away. I promise, I'll find who's responsible for this, I know this is exactly what you were trying to avoid. I have to go. I love you," he murmurs softly.

Although our conversation ends on a placated note, I'm embarrassed and can't shake my suspicions of Dawn's trickery. But what can I do now? He has to go back to his meeting.

"Love you, too," I return, just above a whisper.

I stay, stuck in place at my desk, still chewing on Azmir's words. I even hold the phone to my head, enduring the blaring disconnect alarm. His analogy of the type of status he holds rings in my head. Though I still have yet to understand Azmir's rise, I have to admit I signed up for it when I agreed to marry him. I don't want the fanfare, the constant fissures in our bubble, the sharing of traditional personal events with people I don't know. *But I've chosen him. I've relented to his chase.* That's what I meditate on while going about the remainder of my day.

It's well after six p.m. I'm sitting in my office, going over x-ray films, when I get a text from Azmir:

Sorry for being so short earlier. It's been a stressful few days returning to work. Facetime tonite @ 9. Grab your iPad.

iPad? I haven't thought of that thing since our breakup, last year. I have to think of where it is. After a few beats, I recall Azmir having it delivered here and me tossing it in an underused drawer. I turn to open it, and sure enough, it's here. Nice and dead, but here after months of abandonment. I text Azmir back, agreeing to it and then make my way home. After locating and plugging the device into the charger, I go into my regular night regime.

Finding time to kill before he calls, I start to reacquaint myself with the *iPad*. I didn't set up much in it before my breakup with Azmir, but I recall feeling it was such a cool device. When I unlock it, I immediately see a picture of Azmir and me at the charity he invited me to right after our blow up about him paying Sebastian off. We were seated at our assigned table, leaning into each other for the camera. My smile was barely stifled and the look in Azmir's eyes was soft...peaceful-like. I know I didn't set the picture on here, so my curiosity carries me over to the photo app to see what else I can discover.

My breath catches when I see there's actually an album, created at some point. I start sliding through at least two dozen pictures of me, and others of Azmir and me. Many of them were taken while I was asleep, a few when I was gazing introspectively out at the water in his cabin cruiser, some of the two of us at social events, and a handful of me laughing away from the camera. What amazes me are the ones of me naked from the shoulders up with a flushed face and glistening skin, hair damp and stuck to my face, lips swollen and parted, dozing, clearly after having just made love. All of these pictures capture me in delicate states. I'm not angry, sheepish—or fleeting in the pictures. I'm very much happy and in love. I'm soft, feminine, and valued. I'm his to adore. To love. Azmir had loved me, even back then.

The emotion lancing through my belly can't be explained. I never knew these photos even existed. I had no idea Azmir is the memorabilia keeping type. They are intimate photographs of shared experiences by us, revealing a sentimental side of him. Now it makes sense why he had the iPad delivered to me out of all my other belongings. Maybe I'm reaching, but I believe Azmir wanted me to see myself through his eyes. He wanted me to capture his love for me at a time when I didn't think it existed.

I must run the slideshow of the collection of photos ten times, losing myself in the message of it. When the *iPad* trills, I look at the time on the nightstand and note Azmir is six minutes early.

My heart pounds like elephants in a safari while I wait for his image to appear. When we're connected, I notice the weariness in his eyes. As beautiful as he is encased in dark chocolate, I know Azmir is overworked. He's lying against a headboard, wearing a tank T-shirt exposing his bubbled arms and the lumps of his carved chest muscles. I swallow deep in fortitude. For the first few seconds after being connected, he doesn't speak, just studies my appearance in the box contemplatively. I attempt to break the awkwardness it causes me to feel.

"Quiet much? This feels a little stalkerish instead of communicative," I jeer on shaky vocals.

Azmir cocks his head to the side, bringing that tongue to his molars. "You don't usually stalk something belonging to you."

Awwww... Azmir...

I fight through my cheeks heating.

"How have you been?" he asks softly, in clear contrast to our previous exchange.

"Lonely, angry...downright miserable without you," I easily admit.

Azmir nods solemnly. Though he doesn't offer words of comfort, I somehow sense his regrets through that simple act of nodding as if he's somehow slipping his long, capable arms through the screen and wraps them around me. Suddenly, I feel overwhelmed with emotions needing to escape my tormented heart.

"Clear your weekend schedule for me?"

"Always," I almost cry. Even over the telephone, Azmir breaks down walls inside of me.

There's a pause before he murmurs, "Richard has been bouncing off the walls with proposals, trying to take over the world and drag my black ass with him. The *Mauve* project has been hugely successful but demanding seeing I'm the front marketing man for the US, South America, and Canadian markets. Brett has been out sick...some flu-like bug." He lets out a long and deep breath. "And when my ever-efficient executive assistant is away, the mice play. I have very small eyes and limited vision on the home-front." Then his eyes land on my breasts clad in one of his worn tank T-shirts. My nipples immediately tauten. "And—"

"When you have a new wife, at home, causing more grief than relief—emotionally...physically—it makes for a tight Azmir Jacobs." My eyes slam shut as my exasperation for myself stirs.

First Lady Twanece's voice pops into my head when she heeded during one of our premarital counseling sessions, *"Men of leadership and those who govern others have a short attention span for complaints. They are solution-driven and can quickly become dismayed by cries of discontentment, even from the home. As his wife, it is your job to filter complaints, and what little you do bring to him, be sure it's accompanied by solutions. Minimize those concerns that are not."*

Discovering those pictures has tipped me over the ledge. I feel aroused and guilt-ridden simultaneously. I don't have a solution, or proof that it's Dawn who leaked the pictures. All I have is gut intuition. I don't want to be that type of partner to him.

"Azmir, I'm sorry...for everything. Sorry for not telling you about my past—the shootings, the money, the murders, the secrets...the demons. I'm sorry for the nagging, the pushbacks, the pouting, the neediness. I'm sorry for trying to turn the blame on you for going the lengths you did to learn about my demons. It's all still tender, but I'm glad you're now in the know. I have nothing else to hide." I exhale. "I just want to try to give you what you give me every day."

He nods again, seemingly taking in my words. There's a peaceful stretch of silence for a while. Then his telephone rings.

"Shit," he swears underneath his breath after checking the caller's I.D. "I gotta take this, Mrs. J."

I nod, not feeling as sad as I did before unloading on him, but disappointed that he has to go.

"Since Brett is out, I'll have Dawn forward the details to his temp that will, in turn, forward you an itinerary for this weekend; I'll be doing *Mauve* promos."

I steel against the plush pillows of the bed at the mention of her name. I haven't forgotten my suspicions of what she's done, but momentarily escaped them to reconnect with my husband. I don't want any dealings with Dawn, don't even want her name pouring from his delicious lips.

"Aye," Azmir calls my attention back to him. "Don't pack panties, you won't be needing them."

My mouth waters at his carnal promise, "O-okay," I squeal and readjust myself in my seat, feeling all of a sudden liquidated that quickly.

Tonight, I dream my favorite dreams: those of six feet and four inches of dark chocolate blanketing my needy body.

Time speeds up considerably after that soul cleansing conversation with Azmir. I attend my counseling session, Bible study, and dance class for the week. My travel itinerary arrives the following day via email, detailing my flight plan and car travel to the hotel where Azmir will be staying in Washington. Overlaying my disdain from Dawn having a hand in this wonderful information is my excitement of seeing Azmir. I'm looking forward to doing absolutely nothing with him but raise his heart rate and race his breathing with varied parts of my anatomy. I also have an evening with Erin to look forward to.

While on our way to the restaurant, I get a call from April, reminding me I never followed up on her voice message to me a few days earlier. Certainly, nothing April has to offer is a topic I want to hash out in front of Erin, so I let the call go to voicemail. After listening to it, I tell myself not to forget to contact her next week sometime, seeing I'll be leaving for Washington Friday morning and won't return until late Sunday.

Over dinner and while delighting in Erin's imaginary play with chopsticks, I decide to check my calendar to mentally prepare for my weekend. I know I have a light schedule at work tomorrow, which is great. I want to preserve all my energy for the big guy. Other than picking up my birth control pills, I have very little else to do before my flight. I'm slightly annoyed that I punked out of getting the birth control shot after Azmir's reaction to my mention of it to him that day in his office when Dawn and Shayna were meeting with him.

He predictably brought it up later when we were alone. He was extremely gentle in his approach, but it annoyed me that I had to make a production out of choosing *my* birth control. I want the convenience of a one application method; he doesn't want the long-term commitment. *It's my body!* For every argument Azmir presented as to why I should continue with my current regimen, I gave him pushback. I fought him on it simply because I felt it was not his decision. But I digressed remembering First Lady Twanece's heeding: *You don't argue just to have a voice in a fight, you fight for a resolution. Love is yielding.*

Still partially listening to Erin's pretend chat, I then move on to glance at my email. We're waiting on dessert, and I want to be sure Jim Katz has responded to a report I sent him this morning. In search of it, I see Sharon sent me an e-mail about thirty minutes after I left the office. It's a forwarded email from Brett: Azmir's itinerary. It's strange getting it on a Thursday; they typically arrive on Mondays.

"Let's go on the boat and fly kites," Erin trills, totally engaged in play. I snicker, knowing she's referring to Azmir's cabin cruiser when we took her sailing and Azmir taught her how to fly a kite while we cruised against the mild winds.

I absentmindedly open the email out of pure idleness while we wait. I see the itinerary is from last week, stretched into this week. My concentration lands on this weekend's schedule, hoping my lazy plans won't interfere too much with his promos. That's when I discover Azmir is due to appear, two hours, at a function at *The George* in Georgetown. *If my geographical logic is working, Georgetown is not in the state of Washington where Dawn has set my itinerary.* No. In fact, my itinerary from Dawn is set across the country from where Azmir is scheduled to be in less than twenty-four hours.

I check Brett's information against Dawn's via his assistant again, and then three times over for clarity. Nothing changes about the locations being two separate states. *This must be a mistake.* Then again, probably not. But I have to be sure.

I send a text to Azmir:

You think you can arrange a tour of the White House while I'm out there this weekend? Don't try to front and tell me you're not cool with Barry.

He replies seconds later as ice cream and cake is delivered to our table.

I don't want your hospitality out here to be by your president. The only type you'll receive is by your layman of a husband. I think you'll enjoy mine better though.

That does it!

It seals the deal. It confirms Dawn has sent a fraudulent itinerary.

Throughout dessert and Barbie shopping afterwards, with Erin, I brood over this sting of Dawn Taylor, trying not to tip off a shadowing John. *This security thing is for the birds!* This time, my first thought isn't to go to Azmir. I have to handle this on my own, starting with finding a redeye out to D.C.—where my husband is. By the time I drop my princess off home, I have my flight booked for ten fifteen tonight. I also concoct a plan to ditch John for my early trip. He'll think he's seeing me home for the night, but I'll slip into the car later and drive myself to the airport. He's not contracted to travel with me to see Azmir anyway.

On my way to the marina, my phone rings and it's April. Frustrated, I growl as I hit the screen to accept the call. I'm not in the mood to discuss why I didn't invite someone to my *private* wedding. But it's clear April isn't backing down.

"Hello," I speak, irritatingly into the blue tooth.

"Rayna! Oh my, god, you answered!" April sounds almost out of breath.

"What choice did I have?"

"Rayna," she sighs. "I didn't call to fight."

"Well, I hope not considering I have a flight to catch in a few short hours," *I hope John didn't hear that.*

"I just... It's just that," she can't catch her words. "Geeze, Rayna, I've changed! I don't want to fight with you anymore—not that I ever wanted to, but you made it a sport almost right after meeting you." My brows rise at that statement. *What's she hitting at?* "You know, I never really got you. We never had real beef...a legitimate fight, but you never liked us...Britni and me. For some reason, all we were ever met with from you is the typical rolling of the eyes, mumbled sarcasm under your breath, and an overall cold regard. We'd never done anything to you! You know, I hate to say it, but you were that...stereotypical black woman we eventually regarded *you* as. And that became easy, because at least it made some sense."

"Stereotypical black woman?" I bark, ready unleash the brewing anger onto her that I'm trying to reserve.

"Yes!" she exclaims. "It was immature, but that's all we had to combat ourselves against you. You've always been so mean and angry towards us...for no reason! We never viewed you negatively. Heck, when others tried to paint you as an opportunist to Michelle, secretly Brit and I went to bat for you on several occasions. We never understood your bond, but what we could see was reciprocity. You adored her and...well, we couldn't understand why you didn't give us the same opportunity of friendship. So, yeah," April's voice turns definitive. "We teased you and got silly in your presence to have fun at your expense."

My mouth pries open. Revelations begin hitting. Her accusations sound vaguely familiar of me, but spot on for...*Syn*? My head won't slow its spin. These are thoughts I've had of how Syn regards me: angry to the degree of antagonism.

Oh, my god!

Suddenly, I understand all of my flaws and self-discoveries aren't limited to counseling sessions with Pastor Edmondson, or via fights with Azmir. This time they're coming from a different source. However, I don't understand the nature of her call, her insistence of getting in touch with me.

"Is this the imperative conversation you said we needed to have, April?"

"Some of it, yeah! I didn't want to dig right in like that, but you..." she sighs again. "Hear me out, Rayna. For crying out loud, we are sisters in Christ now, right? I mean, I've heard bits and pieces about the new Rayna through your pastor while with my in-laws. He and his wife adore you and that's saying a lot."

"Is it so hard to believe good people like me?" my voice cracks.

"No! God, no, Rayna!" she assures. "It's just that since Michelle died, you up and left contact with us. It's just weird hearing about your life through an unlikely party," she murmurs.

"Well, April, the last place I expected to see you settle into is a pending first lady role, myself," I softly challenge with humor.

"Shit—*I meant*—crap! Me, too! But people change. They see better and then sometimes want it for themselves. I've been lucky or should I say—"

"...blessed," I insert, certainly understanding the sentiment.

"Well, I know you have to go, but I want to say a few things to you," she informs.

"Finally, we're getting to the point of the call," I sputter on a giggle. April joins me for probably our first shared laughter in all these years.

"Anyway, I heard about you and Erin. I'm very happy about you reconnecting with her. Believe it or not, I fought for you to Amber. No one deserves to be in that little girl's life like you, Rayna. I mean that," she almost chokes out.

"Thanks, April. I appreciate that," I breathe into the phone. Instantly, her words mean a lot. "I just dropped her off before you called."

"Awesome!" she cheers, and seemingly authentically before going silent on the line.

"April, you still there?"

"Yeah," she nearly whispers.

"You alluded to calling about several things," I remind her as we turn onto my exit.

"Yeah, I know," she confirms shakily. "There's no easy way to get into this," her voice grows with fortitude. "About that sex tape in The Bahamas..."

I can't believe the latter part of the conversation...

CHAPTER 14

Rayna

Drenched in anger. That's how I feel. It's as though my entire body has been subdued in an oily batch of fury. So much so, I don't recall packing, neither much of my flight. I didn't sleep, didn't eat the entire four hour and forty-two-minute trip. When the plane landed, I grabbed my *Pagase 45* and made a mad dash to a cab. Although I observed, unseeing, the city, I didn't take in the beauty of it all. I didn't even admire the epic *Lincoln Memorial* when the cab passed by it. All I can think of was what those bouncy curls will feel like, stretched and twisted against my fingers and bawled into my palms.

I reach the concierge at the *Mandarin Oriental* without batting an eye to the opulent reception area, vaguely appreciating plush décor from the carpets to the walls, and up to the chandeliers. I'm looking for my destination.

"Good evening!" the café au lait male with a shiny head greets. Even his ideal smile can't warm my cool veneer. "Welcome to the *Mandarin*. How may I assist you this morning?"

His question makes me wonder about the hour. It's after seven in the morning on the East Coast and I don't even feel the lack of sleep.

"Checking in. My name is Rayna Jacobs. My husband is here: Azmir Jacobs," I offer.

"Okay..."

That's all I take in from him until he instructs me to the fourth floor with a key. But the biggest phase of my plan hasn't been determined. I don't know how I'll accost Dawn; I have no clue of her room. So, I back up, literally, in reverse to the desk.

"Yes, ma'am?" he asks.

"Before I settle in, I'd like to run a few things past our staff. Could you please give me the room...or suite," I include suite in case A.D. rolls that way with his contracted staff. That possibility is thought of begrudgingly. "...of Dawn Taylor or *Bacote & Taylor's Planning and Public Relations Corp*?"

My mind honestly goes blank, I only recollect several things after that. The next patch of consciousness I have is knocking at the door of a room. With my left hand, I hold onto my luggage handle, and with my right, I give unyielding, modest knocks.

I hear movement from beyond the door, and my heart speeds up in beats. I even sense someone looking through the peephole seconds before opening the door.

Lord, forgive me for the next twenty minutes or so. Please!

"Mr. Jacobs, is that you?" I recognize as Dawn's playful voice.

I'm not falling for that!

My body goes cold. When the click of the knob sounds, I brace myself. And when the door swings open and I see dark brown, bouncy curls and long, coffee bean shaded legs that run a mile long under a black lace slip ending just below the pelvic line, and all of this is covered by a white, plush housecoat, my brain goes haywire. Dawn looks very sensual, holding a petite porcelain teacup to her face, barely hiding that crafty smile. I want to break it, so I do—the smile and the cup.

"Wrong Jacobs, bitch," I calmly inform, using the palm of my hand to smash the tea mug into her face.

I hear her shriek in pain and get excited by the sound of alarm in her cry. Dawn stumbles backwards, away from the door and I move fluidly towards her after slamming it behind me.

"I tried to be so nice to you, Dawn. I tried with every inch of me, but you don't know how to let me breathe," I barely register the sound and feel of porcelain breaking beneath the soles of my sneakers. "But I can show you better than I can tell you."

Before she can process what's about to go down, Dawn examines the blood from her fingers and wipes that from which is pooling into her mouth, down to her trembling chin. She looks at me in disbelief, and I nod my head before punching her square in the nose.

Dawn screams, "Uhh!" and I go in for another jab.

By this time, she's backed up on the bed and falls backwards onto it. And from there I go wrathful with punches in perfect sequences everywhere on her I can land them. I hold her by the roots of her perfect bouncy curls and anchor her face for my pounding. And when I'm done with that, I pull her from the bed, unresponsive to her screams and the banging at the door—those are extraneous sounds behind my deafening rage.

Dawn begins to fight back, flailing her arms in defense. She even lands a few slaps. I pull her from the bed and haul her to the foot of it where I have more space to stand her. When I land my first uppercut into her face as her upper torso is bowed before me, I fade to black. In other words, I beat the living hell out of Dawn Taylor with no consideration of consequence.

You can take a girl out of the hood...

You can even let her marry a multi-millionaire, but...

Azmir

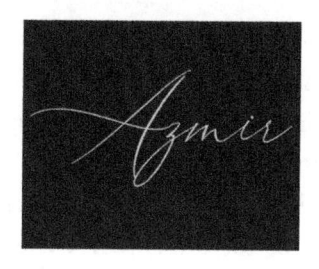

"You good?" I ask. My tone is low, indistinct.

Rayna's neck jerks up from the water. She's slouched chin deep in the Jacuzzi, soaking her muscles. She appears slightly alarmed, but quickly she composes herself, stubbornly submerging back in the water until only her head is out.

"Perfect," she replies after a few beats.

"You must be ready to eat something."

She shakes her head softly, still being ornery.

"No."

I observe her for a few more moments before muttering, "Come see me when you're done."

I then leave the bathroom, deciding to give her more time. I have no choice; she's been cleared medically by a physician—one I used to fuck no less, but someone competent and who could provide discretion—and is still a free woman considering her stupid actions.

She's fine, Divine, I tell myself.

I'm still baffled at how Rayna spazzed the way she did. I'm just happy I was there from the moment it popped off to offset any legal liability, or further physical harm. I was coming from running with Tyler, who's traveling with me this leg of the *Mauve* promo, when we noticed her in the lobby. I split up with him to attempt a playful sneak attack on my wife who had arrived earlier than I was expecting her. I even thought it was cute that she'd gotten off on the wrong floor; I assumed she was that delusional from clearly having caught a red eye to surprise me.

I even let her knock on the wrong door, stood back, and was

prepared to laugh my ass off. It wasn't until I heard my name from the other side of said door that I became concerned. And when I realized it was Dawn's room, I knew shit was about to go down. She asked if it was me knocking at the door when I didn't know where she was staying. However, when I sprinted to the door it had already shut.

I heard Dawn's scream and Rayna's seething words, though not clearly. I knocked on the door, but they'd already been too engaged in ruckus to hear. I called out Rayna's name frantically but tried not to alert other hotel visitors with my alarm. I called Marcus, my muscle, and asked him to discreetly find someone who could open the door without calling the cops.

It seemed like an eternity before they arrived, and by that time several hotel guests had opened up their doors for answers. I couldn't worry about them; I had to make sure my wife was safe. When we entered the room, I saw Rayna, wearing Dawn's ass out. At first, I felt relief knowing my wife wasn't being victimized. Then, I saw the brutality of the situation.

Now, I'm a married man and very aware of whose team I play for between the two women, but when I saw Dawn, helplessly hunched over, having recurring jabs thrown into her face and upper body, I felt a bit of sympathy.

I grabbed Rayna, demanding no one to touch my wife but me. The hotel staff, Marcus, and Tyler, who appeared out of nowhere, respected my wishes as we separated the femme warriors. After the screams, threats, and heaving for air by the two, I was able to get Tyler to take Dawn to seek medical attention. Marcus stayed behind to play the role of the *Cleaner*. With him being former *One-Time*, he knows the language to convey discretion of this matter.

I was able to extract Rayna from the scene and into my suite where she was seen medically and cleared to bathe. At first, she appeared tired and...hard assed. She argued I was overreacting, but I couldn't give a fuck.

My wife just beat the shit out of my PR rep.

Sometime later, while in the living room, going over blueprints for a new *Global Fusion* office building, I sense her presence. I glance up from the coffee table and see her glaring at me tentatively. I know this mood she's in. Over the past few months, Rayna has adopted this hard veneer dissimilar to the one she had when we met. This time, her attitude encompasses me and our relationship. She's been more assertive in arguments concerning our *bubble*. I can see right through that layer of protectiveness, but totally respect her switch in gears. It's all about her process of bettering herself.

"Well...?" I ask while I observe her in a long taupe silk robe, inadvertently matching the motif of the suite.

"Well, you said you wanted to see me." The crisp in her tone can't be missed. Her hood persona is still lingering. I have to take it up a notch to effectively handle her.

"Okay. So can you now tell me what the fuck happened downstairs this morning?"

"Are you going to listen to absorb or listen to develop your argument?" She folds her arms into her abdomen as her hip rests against the sofa, keeping her distance.

I straighten in my chair, tossing my highlighter aside. "Let's cut the bullshit already. I've given you time alone to get into a calmer state of mind. Damn, Rayna, a couple of hours ago she was a contracted employee. Now, she's a *battered, former,* contracted employee I have to negotiate out of pressing charges against my fucking wife. Give me something!"

"Give you something? Are you ready? Because I have lots to give you on the woman who we know you have a checkered history with going beyond public relations—"

"We're beyond that, Rayna—"

"Like hell we are! You should have never kept her on! Not only was she connected to you through business, but her access was too immediate. To you, that kiss was nothing more than a revelation of the flaws in our relationship, but to her it was only the beginning.

And you, keeping her around—and so close, no less—fueled her obsession." She advances toward the desk. "Dawn sent me a botched stylist for the *Mauve* event. I have pictures to prove the satire in that attempt. She dressed like *your* date for the event, in anticipation of me taking on said faux designer! She purposely put me on a wild goose chase that night so she could be photo'd with you as a date. Dawn took and leaked those wedding day pictures to the media—"

"Oh, we're on this shit again?" I snort, interrupting her finger count. "I deal with facts, Rayna. We have no evidence of that."

"Oh, yeah?" she asks, now directly in my face. "I got a call from April last night. She tells me she spoke to Britni about that leaked tape, trying once again to get answers. Well, Britni tells her about an evening after a Trey Songz concert when she and Spin were approached by a woman who claimed to have had a beef with Azmir's girlfriend. What a coincidence that so did Spin. The three of them got together and planned how to embarrass Rayna and humiliate Azmir at the same time. Of course, Britni didn't describe this woman to April, but she did mention this woman said she worked with Azmir and had enough access to hurt him."

There's complete silence for what seems like hours. I'm trying to process it all. I had no fucking clue of Dawn's trickeries but can't deny her being capable of them. I've always known she's like a cat ready to pounce. However, I thought her ideal pouncing was a sexual relationship with me, and as long as I made sure there was no way that would happen; we were fine. I see I've underestimated her. So many thoughts are running through my mind. I need to know how I'll get my wife out of this situation unscathed. I also need to contact my attorneys and Shayna Bacote. I'm getting the fuck out of the contract. This requires no further consideration.

"Still don't believe me? Fine!" Rayna's yelling snaps me out of my own head.

I don't want to fight. She doesn't need another punching bag. I have work to do before going to this event this evening. And my wife needs food and rest. If she doesn't eat, she's certainly going to rest. I stand from my seat and immediately tower over her.

"No need to get tight. I never said I didn't believe you." I take her at the small of her back and gently push her into the bedroom. "You said you're not hungry, but you will sleep."

I tuck Rayna in bed and turn down the shades to darken the room.

"I need to get a few things done. Let me know if you need anything," I offer before leaving the room.

Damn, this isn't how I thought I'd be putting her ass out this weekend!

For the past week or so, I've been able to effectively rid my life of Dawn Taylor. Chesney presented her with Britni's story, quickly quieting her threats of pressing charges against Rayna. I've given my parting words to Shayna. It's unfortunate she's caught in this shit, but it's only business to me. I assured her that if she ever decides to part with Dawn, I'd give her a reference.

Things have also begun to heat up with the defendants of the sex video scandal. I relayed to Chesney my desire to have their asses prosecuted to the highest extent of the law bearing in mind the damage they were attempting to ensue on Rayna, and not to mention the memory of her best friend who is now deceased and unable to defend herself. Announcements of lawsuits went out last Monday morning, and by lunchtime, Chesney had heard back from the radio station owning Lady Spin's show and I received a call from Spin herself.

Though tactful, she tried to go the journalist route by using the excuse of reporting a story without bias. Conversely, I wasn't enthused; she fucking violated my lady to spite me. Rayna was devastated and justifiably. Michelle's daughter could one day get a hold of that footage. I was advised not to speak directly to her. Beyond that, I could only tolerate a minute and a half of Spin's cries of indignation. I now know the truth of the matter wasn't that I'd stopped fucking her; she had said she was going back to Dalvin. *Hell, she's still with the dude!* But it was because I found someone who had stolen my attention from casual relationships entirely. That's the typical selfish and malicious move of a woman who wants to be *Queen B* to a man she never belonged to in the first place.

Rayna has gotten calls from Britni and April. And just like me, Rayna had to dismiss Britni's call per the advice of counsel. Rayna is still shaken by the web of lies and conspiracy that had taken place underneath our noses. Who would've thought Dawn would be so keen to connect all of those women that night and hatch such a plan. She had to be damn convincing and thorough, as she never knew about such a recording. What a crafty one she is. According to April, Britni said Tara had declined Dawn's offer. I'm sure it was because I'd been throwing her money at the time, and she didn't want to compromise that.

I decided to take Rayna away the following weekend to help get her mind off all that estrogenic bullshit. We jumped on a flight to San Francisco for the weekend.

It's been too short for me, and against my preference of going farther for a longer amount of time, but Rayna has to work. I couldn't help but feel like so soon into our marriage we need regrouping and can use a change in scenery and arranged this trip. We've had a relaxing time, doing the tourist thing. We rode the cable car, something she was adamant about doing the first evening we arrived. We also toured Chinatown and explored *Pier 39*.

It's our last night there and I'm returning from the balcony off the bedroom of our suite. As I approach a resting Rayna, laid in the bed, naked beneath the comforter, I notice she looks a little pale.

We've just made love minutes ago, before I went out and now that I'm returning, I see her caramel skin isn't producing its natural honey glaze, especially after having made love. Her eyes look glassy, and her body doesn't possess the usual feminine poise.

"You okay, little girl?" I go to touch her head, not knowing what the fuck I'm searching for, just believing it's the right thing to do. And quite honestly, it's disconcerting.

"Mmmmm..." she sighs and applies a soft smile, but I don't know if she's simply quelling what she can pick up as my start to a worrying state.

"That's not an answer, Mrs. Jacobs," I push.

"I guess I'm a little tired. We've had a long day and just topped it off with a happy ending," she smirks.

"You sure? I've seen you tired before—*hell*—I've even worn you out past exhaustion a time or two, but you've never looked this frail."

Rayna giggles, causing my stomach to flutter at her delight. I look at her and all of my stressors are suspended, my worries take residence in the recesses of my mind. I love her so much and still can't believe she's taken me up on my offer of spending the rest of her life with me. *How the fuck did I pull this off?*

"Either that or I've caught Erin's little bug," she murmurs. "I tried seeing her before we left, and when I spoke to her, she sounded off. Brenda answered my call and said Erin apparently caught a cold going around her school."

"Oh," I consider. "I wondered why you didn't do dinner with her on Thursday."

Amber still hasn't come around to Rayna being back in Erin's life. Gracefully her partner, Brenda, has. Brenda acts as the mediator for the two. It's fucked up of Amber, but at least she knows she can't continue with her control games.

"I'm gonna order room service," I say as I get up to grab the menu. "You want something?"

I don't hear anything right away and figure Rayna's pondering her answer. Then she mutters, "Not really...*maybe a brothy soup?* I'm not really hungry."

"Yeah, you're coming down with something all right, Jacobs," I snort while spying the menu. "You never turn down food after smashing." I turn to find her subdued smile. Poor thing is fading.

I don't particularly have a taste for anything. I'm just hungry. We had an early dinner, trying out a restaurant at the Pier Rayna was eager about, but that was so many hours ago. I notice during my search, the hotel doesn't have the lengthiest dinner selections.

"You know what my biggest fear is?" Rayna asks from behind me. Her voice is soft and almost unrecognizable.

"No idea," I murmur as I walk back towards the bed, still studying the menu. After deciding on a steak for me and chicken noodle soup for Rayna, I return my attention to her.

With the most austere regard she softly says, "Not being able to be whatever you need me to be whenever you need it." She swallows. "I have this fear of waking up from all of this," she gestures to the space between the two of us.

I chuckle as I lay the menu on the nightstand. It's more out of nervousness than anything else.

"Hey," she nips my arm between her thumb and index finger. "That's not fair. I'm pouring out secrets here. What's so funny?"

I try to never leave Rayna out there emotionally, particularly when she's revealing her core. She's getting better and I make it my business to facilitate that.

"No humor, just irony," I say as I gaze into her sleepy eyes. I'm not sure if her drowsiness is causing delusion or there has truly been a turning of the corner in our relationship, but since we've become one, we talk far more frequently and share almost as much. "My biggest fear is one day you'll wake up and realize I'm not this all-knowing, larger-than-life...formidable entity of a man. That I'm just a jack of all trades; master of none. A mere man behind the smokescreen, trying to hold on to a piece of joy...that is you."

Damn, that felt good to release.

I'm not prepared to spill my guts right now, but I'm able to share that with ease. My faith in her sustainability is gradually returning.

"I need you, Rayna. I need you to know I'm working hard at making you feel secure, here with me. There is no other woman for me, nor has there been since you entered my boardroom. My soul rests with you."

She gasps, and I can see the tears threatening to spill. I don't want her crying, that's not what this moment is about. Happy or not, I don't relish seeing my lady cry. I hold my breath.

"Well, aren't we the needy pair?" Our eyes lock for a beat before we fall into laughter.

"Indeed...just hopeless." I kiss her forehead, which feels a bit warm. "But I couldn't be in better company."

love ∞ belvin

The next morning, we fly home. Rayna hasn't improved. In fact, against my judgment, she forges ahead to work on Monday, only to be forced back in bed by noon. When she doesn't get any better by Tuesday, I roll her into the doctor, who confirms she indeed has a virus of some sort, doubling with an ear infection and prescribes antibiotics. The doctor explains her bug will run its course on its own, but the infection should ease up in a couple of days. I'm just happy to have a diagnosis and solution for recovery.

I move around my schedule so I can play doctor to her for a couple of days and work from home. The routine turns extremely domestic and quickly. Rayna stays in bed, sleeping on and off, and catching a little television in between. I work on my laptop, next to her unless I need to be in my office for a call. Azna finds his place right underneath Rayna.

When Rayna's fever reduces, she ventures into the sitting area of the master suite, and I set her up comfortably there where she sleeps less and watches more television. I cop a spot on the other side of the L shaped sofa and work, avoiding her fatuous reality shows. And Azna lays right underneath his maternal owner. It amazes me how dogs can sense when their caretaker is ill. He's very protective of her, not even letting Rayna take a piss unsupervised. When Rayna shoos him out the door once she starts to regain her strength, Azna patiently waits outside until she's done.

Eventually Rayna grows tired of the master suite, something surprising me. She's coveted that room since laying eyes on it. I caught her in there molesting the bed during her first visit to the marina. I recall that night, thinking the room would increase my chance of tasting that ass. And I'll be damned if I didn't enjoy it the first time I had it in there.

When she moves to the great room, insisting she needs a new view, Azna and I follow. She also starts eating, even if just a few spoons full of chicken broth. I feel victorious in aiding her back to health. I'm slowly regaining my Rayna. This lasts until Rayna's fever lets up; she begins to feel better and all but kicks me out of the crib. That much about Rayna hasn't improved as much as other facets of her; she still maintains the independent streak I continue to rival.

∞

I shut the door behind me and can immediately hear Azna's paws pouncing against the Italian marble floors as he heads my way. This small ritual thrills me this moment, as I've been stress as a motherfucker over this D-Struct search and police investigation. I toss my messenger bag and the bouquet of flowers on the foyer table and reach down to pick him up.

"Somebody was groomed today," I say as I ruffle his hair while petting him. Azna's tail wags in my arms as he tries to catch my hand to lick it. "You didn't let them snip your sac, did you? We need more testosterone in this piece, man."

I let him down as I chuckle to myself then yell out, "Where's the Missus of the house?" to no place in particular.

Then I grab the flowers and head to the back of the apartment. I don't hear movement, but that's plausible considering the size of the place. Rayna isn't exactly a phone chatterer so she could be anywhere, quiet as a librarian. I make my way into the master suite and scan the bedroom area and then the sitting room from across the way. I then give a cursory glance in the walk-in closet where I discard my suit jacket and tie, to no avail. By now, I know she's in the bathroom.

When I enter, I find her standing over the vanity, removing her makeup. She's wearing a pencil skirt and a soft silk ivory blouse, which, though aren't skintight, still reveals the contour of her delicious frame. She's shoeless, but still in her hosiery. My groin tingles.

I'm starving for my wife, horny as a motherfucker. It's been almost two weeks since we last made love in San Francisco. I've been out of town, and she was so sick I didn't think of touching her, even when I dreamed it. Rayna still has a lingering dry cough, remnants of her bug, which coincidentally she did catch from Erin. But her glow hasn't fully returned. And there are slight dark circles under her eyes, telling of exhaustion and evidence of recent illness, which is why I assume she's wearing more makeup than usual to work.

Other than that, she's back to her feisty mannerisms, even let go of an intern earlier in the week for good reasons. My need for her has now risen to a volcanic level. My need for her has grown so severe, everything feminine I've seen and smelled over the past few days has reminded me of Rayna. And I'm randy and ready to fuck Mrs. Jacobs. That's what I do and do well, I'm sure of it. I sidle up behind her embracing her small frame beneath me, pressing my intolerable erection into her ass.

Damn I miss this!

Azna exits the bathroom, I guess understanding Rayna no longer needs his protection.

That's right...Daddy's home to give mommy her medicine. You're dismissed.

I see her pleased smile reflecting in the mirror in spite of my solemn expression of need.

"Flowers," she notes.

I toss the bouquet on the vanity bench and then turn back to her.

"*Mmmmmm...*" she purrs as she lifts her one arm to extend behind my neck and the other hand gripping the back of my head. "Somebody's not finished with their day yet, I see."

I don't speak right away, my eyes land on her pebbled nipples protruding through her blouse. It's telling of her wearing a lace bra, and I can't help but pull the thin material closer to her breasts to see her nipples push through the fabric even more. My eyes find hers in the mirror and she arches her back felinely in my arms as she smiles bashfully. Rayna's turning me on like a motherfucker. I raise my right hand to cone her breast, and when I reach the vertex, I squeeze her nipple in a flash.

"*Ahhhh!*" she screams out in pleasure and then begins to shiver in my enfold. Seductively, she rubs her ass into my pelvis, missing the target because of our height differential. But I get the message and squat until she feels most of me.

"My day being complete is contingent on my wife's agenda," I murmur, before kissing that spot just below her ear.

"My agenda for this evening consists of feeding you dinner," she speaks softly with her eyes closed.

"Oh, I need to be fed, but food can wait."

I rake her blouse up from her sides with my fingers and lower my mouth to the right side of her back, just at her waistline, and apply small chaste bites before licking and then sucking on it. Rayna grips the sides of the vanity with her left hand and the back of my head with her right. I know she's awfully sensitive there.

"You know what those...*be*—bites...are reminding...me *uh*—of?" she shutters.

I unzip her skirt as I rise, brushing myself against her. I push my hand down the front of her, into her skirt and panties and dip my fingers into her slickness, rubbing her pliant folds. She releases a long moan.

Damn, Rayna...what you do to me!

"Do tell," I whisper between teasing her neck with my tongue.

My thumb starts circling her swollen clit and my fingers slowly push into her hot valley. Rayna's mouth collapses into an O and she has this impending grimace as though she wants to shout angrily. But I know better. My other hand slides up her blouse against her soft skin and releases her left breast from the cup of the bra. I stretch and flicker her tan nipple and watch her buckle underneath me.

"Azmir..." she cries out with urgency.

As my hands fine tune her brewing body, I run my tongue discriminately over her neck and observe her quivering reaction in the mirror.

"You were saying?" I ask, mockingly.

Rayna grinds on my fingers as I drive them into her valley. Her hands are in a frenzy searching for something to grasp, preferably something on me. One reaches behind my head and the other searches frantically for my waistband, fumbling to get to my cock. Rayna works with me, creating a rhythm to drive her pleasure. Her inexorable hip thrusts meet my cyclic plunges into her. We always work beautifully in tandem, and this is no different.

Now she's ready. I can feel her walls contract around my fingers, her thrusts onto my hand growing urgently, and less rhythmic. Rayna's eyes are sealed shut, her mouth open, tongue limp, and her entire body vibrates preparing to erupt. She's fucking beautiful.

"Oh, Azmir!" she shouts.

"I know," I speak directly into her ear. "Let it blow, baby."

And she does. She shutters all over me, expelling her sweet juices onto my right hand as I hold her shuddering frame with my left arm. My body is at war with my mouth envying my hand. I can't get enough of this woman who occupies every corner of my mind. She's mine. *All mine!*

When Rayna comes down, I watch raptly as her lids peel open and she sucks her bottom lip into her mouth, scraping her teeth against it as it rolls out. I know that look in her eyes. My lady wants more, and coincidentally, I need it. I withdraw my hands from her, bringing one to my face, creating a happy medium between my hand and mouth. Rayna watches in the mirror as I taste her on my fingers. She enjoys this shit, but not nearly as much as I love tasting her. She slowly turns to face me, still fixedly observing my caveman proclivities.

"You didn't tell me what it reminds you of," I tease as I smirk self-assuredly.

Rayna launches at me, kissing me with wild abandon, apparently contending with my hand and mouth for her essence. She moans deep into the back of my throat as she throws her pelvis into mine, confirming her extended desires.

She snorts sans the usually accompanied smile. "You in my mouth," she whispers then nudges me backwards until the back of my legs touch the bench in the vanity section of the bathroom. I watch as she, *this time*, successfully unbuckles my belt, opens my pants, and allows them to drop to the floor. She moves quickly, dousing my boxers, and before I know it, she's moaning at the sight of my throbbing strongman suspended in the air and moist at the tip.

I'm ready for her. Rayna doesn't waste any time flickering her stiff tongue on the tip of my cock to lap up my fluids. She rolls it over the head, around and around, increasing speed each time. *Goddamn!* Then her wet tongue trolls the length of me. Rayna angles her head and licks me horizontally. My head falls against the wall in tantalizing expectation. She returns to the tip and applies soft scrapes, taking me in deeper each time she does it. When she gets midway, Rayna pulls back, softy scraping me until she makes it to the apex, sucks then plops me out, making the popping sound. That's new and I like it. *My wife the G.* Too much of it and I'm prepared to explode.

But then Rayna attempts to take all of me into her mouth. I can feel her tongue flattening and then her throat starts to expand. She pulls up and then when she descends again, her neck snaps back, she retches, and makes a beeline to the toilet.

What the fuck!

"Rayna, you okay?"

"*Gooooob!*" That was the first upheaval, there are three more to follow as Rayna upchucks the contents of her stomach. I can't believe she's vomiting. She *never* gags!

I go to grab a cloth to wet it. When I place it on her neck she screams, "Get out, Azmir!" Then hurls again.

"Rayna," I call out to her. *How can she ask me to leave her in this condition?*

"Go!" she yells again hurriedly this time, anticipating another round of vomit.

Out of nowhere, Azna barks, alerting me of his alarm because of Rayna's excitement. I'm outnumbered and decide to leave the room, feeling as useless as Azna did earlier.

I don't go far. I find shorts and a T-shirt to throw on and grab my phones. As I walk out to the bedroom, I keep one ear to the bathroom vicinity to listen out for her. Initially, I hear nothing. I check my email and even return a few in an attempt to keep from going back in there to check up on her.

I'm well beyond mystified by what just happened. I've had several gaggers in my day, but that's usually during the first few encounters. Rayna is precisely acquainted with my girth and has always accommodated my length. This is some bizarre shit. I can't conceive of hurting her.

"Pssssssst..." I hear from a short distance.

She's standing in the doorframe of the bathroom, water running from her dripping curly mane to her caramel shoulders, and down her toned thighs. My cock stands at attention, awakened from its repose state and painfully growing by the second. I bite my lip.

"I'm almost done," she utters seductively. "You better hurry up if you want reciprocity." Then Rayna swings around gracefully, returning into the bathroom.

I chuck my clothes in a nanosecond and I'm right on her heels. The bathroom is steamed, but I find my way to her glistening curves and can even observe her knowing smirk.

"You sure you're ready?" I hope like hell she doesn't take the out. I don't want to force myself on her, but my body is in desperate need of a release and something deeper inside needs to connect to her essence. "Do you think you need a few more days to recover?"

Rayna turns to me with heavy eyes and brings her arms to my shoulders, melding her body into me. My cock twitches against her belly and I feel like a Neanderthal for the brewing need I have for this woman.

"I need you now," she speaks into my mouth, her lips are soft and warm, her breath minty.

"But I'm hurting so bad," I hear myself growl as I place my hands at the top of her mounds. "I don't think I can take you with delicate hands." I warn with sober eyes. My need exceeds the softness making love requires.

"You need to smash," she accurately secerns.

I slowly nod my head, feeling the heaviness in my sacs from her proximity. I know Rayna and can tell she's nowhere close to the level of need I'm saturated in at this moment, but her stubbornness will never allow her to pass up on the opportunity to pleasure me. I don't know what my next move will be. I just don't want to take advantage of her near feeble state.

Rayna lifts her left leg, followed by her right and climbs up my body, hooking her hands at my shoulders until she's straddling me. Then she uses her tongue, slowly trailing the seam of my lips while she gazes into my eyes. She's relinquishing her body over to me. She wants to help me in my need of a relief. Her tongue darts into my mouth and I join her in an impassioned kiss. As my hand reaches up to grip her short wavy hair, all I can think is how I could never resist this woman. She's my weakness, my personal carnal oasis.

Rayna reaches between us to guide the head of my cock to her hot, milky labia, but I'm still hesitant and take my time enjoying her mouth. I slowly taste her freshly minted breath. I eventually rotate us and rest my hands against the wall as her body clings to me. I pull back to observe her again. I want to see if she's now closer to where I am in need.

Rayna's eyes dance in mine when she murmurs, "You know you want it, Jacobs," using my mocking from that night after the *Mauve* event in the limo.

I rock forward, slamming into her, breaching her tight muscles.

"*Ahhhhhh!*"

"*Gaaaah!*"

We cry out together. She's fucking tight, but damn wet and hot. My cock is twitching inside of her. I'm not ready to move, she feels so snug, and I don't want to hurt my wife.

Shit!

Panting, Rayna urges, "Move, Jacobs!"

"You a'ight?" I can't believe I'm acting like a pussy. My self-control is thinning. I'm about to lose it.

"Now!" she screams.

I retract almost entirely and plunge back in, now buried to hilt.

"Mother...fuck!" I growl through gritted teeth. I can feel every muscle in my body strain.

"No! It's me. Your incredibly hot wife," Rayna scorns.

Smart ass, aye?

I start grinding, increasing to a jackrabbit rate almost immediately. I feel Rayna's thighs and arms tighten around me and I can't stop now. I'm pounding into her, trying to not hit her back against the wall. Even in my caveman state, I know the force I'm pushing out can hurt her. But I can't drive into her wetness like I need to because I'm not holding on to her, my hands are still on the wall.

I stop and pull Rayna from her grip on me. "No!" she cries.

"Turn around and grip the bench," I growl to her more on a command than a request.

Rayna scurries into position and before I know it, I'm ramming back into her tight pussy. I begin my thrusts and in no time, Rayna is moaning. She feels good as fuck. Her walls are recollecting its dweller and welcoming me in as I anchor her at the waist. With each plunge, a flesh smacking sound reverberates off the walls, fueling my ape like dives into her. In next to no time, I feel my orgasm tipping.

"I'm about to blast," I demand. "Are you close?"

Rayna tosses her head back, indicating her wanton zone. But she shakes her head. That's odd. But there's no time to think about it. I'm not going to let go until my lady gets here first. I swing my hand between her thighs in route to her swollen nub. When it's located, I rub with measured circular movements. Within seconds, Rayna's head tips back and her moans intensify.

"Fuck, baby!" I cry out, incredibly turned on by her cries of ecstasy. I'm full on impaling into her now. "I'm about to blow!"

"Go...go...I'm com—" her shoulders start to flap and her back jerks up and down feverishly.

Rayna's legs kangaroo like a rubber band as she convulses all around me. I execute three more plunges before my body jolts, extracting some unfamiliar sound from the back of my throat. My orgasm shoots out of me like fucking rocket in to orbit.

As I rest a moment to catch up with my racing heartbeat, slowly grinding around inside of her, I'm concerned about Rayna not coming from my wood. This is unusual. I've always been in control of how she comes and when she comes, and there's never been a time when she hasn't orgasmed from penetration. I don't dwell on it too long because if I do, it'll start to fuck with my mind.

It already has.

※

Later in the evening, Rayna and I are in the kitchen, preparing for dinner. Rayna's plating the food, stuffing her face with carrots, blueberries, rolls—anything in her line of sight. This is an indication of her recovery. She gets the munchies after a good smash session.

"You wanna eat here in the kitchen?" she asks as I observe the menu for the upcoming month.

"Sure," I answer half-heartedly. "Why are there such heavy meals for next month?"

Rayna shrugs as she brings the plates to the table, "I dunno. I know he needs it by tomorrow, so I threw things in there to meet the deadline." She heads out into the great room as I go over the form. Rayna returns with a glass of brandy for me then goes to the fridge for her beverage. "Why are you studying it like that? In all honesty, I did it just before lunch when I was starving." She chuckles, much to herself.

"Indeed," I acknowledge her explanation. "I'll make a few changes before bed. I don't think Tyler would be amenable to consecutive meals with all this red meat and heavy starches."

I glance up to Rayna who has already started digging into her spinach and Gouda cheese wrapped in chicken breast. When she comes up for air to find my dubious glare, she simply shrugs. I can't help but think she's preoccupied.

"Who did you look like as a baby?" she asks.

"Are you trying that desperately to change the subject?" I reply as I start into my food.

"No. I was thinking about it the other day. We don't have any baby pictures of you."

"The same can be said of your missing baby pictures."

"Uh-un." She shakes her head while swallowing, then goes for her glass of juice. I watch as her throat shifts as she drinks. "I have quite a few baby pictures. My mother brought them back from Jersey after New Year's."

"I'll see if I can get my hands on some. Are you going to hang them?"

As she cuts into her food, she shrugs her shoulders. "What time does your flight leave tomorrow?"

"Not until the afternoon...about three or so." I take a sip of my brandy, while observing her. "You cool about earlier?"

"What about earlier?" She avoids my eyes.

I finish chewing my food. "Your gagging."

"It only happened once. It's no big deal," she insists.

"Just thought it was unusual for it to happen at this stage in the game."

"It won't happen again, Azmir. And if I'm not mistaken, I more than made up for it in the second round." She's finally looking at me. "Drop it."

We lock eyes for a minute. And here is my fiery Rayna. It's a welcoming reprimand to have her visit every now and then, but I have no desire to exasperate her. I decide to forfeit and go back to my food.

"I just wanted to make sure you didn't need a refresher course is all," I speak just above a whisper.

Rayna drops her utensils in her plate and cries, "Azmir!" She then belts out an enthusiastic laugh, lightening my shoulders.

I chuckle at my wits and continue to eat, enjoying her mirth. She eventually calms down, and we enjoy agreeable silence as we eat. When I'm done, I observe Rayna finishing the last of her mashed potatoes and I take my plate to the dishwasher, feeling like a trained domesticated dog.

Before Rayna moved in, I'd leave the dishes in the sink for Chef Boyd or Louise to find in the morning along with the half-filled pots and pans accompanying them. Rayna shut that down, saying it expressed arrogance and a lack of consideration regardless to me paying Boyd to cook and Louise to clean. I didn't necessarily agree, but certainly yielded to her request. I even put my soiled clothing in their respective hampers instead of tossing them into a pile for Louise to sort. I've come a long way.

"Why do you monitor my cycles?" I hear underneath my introspective thoughts.

I turn to Rayna, "Pardon me?"

"Menstrual cycles. Why do you keep up with them? Is that something you used to do with all of your lovers...or smash partners?" Her lips twitch as she inserts humor.

I don't know how to answer right away. I finish rinsing the plate and fork and put them into the dishwasher as I ponder her questions.

"I've done it a time or two, yes. Though it's not something I've made *my* thing."

"Why do you do it?" she asks as she sits, raptly anticipating this exchange. I hope I haven't offended her by keeping up with her periods.

I find my forehead pinching as I consider her question, deciding how transparent I'll be in my answer.

"Well, I started it with an older woman I was dating when I was about your age, give a year or two...younger. I knew she'd been around the block and had an idea of my income. I didn't want the entrapment, so I decided to keep an eye on her cycle...in addition to not slipping with strapping up."

"And the other?" Rayna retreats from her seat, traveling over to me with her plate, knife, and fork for me to rinse while I'm still at the sink. *Yeah, I'm housebroken like a motherfucker, and unapologetically so.*

"Huhn?" I ask as I take the dishes.

"You said a time or two. Who was the other woman?" She rests her hip against the counter and folds her arms, appearing very much into this conversation.

"*Uhhhh...* Tara." I turn to rinse. "I knew she wanted kids about four years into our relationship. I didn't. We didn't exactly use..." Suddenly discussing my former sex life with my wife isn't so fluid. "Well, you know...birth control was entirely her responsibility, leaving me little control. So, I did the math to stay on top of things."

"Is that why you count mine?" Her eyes are wide though her tone is soft.

I turn off the faucet and motion for her to scoot back so I can open the dishwasher door. When I load it and switch the latch, I rest my hip against the countertop myself. This is hard...really hard.

"No. I counted yours because of my quick fascination with you. You were so closed off emotionally that when we started sleeping together and I learned of that first cycle, I wanted more...I wanted... intimacy and that seemed to have been my only connection in a sense." I shrug. "So, I started to count not only your menstrual cycle, but each time we smashed. It became my little obsession."

There's silence. I know my lady's phasing; incommunicado mind is hard at work. I can only imagine with what.

"Do you still do that? Document each time we...smash?"

"Not in a *write it down* matter of speaking, no," I answer honestly. "Why do you ask?"

Rayna moves from the counter and makes her way to the

doorway off to the great room when she shrugs. "I don't know. I was just going to ask how you'd record round two of this evening."

My cock springs up as she leaves me in the kitchen alone.

CHAPTER 15

James Lombardi

I smooth my dress shirt and flatten my tie as I sit in this sterile conference room. I hate wearing this formal shit. I know it's policy, but the moment I'm out in the field this clown costume comes off. I'm anxious about this meeting. My optimistic side is telling me I'm being acknowledged for successfully apprehending the region's third largest gun trade organization. Last week ended a six-month sting operation that drained the fuck out of me. I worked twenty-hour days with the South Bay Metropolitan Task Force to bring Louis Suarez and his crew down. That had me in San Francisco with a temporarily assigned group Captain Munick loaned me out to.

It was good work I did up there, and hopefully now Captain will come off my ass and loosen my leash on the Jacobs case. I came home for a few days in October and paid Jacobs a visit at the club he owns on Santa Monica Blvd. I'd learned of Harrison's arrest and thought to use that to ruffle his feathers. He came off high and mighty like a king in his damn minstrel's gallery overlooking the dancehall instead of the great room.

He's a reserved man. When I hit him with the news, he didn't react the way I thought he would. He didn't even blink an eye when I mentioned Harrison's arrest. I'll bring his cocky ass down now that I'm done with the Suarez assignment.

I wish they'd hurry...

I'm meeting Tracy in an hour. Drumming my fingers, I hear the door open and in comes Captain Munick, Major Pennington, a few Lieutenants from the division and—*Attorney General Kamala Harris*? What the fuck is this? My fucking heart is about to beat out of my chest. A.G. Harris doesn't meet to congratulate on a job well done for a case the size of Suarez's. Like a nervous prick, I stand and assume the salute.

Not even half of them acknowledge it as they take to their seats. Captain Munick nods and once all are seated, he offers me to take mine. At this time the table attendees are opening files and folders, scrambling for pages. I didn't receive a fucking agenda.

This isn't looking good for me.

"Sergeant Lombardi, thanks for being here. You're versed with who's here at the table so let's get right to it. This deposition—" *Deposition?* "...will be recorded starting now." Major Pennington hits the tape recorder and Munick begins to call out the names of all present. When he mentions the *reprimand of Sergeant James Lombardi*, I nearly shit my trousers.

He shifts his head from the recorder in the center of the table and looks over to me. "Sergeant, authenticate your presence; please state your full name with ranking."

I clear my throat and straighten in my seat. "Sergeant James Lombardi."

"Sergeant," Major Pennington takes over. "...have you just concluded the South Bay Metropolitan Task Force special assignment that resulted in the apprehension of Louis Suarez?"

I'm so fucking lost right now. What is this? I swallow.

"Yes."

"Which case were you assigned to prior to that mission?"

Clearing my throat again, I answer, "I wasn't exactly assigned a case in particular, but as you know in the *CBI*, we can make inquiries into suspicious or potential illegal activities in between assignments. So, I was looking into the Harrison/Jacobs' pros/case."

Munick moves forward in his seat. "You've used two acronyms, Sergeant. This goes against policy when giving an official statement."

I know we aren't supposed to use short titles and acronyms, but my ass seems to be on the line here and I don't know why.

"Please clarify," Munick grills.

Goddamn prick!

"*CBI... Criminal Bureau of Investigations,*" I grit through my teeth. "Detective Darryl Harrison and Azmir Jacobs...pros/case... prospective case."

"Thank you," Pennington offers. "When did you start looking into the Harrison/Jacobs' prospective case, Sergeant?"

So, the question earlier about my South Bay Metro case was just to assess my honesty and had nothing to do with this deposition. *What the fuck has Harrison pulled off?*

I take a moment to think. "Unofficially, last May when it was brought to my attention. Officially, last June when I'd gotten low-level clearance from Captain Munick."

"And you are aware that once you receive clearance, at no matter what level, the case is then officially open to the *Criminal Bureau of Investigations*, correct?"

"Yes," I mumble.

"Please speak up, Sergeant Lombardi," A.G. Harris commands.

WHAT THE FUCK IS THIS ABOUT?

"Yes," I state affirmatively.

"Have you questioned either of the unofficial persons of interest?" Pennington continues.

I watch as the Leu's and A.G. Harris scribble busily into their pads and notebooks.

"Yes."

"Please state which unofficial persons of interest and when you questioned them," Pennington follows up.

"Spoke with Detective Harrison on two occasions last year: once in May and a second time in July. I met with Azmir Jacobs in October. I'm sorry, I don't have the specific dates to present, I wasn't exactly prepared for this...event," I offer candidly.

"No need," Pennington returns. "We have them." He goes on writing for a few moments before continuing with, "In October, when you met with Mr. Jacobs, did you also encounter a Ms. Tracy Edwards?"

My mouth goes fucking dry. I find my eyelids falling as I exhale harshly.

Mother fuck me! This is my ass!

As I walk to my pickup, feeling light from the confiscation of my desk revolver, I'm seething. This is one of many issues I have with CBI policy: they focus on the wrong shit. I'm being reprimanded for compromising an investigation by having an affair with an associate of the *unofficial* suspect.

Fuck!

Tracy has no idea of the investigation.

And as a result of poor policy by California's finest, a goddamned drug lord gets to flood the streets with his fucking poison. The shit infuriates me!

I slam the door to my truck closed. Anger builds from my belly, and I explode, pounding my palms into the steering wheel. Once I let up, I rest my spinning head on the wheel to allow my racing heart to slow.

I swear to fucking holy hell, Jacobs. I'm going to get you. I will hit you where it hurts. I don't know how...and I know where just yet, but you can bet on it!

love
believin

Rayna

I'm standing in front of a refrigerator display at a bodega in South Los Angeles. It isn't the safest of neighborhoods, but I don't feel threatened or intimidated at all. I'm armed with personal security, compliments of one A.D. Jacobs. An A.D. who would blow a gasket if he knew of my whereabouts, no less. John, my assigned security—*God, I can't believe I'm using this term*—will likely include this in his report to Azmir, but I'll cross that bridge when I get to it.

I just left Karmen's, one of the women in my Bible study group, in Athens. After hearing once again about her devoted dildo, I need a sugar fix. It could also be for the fact I haven't eaten since breakfast, working tirelessly on my monthly reports. Before coming in, John admonished me about taking too long in here considering we have an unattended luxury car outside. I mollified his heeding by explaining I'm aware of the neighborhood we're in and promised I'd be two minutes.

Right now, I'm dealing with a far more pressing issue: deciding between a *Snickers* bar and *Ben & Jerry's* pistachio ice cream. *Which is the lesser evil?* As I pull open the refrigerator door, I hear sensual giggling from a distance. The distance, though, is close enough to distract my decision making process.

I glance up and toward the direction of the shrilling sounds. I swear, I'm not being nosy; it's just the sound that is distasteful. It doesn't take long for me to find the culprit. The store is relatively small, larger than a Mom and Pops convenience store, but certainly nothing you're able to get lost in. What isn't expected is recognizing a pair of eyes from the rumpus couple, engaged in a tasteless public display of foreplay.

"Brian?" I practically whisper in disbelief, totally stupefied. The last thing I'm expecting is running into Brian Thompson here in Athens.

I'm not alone in shock, even through his visibly besotted gaze, I can tell I'm the last person Thompson thought he'd see tonight. Outside of his drunkenness, Thompson appears to be a different man than I knew from all of those abrupt visits to my office. His shoulders aren't squared, eyes aren't discriminating, and he doesn't have his usual air of superiority. He does develop, in recognition of me, a discernible sneer. And naturally, he isn't sporting an Italian suit aligned so well with his haughty demeanor.

Even the woman he's with is outside of what one would ever think Thompson would associate with. She's nearly his height without shoes, but in her scuffed closed toe, strappy heels she towers him just a little. She's his café au latte complexion and is sporting a horrible auburn wig cut into a silky bob passing her shoulders. The ornery strap of her thin tank keeps slipping from her shoulder, I notice her pulling back up several times. Underneath her miniskirt, her black stockings have a run going from her thigh to well into her shoe. Her magenta lipstick is smeared beyond the lining of her full lips. Her thick eyeliner is smudged outside of her pink eyes. They are blissfully and sloppily wasted.

"Whoa," he slurs slightly. "What are you doing in these parts, princess? Or maybe I should ask who let you out all alone?" As he speaks, his body slowly pivots towards me, almost as if he's drawn to me.

In an answer to his question, John steps closer to me, abandoning his *eight feet away in areas where there aren't many people* standard practice. Thompson freezes at the sight of him, but then I see a hint of a smirk crack upon his face. His drinking companion becomes aware of his new fixation, and turns in my direction as well, wearing a similar expression.

"I see you still have your guard dog, even if it's assigned armor." I opened my mouth to counter his comment, but defeat engulfs me right away.

This security thing is ridiculous. However, it's been for so long that, just as Azmir assured when he decreed it after the fire months ago, it's become an accessory I've eventually forgotten about being odd.

Thompson snorts and turns in a one hundred-eighty-degree angle, quickly ending our abrupt run in.

"Brian, wait!" I call out.

I haven't seen him since the parking lot fiasco last fall and don't want to miss an opportunity to apologize to him for that day. Call me crazy, but not having made peace with Thompson for it still feels like I've wronged Azmir. Though he's never brought it up again, I still had remnants of guilt floating in my heart about how I allowed that ordeal to get so rampant. It was so out of control it forced Azmir to react in a manner barbaric and outside of his calm and aplomb nature.

Thompson turns back toward me; a dubious expression develops across his face. Even John shoots me a questioning glare.

"John, just give me three minutes," I murmur to him with stern eyes. I will not be told whom I can and cannot shoot the breeze within a local convenience store.

"This Thompson guy is very high on the no access list, Mrs. Jacobs," John warns. I can't believe there's a list of people I'm forbidden to be within mere feet of!

"I was never made aware of this list," I emphasize the syllable in the word. "But I can assure you it will be addressed with Mr. Jacobs quicker than you can write this two minute chat with Brian

Thompson in your little report to him," I hiss. John, who I've always shared an amenable relationship with, and I do the stare down game. The game I will not lose.

The moment John's eyes blink, I turn back to Thompson and incline my head to the top of the aisle, gesturing the location for our talk. With a short period of hesitation, he acquiesces and follows me, but not before whispering something in the ear of his acquaintance causing her to giggle lasciviously into the air. It's annoying and makes me idly wonder if that's what I sound like to the walls of the marina when Azmir and I are lighthearted with our affection.

Once at the corner of the aisle, with my back toward John and his friend, I go right in.

"Brian, you up and disappeared from the practice..." I don't exactly have a script prepared for him. I had no idea he would never answer the invite issued via voice message to meet for coffee months ago. And so much has taken place in my life, pushing this unfinished business to the back of my list of priorities. "I left you a message a few months ago, asking to meet so I could apologize for what happened that day behind the recreation center. I thought I'd have time to formulate my words, but then I learned your firm left the practice—"

My flow is interrupted by Thompson's scoff.

"Is that what happened? It was more like a *move on or have your life ruined* type of thing," he grates much to himself before speaking up and more clearly with an exasperated shaking of his head. "Listen, Rayna, what happened that day is water under the bridge. As you know I've moved on. I'm sure you haven't had a problem doing the same." He glances down at the rings on my left hand. His tone and body language reads impatient. He isn't comfortable or happy to be in my company. I don't know how I feel about that.

"I just... I've always felt guilty for how things went down that day. You were just being a...guy...and I led you to believe I was available when things hadn't been settled between Azmir and me."

I pause to blow out a frustrated breath. "*Eh*—I'm sorry is all I've been wanting to say and apparently I've dragged my feet on it, and you left the firm to put some room between you and the drama..."

"Let's get one thing clear: I didn't leave *Smith, Katz & Adams*. My abrupt departure was not voluntary. What is clear is you don't have a fucking clue about what went down right in front of your eyes," he speaks through gritted teeth. I can see anger, slowly stirring within his eyes. He throws John a cursory glance over my shoulder and then roughly brushes his head with his hands as he slightly turns. He's wrestling with something, but he's right I don't understand what's happened.

"Did they fire you because of the fight?" I'm grasping at straws. "I mean...I was expecting you to press charges—*and I'm grateful you didn't*—but I didn't expect for you to drop us as a client, Thompson."

"Oh, I wanted to do more than press charges. I wanted to sue that fucker for what happened. His hands used to be registered for Christ's sake!" I know he's referring to Azmir's days as an amateur boxer. That mention brings back images of Azmir executing measured jabs into Thompson's face. I grimace at that. "But he had the footage proving I hit him first—several times—before he was 'forced to defend himself,'" Thompson uses air quotations. "Oh, he was quick to throw that argument into the ring. And the more I think about, I believe that S.O.B. planned it that way. No matter how random and chaotic things got that afternoon, there's something very strategic about Jacobs' involvement in it all."

Suddenly feeling eerie, I transfer the weight from one leg to the other while holding myself. He's speaking about my husband as if he's some sinister mastermind.

Nope. Azmir will never approve of this, Rayna!

"He not only took my job, Rayna, that fucker took my life! I've been on leave from my own firm for months behind some *catch-a-tail* game that turned legal before I could recover from the bruises from the fight," Thompson speaks so hard, his breathing gives out.

The anger has surfaced, and I don't know how long it will be before it overflows. "And his arms...his people...his influence." Thompson exhales hard again. "Being an attorney, I thought I'd fight back by looking into him, hoping to find something that would pump his breaks," he snorts before looking directly into my eyes. "Jacobs is a *very* connected man. The things he's been able to pull off. The way he's been able to put my life on hold...put me in a tailspin."

"Brian," I caution. He's speaking words of my husband that have a semblance of Mafia in it. *My husband.* As if he's at the helm of an organized family. Or is a Keyser Söze reincarnate. "You've demonstrated how there has been a bit of a war going on beneath my nose. And I see it's caused you some trouble with your *Smith, Katz & Adams* account and possibly your firm—I can assure you I will be talking to him about that tonight. But, Thompson, Azmir isn't some ruthless underworld leader. He's an astute businessman, albeit one who allowed his personal life to take over his better judgment. I'm sure now with cooler heads prevailing, we can right some wrongs."

Thompson squints his eyes in incredulity. And I don't know how long I can hold on to my cool veneer. I'm two minutes from cussing him out something proper.

"How much do you know about..." He gives a cursory glance to reference my rings. "...the man you're most connected to in the biblical sense? I mean..." He inches closer. And in the rear of me I can hear John issuing clear and terse words of warning, to which Thompson completely ignores. "I can't say too much because of the gag order, but you should consider the man you've taken on a life with. He has loads of dirty laundry in his warehouse of a closet."

"That's it," John yelps forcefully, but without alarming outside parties.

Thompson's heedful glare stays on me as John shoves him back towards his waiting companion. A chill runs through me. One I cannot identify. He's spoken so hauntingly, and I don't understand the source of his audacity. How can he be so assured about someone who's a virtual stranger to him?

I pay for my *Snickers* bar, and we leave for the marina. I wanted my closure with Brian Thompson, and I got it. It's just that I don't quite know what to make of it.

love
believe

Azmir

I just left a lucrative signing at the *Sunset Marquis* with Richard. Now, I'm headed into a much different meeting, one with law enforcement. I walk into a low-key bar on a lower level from the outside, so when I enter, I skip down several steps. The place is half-full with patrons at the bar and those at tables. Televisions dispersed in the front area, near the bar plays various channels.

The bartender nods my welcome, to which I reciprocate. Towards the rear there's more of a restaurant feel than the front. The place has dim lighting and I can smell the aged carpet beneath me. I presume the place has been in establishment for decades, and the stale aroma corroborates that theory. I've been here before, creeping with a local assembly woman with a propensity for fucking for donations to her cause, so the layout isn't new to me.

The place is so small, yet still I have to scan the room in search of my party. I see David, waving with sheer enthusiasm. I make my way to the back of the room where I see the men are finishing up on their meal.

"D, man!" David rises to draw me into a sincere embrace after giving me some dap. "I'm glad you could make it. I know how busy you get, bro."

"Never too busy to break bread with my peeps," I greet with genuineness in return before turning to David's guest.

He also rises from his seat, eager to make my acquaintance. "Divine, a pleasure," the older man murmurs before we shake hands.

"The pleasure is all mine, David," I return.

"Dave, please," he insists. "Join us," the senior David gestures to the available seat.

This is only my second time seeing him face-to-face. The senior David has given his son several of his distinctive facial features. And I wonder with age, would he inherit his father's pot belly and salt and pepper hair. It's kind of odd to experience his aura. As humble as he's coming across, nothing can hide the authoritative air he exudes. I'm not too fervent about this meeting, but he was insistent.

I take a seat and ask, "How was the food?"

"Oh, delicious, man! Wanna order something? It's all on me, D," the younger David offers in earnest.

"Nah, man. I'll just have a drink, if you don't mind. The lady will kill me if I come home fed," I say in jest, though it's partially true.

Rayna should be finishing up in dance class, and we've agreed to meet at home for a late dinner.

The waiter appears and takes my order.

"Well, I appreciate you coming to meet my old man," David glances over at the elder with gleam in his eyes. I know the look. After being in leadership for so long, I know when subordinates need and thrive off approval. David needs that and in my opinion is due it. "I gotta shift I gotta start in like thirty minutes, so I'm glad you stopped by, even for a few minutes.

"It's no problem at all. If you're free next Thursday night, the

Black Eyed Peas are trying out a few cuts they're working on at *Cobalt*. It's a private party, but I'd like for you to stop by and meet my lady."

David's cup stops short of his mouth, midair. "Sure, man! That'll be great, bro." He can't façade his excitement.

It's weird with him. I've never been in the practice of exposing Rayna to much of my world, particularly anything relating to my dark world. However, David resembles a part of me that's relative to Rayna. His turnaround from a formal morbid life into a promising horizon, encouraged my plan to give the drug grind up. If David could reform, so could I. Rayna may never know what significance David plays in my life, but I'd like to share his eager energy with her.

"You think I could bring Sabrina?" David asks, throwing me.

With narrow eyebrows, I ask, "Who's Sabrina?"

David's cheeks go from pale to pink in two seconds. "My girl, man," he offers bashfully.

"Oh, shit. That's what's up, D," I respond in earnest. "This is news, man!"

Sheepishly, David smiles as he throws a cursory glance to his father. Whoever the chick is, she got my dude blushing. But that's David. Since his sobriety, everything is a new and unadulterated venture. You couldn't be anything but happy for him. The waiter returns with my brandy.

"I know. I was just telling my old man and couldn't wait for you to get here to tell you, too," Almost instantly, David's crestfallen smile catches my attention. "Don't worry. Dr. Halsom has agreed with certain *"provisions"*," he uses air quotations. "Whatever the hell that means."

I'm sure it means David shouldn't, at this stage in his recovery, involve himself in a relationship that could distract him on his journey; something I agree with wholeheartedly. I won't crush his spirit though. He's had enough of that.

"You'll do what's right," I nod.

His father reaches across the table to grip his shoulder. "I believe you'll be just fine, David". And here comes that look of ease in his eyes at his father's approval.

"All right." David wipes his mouth and drops the napkin in his plate. "I have to jet." We rise after him. I offer my hand and he says, "I'll call you about next week. I'm sorry to drag you out here for just ten minutes, but you being my boss and all, I'm sure you understand."

"Indeed."

"Call you tomorrow, Dad." He turns to shake the senior David's hand before being pulled into a bear hug.

"You bet, buddy," Dave replies before David drops a few bills on the table, feeling proud no doubt, and heads for the door.

I'm no emotional man, but between Rayna and David, these last few months have made me appreciate and feel things a G should never be so affected by. It's all good. My eyes go to the senior David—or Dave, as he urged me to use earlier. He gestures his head toward my chair for me to sit, and I oblige.

"Thanks for agreeing to this," his voice strains as he takes to his chair. I guess that's what an expecting-sized belly will do to you. "When he asked if I minded if you showed so I could meet you, I took it as the perfect time for us to catch up."

I nod just before taking a nip at my drink. He takes a deep breath, drawing limited air into his long and narrow nostrils, making a whizzing sound from the inhale. With hesitation, he continues, "This is hard...extremely difficult." I offer another sympathetic nod, presuming he's referencing observing a son, fighting addiction. Again, I'm moved by David's road to recovery. "Never did I think I'd make an ambivalent call I'm so sure of." Dave's eyes rise to mine and now I'm a little thrown. I can tell he senses it before he speaks again by the way his chin jerks in the air, mustering dignity.

"I've never respected a drug dealer, Divine," Dave pauses tentatively.

I take the opportunity to correct him. "Azmir." I nod again, not removing my gaze from him. I'm not sure where he's going with this, but I do know I will not tolerate insolence from *One-Time*, considering they are some of the most corrupt motherfuckers on the planet. I know this because I've employed dozens of them—legally and non-so. "And, Captain, contrary to what you might perceive, based upon our sole *and* purely legal and moral commerce, I am a businessman. One with varied resources." I give him cutting eye action to be sure he understands that in spite of his law enforcement authority, my tail never folds between my fucking legs.

After a moment or two of him processing my verbal—and nonverbal—message, he continues, "When I called you last summer after learning my only child was locked away in some drug house like a fucking meth slave..." Spit slings from his mouth as he speaks his memories of the David I found, strung out and hopeless. I can understand it was some shit that may still be difficult to swallow. "Well, we know what condition he was in." Dave shakes his head, trying to free it of the despicable memories of that ordeal.

"I didn't *know* about you," he emphasizes the word and I comprehend he'd only known me as a legendary character, not as a well-documented criminal whose file you could easily pull for reference, because *that* I've never been. I've always laid low, always avoided arrests and serious investigations, until now. "I'd heard through microscopic whispers that you were a very resourceful "conduit" for *unconventional* matters."

I want to clarify that I'm no snitch. I've never cooperated with law enforcement for legal matters. I'd always brought them over to my side when they needed extra bread and I needed to "enforce" my hustling agenda. I've also only worked directly with less than a handful of those fuckers, never wanting to get too acquainted with them. Theirs was a necessary association. It was a mutually beneficial exchange of powers.

"David is my only child." Dave's eyes shoot over to me, breaking my reverie. "I knew that my time on the force pushed my parenting to the back burner and I neglected him, but I'd be damned if I lost him to the fucking streets, I spent a career protecting." Dave's face turns a shade of burgundy. I sit back, placid, giving him my undivided attention.

"I was so damn desperate when I made the call for your help. Damn it, it was either my career or my son's life! For once, I chose him. It seemed fair." Dave's glazed eyes meet mine. "Without question or an in-kind request, you agreed to get my child out of there, even if by an inch of his life. I will be indebted to you far beyond my pension's depletion."

I continue with my silence. Quite honestly, I have nothing to say. I helped him without even informing Big D as a reference for Munick, something I did occasionally, not always wanting to merge or match associations with him. Right now, it's clear to me Dave is beleaguered. Whatever he's attempting to get off his chest is heavy. His eyes pace the table below.

"All of the suicide attempts, monies stolen, jewelry disappearing into midair. Christ...the kitchen window being broken after we'd taken his house keys—none of that compares to having your child missing for months, fearing him dead. I had to step up and do something most unconventional." Snapping out of it, he squares his shoulders and moves his gaze to me with newfound determination to get through this conversation.

"You're being investigated by one on my team." Dave eyes me cautiously for a reaction. I give none. This isn't news to me. My people informed me months ago that Lombardi reported to a Dave Munick. I could've reached out to him to gauge his position, but I didn't jump to play that hand; I kept it in my pile of cards to pick when needed. Even since Big D's arrest. I've doled my cards methodically. "And I'm sure it comes at an inconvenience to a man of your...repertoire."

Still, I give him nothing. He isn't speaking with the right type of clarity. I'll just wait. We play the eye game for what feels like hours. I will not fold until he shows his fucking hand.

Then there's a spark in his eyes, a sudden revelation. "You invited David to meet someone. Am I correct in assuming it's a *special* lady? Men of your stature don't go around introducing Betty from the Blackbook. I know you're a private man, so I'll have to take a guess. Is she your leading lady...wife perhaps?" The flicker in his eyes tells me he's done some research, but I don't confirm it.

I go for my brandy. "I'll tell you like a friend of mine has so eloquently coined it." I take a sip. "I got ninety-nine problems, but a bitch ain't one, Captain."

He gives a snort, apparently picking up my connotation. "Not only is the case, leads, and evidence futile—consequential inspiration at best, but Lombardi has blown his self-initiated case by sleeping with an associate of the suspect," Dave says, conspicuously as he sips his drink, not removing his eyes from mine.

"An employee?"

He nods. "Of *Cobalt*. A Tracy Edwards?"

Tracy, my assistant manager, is fucking Lombardi? *Get the fuck outta here...*

"You don't seem very surprised, Azmir..." Dave is eyeing me questioningly again.

"Surprised is an understatement," is all I give him.

He expects me to be shitting bricks right now about the threat of my former empire being infiltrated. However, what he doesn't know is I don't double dip on employees. My legal associates remain legal, and my illicit acquaintances stay on their side of the tracks. Ain't shit Tracy could give *One-Time* unless she manufactured it.

"Well, be that as it may, Lombardi has been reprimanded. Not sure of his sanctions, but he will be of no consequent to you moving forward." Dave exhales long, indicating the wrapping of this extremely informative confab. He empties his glass with his body inclined, "I may never be able to utter a formal *thanks*, but I can get that pisser off your back before I retire. And hope this Sabrina, David has mentioned, will give me grandbabies." Dave takes from the table.

"Goodnight, Azmir," he mutters as he takes to the door. I make note of his obedience to the name reference immediately. I'm not too far behind him, on my way to the marina.

I feel weightless with this news. Although Lombardi wasn't pushing with much, it's never a good look to have *One-Time* on your ass. The last few months of my reign in the drug game had been risky with him on my heels. Nobody wants to fuck with a marked man. Although I've been retired for months, I'm a very lucky man to have dodged several bullets stemming from Lombardi's investigation. I race home to my wife. My life.

When I get in, Rayna's sleeping on top of the beddings. Her laptop is open, and I see she was working on staff reports when she fell into slumber. I remove the laptop from the bed, then the decorative pillows before pulling down the bedding to plant Rayna inside. I carry her delicately because that's exactly what she is to me. I've gotten my piece of joy and now I can enjoy her without the threat of losing her to my dark past.

As I strip down to just my boxers, anxiously ready to join my wife in bed, I deliberate on how I've just gotten newsworthy of celebrating. The irony in it is the only person I want to celebrate with is precisely the one I don't want to know a damn thing about it. I study her while she sleeps and realize Rayna has brought me the motivation, I needed to finally leave the game. It was certainly in the plans, but her abrupt presence propelled me to walk away from it all.

If you told me I'd lose my fortune in the near future, I would still decide to leave my organization, if it meant I could keep Rayna by my side. I'll be a hustler until they bury me, I can always make a dollar. But I could never get another woman who makes me believe in possibilities beyond me. The possibility of love.

I close my eyes and contemplate the phrase from Rayna's vows —*love's improbable possibility.*

Rayna

As I walk to my car, all the way in the rear of the recreation center's parking lot, the sun's illumination is dim, but there are still hours left before it will retreat and I'm glad to still have the energy to make it to my counseling session. First, I plan to stop at the mall to pick up Erin a *Hello Kitty* cover for her *iPad*. I called ahead and was told there were only three left.

Unexpectedly, I hear footsteps behind me. Usually, I wouldn't be so alarmed, but since John was called away on an emergency this morning, I'm somewhat alert. His presence has given me a security blanket effect. I turn to chance a glance over my shoulder, but I'm unable to catch an image so quickly. I hate having security, but in this moment, I wish I had someone with me.

Calm down, Rayna! Don't be ridiculous, you're in a huge parking lot.

But no one I know is around, at least anywhere I could see. Azmir said he'd have someone observe me to my car, but I was too impatient to wait for that arrangement, I have things to do. I hear the footsteps speed up, gaining on me. I then increase my sprint towards my car...as does the stride behind me. My heart begins to race. Similar to the incident with Azmir in Puerto Vallarta, it's fight or flight. *What to do?* Once I make it to the car, I'll need time to get in and lock the doors. I could be attacked trying to do that. I can't help it. I have to confront this.

I jolt around to meet whatever is behind me, and when I do, I yell, "For what...why are you on my ass?"

Out of nowhere, Marcus calls out, "You gotta problem here, homes?" as he races toward my perpetrator.

The man is tall, with dark hair and olive skin. He wears a blue jacket, a black shirt, blue jeans, and thick black shoes, which can be confused for boots. He's scowling at Marcus whose presence has apparently surprised him, too.

Marcus is close up on him at this point and is preparing to grab the guy before he screeches, "I'm law enforcement!" He flips out his badge and goes for his gun at the same time. Marcus attempts his gun as well, but clearly quickly registers he's an officer and doesn't expose it. The cop must notice and warns, "I'm gonna assume you were about to scratch an itch that's instantly disappeared rather than preparing to pull a gun on an officer," in a quirky tone.

Marcus wears an expression of, *Your badge is the only reason I'm not kicking your ass.*

"What are you doing following me around then? And don't say you weren't because Marcus wouldn't be here if he, too, didn't consider you a threat!" I demand.

"Consider it an act of kindness from the *Federal Bureau of Investigations*. I'm sorry if I've alarmed you," he ends apologetically.

"Well then, what is going on? Do I need to file a complaint?" I grate.

"Mrs. Jacobs, I need to talk to you about Divine. There are some —" he attempts.

"Who?" I belt.

"I'm sorry. Azmir Jacobs...your husband. There are some things you need to know about him...for your safety," he continues.

Now, I know my husband's full name, but it doesn't register

with me right away. Maybe because of the way he enunciated it, or that was the last thing I thought I'd hear, but initially I have no clue of who this man is referring to.

"Rayna, man, just go 'head home. You ain't gotta listen to this pig!" Marcus pleads before turning to him and saying, "Unless you're gonna arrest somebody, you need to get the fuck outta here. This private property, fam," in his rich Compton cadence.

The detective chuckles while giving Marcus a sly smile. He then turns to me while fumbling in his back pocket. "My name is Agent Lombardi. Mrs. Jacobs, I think you should know Jacobs is a very dangerous man who's being investigated for being at the helm of a major drug trafficking and distribution operation. I just thought you should know seeing you're married into something you likely had no idea existed." He then tries to hand me a manila envelope.

"Yo, man!" Marcus yells as he extends his arm. I can tell he wants to prevent me from hearing what the detective is saying.

What is he saying? This can't be. I'd know if my soulmate, the man I've committed my life to was a lowlife drug dealer—or kingpin no less. This was out of this world ridiculous!

"Be easy..." this detective guy, Lombardi, warns. "...before my perception of your hand going towards your waist area changes and we drive out of here with you in cuffs for illegal possession of a firearm and attempted murder of law enforcement," It's all happening too fast.

"Why the hell do you assume I don't have a gun permit or that my weapon isn't legally registered to me? You wanna try me?" Marcus counters. I can tell he's up for the challenge.

His eyes are locked on the agent. All I can wonder was *what in the hell is going on?* If the agent is awaiting a response from me, he'll surely be disappointed because I'm at a loss for words. And I'm certainly not about to accept an envelope from someone who has clearly marked Azmir as an enemy. This is insane!

Lombardi slowly turns on his heels to leave. There's something smug about him; his claim to be looking out for me aside. *Is that why he stalked me to my car? Is that what a good Samaritan does?* He quietly walks off as I stand, looking dumfounded, staring at the back of him until he disappears from my line of sight.

"You a'ight, Rayna?" Marcus asks.

This is all so eerie to me. It's perplexing that Azmir has insisted I have security with me at all times. It's more unnerving to think I could be attacked at any time. So, I complied, but limitedly. I was insistent on not having anyone replacing John just for a few hours, in tow like I'm Kate Middleton or someone of social status. And almost immediately this happens. I've also been followed randomly by paparazzi. *Talk about a lifestyle change.*

"Rayna, you a'ight, yo?" Marcus asks again, interrupting my thoughts.

"Y-yeah...yeah, I'm all right. What was that all about?"

"Don't sweat that pig. They always hating on Divine." *They... always?* "You just go 'head 'bout your business. Im'ma make sure he ain't on the property again unless he's got real business here. Matter fact, you want me to follow you home?" he generously offers.

"No, that's all right. But...thanks." I'm floating in bewilderment as I open the door to my car and slip in.

CHAPTER 16

Rayna

During my ride to the mall, my first thought is to call Azmir and ask for an explanation for why an *FBI* agent would be creeping around his place of business. *Drugs?* That's a crazy accusation, by law enforcement, no less. *Who is this guy I've known a little over a year?* My thoughts race to Brian Thompson and his comment in the bodega that night. This isn't adding up. Azmir is going have to explain this if he wants this marriage to go any further.

The FBI is accusing him of being a kingpin! The rumination wouldn't stop.

I send him a text:

Where are you?

About a minute later he replies:

SMB @ a mtg Which is short for *in a meeting at Cobalt on Santa Monica Boulevard.*

I'm immediately en route there. On my way, I keep thinking about how I've missed very pertinent factoids about my *husband*. I begin to rolodex all of the clues that were dropped: the time in his bathroom at the marina when he tried to mollify my insecurities and told me he earned four hundred thirty-nine-million dollars in three years; the car he'd gifted Kid in Vegas; the need for bodyguards all the time; his informing me of being a millionaire since he was twenty years old while at *The Peninsula* hotel in New York last fall; in my bed in Redondo Beach after our week-long breakup when he shared, *"It's closer to a billion, but as far as the IRS is concerned, my assets and earnings amount to about Five hundred seventy-three point eight million dollars, per last year's filings."* Why would he not file *all* of his earnings? Only a person with something to hide kept money like that from the government.

My stomach toils as the revelations come rushing through the front of my mind in spades. I can't believe I've turned into one of those women who don't use general common sense when falling in love. Azmir has dropped so many substantial hints over the past year that I wonder if he's wanted me to discover his alternate life.

Oh my god! The trip to Puerto Vallarta! Why did I not question what business he had in Mexico with a group of thugs? Where had my sense of realism gone?

I storm into *Cobalt*, brush past security into the empty ballroom, barge through the crowd of people coming out of the elevator and eventually burst through his office door. I immediately spot Petey. He nearly jumps as I enter the room. Azmir sits tall at his conference table with one hand thrumming his goatee while the other grips the arm of the chair. He's wearing a contemplative expression as if my demeanor comes to no surprise to him. In fact, it's almost as if he's anticipated it.

His expression of equanimity triggers something deep within me. Something inside me abruptly explodes. Every ounce of decorum, every attempt at class, each morsel of good judgment and grace recedes, giving way to a violent on rush of fury. Azmir's customary placid veneer now appears arrogant to me, and I fly into an emotional frenzy.

"Oh, so the goddamn joke's on me? Everybody knows a secret about my life except of fucking me? Who the fuck do you take me for? You think I'm one of those fucking birds who patron your spot in Compton? You put my livelihood and reputation on the line as if it's your choice and not mine? And then...and then you lie to me like I'm some fucking child or subservient woman you can manipulate as if it's fucking okay! Who the fuck do you take me for, Azmir, hunh? What the fuck do you take me for?" I rant at the top of my lungs so much they burn as I lunge toward him.

I hear Petey yell, "Hold!" And he grabs me from behind.

"Get the fuck off me! Who the fuck do y'all think I am?" I scream as I try to yank my arm from his grip. *He's about to get it, too.*

Azmir stretches from the chair and reaches out for me. His long body grows taller by the second as he rises. Within seconds, it seems as though I'm engulfed in his black shirt from of the bear hug he draws me into.

"I got her...I got her!" Azmir informs, urging Petey not to touch me. In the moment, I don't realize Petey is simply protecting his leader.

As his arms enclose around me, I become submerged in his miscellany of fragrances, his natural body oils, cologne, body wash, and moisturizer. His proximity, the armor of his hold, the vibrations in his chest as he speaks over me; all of the things deluding me into the quandary, which brings me here.

Instinctively, my knees grow weak, and I'm stammered by his virile countenance. *No!* No! I have to fight for lucidity; this all-consuming attraction to him is how I've arrived here in the first place. I wonder am I the weakest target for him, because he has many. If Azmir is saturated with anything, it's willing dames wanting to drink from the *Divine fountain*. I could be a number of women; Tara, Dawn, Spin, the intern I had to fire just a few weeks ago for obtaining his contact information and soliciting him. But no. It's me who's taken the total plunge with Azmir, apparently turning off all sound judgment.

Not anymore!

"No! Get the fuck off me! I'm no piece of property you have

control over!" I scream while aimlessly throwing punches and slaps that don't travel very far because of the bear hug he's holding me in even tighter to avoid them. I yell even louder.

Azmir howls to Petey, "Is the car ready?"

I assume he answers yes because the next thing I know, Azmir's carrying me out of the office and into the elevator in this bear grip.

I scream, "Let me go! We're over! This marriage...over! Your lies...over! The games...over! The manipulation...over! Rayna being a fool...*over!*"

Azmir effortlessly lifts me into his *Range Rover* waiting in the back of the building. As I continue to demand him to let me go. I notice the muscles in his jaw flexing as if he's extremely agitated. I don't know what's going on. *Am I being abducted?* I certainly don't want to be anywhere with him. I now feel like I've opened up a can of worms by confronting him. For the first time, I'm shockingly fearful of him.

What type of person takes someone against their will? Suddenly the *FBI*'s admonition of *"There are some things you need to know about him...for your safety,"* pops into mind. I almost piss my pants. Out of nowhere, I think of the kid, Mikey, and his disappearance. Did Azmir have him murdered?

Oh, my god! Please...no!

"Azmir, let me go! I swear...you won't hear from me again! Please, just let me go. I will never bother you!" I plead as he forces me into the truck.

Once we're inside he orders, "To the spot, Ray," urging him to pull off.

I then hear Petey yell, "Yo, you want me to follow you, Duke?"

"Nah, I'm good. Handle that issue. I'll hit you later," Azmir calls out as the truck peels off.

Once we're off, I begin to sob uncontrollably against the door of the truck, folded into a fetal position. I am terrified. Azmir reclines in his seat, brushing his hand over his face as if he's exasperated.

I continue with my pleas, "Please, just let me go! I don't know anything that could hurt you! I swear, I will leave, and you will never hear from me again."

"Rayna, man, I am not going hurt you! You're my fucking wife!" His Brooklyn tongue is fierce, stirring more fear in me. "Why the hell are you wildin' like I'm some fucking animal...like you don't fucking know me?"

"I don't!" I scream at the top of my lungs. "I don't know you!"

I cry for the duration of the trip. After what seems like hours of driving, we pull up to an empty beach. Azmir jumps out of the truck. I stay put. If he's going to kill me, I won't go willingly. In this moment, I'm thinking how difficult it is to believe this man I love so much would ever deceive or bring harm to me. *His touch is so gentle. His words are so sweet. How could I totally be off in my judgment of him?*

I married him for Christ's sake!

Azmir opens my door and reaches for me. I freeze in place. He grabs my hand and gently pulls on me to come out of the truck and my body thaws instantly. I'm so confused. A minute ago, I thought my life was over and now his familiar touch has returned.

"Azmir, what's going on? Where am I?" I beg. "What are you doing?"

"Rayna," he delicately reproves as he wears an expression of concern for me. It's the old Azmir again.

What in the hell is going on?

I get out of the car, but don't take his hand. My face is wet, stinging, and itchy from tears running down and snot dripping from my nose. I don't have control of my lungs. Azmir motions for me to start walking. Following a brief pause, I begin taking timorous steps.

After walking for a few moments in obscure silence, he exhales. "Rayna, I don't know where to begin other than saying I'm sorry," his voice is hoarse and his approach regretful. "I haven't been totally transparent with you about who I am. And that's because *we* happened so fast and unexpectedly." Although Azmir maintains equanimity, he's very much restless. His beautiful nostrils flare in frustration. He can't stop brushing his face with his hand. He's afraid.

How did we get here?

He continues, "I've never been the type to show all my cards, you know? That was how I was built. I was taught to never let your left hand know what your right is holding. And when it comes to your woman, you never expose her to your business because she's the weaker species...almost substandard...too emotionally vulnerable...a risk. Love was only an accessory to life, not an essential and significant part of your existence—"

"Cut the bullshit!" I scream, emboldened by the ease in his execution of words. "You are a deceitful, manipulative, and narcissistic bastard, and I can't believe I...I believed you!" My emotions are pouring out faster than my thoughts are being formed. "What do you do for a living? How is it that you are able to afford...the *Bentley*, the *Porsche*, *Wrangler*, the *Benzes* or the *Range Rover* that just drove us here, the driver who's over there waiting, the posh apartment we live in? How were you able to fund the rec...come up with the money for the clubs, beauty salons, rental properties, movie theaters, restaurants and other businesses you have? The trips you've donned on me...the boat...our wedding...the gifts you've lavished me with? Explain that—you know what," I quickly think. "...don't! I don't want to know anything more. I'm not trying to be an accessory to crime!" I lose my breath.

"Wait, Rayna!" he inches toward me. "I'm not this hardened criminal you're accusing me of being!"

"Oh, no? Well, why is an *FBI* agent following me around and telling me you're under investigation for being at the helm of a major drug trafficking and distribution organization? What elaborate explanation do you have for that?" I hiss sardonically.

"Rayna!" he roars before quickly reeling in his exasperation, bringing his fist to his mouth. "That wasn't an *FBI* agent. He's just a detective and is stirring the pot. Lombardi decided to rattle your nerves to get to me. It was his final attempt at bringing me to my knees when he couldn't legally," he provides. "And I'll be damned if he didn't get the last fucking laugh." He turns and kicks the air.

I'm now even more confused. "Couldn't legally? Either you're a hustler or you're not, Azmir! Point-blank-period! What is it? Are you a drug dealer?" I demand.

He turns to me and gives the longest and most piercing regard deep into my eyes. He breaks it with a painful grimace etching across his dark, handsome face as he stares into the distance. Azmir exhales deeply before uttering, "Rayna, I haven't been a criminal-act-free type of guy. I've done some things that are...illegal, but that's not the man I am shaping up to be—"

"Don't give me a pity dissertation! Drug dealers don't get to fluently articulate their indiscretions!" I cut him off, not wanting him to manipulate his way out of this with his expansive and lucid manner of speaking. We are not in his boardroom. I am not one of his subordinates.

"And you think you're better than me?" he howls as his gaze turns dark. "You, the one who stole money earned by a dope boy who pushed the same shit you appear to be so revolted by. The money that allowed you to escape your personal hell. The money that afforded you a new fucking identity, leaving that poor, ghetto, uncultured, Syn-like, 'round-the-way-girl back in those... deplorable projects in Jersey," he sputters.

His scowl burns me. *"ARE YOU ANY BETTER?"* he yells directly in my face.

And I wonder is he questioning my life improving from me having fled Jersey with O's dirty money, or me being more of a morally encompassed person than him. I could only answer no to one of those questions.

"My businesses are all legal and legit! Before I acquired this financial status, did I peddle? *Yes.* Did the money from those activities put me on the map? *Yes.* Do I have this major drug ring hidden behind my businesses? *No!* Those businesses are up and running—most are even flourishing off my vision, ingenuity, and impeccable leadership...my fucking blood, sweat, and tears! I hustled on the streets and then decided to become a man and achieve the good ole "American Dream." I've worked fuckin' hard to get where I am and that shit could not be done standing on the corners, pushing fuckin' crack, hand to fist. *KNOW THAT!*" he roars, rivaling the gusty winds picking up at this hour.

Azmir takes a breath. We both need one. Things are spiraling emotionally out of control for the both of us. I can't believe I've fallen for the same thing I ran from so many years ago.

After a while, Azmir speaks again. "The man who has mentored me over the years...he's even assisted me in getting into that line of work—legally and illegally," he begins filling in gaps of what I've known of his life. "I dated his daughter, who coincidentally is Tara. And breaking up with her just before meeting you had him foolishly believing our breakup was because of you. That began the dissension in our business and personal relationship." His stormy chestnuts divert for a minute. It is clear speaking about this makes him uncomfortable.

"Yazmine reentered my life, and she was able to shed light on lots of details of my parents' relationship with Daryl. Funny thing is, I was convinced my mother had been a perpetrator, which of course, was eventually disproved. At that time, I panicked, and looked into every person I was affiliated with, starting with those new in my life and that caused me to look into your past to see if you were a mole."

Bile rises from my stomach, pushes into my esophagus, and eventually exits from my mouth. I feel so ill. Azmir jumps to help me, and I jolt back with my hands out telling him to stay away.

"I'm fine," I manage with all the strength I have to sound

convincing. It works. "Continue," I demand. He continues when I'm able to raise my body into a full standing position.

"Once I came up with just your skeletons after Tahiti, I was relieved. Everything happened so quickly...the traveling for work, my fear of losing you, getting up the nerve to ask you to marry me...it all demanded my attention and simultaneously caused me to protect you from it all..." His words trail off. And my stomach toils. "I never wanted to reveal my former lifestyle, but fucking Lombardi..." He exhales. "I swear, Rayna, I never wanted to hurt you. I only wanted to give you the world you deserve."

And Azmir really seems sincere in his delivery; so sincere I could swear someone has cued the violins. No matter how earnest he comes across, he still hasn't explained a lot of things. I grow angrier by the second. The more I listen the more my head spins, and my breathing becomes erratic. I can't take it anymore. I need him to stop. He needs to stop trying to circuitously coax me into believing all of this is okay. I can't hold it in any longer.

"Stop! Just stop it, Azmir!" I yell at the very top of my lungs. "Just cut the bullshit! You can stand here and cry me a fucking river about your upbringing and experiences leading you to become a scum-of-the-earth drug kingpin, but that still does not justify you thinking you could play God and involve me. You've had countless opportunities over the past year to tell me who you were and give me the opportunity to decide if I wanted to intertwine my life with a Teri-fucking-Woods novel!" I move away from him while shaking my head. "How dare you...you arrogant son of a bitch! More than I hate a fucking drug dealer, I detest a liar! I can't believe you made me...you made me...you...made me...love you...for nothing," I cry, my voice beginning to squeak from being overcome with the strongest of emotions.

I try covering my tears with my hands. Abruptly, I don't like being so emotionally transparent anymore and need to go. Besides, there is no way I can stay in a marriage with this man. I barely know him. I begin walking back towards the truck. I'm done. He is a narcissist, and I can't believe I didn't know that until this very day.

"Rayna!" he calls out to me, to no avail. I maintain my stride.

"Rayna!" he attempts again as his voice competes with the waves of the ocean. I'm awash with emotions. I can't further process his reasoning.

"*FUUUUUUUCK...RAYNA!*" he cries out in a forceful bellow.

It's so powerful it halts my tracks. I can't manage to face him, though. For a few seconds I am motionless. My mind is telling my legs to move, but they won't listen. Per usual, my heart, mind, and body are out of sync concerning this man.

For seconds the ocean sings long and loud. Then I turn to him, wondering where he's gone. I see him, eyes glazed, and shoulders sagged.

"I...have nobody else—" he begs before his voice gives out.

Azmir is broken. Crumbling is the placid veneer. And it hits me, he isn't asking for me to be a front woman or to be an accomplice to his illegal activities. He's begging me to not desert him in this dark hour. For the first time in my life, I feel something far from physical by someone other than Michelle. This is a different emotion, however. It is unconditional, partnership love.

I immediately feel an exclusive connection to another human being like never before. In this moment, all of my feelings for Azmir come flooding in and then some. The realization is so powerful it overwhelms me. It weakens me. My frozen state doesn't relent. My body goes cold and then hot. I'm in a trance until I feel Azmir's arms wrap themselves around my upper torso. With his face buried in my neck, he sobs silently. With each heavy exhale he pushes out, my knees fail. My tears won't stop falling. We stay in this position for what seems like days.

At some point I'm eventually able to regain control of my body and stand on my own. When he feels he no longer needs to support me, Azmir lets up on his grip and turns me around to face him.

He peers directly into eyes and murmurs, "I was wrong, and I am sorry."

Our embrace is stapled to this very spot on the beach where we stand. This formidable man...my loving and capable husband seems so vulnerable and wounded. I want so desperately to reach for him and provide loving arms to console him. To tell him everything will be okay but...I can't. I can't live past today. The day I learned he's lied to me and kept another life from me. It is so close to what my father did to us as his family. He totally became a different man...took on a different life in spite of us. Azmir didn't just keep troubling information from me, he's withheld an entire world he had created from me. I could never trust a man who was capable of such grave deception.

I break our clasp. With tears still streaming uncontrollably from my eyes as I focus on the sand we're standing on, I whisper, "I'm ready to go now."

From short glances up to his pain stricken face, I can see his eyes are glued to me, trying to find a clue as to what I'm feeling. I guess he's discovered I'm over this conversation and there is no need for us to stay here. I hope he won't press me for any answers about our future. He doesn't. He grabs my hand, and we slowly saunter to the truck.

The ride back to *Cobalt* seems eternal. It gives me lots of time to think, but in that long duration, my heart can't open to what it once was. He's lied and therefore is a liar. He's disappointed me, and is, from here on out, untrustworthy. He, like me for the most part of the ride, stays glued to the view of his window unseeing. When we arrive back at *Cobalt*, I don't give Azmir or Ray a chance to open my door. I expeditiously, yet calmly exit the truck. But I do wait for him to approach me.

"Give me a minute to close up a few things here and I'll ride home with you," he murmurs.

No. "I'm going to the apartment to get a few things. I need time to think this mess through. I've heard you out and now need to process it all," I inform. Azmir immediately looks torn. It's clear he wasn't expecting this.

I continue, "You hit me with a lot out there, you must admit." He sighs in agreement. "Now finally give me the time to decide if I want this. Azmir, you know I've come a long way with personal and spiritual development since...us. I need time..." My voice gives out on me, and my tears return.

He reaches for me. I back out of his range before walking away. As I peel out of the parking lot, I see him in my rearview mirror, standing in the same spot where I'd left him. He has one hand on his hip and the other on the back of his neck.

I burst into the apartment and fly into the master suite closet. I find two large duffel luggage bags. I go into the drawers and begin throwing essentials in them. I then go into the bathroom, depositing a toothbrush and facial moisturizer, then hair products. I dump everything I can think I'll need. Then I go for Azna's things.

The last thing I grab is Azna. I have no idea why I'm bringing him; all he'll remind me of is Azmir. I don't want any connections to that man. I lower my dear pooch onto the floor. "I can't take you today, lil guy. Perhaps in a few days," I promise. The tears flow yet once again as I turn to leave.

I check myself into a hotel. I know it's a place Azmir can easily access me, tracking my card, but I just need time to clear my head. I'm in a great deal of pain and attempting to process it the best way I know how. Alone.

I swear I'm here but an hour before my phone begins blowing up. It rings and pings of calls and texts. Azmir is in the lead, but my mother, Yazmine, and Chanell are just behind him. Hell, even Kim texts with a prayer. I feel like a bullet has been shot through my soul. Azmir has been so much of my life for over a year, even when I've fought against it. His circle has become my circle; my victories are won parallel to his. For Christ's sake, our once vanishing mothers are now roommates. I set my phone to silent. I need time to think.

For four days, I stay at the hotel. I barely go out. I've called out of work and canceled all of my weekly appointments via text, taking the cowardly route. I'm too tender to speak to anyone, I don't need to be influenced either way. I just need quiet. And I'm content until I receive a note under the door to my room. It's handwritten by Azmir, saying he knows where I am and is happy, I'm safe, but if I don't want him around, I'll have to at least pick up the phone and take calls from someone, so they know I'm okay.

So he knows I'm okay!

That unexpected letter is what causes me to move back to Redondo Beach with Samantha and Yazmine.

"Are you sure you don't want more, beloved?" Yazmine asks, taking my bowl.

I shake my head. "No, I'm full," I murmur as I tuck my legs beneath me and pull the blanket over my shoulders.

Across from me, my mother watches curiously. We're outside in the yard Yazmine has transformed into a botanical oasis. There are flowers strategically planted all around the small yard. She even has potted ones around the lip of the Jacuzzi they're not making use of. She has flower beds encompassed by stones and even installed a small fountain in the far corner, against the fence.

"It's very peaceful out here," I murmur. "You guys have turned this place into a home."

"I gotta give Yazzy all 'da credit. She just tell me what to do," my mother replies.

"So, you guys really hit it off, I see. That's great," I say, staring at the water trickling down the quiet fountain.

"You know, Azmir put that in."

I glance over to Samantha quizzically.

"Yeah," she answers my silent question. "He came over a couple months ago and help 'da man put it in. He come 'round here to check on us a lot. He good like 'dat."

Yazmine comes back out with a saucer of pie and hands it to me.

"What's this?" My mouth begins to salivate at the smell of tan mush.

"Bean pie. Ya' momma told me how you go coo, coo for her sweet potato pie. I told her you should love my bean pie then. She say bean pie is different from sweat potato. I say not really. I wanna see what you say, beloved," Yazmine challenges.

By this time, I'm swallowing my second forkful, going for my third. With a stuffed mouth, I garble out, "Well...you're both right. This isn't sweet potato pie; it's spicier. But I do love it! It sure is delicious."

They laugh equally. Yazmine slaps my mother's thigh. I inhale the pie, fighting myself not to ask for a second serving.

"How are you guys making out with the security detail?" I ask curiously.

They have to be half past crazy with it as I am. John has been doing his usual shadowing of me since I left the hotel. I have a sneaking suspicion he stood guard outside of my hotel room while I was there. Only this time I don't mind. Now that I know the type of man I've married, I find it a necessary inconvenience.

"We used to it now," Samantha notes.

"Yeah, beloved. We feed 'dem our leftovers. They like 'da trees outside; they just there," Yazmine adds.

Interesting.

"I spoke to Azmir earlier," my mother murmurs.

"You know the *IRS* is now tryna' get at him? I can't believe 'da trouble 'dat pig putting him through," Yazmine hisses.

Azmir has been in the news lately about his affiliations. Nothing significant has hit the circuit, but the *IRS* audit has been on the rumor mill. If I'm honest with myself, I'll admit to being worried about him. I wonder how he's making out. If he's he eating? Where's he sleeping? *Is he thinking about me?*

It's been nearly two weeks since I left him out on that beach. I've returned to work, counseling, dance, and Bible study. But I haven't gone back home. He stopped texting and calling when I moved my things in here a week ago. I've had plenty of time to think, and while I don't believe I'm dismissive of his major infraction, I know I can't live without him. *Does that make me some type of post-accomplice to his drug world. Am I like First Lady Drug Lord?*

Was he a real kingpin?

If I could stand the sight of him, I could get a better understanding of what he *was*. Nothing about his drug world is being reported on the news. Yazmine hasn't uttered a word about it and neither have Chanell and Kim who I met for lunch over the weekend. I don't think his silence has ever been so painful.

What's bizarre is how my period was late until earlier today when I found my panties lightly soiled. I came in from work today, threw on a tampon, and I've been feeling a pinch of blues ever since. A few days ago, in my crazy mind, I had flights of the fantasy of being pregnant, though, I'm sure, loneliness was driving that wish. I still don't want kids. But I want him—a piece of him if that's all I can get.

"What's on ya mind, beloved?"

Things go quiet. I don't know how to respond. I've not discussed Azmir with anyone since our split. I'm embarrassed to speak my truth aloud. Silence spans for minutes long as I fight my emotions. I'm struggling to keep them within.

I lose.

"I miss him," I cry...like actual tears, tears that won't hold or slow. It's almost like breaking a dam.

Within seconds, I feel two sets of warm arms surrounding me. Though I can't stop the tears, I don't understand why I feel so sad. I know if I returned home to the marina, Azmir would welcome me with open arms. It isn't that complicated a situation. Yet, my emotions can't take my circumstances. My reasoning doesn't resonate with my feelings. I'm a mess.

"You want me to call Azmir, honey?" my mother asks thoughtfully. "He'll be right over, I know it."

"Yeah, he would," Yazmine confirms.

"No!" I choke out, suddenly finding an anchor for my rabid emotions and unrelenting tears. "I'll be fine. I'm not ready yet."

Samantha throws Yazmine a knowing gaze. What it means, I don't know and quite honestly, right now I'm feeling extremely sleepy.

"I'm going to shower then to bed. I'll be fine," I murmur as I toss the blanket off and saunter into the house.

As I lay on the most distressing air mattress, trying to find my way to sleep, suddenly I heard the doorbell ring. I wonder who it could be, seeing that neither Yazmine nor Samantha know many out here that could visit at this hour. It has to be close to eleven at night for crying out loud.

I hear animated chatter from afar. *What in the world is going on?* The voices are getting louder as they come closer to the back of the house.

Ahhhh...

Now, I can hear, in detail, distinct voices!

"Azmir, beloved, just give her some time alone. Don't go running her off," Yazmine admonishes.

Azmir? Here? What does he want this late at night?

Immediately, I hear my mother chime in, with her not so inconspicuous whispering, "We making strides. You sure you wanna risk 'dat, barging in here, forcing her to talk?"

"Time, baby, time," I hear his mom beseeching.

"I just need to talk to my wife," Azmir's baritone is laden in distress. It is a tone I don't recognize. "I'm not here to harass her. Please...just give me a minute to speak to her," he demands in a manner that is not to be wrangled.

The CEO's here.

Right after that, I heard my door open. The light glares from the hall as Azmir's lengthy frame appears larger than life, quickly opening and shutting it behind him.

I lay on the air mattress frozen, unable to move, barely able to breathe. This man still has that effect on me. I don't know what his purpose is for being here. I faintly hear him finagling with his possessions—at least that's what I presume—before approaching me.

Suddenly, I feel him reaching for the bed, in search of me. He immediately locates me. I'm still lying stiff as a board, in total shock of his presence.

Is he angry?

Will he harm me for staying away for too long?

"What are you doing here?" I ask briskly.

He doesn't respond right away. In fact, the silence is so long I wonder if he's going to answer at all. The room is so quiet I'm afraid to swallow, sure he'll hear the awkward sounds of the anatomical workings in my throat. I can't speak. I've nothing to say.

"It's been eleven days since you've left me. And thirteen since I've touched you," his voice is impassive and steady. "Our bed is cold and unwelcoming since you've been gone. Azna doesn't even sleep there anymore. He's been in his own bed." He snorts, "Imagine that."

Under the darkness of the room, I smile. I've missed Azna. Clearly, I miss my bed. I grossly miss the accoutrements of the high rise at the marina. And now that he's just inches away, I realize how much I've missed Azmir's heavenly scent. His virile and robust presence. The way his natural body oils mix with his cologne has always stirred my libido.

I reach over to the floor lamp, switch on the dim light, and have to give my eyes time to adjust. When they do, I see my husband, kneeling over me in dark suit pants, and a lavender dress shirt with the first few buttons undone. I grab my cell to check the time.

"Why are you here...dressed like this at this hour?" I ask, sounding more annoyed than curious.

Funny thing when you're beefing with your spouse; asking trivial questions such as their whereabouts isn't supposed to feel so odd and inappropriate, but they do in middle of a battle.

"I just left Chesney's office. We've being going over documents—ill-formulated evidence, my business licenses, earnings, employee files, expenditures, business associates, former filings, travel...all types of shit," he murmurs as he rubs his eyes.

Azmir is heavy-hearted, exhausted from the weight of the world resting on his mortal shoulders.

"I'm sure that was daunting," I genuinely sympathize.

"You have no idea," he exhales, massaging his temples as his elbows are planted in the mattress. "But nothing compares to the torment of losing you," he adds on a whisper, looking deep into my eyes, the way he always does when he's in search of my soul.

I shake my head in frustration of him mentioning *us*.

"Azmir, I just need some time to—"

My words are interrupted by his leaping towards me to cover mouth with his own.

In no time, he buries his tongue into my mouth. I'm besieged by the hint of spearmint on his breath and the urge in the lashing of his tongue. Azmir grabs the sides of my face with both hands in an ardent grip. Butterflies disperse in my belly as though it's our first kiss. Naturally, my tongue responds and out of nowhere, my breathing increases. I've been so disconnected from my world I've forgotten about the electrical currents coursing my frame when he touches me. My body begins to shiver, and suddenly he stops.

"It's time for you to come home, baby," Azmir's weary gaze meets mine, and the determined gleam in them bears into me. "I've been sick without you. You've asked for time, and I've given it. I've even used it to think about the confusion and pain I've caused you." His eyes fall. "And what I've come up with is I don't want to lose you. I can't lose you. Rayna, I have very little reference of what life was like before seeing you in my boardroom that day, long ago. I need you—forever. No more secrets. No more hidden cards."

His eyes are so weighed. I've never seen him so desperate or deprived before. His valor is absent. His bravado, on hiatus. His equanimity, completely gone. I don't want to reduce him. I have no intention on further breaking his spirit. I only wanted space to think about if this life with him is something I want.

My feelings of frustration, loss, emptiness, and confusion come rushing back in. On cue, my tears start to fall. "Azmir, you kept an entire life—a *world*—from..." I have no more voice to speak.

"No...no! No, baby. Don't cry!" he whispers as he moves onto the mattress with me. "I only wanted to make you happy. Not betray you. I swear," he continues before throwing his lips against mine and forcing his tongue in my mouth. Seconds later, his soft lips travel down the side of my face, onto my neck.

My intoxicated eyes slowly close, welcoming the passion. An involuntary moan slips my mouth. Azmir's hands find the end of my slip and lifts it up to my belly.

Oh, no! What is he doing?

He then peels the strap from my left shoulder and kisses it tenderly. His lips light a torch to my skin, sending tingles trickling to my groin. Then he repeats the same with my right strap and shoulder. His soft, moist, and full lips cure every internal pain and cause my skin to prickle in excitement as I writhe beneath his exploratory mouth. He pulls the top of my slip down until my heavy breasts are freed and plop out. With wild eyes, he regards them before dipping his head and excitedly licks them. He exhales loudly and groans as he indulges. I feel my insides lubricating and struggle to put aside every carnal feeling to try to end this.

"Wait, Azmir..." I pant.

Mmmmmmm...

His mouth feels so good. My lower abdominal muscles tighten, alerting my conscience of my body being ready for intimacy with my husband, prepared to mate with my primal partner. With both hands he grabs my breasts, pulls my nipples close together, and licks them swiftly with delicious, firm laps.

"*Ahhhhhhh!*" I belt as quietly as I can as my body bows off the mattress. "Azmir, we can't—"

I try warning him before he cuts me off, demanding, "*Shhhhhhh...*"

He greedily tugs at my panties, lacking finesse, but signifying his desperation and peels them off.

Oh, no!

"Azmir, I have to—" he places his left index finger on my mouth as his right finger searches my private area.

He doesn't go straight for my clitoris, which tells me he knows. He finds the string and pulls it out, tossing it onto my panties. He kisses my kneecaps while unbuttoning his shirt. Then he sheds his pants and boxers. My heart pounds my chest watching him. His thick, heavy, and pulsating erection springs out strong. *My, how I've missed it.* I could just kiss it. It looks so delectable my mouth waters in direct response. Azmir is absolutely beautiful. That, sometimes inconvenient, fact could never get old to me. He's stunning in every sense—public and private.

Although everything about this night is odd—the location, the circumstances our marriage is under, our undeniable passion and apparent need for each other on an air mattress—one thing is familiar and that's the indisputable amount of sexiness this man exudes. He's clueless of it, but it's irrefutable. Now that he knows my little...red secret—seemingly before he got here—I'm more relaxed. But I have to say something before we indulge.

He pushes my legs far apart.

"I just don't want—" he interrupts me.

"Baby, there's nothing you can say right now that will keep this hungry man from being fed what's his." He groans gutturally as his body descends over mine.

The next thing I feel is the head of his erection lashing my feminine muscles, spearing me. I gasp at his fullness as he plunges abruptly. It's painful at first, but there's that thing called muscle memory, when my body recalls Azmir's bullet-like presence in this region. It's powerful, he's powerful. This is not his usual style—not that anything is ever typical about our sex. His breathing is erratic with every plunge and pull.

Oh, no! My husband's deprived. He could only behave this way because he's in despairing need of me. Of us.

He feels so good penetrating me. His thrusts are so resolute, withdrawals are regretful. I'm caught up almost instantaneously. My body goes weak. There's that delicious stirring in my belly. This phenomenon is so familiar and can only mean one thing.

"Do you feel it?" Azmir cries out in my ear over the explosive sounds of blood rushing through my head.

With my mouth agape and eyes blinking, trying to hold back my tears of pleasure, I have the most quiet and emotional orgasm to date. The only two events this could compare to this, is the very first orgasm he bestowed our first time together, and that of our first as man and wife. In my euphoria, I'm reminded not just of the magic we make together, but of our undeniable and magnetic draw to each other. The beautiful harmony we create together. The overwhelming love this man expresses to me, and I hold for him in my heart. There is no other being I connect to the way I do with this man. There is no other charge greater than what propels me to him. Here is where I thrive; with him is where I belong. This space we create together with our bodies, hearts, and spirits is in a realm created just for me...and Azmir. It is our home.

Our bubble.

"Don't hold back," Azmir belts as an orgasm falls upon him as well. "Damn...I'm...with you!"

He powerfully thrusts twice more before his entire frame judders on top of me, with quiet vibrations, pulsating inside of me. We lay on this petite air mattress, whimpering together, suspended together in orbit before coming down from our coitus ascensions.

For a while, we just lay, Azmir's imposing weight not factoring in at all. The only thing registering to me is his soothing heart rate racing to the staccato of an animated drum. I'm quickly lost in his all-consuming presence. Delightfully engrossed by his outpouring of passion and plea for me to accept it all. It's frightening and comforting all at once. His warm body blankets me from the coldness of our circumstances. Our pain.

"How are we going to get out of here?" his baritone jolts me.

I didn't realize I've dozed off.

"We?"

"Yes. You're coming home. You've overstayed your welcome," he murmurs while peppering small, chaste kisses from my dampened forehead to the side of my face, and down my misted neck. I'm melting again.

I pluck an eyebrow, "In my own house?"

"My house," he corrects. "You handed over the deed, little girl."

"I haven't signed anything making it legal."

Both Azmir's brows jump. "You also opted out of a prenup, so I can always get it in the end. Trust me, I have the resources."

Although I know he's keeping with the cadence of my humor, I have no doubt Azmir could finagle me out of my home, using his monster legal team. He starts nibbling on my ear, setting my nerve endings aflutter. But abruptly I'm reminded of his persistence in the first place.

"But—"

Azmir's head shoots up to meet my hesitant gaze. Behind the smoldering in his eyes, I see determination. I've seen this mien before. He won't be reckoned with.

"No, Mrs. Jacobs. You're coming home where you belong," Then he slowly strokes his still erect penis inside me, beckoning a moan from the back of my throat. "I can't promise I won't fuck you into insanity but will be agreeable to a sit down where I'll answer all of your questions regarding my past."

"In which order?" I muse.

"I can't predict that. I can't guarantee there won't be some fuckin' before and after said conversation either. It's been a while... too long." I hear the longing in his voice that can't be confused with humor.

I nod slowly, as my eyes are held by his. I don't think I have much choice in the matter. Azmir is giving his dominant CEO demeanor. And in all honesty, I miss this man like crazy. After having been so close to him, having inhaled him, made frantic love to him, I am in no way prepared to separate from him. I'm fully aware I'm in bad shape now. My resistance has waned. I'm leaving here, tonight, with my husband.

Azmir rears to pull out of me. My body jerks in his withdrawal. He then shifts to leave the mattress.

"Wait!" I jump to turn off the light.

"Why? How am I supposed to see to put my clothes on?"

"I..." *Quick, Rayna!* "I don't want you to see the mess made by mother nature over there. Let me sort that out before I turn the light back on for you to get dressed," I whisper.

He doesn't answer, and I take that as an agreement. I shuffled towards the corner where my underwear and tampon landed earlier, and on the way, stub my toe on my purse. I cry out in pain, but never halt my stride.

"You okay?" I can hear Azmir make his way behind me towards the lamp.

"I'm fine!" I shout. "Don't turn the light on!"

"Okay," he shoots back. "Take it easy."

Once I've put on my slip and gathered the tampon I wrap in my undies, I make my way to the door and crack it open, allowing the light from the hall to illuminate a path into the room.

"Okay," I murmur. "You can turn it on now."

And once it's on, I take off for the bathroom.

CHAPTER 17

Rayna

When I step onto the balcony, right off the great room, Azmir senses my presence and his head shoots up.

He slowly observes my Japanese wrap; I'm sure feasting on fond memories of me in this. I left my other housecoat in Redondo Beach, not having a moment to properly pack. Azna is squirming in my arms. I let him down and he takes off back into the house. He's been at my heel since my return, but I guess the elevation in open air is too much for him.

"You're not...clogged, are you?" The child-like nescience in Azmir's eyes melts my heart and terrifies me all at once.

An unrelenting need to smile tugs at my lips, "No, I'm...well padded, though."

We've made love again since arriving at the marina. It was most amazing, and I had to remove Azmir's paws from hips before he took me again. He's been insatiable and under different circumstances, I would be indifferent. We need to take things one day at a time from here on out. So much has come into play.

I move to the bamboo seat across from him and tuck my bare

feet underneath me. On the center table between us, I see a glass of wine next to one of amber juice.

"I took the liberty," he gestures nervously toward the table. "I went with Noir, but if you prefer Riesling, I'll go grab you a glass."

I can tell he's struggling for the placid composure he typically exudes. For some reason, it doesn't seem as easily applied tonight. So much has happened.

We are here to talk. It was verbally agreed that we'd consummate properly, needing to feel that connection, and we did. However, what can't be ignored is the conversation about this man's identities. I need to have knowledge of all of them to decide which, if any, I'll acquaint myself with.

Azmir clasps his hands together, creating a smacking sound. My eyes jump, giving him my attention. His brows pucker. *There is the impassive CEO.* And suddenly I don't care who I converse with, so long as I get the answers I need.

"Are you currently involved in..." my words fail me. I can't believe the ones I'll have to use to question *my husband*.

"...in drug trade? No." Azmir's shoulders are poised, and his big hands are folded in between his widespread thighs. *Oh, he's ready.*

And so am I.

"Since when?"

"Since the end of last year. I've completely resigned and have not been involved with any transactions or meetings, neither have I received any monies from that trade since."

"How long were you involved?"

"That's not an easy answer. I've been making money in multiple streams since high school," he answers.

"You then went to Stanford," I mutter much to myself. Then, immediately, I'm struck with a thought. I continue, "Is that how you hooked up with Mark and Eric?" My lips puff on a breath at the scandal of it.

Calmly, he chuckles before answering, "No. I met Mark and

Eric purely in academic pursuit. They know nothing of that facet of my life."

"And Kid...Petey...Wop?"

"What about them, specifically?"

"How do they tie into your...other—"

"Former," he corrects.

"...former life? How were they able to afford those insanely expensive gifts at Kid's party in Vegas?"

Azmir rolls his neck, cocks his head to the side, and pushes his tongue into his molars, signaling discomfort.

"I'm not at liberty to speak about Petey, Kid, or Wop's income." He gives me a messaging gaze, and right there I get my answer.

"So, *The Clan* is a drug organization," I whisper on an exhale, my eyes diverting into the distance.

"In part. *The Clan* is an organization that does tremendous charity work in various communities," he offers, sounding more PR'ish than anything else.

"Walks like a duck, talks like a duck, Azmir," I hiss. "You put money and resources back into the same communities you destroy." We are not about to morph this discovery session into an opportunity for him to justify what he is and what he's done. Azmir doesn't argue, wisely. Nonetheless, I am not prepared to crucify him. "And you spearheaded all of that?"

He gives a slow nod. Things go silent as I think. I wasn't exactly prepared for this line of questioning. Ever.

"Who are you in the music industry? Why are you so well-regarded by celebrities and people in that business?" And before I can finish with the question, I'm hit with another revelation. "Were you a supplier to the industry?"

Azmir's tongue traces his top lip. He regards me closely before answering, "Initially and unofficially, yes. Like I told you when Jackson and Lenny were here, when I came to L.A. right after high school, I'd already known many artists and producers from Brooklyn and Chicago. I linked up with them and met their people...even met some on my own. I got to know everyone I could. At first, I would get them whatever recreation they needed. Very few asked questions, and I never answered to who was the source."

"So, those rappers and athletes...political figures," I start thinking of the household names he's affiliated with since I've met him. "All those people are in with this *other* lifestyle?" I ask incredulously. I feel my eyes popping out of my head.

"First off, you're using present tenses. I don't know how many ways I can say I am no longer involved in that world anymore," he grates, losing patience. And so am I; *I want answers!* "None of the well-known people I've exposed you to had *anything* to do with that world. In fact, they likely know nothing of it, which is the only reason I've had you around them. The ones that do, I keep at a distance."

That's good to know.

"My name got around, and referrals increased. I created an image of a broker for clients, not a direct supplier. Then, because I knew so many people and had this...swag transcending one particular region, I would be asked to A&R. Eventually, I started doing that...legally," he states emphatically. "I wore these hats for a number of years, but not really feeling fulfilled or like in the industry was where I belonged—"

"But you were also upstarting businesses; beauty salons, bodegas...your club in Compton," I interrupt, suddenly deciding to use my delayed reasoning skills. I can't believe I didn't piece so many things together—*like when I was on a plane, headed to Mexico on a business trip with a CEO and his thug subordinates!*

Azmir nods, tentatively. "Yes, I did. And all those ventures were part of my hustler's mentality. I was hungry. I'd always known I would cultivate a conglomerate, but I eventually desired it on a corporate level. Many of those celebrities you're alluding to have no clue about my grassroots efforts. They only, at the time, knew my eagerness and aptitude to grow and learn. For years, I'd tag along with those rappers I came up with and rubbed elbows with their CEO friends, their president buddies...rich ass Jewish venture capitalists. I made friends and deals. I met people and made shit happen."

Azmir shrugs and sits back. "I did well in real estate before the market crashed...got bored with that but liked the flipping concept and thought to transpose it to businesses. I looked into a well-versed partner, hooked him, and the rest is history."

He pauses but for a brief moment before he brings his elbows to his thighs. "Rayna, I worked hard for every penny I've earned. I didn't sleep; I ate each meal on the run. I strategized for days, weeks, sometimes months on my next move. At night when everyone else slept, I orchestrated the streets. During the day when my goon contemporaries slept, I legitimized my reputation by rubbing elbows with corporate America. I'm not your run-of-the-mill block hugger. I've always had an end game. And separating me from the rest of those cats is that I pursued my plan and succeeded. I fooled the best of them being two different men; orchestrating two different careers—"

"Oh, my god...you *are* Keyser Söze!" I cup my mouth on a slap.

"Pardon me?" Azmir plucks his brow. I didn't mean to let that slip.

"Nothing," I quickly retract. Right now is not the ideal time to open the Thompson can of worms... *Then on second thought*...now that all of our cards are up, why not? "I ran into Thompson a few weeks ago. He..." I find myself chewing on my bottom lip.

"He what?" Azmir grates impatiently.

"He warned me about you...made it seem like you were this menacing mastermind." As crazy as it sounds, I'm spooked right now.

Abruptly, Azmir stands and walks inside of the great room. I don't see him much beyond the sliding doors. It's not his style to walk away from a conversation; I coined that behavior entirely. I wait perhaps a minute or two before I see him make his way back on the patio with a folder. My stomach toils. The last time he presented me with one of these it was laden with the bones making up the skeleton of my past.

I open it with shaky hands as Azmir takes to his seat, grabbing his tumbler on the way. The first recognizable name I see on a legal document is Brian Thompson. The packet is filled with legal verbiage, much of which I can't decipher, but I struggle through it.

And that's when I identify the words *plaintiff* and *defendant*.

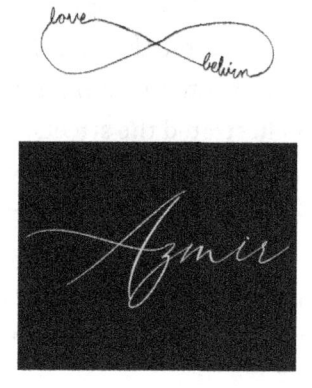

Rayna's mouth hangs agape, then she brings her left hand to cup her face. I've held on to this news because I didn't want to concern her with it. I told her to stay away from him and per John's reports, she had…well, for the most part. He did relay to me her running into him in some bodega in South L.A., but I decided not to confront her about it. She was safe from that son of a bitch and that's all that mattered. However, now that she brings it up, in the spirit of sharing, I fully disclose what I know.

After confronting him in *Wino's* back in San Diego, I had him looked into. It was for purely jealous reasons; I'm man enough to admit Rayna brings out the bitch in me. And going to the extent of having him checked out was worth being a jealous and perhaps insecure lover. Washington uncovered Thompson's penchant for drugging unsuspecting women and raping them. His track record was to have a few drinks with them, get them alone, slip them something that would knock them out for hours and have his way them. There were charges filed against him in at least two states, but his legal savvy has been enough to keep them tied up in processing.

When John reported Rayna's run in with Thompson, instead of getting upset, I thought it was good for her to see him with a woman who was under the influence so, in the event I'd have to confront her with this news, she'd see the seriousness of my call to stay the hell away from him. It seems to be playing out in my favor.

After studying the document for some time, Rayna mutters, "I-I need to lie down. I'm sleepy."

She places the file on the table and saunters into the apartment without another word. This time her silence doesn't trouble or send me into a self-doubting fit. I know what she just learned is weighing heavily on her mind.

I clean up our glasses—Rayna's oddly still being full—and go inside myself. After my shower, I crawl into bed, pulling a sleeping Rayna into me without disturbing Azna.

My chest feels light and all seems to be well with the world, in spite of the other stressors I face, *like D-Struct still being on the loose*. Rayna *was* the biggest of them all. Her being back in our home, in our bed, and in my arms ebbs the mental tension weighing me down. As I breathe into her hair, my lungs loosen, my heart flares, and my mind is able to rest for the first time in eleven days.

Over the next few weeks, our regime returns. My contentment is being restored. We spend time with Erin who has a penchant for boats. Rayna has dinner waiting when I get in and sometimes we leave together in the mornings. I get busy with work, per usual, and this includes ripping into to Kid's ass about locating D-Struct. I'm baffled by the hold up and don't waste an opportunity letting Kid know.

The *IRS* probe subsides as my team, and I provide what the government asks for and then some. Chesney's inclination to outwit them also keeps my head above water. The attack will take months to victor, but the turbulence recedes in almost no time. That fucking Lombardi set off alarms I insulated myself from over a decade ago when I mapped out my plan of one day getting the fuck out of the game. He may have rattled my boat with informing Rayna of my former life, but she stuck it to his ass when she decided to stay with me. I plan to finish his ass with a multimillion-dollar lawsuit for fucking harassment as soon as I'm cleared with this *IRS* bullshit.

I eventually realize Rayna's sick again. I suppose spending so much time with a toddler would wreak havoc on your immune system. She's been sluggish getting out of bed and takes long periods in the bathroom in the mornings. Even her breakfast orders to Chef Boyd are light and barely eaten. One day, I came home early to grab something from the office and found her sprawled out on the couch in the great room. I didn't question her, just made sure she was okay and had everything she needed before heading back out—actually I was shooed out in her crankiness. A sleepy Rayna is a cantankerous Rayna. It hadn't bothered me in the least bit. My lady is home. The castle is now perfectly settled because of her return.

It's the night before I'm due in Phoenix, when I come through the door, a waggling Azna meets me. I'm damp from sweat. I balled with Mark and Eric, which was less of a recreational activity and more of a sport in comedic comebacks and staying above the physical fray for Eric and Mark. They really need to invest more time in their bodies. I enjoy being with my corny ass friends and took it all in good fun.

In the master suite, I let Azna down and crawl on top of the bed to lay behind Rayna. Her back is to me and she's underneath the sheets with her housecoat on. I don't know if her current illness has caused her to feel a delusional sense of cold or what, but she's snuggled tightly under all the fabric. Her right arm instinctively comes up and wraps around my neck. She's chewing gum, something she's been doing lots of lately, either that or sucking on candy. I cup her at the waist and breathe into her neck, getting aroused by the familiar scent.

"*Ewwwww...* Jacobs, you reek!" she screeches as she crunches into a fetal position.

Rayna never minds my odor after a workout or playing ball, in fact, she never utters a complaint. So I roll my tongue over the smooth skin of her neck. Rayna moans as she recoils, innately yielding to my need of her. That's all I need to know. I still impact her sexually.

"Be right back. I'm gonna shower," I growl in her ear and regretfully leave the bed.

As I shower, I concoct a plan as to how I'm going to take my wife and bring her to another spine trembling orgasm, even consider bringing out the cuffs, making her ride me rodeo with no hands. I rush through my shower and hurriedly rinse off, foregoing the usual beating of my muscles underneath the scorching cascade. Once I'm toweled dry, I all but leap back into the bedroom only to find my wife, not only sleeping, but snuffling in slumber.

Fuck.

I feel brute for sulking, but I can't lie, my sacs are heavier than a motherfucker. It's been a few weeks. Nonetheless, I won't wake her healing body. As I peel her out of her robe and tuck her in, I hope whatever new germs she's caught from Erin quickly dissipate and when I return from Phoenix, I can indulge in her playground again.

I end up back in my office to make a few calls and send out emails in preparation for my trip.

love ∞ belien

Rayna

"Hi, Rayna!" Dr. Barnes greets with her *Ruby Woo* stained lips.

Although I've been waiting in here for over a half an hour, I can't help but appreciate she's definitely a diva with her straight bangs and long tresses falling beneath her shoulder into a bob cut to precision.

She hooks her black *Charlotte Olympia* pumps into the roller stool and gracefully slides it underneath her and sits. I know these shoes because the last time I was here for my annual, I'd worn the same *Charlotte Debonaire* platform pump and she animatedly commented on how she had the same pair she primarily wore for work. That struck me as funny as she was wearing a pair of *Yves Saint Laurent Tribtoo* patent pumps that day. I recall because they were patent leather, and I don't do patent leather...well until that day when I saw how Dr. Barnes rocked them fiercely.

My phone goes off for the second time since I've been here. It's Azmir, and I'm afraid to answer for fear he'll ask where I am. If I mention GYN, all types of bells will sound in his over-involved-in-Rayna's-feminine-world mind. I send him to voicemail and returned my attention back to the task at hand. I recall how I've sent him out of town without a release. That's something I don't typically practice. I make it my business to drain Azmir before each departure unless something unavoidable presents itself.

"What can we do for you today, chica?" Dr. Barnes smiles her dazzling, two-million-dollar smile. She's up there with Azmir per her alignment. "You were here hardly six months ago," she comments while skimming my file.

This doctor is fierce and that is the only way I can describe her.

She looks to be barely thirty years old and always wears a full face, primed with tactful colors against her flawless chestnut skin. She runs her own practice and is very responsive to my questions about my body. I know of her through Michelle from years ago. When I decided to dump my old GYN, Dr. Barnes was the first practice I looked up and I've have been hooked since my first visit. There aren't too many young, stylish, and competent professionals I come across. Michelle used to say Dr. Barnes reminded her of me. I didn't see it. This chick could sit me in a corner with all of her swag.

I lick my dry lips as I try to formulate my words. "Well, Doc B," I stall. "I've been a little off lately." I trace my lip with my left thumb.

"Damn! I forgot all about your wedding!" she trills in her valley girl manner, lifting my hand to admire my rings. "How was it? I've heard about your husband, chica. He's a big fish!" She's all teeth, full-on glittering smile. "Girl, you know how hard it is for us black professional women to hook a good one! You did that and beyond," she gleams.

"Yeah," I sigh ruefully. *I do*. "He's definitely been hooked," I retort with a faux smile, thinking about how Azmir would *really* be hooked if I am, in fact, with child.

"Okay, chica. What can I do you for today?" she flicks her long and behaved weave I struggle with if it's a weave at all, this is how immaculate this woman is.

"Well, I've been sick lately. I was diagnosed with a virus and an ear infection a few weeks ago, and while I think I'm over them, I'm now feeling queasy a lot—"

Dr. Barnes' phone trills, and she pulls it out and punches the keys to reply to it.

"It's just that it's been a whimsical month, at best," I murmur pathetically.

Dr. Barnes narrows her perfectly arched brows. "No honeymoon period in newlywed land? I can hardly imagine that if you're here," she observes pretty accurately on a lifted brow, which helps break the ice.

Okay...I can do this.

My phone goes off again. It's Chanell calling. I send it straight to voicemail.

I offer a light smile, a fortifying move on my part. "I missed my pills for two days last month...about a week after the wedding. I hopped on a plane and forgot to pick them up before heading to the airport." I shake my head. "I didn't realize it until I was on the flight back home."

"Okay," she gives a comforting nod as though she knows there's more to come.

My phone sounds again. It's Azmir again. I've honestly been here way longer than I anticipated. I can't continue to ignore my husband's calls, especially when he's out of town.

Just a few more minutes, A.D.

"And then I got sick about a week after. I was prescribed antibiotics. My admin assistant so happened to have walked in my office one day while I was taking one of the last pills and reminded me the antibiotic can contravene birth control pills. And now I'm late...and sick."

"Yes, their concomitant use causes the contraceptive to fail," she affirms. "What kind of symptoms, chica?"

"Some are not all that dissimilar to the ones I experienced last August. But then, just a few weeks ago, I was spotting. It wasn't my usual flow, but enough for me to use tampons for about a day and a half," I hint over.

"Ooooooh," Dr. Barnes recognizes my panic.

The phone in the exam room buzzes and her front desk person says she's needed for a code red in another room. Dr. Barnes goes into a cabinet and pulls out a plastic cup with a lid before strutting back towards to me.

"Okay, Rayna," she turns to me. "I have to respond to that. I'll have Patti come in and collect your urine and go over some information with you while we wait on the results of your pregnancy test." She pats me on the leg, "Don't panic. I'm sure either way, that hunk of a man of yours will be just fine." I'm hit with a waft of her, I'm sure, designer eau de toilette as she turns on her heels for the door. "And thanks for your patience with me today. This place has been a zoo," she sighs just before closing the door.

My shoulders collapse. I think in a perfect world, I was expecting her to tell me I was premature in my concerns. I can't believe I'm taking a pregnancy test less than two months after being married!

I throw my sagging body off the table and saunter over to the en suite bathroom and do my duty. Once I'm done and sitting back on the table, my mind starts racing with fear. Fear of losing him. *What if he thinks this was all a scheme to get his money? What if when he told me he wants kids he didn't mean this soon? What if he's changed his mind about wanting to be a father at all?* Would *he* leave *me*?

My phone goes off again. It's Chanell and this time I could use her trivial gossip as a distraction.

"Yeah, C?"

"We been tryna' call you for a mad long time, yo'!" I can hear tears in her voice.

"What's wrong?"

"Divine hopped on a plane. He tried to call you before he took off. Kid got capped. It ain't looking good, yo'," Chanell shrieks and then I hear the pending cry. My mouth drops.

"I'm so sorry, C. What can I do?"

She sniffles, "Divine said meet him at home and don't move 'til he gets there, okay?"

I nod my head, before catching myself. She couldn't see me. "O-okay, C. Please keep me posted."

"A'ight, yo'. I gotta go. Wop just pulled up. We going to check out dude now," she advises before hanging up.

I jump off the table and pace the room. Azmir must be beside himself. I don't know if this is a common occurrence in his other world, at least he's never said. I don't recall hearing about shootings or deaths this close to his circle. I will myself to stay and wait for Patti, even she's behind today. I eventually decide to get dressed so I can make myself available for Azmir when he returns from Arizona. I'll just have to come back to sort this out later with Dr. Barnes.

love ∞ believe

It isn't until well after midnight when Azmir gets home. As he saunters into the master suite, he appears zombified, making his way to me. His shoulders don't hold their usual grace and confidence. His head is dipped and not well supported by his neck. His eyes are heavy and haunted. My fearless, commanding mogul is visibly wretched.

He stands there for long seconds before saying, "I'm sorry. I'm sure you've heard about Kid's death. I had to make sure to touch his family and talk to a few friends."

I nod slowly. "Yes, baby, I've heard. I'm so sorry," I barely breathe out.

Chanell sent a text with the horrific news hours ago. I'm still in shock. I can't believe Kid's dead.

I'm frozen, numb in fear. I don't know if I can grab his long, solid frame into me the way my arms itch to console him. I've never seen him so doleful.

"Is there anything I can do?" I feel like an idiot for uttering that, but I have to say something...offer something.

"I'm going to take a shower," he mumbles before turning on his heels.

My heart constricts in my chest. A pang runs through my upper torso as I observe his desolate gait into the bathroom. Moments later, after I hear the shower running, I crawl from beneath the bedding and go into the bathroom. Our connection is so magnetic that being even in the next room feels inadequate. I see Azmir has doused his clothes into a pile on the floor. I quickly sweep them up and discard them appropriately to be laundered. Then I briskly skip into the walk-in closet to retrieve his favorite house attire: basketball shorts, white tank T-shirt and black ankle socks.

Once he's done with his shower, I watch Azmir dry and clothe himself, helplessly from the bench. Like the foolish woman I am, I even turn away while he's indecent as to not give a second to ogling. His sheen, chocolate shell never fails to do things to me, even in my body's mercurial state. I feel useless. I don't know what to say or what to do.

We walk out into the master suite and climb into bed. I wait for Azmir to find his comfort before I snuggle behind him, roping my arm around his bubbled abdomen. Azmir audibly sucks in air, and I can feel his body go rigid, but I plant myself against his long frame. I know this is unusual for him; I always stay to my side of the bed while sleeping unless he calls me over. But tonight is different. My big guy is hurting and it's my job to console him, being what he needs when he needs me to be it.

I'm thrown from my sleep by a frightening yelp. I twist around to find a trembling Azmir sitting on the edge of the bed. He's out of breath, skin is clammy, and goose bumps are disbursed throughout his torso. This time I do throw my arms around him, needing to help him land from whatever nightmare he's just escaped.

"It's okay. It's okay," I whispered in his ear, my face pinned against the back of his head.

His body eerily jerks. Any other time I would have been scared out of my mind, but in this moment my first inclination—my natural inclination—is to comfort him. I squeeze him and rain scant kisses from his face to his neck, not in a salacious manner, but a soothing one instead. We stay this way for long minutes until I'm able to coax him back down into the bed and shower him with words of assurance and comfort as he does me when my nightmares surface. It works. Azmir is asleep in my arms within minutes, breathing softly. This time I don't return to my corner of the bed. I remain at his side until we're both awakened by sunlight.

The next few days are similar to that night. Azmir is a ghost of himself, somewhat despondent, uncharacteristically taciturn. He goes about his days, but I'm worried about him, constantly checking in with Brett who reports of his reticent behavior but assures his business astute is still intact. I orchestrate shorter workdays, even covertly contacting Richard, his *Global Fusions* partner, to take on Azmir's travels for the next week at least. Azmir is so aloof that either he doesn't realize his early arrivals home to me at night or doesn't have the energy to fight me on it. He retreats into his office until I call him for dinner and a bath. We do lots of quiet bath time. The silence doesn't disturb me at all; I have my own cross to bear…alone.

The day to put Kid to rest arrives. It's the greyest day, reminding me of Michelle's funeral. Azmir's rigid the entire event. I almost feel every bunched muscle of his frame as I sit just about underneath him the entire service. It's a sad event. I've never seen so many hardcore thugs, bawling into their knees in one place. Their wails are frightening loud pitches. It makes me clench to a stoic Azmir even tighter.

Azmir holds it together well. He and Petey sit tall and military-like, just behind Syn and Kid's immediate family during the service. They don't flinch and hardly blink. I don't know how they're able to hold a public face. I know Kid's death is taunting Azmir within. I'm not able to hold on to my tears. They seep of their own will. Kid was such a respectable guy to me. Of his memory, all I can think of is his little bop in the club in Vegas for his birthday. He held his bottle of bubbly, contently smiling and dancing blissfully by himself.

love ∞ believe

"You gotta get duke up outta here, Rayna," I hear from just behind me, perhaps a little too close because it startles me.

I nearly leap in place before turning around to find a pensive Petey, peering into me. We're standing in the hallway of Syn and Kid's home, facing their kitchen. People are moving all about the house, attending his post-repast gathering. Children are running about. There's a game of football going on outside with thuggish men, sporting casual attire, attempting something appropriate for a funeral. Azmir has been standing here for nearly ten minutes now in a grieving fog. Like his shadow, I'm glued to his back as I hold a Styrofoam cup of ginger ale to help with my queasiness. I need to eat but won't dare utter a complaint to Azmir. If he hasn't eaten, neither will I. The soda has helped marginally.

Observing Petey, my belly toils even more. I knew something was majorly off with being here, but he just solidified it with the signaling look in his eyes. I don't say anything, don't have to. With my eyes glued to his, I give a slight nod and turn to a haunted Azmir.

"Jacobs," I whisper to him, pretty much in his shoulder as I can't reach his ear without standing on my tipsiest of toes in heels. "Petey is saying we need to leave."

A melancholy Azmir beholds me from above, and while processing my message, turns his attention behind me to Petey. I glance over to Petey and catch him giving Azmir an affirming nod. It's all so strange, but I'm accustomed to their peculiar dynamics by now. Petey's eyes make their way back to me, silently messaging his urgency. I slowly grabbed Azmir's hand and start making my way toward the front door. And without dispute, he follows obediently.

As we're just mere feet away from Azmir's truck, I ask for the keys so I can drive. He pauses, considering my call. I'm prepared to be stern in my request. It's clear Azmir is a shell of himself and rightfully so, he'd just buried one of his closest friends. I feel the overwhelming urge to cover him in my bosom and nurture him until his strength and resolve returns.

Azmir goes into his suit jacket pocket and as I watch him pull his arm out, I hear, "Yeah, that's what I thought! Don't bring her ass back 'round my way again!"

Simultaneously, Azmir and I stop to see what was going on. I turn to find a brazened Syn. It seems as though she's just been made aware of me being in her home. I can't believe her balls to take me on after having laid her lifelong partner to rest merely hours ago. A few people, including Petey, ran to quiet her, some, I'm sure, to comfort her.

"No! I hate 'dat bitch!" Syn spews and I realize her eyes are directly on me. "You's a stuck up, high saditty bitch who think they shit don't stink! Bring yo' ass 'round here again and next time ain't nobody gon' keep me from whooping 'dat ass!"

Syn's eyes are wild and bloodshot red. It doesn't take a rocket science to conceive she is drunk and beyond deluded. Immediately, I know I cannot be affected by her combativeness. I know I can't react in the manner she's hoping for. It just isn't right. If she wants to get a rise out of me, today won't be that day.

Kid is dead for crying out loud!

"What the fuck?" Azmir mutters as he starts making his way toward her. That's when voices get louder, and even more people try to calm Syn. She's outraged and absolutely bold with her verbal lashing.

Just before he gets beyond me, I catch him by the arm. "No," I bite out. "She's in pain. You're in pain. Everybody here is in pain," I speak firmly as I steady myself against his strain to move forward. Grabbing his chin with my left hand, I moved his face down toward me. "She will not get a reaction. Not today." I then quickly turn toward Syn and nod, "Okay. I won't. No worries."

I grab the key from Azmir and pushed him toward the truck. After some resistance, he acquiesces and gets into the passenger side. I close the door and make my way over to the driver's side as I throw Syn the nastiest warning glare I could muster without running over there and putting my foot in her face. A part of me wishes she was able to break free so I could finally put her over my knee. But the more logical side of me prevails. She isn't worth it.

As I mount the driver's side and adjust the seat to my comfort, I give a cursory glance to Syn in the rearview mirror. She's covered by her loved ones in an embrace.

"You okay? Sorry about that shit," Azmir grates. His voice is distressed. My heart starts to bleed all over again. That's all it takes to snap me back into missionary mode for my husband. He's wounded.

I start the Range and then forge a smile. "I am absolutely fine. Don't worry about me," I caress his left cheek. "Let's get you home and comfy," I murmur, trying badly to façade my trembling core. I realize I'm so upset Syn blasted me like that publicly without me retaliating, I could cry. But not right now. Not today. Today and moving forward will be about aiding my big guy.

Our ride to the marina is quiet. I don't have the "right" words articulated in my mind, so I won't let anything stupid and not well thought out slip from my lips. I just want him to not feel alone. My chest squeezes each time I revisit *that* dark place, realizing Azmir could be there himself. The time in silence gives me time to come up with a plan to relax him and keep him with me.

When we arrive to the marina, before I can shut the door behind him and have him set his own agenda, "To the closet and take off your clothes," I order. "And while you're at it, shut your phones off. DND for the rest of the evening."

Azmir's large frame halts and slowly pivots an about-face to face me. I can tell it's the last thing he expected. With his eyes, he questions my authoritative call, but it never rolls from his tongue. Though his glare is intimidating, I will not falter. I give him my poker face until he turns for the corridor, leading to the master suite.

On his heels, I drop my things on the chaise there in the bedroom and head to the en suite bathroom where I run a hot jasmine oil bath. The temperature is set to his liking, so I won't be joining him. Azmir prefers his water at a temperature I can't take.

Azmir arrives in the bathroom as I shut off the water, wearing just his *Calvin Klein* boxer briefs. His head is cocked to the side, messaging the need for further instruction. The only thing keeping me from drooling is the absence of his tongue being pressed into his molars. But damn if his columnar thighs don't arrest my attention and cause me to stagger. I feel my mouth drop.

Needing a comeback—and quickly—I quip, "I don't think those are needed in here, do you?"

Azmir snorts ruefully after a beat and then bends to remove his boxer briefs. During the brief descension I quickly decide not to be a peeping Tom. This comforting thing is not about me and the annoying fact of me never getting my fill of Azmir. He needs soothing. Though my eyes are now facing the Jacuzzi, I can sense Azmir tossing his underwear in the hamper and making his way over to the tub.

I give him time to settle into a place of comfort before I lather the sponge and wash him from his neck to his toes. When we're done, I dry him off and have him lay across the bed. I'm torn about his obedience. Azmir has questioned very little of my instruction. He does everything I ask, which further coils my heart. He just isn't himself.

I have him lay on his stomach while I change into something more comfortable, yet aesthetically pleasing, which is a yoga lounge set. I then grab a small bottle of eucalyptus oil from the vanity in the bathroom. When I settle onto the bed, I take my time and massage his glorious lengthy and muscular frame. I start with his feet, as I straddle him backwards. I then work my way up from his ankles to his calves, kneading every muscle attached to each bone as I ascend to his lower back. I don't touch his butt. Some men have this no-bother-zone thing with their derrieres and Azmir is no different. On a different day, I'd rile him up by hinting to it, but again today is about relaxing him.

I try to focus my mind as my hands explore every inch of him—every scar from childhood, skin-tone blemish, and smooth patch perfecting this man's exterior. When I'm done with his back, I have him roll over and I place a small towel on his private area to keep me from violating the pact I made with myself when I conjured this therapeutic plan of mine. I don't even straddle him this time but sit at his side instead to keep the course. It's difficult. I'm unaccustomed to not having Azmir's body as my playground when it's fully exposed. His glaring erection also doesn't help. I train my eyes everywhere but there.

When I'm done, I check and see his eyes are still closed. I don't think he's asleep, so I go into the walk-in closet and grab some clothes for him to slip on. When I return, he's sitting up with his back resting against the decorative pillows. I feel like a deer caught in headlights. Emotionally, I'm able to identify, but not so much verbally. I hated it when people tried to soothe me with words when I was in mourning.

Azmir doesn't look at me as he sits, staring blankly at the adjacent wall above the flat screen ahead. I'm stapled to the floor, not knowing what to do. I'd do anything to comfort him right now in any way. I know he and Kid weren't exactly best friends like Michelle and I, but when I lost her, there was a bit of comfort being alone in my own head. If that's what my husband wants, I'll give it to him without resentment. And if he wants me here, I'll—

"Come here," Azmir's raspy voice can hardly be heard, but I hear the pain in it.

Within seconds, I mount the massive bed and shuffle around until I'm settled behind him, assuming the support position. I have his back and here's where I'll rest in hopes of him laying his concerns on me so I can help him carry the load. *I want to be what he needs when he needs me to be it.*

"I feel..." he attempts. He doesn't pick up right away and that's okay. We'll stay here as long as he needs to. "It's my fault...Kid's death."

I don't know where he's navigating this conversation to because there is no way I can believe Kid's death is in anyway Azmir's fault. He goes quiet again. And again, I wait.

"In *The Clan*, we all had roles," he starts again. "Mine, you know was the general. Petey's was the enforcer. And so to speak, Kid was the terminator. I won't speak too much on it, but..." He takes a long and heavy exhale, blowing out his grief on the way. It's so thick I can feel it. "When the fire happened last fall in Pasadena, it was Kid's role to find the fucker who did it. We'd easily learned who the perp was on the street. He ended up a ghost and I had been on Kid's ass about recovering him for months. I was marrying you and..." This time he inhales, and I can feel his wide back expand against my chest.

"And even though I'd retired from the game, I couldn't have that situation unresolved. It wouldn't be safe for you or good on *The Clan's* reputation. Kid kept saying he was working hard at finding him. And I kept pushing and threatening his new crown in the organization. He was putting in long hours and wasn't sleeping enough to think shit out. D-Struct walked up on Kid while he was getting out of his car late that morning, after a stakeout shift, looking for him. The report said D-Struct got in several shots before Kid's one accurate blast killed him instantly."

Azmir's body shakes. I straightaway threw my arms around his wide upper torso to anchor him. His cry is dry and soundless. He's grieving. My heart is bleeding for him as I plant the side of my face on his shoulder.

"When I got the call, after processing the fact of never seeing Kid again, all I could think was I'd given up my crown only to lose a solid soldier and..." He can't finish his thought. I assume it's too painful to pursue. I held him tighter. His hot solid body suddenly develops goose bumps all over. I provide chaste kisses from his ear, down to the end of his shoulder. "You're going to leave me," his baritone chokes out.

"Oh, baby!" I implore.

I can't get close enough to him. Can't embrace him tight enough to bury him inside of my protectiveness. I know I can't conceivably hide his lanky frame in my arms, but I try to engulf as much of him as I could.

I shake my head violently although he can't see me. "Uh-un!" I grunt emphatically. "Never!" I declare even louder. I didn't have a reason to leave him when all things was right with the world, and therefore in good conscience could never see myself leaving him while he's wounded like this. "No way...not now."

Not ever!

"Yes, you are. I've involved you in a world you gave no consent to. I thought I could devise this error-proof exit out of the game and create a perfect world for you. I thought I wielded that type of control." He shakes his head somberly. "I don't control shit," his voice cracks.

"But I do," I state firmly. I grab Azmir's chin to bring his face to mine. I need to peer into his eyes, to beckon his sober comprehension. "I control my actions. I may not always make the call for my heart, the heart you captured almost on sight. Conversely, I'm very much in control of how I react to what my heart feels. I don't like that you kept an entire life from me, but I know who you are, the man you are at core."

"Do you?" Azmir asks with ghostly eyes. "Do you have confidence in who I am now that all of this shit has been dumped on your lap? I thought I could insulate you from it all, and look what's happened. God only knows what shit can jump out from my past that will have you hightailing out of my life for good. I couldn't survive that shit." He entreats me with his defeated eyes.

There's silence as we regard each other intensely, our strong willed spirits battling for dominance. I search for the convincing words my soul wants to convey, but I can't. I'm not confident they'd accurately communicate what I need Azmir to know. There's only one way coming to mind.

"Are you committed to me and only me?"

"*Yuh*—yes," he sputters.

"Will you always protect me?"

"Always," he declares without a second of hesitation.

"Can you love me forever?"

Azmir's chestnuts dance in my eyes as he decrees, "With every breath in my body, using every fiber of my being."

My lips twitch into a smile, feeling relieved for using his words from that night on the beach of Tahiti, after he'd proposed to me.

"Why, Mr. Jacobs, I do believe we have an official Jacobs' language," I smile, feeling an overflow of contentment with his big body wrapped protectively in my arms.

Azmir doesn't reply. In fact, his scowl is still in place, confusing me until he brings his hand to my face and covers my mouth with his own. It starts slowly and melodic with his tongue timidly darting in my mouth. His confidence hasn't fully returned. Right away, I recognize I have to give him more time, and possibly coax its resurgence.

Breaking away momentarily and regretfully leaving the warm dwellings of his delectable mouth, I reach over to the nightstand for the bottle of eucalyptus oil. Azmir watches absorbedly as I position my arms beneath his, reach for his semi-erect penis, and stroke it in my hand. He grows steely in my palm and once I see his gaining, with my right hand I manage to unscrew the top off the bottle and pour it onto him, measuring the tilt of my shaking hand. After closing the bottle, I bring both hands around him and slide up and down, dispersing the oil around its length. His skin is silky and smooth around a steel rod. Per usual, Azmir's abdominal muscles roll at my stroke, telling of his pleasure. I observe his clutched eyelids and slack jaw from his profile.

"Feels good?" I whisper teasingly in his ear.

Azmir doesn't answer, he opens his eyes and watches fixedly and I feel the echoing of stifle groans in his back. I tighten my grip on him and can feel the evidence of my own arousal in my crotch. *But this isn't about me; it's safer this way.*

I kiss his shoulder, then trail my tongue to the crest of his ear, applying soft bites. I stroke him strongly, feeling empowered from holding his massive extension in my hand. The most intimate firmness belonging to a virile commanding leader of a thriving conglomerate is being commandeered under my ministrations. This type of power is heady, dangerous even. He is at my control. He needs this release. He needs me to anchor him, to level the pressures of the world.

Azmir's face pivots and his hand shoots up, gripping the back of my head, bringing my mouth down to his. His tongue lashes wildly in my mouth, pouring his carnal desires and sentiments into me. He's helpless, vulnerable, in need of me to bring him to this. My hands work feverishly in jerking him and he groans in my mouth his pleasure. His slick tongue holds no prisoners, flapping deliciously into my mouth and I moan my approval. Azmir's breathing suddenly becomes distressed, and I know he's on the cusp of his release. My hands pump harder, and I feel his strong hip thrusts meeting my fists, creating a sensual staccato swishing sound throughout the room.

Our collision is hard, urgent, and wildly impassioned. His tongue threads my mouth just as urgently as his lap thrusts into my fists while I'm propped up behind him. I work diligently and can even feel my upper arms numbing, but I'm too caught up to stop. I'm dedicated to the process. I won't halt my rabid strokes until he says. Which isn't too much longer.

Azmir's neck jerks back and his pelvis slams into my fist midair before suspending there. "*Raaaaayna!*" he cries out as he heaves violently in my arms.

I swallow his cries in my mouth. I moan as if I'm soaring right along with him because that's how powerful this bond is between us. He is me and I am Azmir Jacobs. I am his partner. I have his back. I cover him with everything I have. I will be whatever he needs, whenever he needs me to be it. And right now he needs me to be right here with him, decidedly. And I am. I love this man.

After a few minutes, I pull myself from behind him and take to the bathroom. I return with a warm wet washcloth to clean him and when I'm done, I grab his clothing. I assist with them, starting with his socks, then his boxer briefs. When I rise to his hips, I angle myself to keep from hitting his heavy appendage. I can't believe he's still rock hard. But this is my big guy; always ready for more. I've had too many awkward moments hanging in this arena of his anatomy. I notice he's watching me with lazy eyes. But these aren't defeated eyes, they're exhausted ones.

I take his T-shirt from the bed behind him and move to pull it over his head. He assists. When his arms come down and he adjusts it around his torso, I mutter, "I'm going to get us something to eat. We haven't eaten a meal all day." Azmir nods. "And then I'm going to put you to bed so you can sleep."

I turn on my heels towards the door and on my way, I stop and look over my shoulder to remind him, "DND for the rest of the day."

Azmir snorts and flashes me a bit of that panty-snatching smirk that does all sorts of things to me. I head to the kitchen to fetch some sustenance for my big guy and my demanding belly.

CHAPTER 18

Rayna

"Mrs. Jacobs, it's a pleasure to see you again," the hostess greets me. I wish I could recall her name. I believe it's Rose. Azmir and I have been eating here so much lately; I should know the entire staff's names. "One of your parties has arrived. This way, I'll take you to your table." Her smile is pleasant, and I follow on her heels, feeling grateful to be without John, a huge concession on Azmir's part. I now feel like a grown-up again.

As we approach the table, April's face comes into recognition. But hardly. Something's different. With each step, I can pick up her features more distinctly. Her face is rounder...slightly plump, and her skin isn't its usual porcelain shade. She's glowing as she rises in my approach.

"Rayna," she greets with a guarded grin. I'm sure that's because of her history with my foul reception. "I'm glad you could make it."

I go to extend my arms to hug April and at the same time, I thank the hostess who leaves. I take the seat across from her.

"I'm glad we could meet, too. It's been so long. So much has changed," I mention with my life transition in mind while trying not to eagle eye her plump belly rubbing against mine during our brief embrace.

"I know!" she exclaims, clasping her hands together. I settle my blazer and purse as she speaks. "And this restaurant pick is awesome! Gerald and I heard about this place and said we're going to give it a try. It's been the talk for a couple of months now. I'm glad you chose it. Have you been before?"

"Ummmm...yeah. A lot actually. It seems to have grown to become Azmir and my favorite spot as of late."

Especially since he now owns it. But I wouldn't dare utter that. Azmir's money still makes me uncomfortable. It's so easy to forget about because when we're together, he's far more than his prestigious reputation to the world.

"I was checking out the ambiance. Look at these benches and chairs. Very chic." She compliments as though she knows, though I doubt she does. Unless you're in the know of local business and investments, you'd never think Azmir would finance an Italian restaurant.

"The food is just as good, if not better," I add.

"Mmmmm! Good, I'm starved," she says picking up the menu.

I notice she rubs her belly and I'm just about to toss a question when the hostess announces, "Mrs. Jacobs, the last of your party has arrived."

I look up to find a Britni with a nervous grin applied to her well made up face. She's wearing a fitted, green mini dress with a cropped denim jacket and military ankle lace up boots, making the look appealing. Britni has always been able to do that.

"Yes! Brit, you're here. Now we can order," April squeals as she trains her eyes back to the menu.

I notice she doesn't stand to greet Britni like she did me, but I guess it's because they are in touch. Britni sits at the head of the table, so none of us are seated next to each other. As if on cue, the waitress comes and takes our order then sets off to put them in to the chef.

"Rayna," Britni calls out tentatively. My head shoots up from the menu. "I'm glad you agreed to meet up." Her eyes speak more than her mouth. Britni knows she crossed the line with that video.

"*Hmmmmm!*" April hums facetiously from across the table. Even she's been compromised by that video.

I settle my eyes back onto Britni and give a peaceful nod. "I'm looking forward to getting things out in the open," I offer because I am.

I've been having mixed feelings about this viral video since my conversation with April. There are so many things I'm responsible for regarding my relationship with these two women, which is why I easily agreed to tonight.

"Well, Rayna," April begins as she reaches for the bread and butter. "Brit and I have squashed our beef about the video. Before coming back to you about it, I had to discuss it with my fiancé first. It was difficult to do, but I knew it was the right thing and had to be done. Needless to say, I wasn't very happy with Ms. Thing over here." She tosses a manicured nail across to Britni who looks to be reduced to a petulant child.

"Anyway," she stuffs bread in her mouth. "My Gerald is still all for marrying me despite my former loose ways and wild days. You got hitched since it, so it didn't exactly end your life. So, Brit and I have squashed it and I'm hoping you two can too, Rayna." April managed all of this with a full mouth.

Before I can speak, Britni says, "Rayna, it was wrong what I did. I was being reckless and immature. I didn't think of what it would do to you. And please don't think I hate you or anything because I've never hated you." Britni's eyes are glossed. I can't believe she's fighting back tears. "It's just that you were always so…ironclad that when the woman came and asked for something that would rattle your cage, *and I knew it wasn't you on the tape so it couldn't ruin you exactly*, I didn't think you'd be all that upset. I was drunk when

Spin and I met up with the Dawn girl the night after the concert. I told her I went to school with you, and she asked about racy... perhaps drunken pictures and that's when I thought of the video. It was the first thing that came to mind. And when I told them you weren't even there, Dawn said it didn't matter." She sniffled.

"It was stupid of me, I know. I didn't think of Michelle...didn't think of Erin," she choked on a cry. "I swear, I'm so sorry."

April grabbed a cloth napkin from the table and offered it to Britni. I wasn't expecting this Britni. She'd always presented like a carefree wayward preteen to me. People change. And her admitting to tarnishing Michelle's memories lightened me. She seemed genuine and that appealed to my resolve.

"I forgive you."

I notice April's hand that had been caressing Britni's from across the table halt. Britni's red eyes shoot over to me and her brows furrow. April's face mirrors Britni's.

"C'mon, guys. I'm not ruthless or cold-hearted. Britni made a bad call," I explained. "...a horrible call. But April's right; all is well in spite of your callous actions. I'm in a different head...and heart space right now. I'm..." I take a moment to decide on my next word that describes my current state. "...happy. I don't know...maybe I wasn't happy until recently...or perhaps I didn't know how to be more than just content with living so independent of everyone except Michelle." I shake my head and allow the smile begging at my face despite myself. "But now I know there's more to life than holding on to things that will allow you to miss out on being happy. So, yes, I forgive you, Britni."

"Oh, my god!" April releases a hefty breath and slaps her chest. "I thought I was going to have to hold you down and beg you not to continue with that nasty lawsuit!"

My head jerks back and a grimace forms on my face simultaneously. "Oh, I didn't say I'd abandon the recompense for the damage," I state vehemently.

"Rayna!" April gasps.

"Not that it changes that what I did was wrong, but Rayna, I don't have two million dollars just laying around in my trust fund." Britni sniffles, sobering from her previous emotional breakdown.

"No, you don't," I retort. "However, you do have a substantial amount in them." Over the years, Britni has made it known both her parents and two grandparents had created trust funds for her.

Her parents separated when she was young and both did well, as did her grandparents. Although she still works, Britni could have taken off time after school and traveled, per her father's suggestion. She can afford it. The amount of the lawsuit is steep under the advisement of Azmir's fire-breathing attorney, Chesney. Lady Spin's doubles Britni's, and the radio station's lawsuit exceeds them all.

I exhale as I fight down the threat of my anger resurfacing on this matter. "Look, Britni, I don't want the money. I couldn't care less about receiving anything from this ordeal outside of a sincere apology. But we don't know how, if, or when this mess will hit Erin. She doesn't have her mother to apologize to her or provide an explanation for her careless behavior. She also doesn't have parents to pay her college tuition. How about we negotiate a number that you will contribute to her college fund, and we call it even? We can agree on a percentage in the single digits of the total lawsuit figure. I can have Azmir's attorney write up the paperwork."

With her little nose as red as Rudolph the reindeer, Britni nods her head ardently. "Of course. I don't have a problem at all contributing towards Erin!" she cries.

"And you can relay the same offer to Spin." I take a sip of my water. My mouth has been unusually dry as of late and talking so much doesn't help. "But don't think her cut would be comparable to yours; she earns a lot more than you do; I've been told." I'm forgiving, but nobody's fool.

"Yeah, sure. I'm sure she'll be relieved," Britni answers excitedly.

"My God is magnificent!" April yelps with her arm stretched to the heavens like a hat lady in the second pew. I see her vocabulary has even changed since being with this Greene guy.

Just then, the sommelier comes over with a bottle of wine. "Mrs. Jacobs, Mr. Jacobs made me aware of your visit tonight with your friends. Please..." He lifts the bottle. "...let me offer you a bottle *of Petrus Pomerol 1998*, aye?"

"Thanks so much," I feel myself blushing at the gesture. Azmir can be so sweet. "I won't be drinking this evening. But let me not stop my friends here." I glance at the ladies.

"Please," Britni motions to her glass.

"I'll pass, too," April declines.

He places the bottle on the table before leaving.

"So, have you told Rayna how your hot ass got preggo by the good reverend?" Britni asks with a plucked brow as she takes a slow sip of her wine.

"Brit!" April admonishes her. "I told you not to open your fat mouth!"

My mouth drops. I knew something was off, April is known for throwing them back. Her refusal of wine should've set off alarms right away.

"I was about to ask you before Britni walked up on us," I share, aghast. "April, he's like the pastor in training! How has his people taken the news?"

April rolls her eyes as she goes for her glass of water. She takes a sip and then murmurs, "They don't know yet. And we can't push up the wedding. His church is part of a worldwide organization. There are people coming in from countries I have never heard of. His parents won't hear of it...if we tell them. So, I don't know what to do with our little love bug here." She rubs her belly gingerly. I find my right hand sweeping across my belly. "I mean, I don't understand what the big deal is. Who waits until marriage for sex nowadays?"

"Well, clearly not your whorish ass." Britni clinks her glass against April's. April forcefully places her glass down on the table. "Awwwww...c'mon, April! Don't be a sour puss. You know that Bible-toting man was not prepared for your sexual prowess." She laughs, and mine sputters out this time.

An unwilled smile hits April's lips. "Girl, I victimized that church boy in his daddy's office after my second Thursday night prayer service." We all broke out in fits of laughter at that. By this time our food is arriving. The waiters go about setting the table as we quiet down.

"Holy shi—I mean, crap! Do you know how much this bottle costs?" April nearly shouts in a forceful whisper out of nowhere.

"How much?" Britni goads her.

"Around fifteen hundred bucks!" April's eyes are wild and wide.

"Well, we've already known Rayna snagged a baller!" Britni shares and April hums her agreement as she stuffs her face with penne a la vodka.

I throw Britni a warning glare. I must admit, I've been having a great time with them. *Who knew!* I don't want to ruin it with any scandalous-like talk of Azmir.

"I know what it's like being with a man of power," April informs, wearing a Cheshire cat's smile. "It makes you suck up his seeds and procreate, even when you're not trying. Men with power are so hot!"

She and Britni squeal like schoolgirls. Despite myself, I smile hard, fighting my own sputter of laughter. Her statement makes me think of two things: my description of what intimacy is like with Azmir the night of the *Mauve* event, and the possibility of what's in my belly.

The rest of our dinner goes surprisingly well, with me finally laughing mindlessly with April and Britni, something I never thought was possible.

The next morning, I make my way into Dr. Barnes' office. I find myself waiting again. I've been here for over five minutes and my patience is starting to wear already. I've taken more time off work to wait. This is unacceptable. My phone goes off and I answer. It's Brenda, Amber's partner.

"Hey, Brenda. Is everything okay?"

"Hi, Rayna," she returns warmly. "Everything's fine. I'm calling because Amber and I have run into a scheduling conflict for today and tomorrow. I know it's short notice, but do you think you can swing by and pick up Erin from school? Amber will be home tonight at six to get her from you and tomorrow, I'll be in at seven to receive her."

"Oh, sure. I can swing that," I agree to it feeling a bit of satisfaction from being needed in Erin's world when Amber's in a jam. All I want is to be viewed as a stable figure for her. "I'll likely drop her off a little later than seven tomorrow. We'll be out to dinner, celebrating Azmir's mother's birthday. I can have her in right after though."

Brenda exhales into the phone. "Thank you so much, Rayna. This is such a relief for me. I appreciate it."

"No, problem. It's my pleasure, Brenda...really," I assure her. "Just text me the address of the school, and I'll get her."

We're saying our goodbyes when Dr. Barnes walks in, clinking her designer heels. She waits for me to disconnect before speaking.

"Rayna, I'm so sorry for my practice's lapse in organization over the past few weeks. It's really been crazy here." She offers a regretful smile as she scoots her stoop underneath her and sits.

"It's okay," I grumble because I'm lying. "As a practitioner, I know the rush."

"Okay," she flips her bone straight hair over her left shoulder, licks her freshly manicured middle finger and fingers the pages of my file. "I won't keep you long. I just want to tell you Patti did find your urine and processed your test—"

"And?" I sputter anxiously.

Her long and thick lashes flip up. "Okay," she sighs as her shoulders sag. "I know this isn't in your plans, but you are indeed pregnant, Rayna."

I cup my mouth. The tears fall. My body trembles.

She gives me a moment before she clears her throat and forges ahead. "So, given the first day of your LMP, your missed pill days, and the days you were on the antibiotic, I have a delivery date of November eleventh."

I still don't speak. I have no idea of what to say. I mean, I knew it was a strong possibility. I know my body has been off...but I always thought if I'd gotten pregnant unexpectedly, Azmir would learn of it before I was able to figure it out. *What is he going to think of me?*

"Rayna," Dr. Barnes gently calls out to me. "I see you need some time to settle this in your mind. I'm not going to inundate you with information, but I'll write you out a prescription for prenatal vitamins and will have Patti make you an appointment for at least one week from today for the first monitoring of the heartbeat..."

That's all I heard before I mentally tapped out.

I go through my day in a fog. I see my afternoon patients with less vigor than I'm known for. I almost forget to eat. *Almost.* I've been starving a lot lately, I guess like April was last night. Before I know it, it's time for me to head over to Erin's school.

On the drive there I ride in silence only hearing the voice of my navigator, my self-loathing thoughts play the background music in my head. *Pregnant.* I have to show my I.D. and sign in to Erin's school before being directed to her class. When I walk in, I'm met with toddlers running amok all through the colorful classroom. It's the end of the day and I assume the two teachers in the room have depleted energy levels.

God, help me! I don't know how I'll handle just one of these little creatures.

"Hi!" one of the teachers greets. "Who are you here to pick up today?"

"Uhhh...Erin Smith."

She turns and calls out, "Erin, it's time to go home, honey!"

Seconds later, I see a little head full of sandy blonde curls bouncing in the air. Erin barrels over to me with such great speed, I think she's going to tackle me, but she doesn't. She places her little palms flat on my belly and shouts, "Baby. Baby. Baby."

I jump and my heart drops to my stomach. "Erin!" I call out.

"Oh, Erin! Not again." The teacher glances over to me and laughs. "You look as though you've seen an UFO!" Attempting to catch myself, I shut my mouth and try to breathe. "No." She shakes her head attempting to slow her mirth. "The head teacher, Ms. Ana, shared with the kids today she's expecting. She allowed them to rub her belly and say hello to the baby. They've been obsessed with the notion all day."

Oh! My belly flutters at Erin's gentle touch. She's still speaking to *it*.

Oh, my god...it!

"Erin, let's go grab your things." The teacher grabs Erin by the hand, still amused by my apparent discomfort, and they take off for her things.

I take Erin to get a bite to eat and chat with her a while before dropping her off home. I head straight to the marina to warm dinner for Azmir and me. My mind is churning with its old acquaintance, pessimism. I try to tell myself this isn't the worst thing in the world, just horribly timed. Azmir has made it clear he wants kids. He is, after all, significantly older than I am and probably should endeavor to parent at his age. It's just that I'm not ready. What if he purposely chose a younger woman who's trim and fit and after I deliver the baby, he no longer desires me? Will he replace me?

Being grabbed gingerly from behind startles me. I drop the serving spoon into the Alfredo sauce as I gulp in air. Azmir catches me somewhere in flight and pulls me into his hard body. He presses his warm and soft lips to my neck and nibbles.

"It's me, Mrs. Jacobs," he whispers into my neck on a snicker, and I fight to relax my body. "I ain't mean to scare you." His Brooklyn tongue is working my skin and eardrums.

"Well, you did," I scold him as my feet find their way to the floor. My legs are shaky, still trying to recover from being frightened. "Dinner will be ready in a minute."

Azmir doesn't let up off me now that I'm standing on my own. And now I feel his erection pressing against my lower back, just above my cheeks. His delicious scent is blanketing me.

"What about you?" he growls into my neck. "Are you ready for me yet?"

I know he's revved up, coiled like a tight wire. It's been a while; my sexual appetite has been off. I've been hiding behind his travel and my enduring symptoms from the bug I came down with in San Francisco. I've never denied Azmir. My body has never allowed me to. It's always betrayed me for Azmir. But since being...*pregnant*... it's been under the weather, cooking up a mini Azmir.

Oh, my gosh! Did I say that?

"I had a bad day at work with spitting up mucus. It's not as bad as it was last week, but all of the coughing has worn me out," I lie. I haven't coughed in about a week, but he doesn't know this as he's been away. "I took something when I got in." I wrap my arm around his neck from behind me. "I'm sorry, baby. That bug has put me in a man down situation," I try to chuckle.

"It's put *me* in a man down situation," he sulks. "I miss you, baby." Azmir rubs my breasts that have been feeling heavier than usual.

"Azmir, we're over the stove," I try to ward him off.

"Jacobs, I'm so ready for you that I'll let you ride me while I sit on the hot racks."

"I know, baby," I murmur weakly. "I'll be ready for you soon." I angle my neck to kiss him. "Now, go get washed up so I can feed you."

I feel him exhale heavily on the back of my neck. Azmir plants another warm kiss there before he walks off, taking his warmth, leaving me feeling suddenly bereft from his tender contact.

I've been up for at least ten minutes and the first thing I do is marvel at the absence of nausea. I don't feel sick. This would be the first time in nearly three weeks that I'm not disgustingly ill!

I don't exactly feel one hundred percent like myself, but thank God I'm not prepared to puke my guts out. Before I get too excited, I decide to sit up quietly without disturbing the men in my bed. Poor Azmir: since moving in, I've laid claim to his incredibly plush bed, and Azna pretty much rivals my entitlement.

I hear the caws of the seagulls of the marina as I slowly turn to my left and lay eyes on a sleeping Azmir. *God, he's beautiful!* His almond crest eyes are closed displaying is long lashes, his narrow nose is inaudible, and his luscious lips are parted and moist. He's sleeping quietly. His left arm rests beneath his pillow, showcasing the knots in it. He looks innocent and serene. Azmir's repose state makes me want to protect him, nestle him. He hardly resembles the formidable corporate thug he exudes when he's roused and in action.

I glimpse down to notice my breasts have slipped out of their holdings. The rim of my gown is below my nipple line and the straps are pulled into my breasts. My nipples... *Geesh!* They're swollen and hard—shaped like the top of pawn pieces.

Then my eyes instinctively roam back over to an unassuming Azmir. He's unknowing, compromised, and...*hot*. His lips are ajar, but the soft air blowing from his nostrils causes fulgurant spikes to course through my delicate frame. The bulb between my lower lips is pulsating.

Oh, my god!

I want Azmir...like in the worst way.

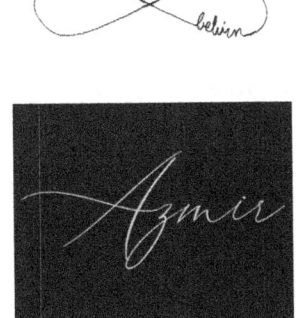

I'm hurled from my sleep. I have no idea why until my vision clears after repetitive blinks and settles on two golden globes with hard milk chocolate nubs at the apex of them. I haven't been this up close to them in so long that they appear a little foreign, but only to my eyes. My cock springs up at the recognition. *Her scent...* that has to be what awakened me. Rayna always spritzes a soft flowery fragrance on her body after a shower and before coming to bed.

My nose is so close to her breasts that her heaving brings them closer for a millisecond before they retreat. Her mounds are pinned against the satin strap of her nightgown, appearing strained enough to pop the delicate material. A warm intermitted air breezes against my forehead from her pants. My eyes trail up her honey shaded skin and when I get to her collapsed jaw, mine reacts in the same manner. Rayna's left arm arches over my head as she's facing me. Her forehead is wrinkled, her eyes are wild, her nostrils are flaring out and retracting just as quickly, and when she takes a deep swallow, unable to keep her lips sealed, I realize what's going on here.

My lady is horny as fuck. She's trying to maintain control. *Is she afraid to tell me she needs her back straightened out?* If it's because she's been unavailable from being sick, she has to know I'm not sweating that shit. I've been *painfully* waiting but understanding.

My gaze traces Rayna's erratic eye movements. She's trying to assess me. And I want to test her. I need to know if she wants me as I suspect because now, I'm feeling the beginnings of tingling in my fucking sacs. They'll be growing heavier any second now. My eyes descend back down to her bountiful breasts, which are larger than they've ever appeared to me, and I flicker my tongue onto her right nipple.

Immediately, Rayna's entire body tenses and she inhales deeply. I'm not quite sure of what it means, so I do it again, only this time I flit it longer. Rayna's breaths are heavier and her chest caves in. Her eyes grow wider and wilder as she stares down at me. Yup. She needs to fuck...and so do I. But before I get happy out my ass, I have to test her a little more. I shift an inch closer to continue my lap on her turgid nipples. I flicker my thumb on her left as I work the right into my mouth and softly suck on it.

"Ahhhhh!" she screams on a husky breath.

Fuck, she's extra responsive today!

I use both my hands to bring her breasts together and go bananas on them with my hungry mouth. I swear I'm trying to suppress the caveman, but her moans are releasing the beast. Rayna's hand squeezes my left bicep, piercing my skin. Her right leg swings over my left thigh as she starts to grind, needing friction where it hurts most. I don't let her. I bring my leg over hers and pin it down as I work her nipples. They've somehow taken on a darker shade in my crazed morning brain.

Rayna cries out in frustration. She needs to work her pelvis, but

I don't let her. I continue my torture. I miss this contact, the intimacy from her shaky frame, heat from her warm breath pushing forcefully from her mouth, hearing her cries of pleasure. There is nothing more that can affirm my masculinity.

"*Azmiiiir,*" she cries out. Her breath is ragged, and her body tremors are violent as I hold her in place to ride out her release. She goes on and on like this, and now the pads of her fingers are gripping my skin as if she fears a long fall.

Oh, shit! That didn't take long at all.

I believe that was a record compared to the last time I did it when I introduced the cuffs to our bed. Rayna's eyes opened heavily...and hungrily. Fuck my own need; my lady needs me more.

"*Awwww... Baby, you want another?*"

I watch as Rayna lifts from the bed, pushes me forcefully to the mattress and straddles me so she's on top. In mere seconds, she's hovering over the tip of my cock with her pliant and gelled lips running against the head to navigate my entrance. Then, without warning, she plummets down onto me.

"*Arrrrrrgh!*" she screams out.

"*Uuuuuuuuuh!*" My throaty cry is nearly silent compared to hers.

She lifts and impales once again. I know this is borderline painful for her. I see the sweat beads forming above her lips and her body is trembling on top of me. We're both panting out loud, neither of us moving for a while. She's so fucking tight; it's been quite some time. But my determined Rayna is moving before I know it. She's rising and falling, using her thighs astride my waist to balance herself as she pulls up and sinks down on me. My vision's blurred and if I don't gain ahold of myself, I'm going to lose it before giving her a second orgasm.

I grab her dampened frame and shift off the bed then lay her back on the edge as I stand over her. Her eyes are harsh, and her breathing is still frantic. Rayna wraps her leg around me as I lower myself, driving into her. She bites her lips and tightens her legs, pushing me into her.

"Harder!" she demands forcefully. "Harder!"

"Gaaaaah!" I push out as I start to go ape shit on her pelvis.

I'm rocking hard and fighting for my own release. My hands cuff her arms above her head as I plunge hard into her, filling her to the hilt. I have to give her at least one more to make her remember what we've been missing. In my libidinous delirium, I take one hand and grab her neck, minimizing her airway, but not totally closing it off. I've only done this with her a handful of times, and just like those times, Rayna climaxes within seconds. My thrusts are hard, savage, and yet all so satisfying. As I let up on her throat, I'm coming right behind her.

My head feels like it's about to spin off from my spine. My heart is making its way out of my chest. Rayna's arms shoot up from the bed and pulls me into her chest, holding me so tight, I can feel her heartbeat almost as much as I feel her inner walls throbbing all around me.

"I've missed you," she whispers breathlessly in my ear.

After a few moments, when I'm able to speak, I mumble, "Give me a few minutes and I can show you how much I've missed you more."

And I do, minutes later in the shower.

In the *Bentley*, leaving a meeting at *Drop It* with Petey and Syn, I'm drained. The day has been long and the conversation I've just concluded hasn't exactly lightened the heaviness of my shoulders. I still can't believe Kid is gone. I've heard various renditions of the story, read the police report, viewed his dead body, attended his eulogy, even buried my *G*. And after that dismal process of finality, I still can't perceive his death.

I've lost very few soldiers in the field during my reign. I never had a large executive circle, so every, thing and person had been abstract, so to speak. Kid—he was family. Therefore, it's only right to make sure Syn and their children are set up comfortably in his wake.

The dilemma in it is she needs to work, and between Petey and me, we could fit her in several places on our payrolls. Only Syn had no occupational skills of value. She couldn't even continue Kid's carwash business because she had no knowledge of that trade. It was an emotional meeting at best. We all spoke ghostly from the shock of having to do this. Syn's eyes were red and swollen, I presumed from profuse bouts of crying.

We were able to work out her coming to work at the recreation center in the LBC with my culinary staff. There is an entry level position there I feel could be the start of a new vocation for her if she gains interest. My head cook has a teaching temperament and would love a captive student. I explained to Syn, by me doing this she has to agree to completely change her regard for Rayna. It wouldn't matter if she weren't my wife; Syn would not be allowed to disrespect her any further simply because she's on my arm. Quite honestly, I'd been planning to confront her about this just before Kid's passing, but the time never came. Then after she spazzed on Rayna at the repast, I wanted to choke the shit out of her. She was fucking lucky out her ass Rayna didn't lose it on her. Syn has no clue of that side of Rayna. But I do. I've seen her black the hell out on several occasions.

When I presented her with that condition, she quickly accepted it then broke down crying. I was shocked when Syn admitted to antagonizing Rayna for no good reason at all. She was a blubbering mess as she poured her soul and cried her eyes out about being an alcoholic. My jaw dropped and Petey jumped to console her, sputtering attempted words of comfort. If it were under different circumstances, it would have been comical. After ironing out a few details, we parted ways.

I'm now on my way to dinner to celebrate Yazmine's birthday. I had my assistant catch us reservations at *DiFillippo's*. The place's popularity has grown in spades over the past six months. The menu has vastly improved, and the ambience rivals the impeccable wine selection. It's been a long revamping process, but well worth it.

We pull up to the restaurant, and just as I'm stepping out of the car, my phone rings. It's Chef Boyd.

"Peace-Peace."

"Mr. Jacobs, how are you?"

"I'm good, Boyd. And things on your end?"

"Can't complain, sir. The reason for my call is to follow up on the upcoming monthly menu. I see a...drastic change in the meals. There are lots of starches—pastas, casseroles, heavy sauces and gravies. This is totally out of the norm," he inquires tentatively.

My mind begins rewinding to the conversation I had with Rayna a few weeks back concerning this. She said she created the list on an empty stomach, hence the richness in her selections. I never got around to changing it that night after she lured me back to the master suite for another round of smashing.

"Indeed," I mutter. "Rayna pretty much has carte blanche in that arena. I'll be seeing her in a few and will ask her about it. You're right; we don't typically go that heavy, at night at least."

"It's no trouble to implement, but I figured I'd ask about it to see if there were some...details I'm unaware of..." he hesitates.

Details—

Pregnancy?

"Oh, no," I chuckle. "No news of that nature yet. Don't scare the little lady off just yet with those possibilities."

Boyd joins me in my mirth. "Okay, Mr. Jacobs. Just wanted to check with you two. I'll wait to hear back on your final selections before I send my list of groceries to Louise."

"Indeed. Good day, Boyd."

"And to you, sir," he bodes before we disconnect.

The hostess leads me to an empty table where we'll be dining tonight. And before she leaves, I ask, "Rose, was Mario clear on the specifics for the cake?"

"Yes, Mr. Jacobs. And your delivery arrived earlier as well. We are on target for the evening," she ensures.

I nod. "Thanks."

As I sit and wait for the women to arrive, I can't get Chef Boyd's call out of my head. What makes it even more humorous is that Tyler hinted at the same thing just this morning during our session. He casually mentioned Rayna's laggard efforts over the past week or so since she's returned from her weeks off due to the bug she'd caught from Erin. I had to explain how miserable the experience was for her. I think that ordeal would've put even a man on his ass for a few weeks. I'd seen her pushing forward, trying to get back to her normal regimen prematurely. That has been our latest theme of bouts: Rayna pushes herself too hard.

Tyler seemed to have tolerated my explanation. He dropped it immediately and went quiet for a while. It was a little weird, but I kept it moving while we sparred. I mean... She's my fucking wife. I'd likely know even before Rayna if she were expecting. We hadn't been indulging as much as I imagined after exchanging vows because of fighting and then her getting sick. But that all changed when Rayna woke up horny as fuck and I was able to quell my insatiable need of her.

I can't lie, before we left San Francisco, I'd had an inkling of hope. But after her diagnosis, I got over it and quickly, feeling foolish because I knew Rayna has made it clear she doesn't want children. She's been good at keeping up with her pill for all I know.

But she did gag that night in the bathroom and hasn't put her mouth on my cock since then.

That was quite bizarre, but again, I fight the possibility. We are moons away from Rayna even considering having a baby. And even though our sexual cadence has been off as of late, I have to consider how it started when I proposed celibacy until our wedding day. And again, the blow up about her past in Jersey, my unrelenting travel, her fight with Dawn, our separation when she learned of my sordid past, and then her sickness, sex hasn't exactly been as regular as it's been explosive. Rayna has gone beyond her typical minx persona, even sending lewd texts and pictures of her body parts. My dick springs up at that recollection.

I pull out my phone as I wait and review the pictures again. She promised to make me taste each image she texted. *Goddamn*—

"Here's my boy," I hear from just above, pulling me from my lecherous thoughts.

I look up to find a beaming Yazmine and Samantha just beyond her.

Fuck.

"And here's the birthday girl." I extend my arm while supplying an overcompensating smile. I can't stand because I'll expose my raging erection.

By the time Yazmine moves to sit and Samantha moves up to embrace me, I'm in the safe zone. You don't maintain an erection while touching your mother and mother-in-law. They put your shit on ice.

"Where's my daughter?" Yazmine asks with excitement. She's never referred to Rayna as an in-law. I guess not having a daughter will cause you to promote someone into that position with ease.

"Yeah, where is my baby girl?" Samantha gleams.

"Rayna should be here any minute. She had to pick up Erin, who will be joining us," I offer.

The waiter comes with menus and asks for our drink order, but not before wishing Yazmine a happy birthday. She can't narrow her smile as she thanks him.

"We still waiting for two more people," Yazmine cautions as she looks over her shoulder, presumably for Rayna.

"We can start with our drinks," I state. "I'll order for them."

I've been spending enough time with little Erin to know she's an apple juice head. Because it is after hours, Rayna will indulge in pinot noir. And I order a bottle purposely to get her twisted. Those racy text messages have me riled up.

"Oh, here they are," Samantha announces as the waiter walks off.

Rayna holds Erin's little hand as she crosses the dining room, wearing a fitted dress falling just below her knees with black leather *Monolos* she's inclined to wear to work, saying they are the most comfortable. As she struts in, I notice her thighs are broad, stomach is flat, but her breasts look more bountiful in this number. Her face is set to a scowl and there's purpose in her strides. I stand as she approaches.

"Hey," I greet her when she arrives at the table. I catch a draft of her *Cool Water*. I place my mouth to hers and pull her bottom lip as I withdraw. In a flash, I see her eyes darken before they go back to their usual browns. It's good to know I still have this effect on her. "You okay?" I'm a little concerned about her frown.

"Yeah, I'm fine," she murmurs. "Just hungry."

Rayna then turns to the table to greet Yazmine and Samantha and I go to do the same with Erin.

"Little E!" I call out, using the nickname I hear Rayna refer to her as from time to time. "You ready to pay up?"

"No, Uncle Mir," she pouts. I'm quite comfortable with the title she's given me all of her own volition. It's very endearing. "You owe me ten dollars. Caillou is not Hawaiian! He's French Ca...Ca..." she struggles with it.

"Canadian. He's French Canadian," Rayna assists Erin from over her shoulder as she chats with the ladies.

"Canadian!" Erin boldly exclaims. "See, I told you, you didn't know Caillou."

Rayna directs the tot to her seat before taking her own next to me. She then pulls the breadbasket closer to her setting.

"Okay, you got me," I play along as I pull out my wallet. "Here you go. You've won the bet, fair and square." I hand her the money.

"Azmir, that's a lot to be giving her," Yazmine admonishes. And while I know, I give a stubborn shrug.

My eyes arrive at my gorgeous wife who is downing a piece of buttered bread as though it's her last meal. I don't think she chews it before swallowing and going for another to butter as she carefully examines the dinner menu. From across the table, I observe Samantha's pensive stare at Rayna. Yazmine is chatting with Erin when the waiter arrives with our drinks.

"Yes!" Rayna cheered under her breath. "I'm starved."

"Erin, would you like spaghetti or chicken fingers?" Rayna asks Erin, knowing although the restaurant doesn't have a children's menu, Mario, the sous chef, will fry Erin chicken fingers and fries.

"Spaghetti," Erin answers.

We all place our orders and nothing's unusual except for Rayna's request for so much food. She orders fried ravioli and calamari for an appetizer, and chicken francaise, as well as eggplant parm for dinner. That's enough for two people. No one mentions it and I wouldn't dare question her need of such heavy foods. However, I do notice Yazmine giving Samantha a knowing smirk in passing before continuing her conversation with an animated Erin. I sit back and sip my drink.

Women are peculiar creatures.

We chat while we wait for our food and well into dinner. Rayna's digging in her meal, seemingly preoccupied with consuming every morsel. Yazmine and Samantha offer their appraisals for the food, which delights me.

"So, Azmir, honey, you own 'dis place?" Samantha inquires.

"Partly," I share. "The other owner is the head chef."

"Oh, nice!" Samantha beams with joy.

"What made you buy 'dis Italian place, beloved?" Yazmine asks.

"This broad I was dating at the time fell in love with Mario's crème brûlée," I answer casually. Rayna's head pops up and she squints her eyes. Finally, I have those piercing brown irises on me. "It was a no brainer from there." Though Rayna was my motivation for agreeing to invest, I'd also believed the new vision for this place was viable.

Minutes later, when Rayna has run through about half of each plate, she comes up for air. We sang happy birthday to Yazmine and wait for her tears to slow so she could blow out the candles. Then she opens her birthday gifts from Rayna and me; a new gold stud nose ring and a family ring holding birthstones of Yazmine, my deceased father and me. Yazmine seems to love it and I have Rayna to thank for the gift ideas. After that ordeal, Yazmine and Samantha happily engage in conversations, which sometimes includes Erin. It amazes me how these two women who were once complete strangers have cultivated a bond the way they have. They are truly companionable, looking out for each other.

Suddenly, I notice Erin pivot over to Rayna, rubbing her belly as she chants, "Baby. Baby. Baby."

Rayna's hands frantically shoot up to cover Erin's little ones, and her eyes are about to pop out of her head.

"Erin!" she whispers forcefully in an admonitory manner.

"Oh, so it's out?" Yazmine asks excitedly. "I can't believe y'all finally gon' tell us on my birthday." She turns to Samantha and cheers, "You was right, Sammy. We gon' be grandmommies!"

Yazmine proceeds to high five Samantha. However, Samantha holds trepidation.

After a few beats, Samantha murmurs, "You ain't tell him, did you?"

My eyes swing over to Rayna whose mouth is agape and her eyes are just the same. I can see her go rigid in her seat. She immediately goes into sputtering, "No... Erin has a teacher...her teacher is pregnant and shared it with the class. She does this to all women now!" she explains anxiously. Then she turns to me, "It's just a phase that kids go through! I swear... Ask her," she urges.

Needing to ask a small child about matters concerning my wife seems quite incredulous to me. I won't be asking *anybody* shit regarding my wife. I glance down at her belly. It now has a little bulge, but that could easily be because she full from all the food she's just inhaled. My thoughts are racing. *What was Samantha right about?* I throw a glance back over to Samantha who, along with her daughter, is holding her breath. Yazmine's eyes deliberately retreated minutes ago. It hits me how Rayna hasn't touched her wine. *Shit!* All of a sudden, I can't remember her last period.

When we'd had sex later at the marina, after leaving Redondo Beach, it was in the shower. I'd figured that was the best place considering her condition. Now that I think about it, I didn't see any blood. I was expecting it but dismissed it knowing I'd never had sex with a woman while she was menstruating, so I didn't know what to look for. *Could it be because she wasn't bleeding after all?* But she hadn't been expecting me that night in Redondo Beach to put on a fucking tampon as a front.

You're buggin' the fuck out, Divine! Rayna would never keep this from me.

Would she?

I know the answer.

My eyes shoot back over to my wife who is now visibly shaking. My glare is sharp and well-intended. I am sure to be unequivocal in my inquisition, annoyed that I'm being revisited by flighty, timid, conniving Rayna Brimm.

"No. I prefer asking you." My eyes scan her small waist once again before I ask, "Are you pregnant?"

CHAPTER 19

Rayna

Is there something about that restaurant that begs my secrets out of the closet?

I ponder this as I walk into the apartment. I immediately hear Azna running towards the door, trotting the same pace as my racing heart. I'm bracing myself for this showdown with Azmir. When we abruptly ended dinner at *DiFillippo's*, Azmir left for the marina, and I returned Princess Erin to Amber and Brenda before meeting my seething husband at home.

As I enter his office, I can hear Azmir finishing a conversation. His daggering eyes pin me in place. *Crap!* This isn't going to be good.

"Tomorrow morning will be fine. I'll see her then. Yeah... Thanks again for agreeing to this at such short notice," he mumbles then hangs up.

"Azmir," I try to cut him off at the path. "I know what you're thinking and—"

"You couldn't possibly know what I'm thinking. And you damn sure haven't a clue as to how I'm feeling, so let's get that shit straight now." His brow line is hiked, telling of anger. Brooklyn is definitely in the house, and I feel like I'm being pushed out of his ring of trust.

I exhale and find my eyes rolling. "I was going to tell you."

"WHEN?" he shouts. I try to hide the tremble of my frame.

"If you would give me a minute, I can give you the timeline of all of this—"

"Fuck your timeline!" he barks as he jumps from his chair.

Azmir treks toward me, but not to me. *Man, what I would do to have him curl his strong arms around me right now.* I've been emotionally crazed for weeks now. Instead, he goes over to the small table in front of one of the built-in bookcases and retrieves his *iPad* mini.

"Your timeline never includes me or my feelings," he grates as he stands, towering over me. The coochie-creaming smile which is now most sinister crests his luscious lips shoot straight to my groin. *Yes! I'm thinking about sex in the same moment I'm fearing my husband's wrath.* This must be the pregnancy. As I'm fighting to keep my tears at bay, all I can think is *he smells delicious.* "But this time I have a say. This time I know you're carrying my baby, and you will not be haphazard about it. No more secrets for you. No more incommunicado decisions. The game has changed."

"Azmir, it's not like that," I try again to get him to reason.

"Oh, really?" he snorts, then he cocks his head to the side and pushes his tongue into his molars. "Is that why you inconspicuously inquired about me counting your cycle? Was that to gauge if I was on to you or not?"

I wet my dry lips with my tongue. My eyes squeezed shut. "Yes and no," I mutter.

"Yes and no..." he repeats, studying my response. His eyes are cold, harsh. "I choked you yesterday! Do you know how fucked up I feel...because you couldn't tell me you're pregnant?"

He then moves behind me and leaves the office. I don't know what he meant by that statement, but I do know I want to hurl over and bawl my eyes out. I feel slighted and ill-targeted. He didn't even let me tell him I wasn't keeping this from him. My shoulders sag as I make my way to the bathroom to shower. I move without motivation and when I arrive at the bed to turn down, I see Azmir isn't in his usual spot in the sitting room, working on his next acquisition while watching several sports channels on one screen. I make it all the way to my pillow before the first tear falls.

love ∞ belvin

The following morning, I'm awakened by faint sounds of clanks and banging. I sit up from the bed and can swear I hear voices out in the hall. I shuffle from beneath the covers, disturbing Azna's sleep, and make my way out the master suite. As my steps progress out of the room, the noise and chatter become louder and clearer.

There are several men dressed in coveralls, holding measuring devices and tools I can't name, coming in and out of the guest bedroom closest to the master suite. One nods as we pass each other. I peek inside the room to see what all the ruckus is about to find it nearly empty, the men stripping it bare. I can't recall Azmir telling me about any repairs being done. Instead of asking the beefy men their business here, I decide to go and look for the man of the house. As I make my way to the front of the apartment, alongside one wall of the corridor, I see at least half a dozen shopping bags with *Vivienne Westwood London* printed across the front in gold. I'm only familiar with the name from Michelle's baby shower. I shake my head and continue my stride.

I don't find him until I'm in the antechamber of the great room. His broad back faces me and I can see from his posture he has one arm wrapped across his abdomen and his other hand pinching his chin. His legs are tall and thick in his stance, clad in basketball shorts and sneakers. I can tell he's been for a run already. *What time is it?* I can tell from his stance he's conversing with someone considerably shorter than he is.

As if he can sense me, he glances over his shoulder, and I can see the mood flip in his eyes the moment he recognizes me. Azmir shifts so I have clear view of the older mocha skinned woman who's wearing fancy medical scrubs. She's somewhat robust and middle-aged. Her smile appears as she registers my presence.

"This must be her," she states rather than question, and I can see her eyes behind her spectacles zooming in on my belly.

I cross my arms over my abdomen, feeling exposed. I'm still in my pajamas and haven't even washed my face yet. There are strangers all throughout the apartment rarely visited by strangers. I notice Azmir's gaze goes soft when it lands on my belly but is hardened once it arrives back at my face. A pang runs through my chest.

"Yes," Azmir confirms. "Ruby Mae, this is my wife, Rayna Jacobs." His intonation is more mechanical than a gushing newlywed, introducing someone to his bride.

"Hi, Mrs. Jacobs! It's a pleasure to meet you two." Her shoulders rise and her upper torso caves in simultaneously, signaling her excitement as she treads towards me and places her hand over my belly.

I flinch and my eyes shoot over to a pensive Azmir who suddenly cannot show me his eyes.

"Azmir, who is this woman?" My tone is curt, and I don't care. I smell something foul in the air.

"This woman, Ruby Mae, is your nurse. She'll be at your healthcare disposal from now until you deliver to ensure optimal health for you and the baby." Azmir's CEO mien appears.

WHAT?

I take a mental breath, not wanting to lose it in a house full of strangers. Azmir is being unreasonable. I really don't know how we've arrived at this battlefield because it's all happened so quickly. I've lost my pace in the race here.

"Why is it necessary for me to have a round-the-clock nurse?" I shake my head, expressing my incredulity.

"Well, given your history of...miscarriage I feel it's necessary," he utters firmly. That stung. Bringing up my past failure is just mean.

"This is ridiculous! I just got rid of one bodyguard only to get another?"

"I'm just doing what's right for the baby," he states coolly.

"And what about what's best for me...for my mental health? Are you concerned about that at all?"

"You have you to look out for," he grates. "I have to look out for me and my child. Somebody has to."

I cup my mouth. Okay, this is on another level. He's waging war. There is no warmth in his tone, no comfort in his sexy baritone.

"Pardon, Mr. Jacobs." One of the construction workers walks up to Azmir and asks, "A word about the flooring..."

Azmir nods and murmurs, "In a minute," rather clinically.

"And who are they? My cell builders?" I sneer.

"No, they're from a boutique in Orange County, stripping and prepping the room for a nursery."

"Nursery?" I gasp. "Azmir, you don't even know my due date. We don't even know the sex of the baby. This is way premature!" I'm feeling light-headed.

"Maybe you should sit down," Ruby Mae takes me softly at my right arm and left shoulder. "You look a little pale." I bite back asking her to remove her hands.

I feel like I'm losing it. My stomach is turning over, my bladder is full, and my head is spinning. I try to take a few breaths before I soil the Italian marble I stand on and corroborate his adamancy of me needing medical care. This isn't my loving and patient A.D. He's turned into someone cold and defensive...against defenseless me. I need his warm arms, not his arctic disregard. His only concern seems to be this baby and not me. A baby I'm still adjusting to having been conceived.

"Azmir, what are we doing?" I sigh while holding my whirling head.

"*I'm* taking control. I have it now...as your husband and the father of that baby," he points to my belly. "I *now* have a say."

"Yes, you do! You've always had a say! I've never challenged that!" I scream.

Ruby Mae gently takes hold of both shoulders now, attempting to push me away from the line of fire. "Mrs. Jacobs, you should really lie down and refrain from overexerting yourself. It can affect the baby."

"You didn't? I'll be damned if you didn't," Azmir continues, ignoring her plea. "Last summer you didn't even tell me I was a father, even if for a few weeks. You took that away from me! You will *not* have that opportunity this time!"

His words sear me. Suddenly, he doesn't regard me as a partner. I'm feeling like someone he has to protect his child from, someone he's protecting himself from. In this instance, his fear is palpable.

"We can work through this together. Alone! You can trust me to do the right thing this time," I beg with Ruby Mae's warm hands, still gripping my shoulders.

"I don't relish taking that risk." His eyes are empty. His voice is unkind. His soul is absent of his words. *This isn't my Azmir.*

I have to think and think quickly. I must change the course of his anger. It has to happen now or we're pretty much doomed. There's no way we can move forward disjointed. This isn't partnership; it's coexisting. I don't want it. Not for me or this man who I love fiercely. I'm desperate now. My mind is running, rapidly flipping through words and phrases to make him see I've changed, and we can do this parenting thing together. I have to get back on the inside of his realm of trust. Now!

"I'm scared, too," I bite out forcefully, just above a whisper.

Azmir slightly jolts in my direction, his luscious mouth goes slack. "I'm afraid the one thing, besides me, you've been consistently clear in desiring, I can't provide." I suck my tears back, afraid of letting them spill only to be rejected. I've always feared his indifference. It's been something he's not been known to express when it comes to me. He's loved me without limits. That's all I know of this man, so in contrast to what I'm feeling in this moment.

"Azmir, I want this. I want to share this experience with you. I want to give you an extension of yourself from my loins. I want to give you the family you haven't had in years. I want this baby to look like you. To persevere like you. To be a warrior just like you. *I want this*. I'm not afraid. Not anymore. Not like before." I choose to quote the lyrics to the Quincy Jones song he shared with me last summer. I now feel it. They've become the theme of my soul regarding our love.

Azmir sucks in a breath and his eyes go wide and stares at me for moments long. I'm panting, beckoning him with my eyes. I feel exhausted and my bladder is now completely full. I don't know what he's thinking, but I have to pee. I also need to eat because I feel my stomach toiling, reminiscent of the morning sickness symptom that have recently let up. I don't want to go back there anymore. I turn and gait down the hallway and into the master suite, swearing if Ruby Mae comes into my bedroom, I'm going to cuss her out.

After using the bathroom, suddenly I feel the need to shower again. I've been in here for a few minutes, soaking my bruised ego when I feel his strong arms encircle my waist. Azmir buries his face in my neck, and I feel the breeze of his cool breath hitting my sensitive skin.

"Where's your crew?" I ask mordantly.

"I've dismissed them all feeling we need to discuss a few things first. I'm sorry," he murmurs quietly. My frame instantly melds into his, warming to his soothing words.

There is silence for long minutes as we stand under multiple cascades, wrapped in each other.

"I'm scared," he eventually speaks hoarsely into my ear.

"I'm scared, too." I feel his arms tense around me.

"You said...out there you weren't afraid," he mentions tentatively.

"I said I'm scared, but I'm not afraid. I'm scared of losing this baby, something you really want. You've always made wanting me seem so simple...making all things right with the world as far as you're concerned. I fear not being able to carry this baby to full-term and give you the first thing you strongly desire from your wife." I turn in his arms to face him. His eyes are soft, and his forehead wrinkled. He's now open, receptive. Vulnerable. "However, I'm *not* afraid of approaching this next frightening stage of my life so long as you're by my side. I can do just about anything with you, here with me. I have the strength I need when I'm here, safely nestled in your arms. I want this baby. With you. For you."

Azmir exhales long and hard, excreting pending emotions I wasn't aware he held within. I can feel the waves of relief lifting from his shoulders.

"It means more than you know to hear that," he utters as he studies my eyes in search of my soul.

"I want it. I also want to eat," I murmur as my eyes fall from his gaze sheepishly. "And I also want to smash...like...a lot. Like now—or perhaps after I eat so I won't get sick." My eyes make their way back to his.

Azmir chuckles beautifully. His panty-snatching smirk has returned.

"I think you should eat first, too." A crease forms between his brows. "You were sick? Was that what—" he's so caught up in his theory, he can't formulate his words.

I shake my head. "No. I *did* catch Lil' E's bug. But then I caught another "suspected" bug I tried to hide from you because I panicked."

"You couldn't tell me? You kept it from me all this time?"

"Your travel made it easy." I kiss his sternum, suddenly feeling like sharing this burden I've carried alone. "I went to the doctor the day Kid passed away." Azmir sucks in a breath. "I didn't get the results then. I left immediately after the call."

"Well, when did you get the news?"

"The day before yesterday."

"*The day before yesterday?*"

"Yes. I had a morning appointment. I'd already given my urine weeks ago and they processed it. The doctor has been calling since for me to come in and chat. I kind of had a clue at that time. My sickness wouldn't let up and I was always tired...still am. She told me in the morning, and I wasn't going to *call* you with the news before coming to terms with it myself first. And I certainly wouldn't announce it to you at the table last night. I guess Erin's new and embarrassing belly-grabbing habit was simply bad timing."

"But Samantha and Yazmine...they seemed to have known," he states, and I know he's confused.

"I don't know," I shrug. "Call it womanly intuition. Maybe she suspected something when I'd spent those days over there."

"But that night we... I pulled out the..."

"I know. The tampon," I nod. "I was spotting, something that isn't rare for pregnant women."

Azmir nods as he sets his ruminative eyes beyond me, processing what I've told him.

"November eleventh," I mutter.

"*Huhn?*"

"That's our due date. November eleventh," I explain.

"That's... Wow!" he sputters. "That's..." Azmir is speechless. There is no thug rhetoric, no airy CEO jargon. Just pure unadulterated jubilation. And I've helped put Azmir in the blissful stupor he's in. I can't fight my smug smile.

"You sure you don't want to keep Ruby Mae on? I mean, maybe the first trimester...until we know you're good," he offers.

"I don't want to think about having another chaperone around right now. I don't have the energy to take that on." I wrap my arms around his neck. "Right now I want you to feed me, smash me, and put me back to bed."

I can feel his erection pushing into my belly as I stand on my toes and cover his lips with my own.

Azmir groans. "*Mmmm*... But I won't hurt the baby, will I?"

"No!" I snap. "But I will hurt *you* if you don't take me. And no kiddie gloves."

"No choking either," he counters.

I concede, using his coined phrase, "Indeed."

love belwin

"And this is one of my best friends from *Duke*. Rayna Jacobs and her renowned husband, Azmir Jacobs," April beams as she stands with her new husband and in-laws.

April's round belly is protruding far from her tiny frame as she unabashedly gleams in her gorgeous wedding gown. Her well-practiced smile is expectant. I know April well enough to conceive she's nervous as all get out in front of the pastor and first lady who are now her parents-in-law. First Lady Greene is wearing a smile not ascending to her hazel eyes. She can't stand April, this I know. She believes April has embarrassed their family with this illegitimate pregnancy.

"Pastor and First Lady Greene," I greet as I take shake their hands. "This has been an absolute pleasure. The day has been gorgeous. Congratulations on the success of it." I then turn to April and Gerald. "Biggest congrats to the bride and groom for standing against all adversities and taking the ultimate pledge of partnership before God, your family, and friends. Gerald, you've chosen an awesome wife."

I fight the chuckle in my throat. April clears her as she straightens her neck. She knows I'm stirring the pot.

"Mr. Jacobs, Pastor John has said such great things about you. He brags as though you're blood." Pastor Greene proffers his hand to Azmir, totally moving past my comedic moment. Thankfully. "We have to have lunch some time. He says you're quite the conversationalist," he continues to charm.

Shaking his hand, Azmir nods with that coochie-creaming smile which seems to have caught the attention of First Lady Greene. I see the sensual slit in her eyes. The poised woman has almond skin, is clad in chiffon, donning perfectly coiffed hair, and cannot seem to get enough eye time in with my husband. I suppress my snicker.

"Oh," she trills. "This is the young man John was referring to. Hmmmm..." she cocks her head to the side, supplying a crocked smile. "Yes, we must do dinner—or lunch..." she corrects herself quickly. "...soon."

"Sure," Azmir agrees obliviously. "I'll have my wife sort out the details with the new Mrs. Greene to make it happen." His big hand slides to cover my round belly. "You know these expectant women are particular with their food preference nowadays, don't you, Gerald?" Azmir invites a pensive Gerald into the conversation. Poor Gerald has appeared withdrawn since circling the room with his parents. I suspect it's because their pregnancy has caused a rift in the family.

Gerald nervously nods as he smiles down at April's belly. First Lady Greene humphs and walks away, leaving her husband to regretfully excuse himself before following on her heels. Gerald follows and April is behind them, but not before we snicker together, and she thanks me for bringing Erin to the wedding.

Erin is the flower girl and since Amber wasn't invited, I was asked to bring her. It, of course, delighted me, it meant more time with my baby girl.

Once we're alone at the table, I turn to Azmir. "Well, Jacobs, looks like this shindig is about over." My voice turns husky, "What now?"

Azmir smirks that panty-snatching smirk as he recognizes my undertone. I've been antsy all evening, dying to get my hands on him, his mouth on me, his strongman—

"Now we get you out of these heels. They've been worrying me since we left the marina, little girl. Then we find Erin," he halts my randy thoughts. "Remember, you're carrying the weight of three, not two," Azmir admonishes.

I'm nearing my second trimester and I've been insanely horny since telling Azmir about this pregnancy. He's been tolerating my bestial hormones and crazy demands for sex—and rough sex—the whole time. It's been most insane with my body constantly craving him, even during work. Oh, my god, poor Peg. She must have endured disruption of work from my lewd cries on at least a half a dozen occasions. I was nearly caught with Azmir in my mouth in the pool room at my job. If it weren't for the delay in the light switch, poor Sharon would've caught an indecent show. Azmir mumbles profanity under his breath each time after we carry on in public, swearing to no more of it. However, each time I accost him for more, he doesn't seem to be able to resist my pheromonal callings.

We learned at my second appointment, at the end of April, we're expecting twins. I nearly passed out there on the table. Azmir was thrown into a daze, but quickly recovered with excitement. He couldn't believe he'll be getting a full fledge family our first go round. Eventually, I accepted it as *one and done*. While each day since my morning sickness phase has been pleasant, I don't think I'll be one of those women who doesn't mind being pregnant.

Just last week, on Azmir's birthday, over dinner on Malibu Beach, he presented me with the blueprint for a new construction of our home in Orange County. It was bittersweet. I love the marina. It's the place where his class and elegance were made soundly clear to me. But I also understand it has more of a sexy air to it than a familial one. We need to prepare for our pending family. After sensing my hesitance, Azmir agreed we'd hold off on selling the apartment until I was ready. I told him it would be ridiculous. Keeping both properties—and not to mention the other properties Azmir owns that I've yet to visit—would be superfluous. He issued his smirk and said, *"I've told you, I like superfluity. I've earned it and now you'll have to adjust to it as well,"* melting me instantly.

After dropping Erin off, we headed back to the marina, enjoying a quiet ride home. My mind is busy, churning over revelations I've collected over the past year since my life has been flipped, turned upside down. Azmir and I make love, sweet and impassioned. He's attentive to my condition, too attentive, but he's improving. I'm continuously reminding him he doesn't have to be delicate, that I'll tell him when it's too much. I guess being a soon-to-be father has him extremely cautious already.

After I shower and leave Azmir to his sports channels, I go out to the balcony off the master suite and take in the nighttime marina. The lights are bouncing off the water, the boats swaying just off the dock. It's a quiet evening, the view is most inspiring, and my spirit is calm. The picturesque view reminds me of how fortunate I am, something I could argue the opposite of just two short years ago. My life hasn't been perfect. I've struggled with pain, betrayal, belonging, trust, and even anger. I was headed down a road of self-exile and willingly because I was too afraid to open my heart. I didn't understand love, so I certainly didn't love myself enough; I'd only functioned in survival. Survival was easy because when you fight to survive the only person you have to consider is yourself.

When I left home for school, I'd only thought of my well-being, preserving *me*. When I came to California, I put myself through graduate school and even irresponsibly borrowed money to suit me. I dated men and even took on sexual relationships with them to satisfy *my* wants, thinking I was receiving gratification in those acts. I only let Michelle into my life exclusively, my heart exclusively to protect *me* from more betrayal.

However, when I met Azmir, I soon discovered the act of reciprocity. Something in me was so drawn to him, I felt things unfamiliar, and he kept pushing me into a sphere which forced me to recognize the possibility of living a life that goes beyond survival. A world where I have to give someone else something I've been lacking for so long—unconditional love. Before I could fully embrace it with him, I had to go seek the original Source first, though. I needed to learn more about love and all it entails. And I'm still learning.

Love encompasses so much. Though one of my biggest lessons is it is unconditional. You don't run from, or shun, or scrutinize love. You embrace it and cherish it.

And though all these years I knew it was a possible, I now know love's improbable possibility.

EPILOGUE

Azmir

"Mrs. J, let's go!" I call out from the base of the spiral staircase.

I've been waiting for nearly thirty minutes. The idea was for her to quickly shower, slip on the dress and shoes I've laid aside for her, and be ready to roll. It wasn't that detailed of a plan. We just left the twins' preschool graduation party and stopped at home to get dressed for an adult outing.

Shit!

I'm reminded she possibly can't hear me from down here. I had this ten thousand square foot home built in Orange County. Rarely is it this quiet with two toddlers, a nanny, and house staff running around, but tonight everyone is out or off, giving me much needed alone time with this slow ass woman!

I go for the phone in the foyer and page the master suite, "Little girl, if you don't bring your sweet little—"

"Chill out, Jacobs," I hear her mumble from behind me.

I slowly turn towards the steps and see her smoothing her dress. There's a twinge of nervousness in her eyes although her scowl is fixed. That aside, Rayna is gliding gracefully down the stairs in five-inch *Sergio Rossis*. Her toned thighs, which are somewhat glistening, hook my attention as she takes the last step and hits the marble floor.

"Goddamn..." I mutter.

"Hey!" she chides. "You've been getting better with the language!"

"I know..." I admit apologetically while my eyes flutter. I've got to get myself together.

"Last week at church, little Dasu told his friend he's the fucking man. Who do you suppose he got that phrase from?"

I arch a brow. "Well, I am the fuckin' man. You know this. And he's my legacy."

"Azmir, baby," she drags out exhaustedly and pinches the bridge of her nose.

"Let's go, Mrs. Jacobs. We're late, thanks to your diva antics." I go to grab her hand. I can't say what I'm really feeling...that if I keep looking at her in this dress and shoes, we may not make it out of here.

"Wait!" she exclaims. I turn back to see her shifting in her dress, once again smoothing it down. "Do you think this is too much...like...for a mom...of two?" she asks timidly.

The dress fits her like second skin, just as I want it to. Rayna curves are on full display, reminding me of how hard she's worked to regain her body after the twins. She keeps a tight workout regime and eats conscientiously. I never complained about the weight she put on right after the kids. Shit, she carried three people on her feet for nearly nine months. Who was I to tell her how to get motivated? I didn't have to. After the kids turned one, Rayna began working on herself rigorously. I couldn't believe the determination she put forth to get back down to her pre-pregnancy size within a year. By the time the kids turned three, Rayna was back to herself.

"Absolutely not," I answer and take her by the hand, successfully this time. As we're approaching the door I inform, "You look like the wife of a luckiest son of a bitch around."

I hear Rayna suck in a breath. "Azmir!"

On the ride to our destination, we're both quiet. I have no idea what Rayna's thinking about, but I'm anxious about this "news" she has to share with me. Rayna has solidified herself as my life partner over the last five years. She's never tried to run since learning about my former profession. She's been a devoted mother to our son, Dasu Azmir, and daughter, Kennedy Michelle. So devoted I have to do things in the fashion of what I'm doing tonight, stealing her away from them for her undivided attention.

Rayna's also been a warrior for me, like when an indie documentary hit the streets last summer by D-Struct's best friend suggesting my former role as a kingpin. The premise of it was how aspiring rappers get into the game today versus ten years ago. The documentary included how to do a demo, to marketing, to signing with a major label, to funding, and that's where I'm highlighted for four minutes and sixteen seconds as a drug lord with investments resources. It was totally fabricated, loosely woven together. I've never funded anyone's career, only lent out cars and jewelry for shoots. That forty-five-minute short film caught the attention of urban radio stations and bloggers. His inch of validity was a former dope acquaintance of mine, Black, who went missing just before my trip to New York six years ago when I took Rayna with me to reunite with my mother. There were even rumors about *HBO* picking it up.

Needless to say, last summer was one of the most trying periods of my life. Although Chesney was on it right away, I feared Rayna's flight habit resurging. However, she didn't waver. Instead, she arranged for our family to be packed and off for a two-week vacation, all in the span of eight hours. The twins were discharged with their grandmothers and Chyna to Hawaii while Rayna and I headed the opposite direction to the Caribbean. Rayna stealthily kept Chesney and his team on course while she tended to me with hours of lovemaking and tourist excursions to bide the time for the scandal to blow over. I was concerned about her being away from the kids for so long. She's so attached to them. However, Rayna never uttered a word of complaint, just stuck by my side. And when we returned home, by way of some rare miracle, things had blown over. Rayna was absolutely amazing.

But I'm still nervous when she says *we have to talk*. I can't imagine what about. As I look over to her, she's staring out the window, seemingly just as pensive as I am right now. I go with the silence because I'm just happy to be back at home with her after two weeks of being away. I've missed the hell out of her.

We pull up to *Mahogany* and the marquee reads:

Mahogany welcomes Raheem DeVaughn.

"Wow," Rayna mutters. "Mark got Raheem DeVaughn again? I haven't seen him since my first time here."

As soon as we entered, we were greeted by Mark. He's wearing a goofy grin.

"Well, if it isn't my favorite couple, Mr. and Mrs. Jacobs!" He welcomes.

"Hey, Mark," Rayna says as she receives him with a hug. She then moves forward to scope out the place. It's nearly comical to see her turn each thirty-degree angle inspective, as if she's going to find something new. "The place is empty."

"Yes," Mark quirks. "Jacobs here has bought out the spot for you two this evening. How 'bout that, huhn! Please," he bows. "Enjoy your time at *Mahogany*."

Rayna's bemused eyes travel to me. "Really?"

I don't answer, at least not verbally. I just stare at her until she makes it clear she understands. A waiter then greets her and takes her to the private booth where we'll be dining. It's the same booth we sat in the first time we came here on a date. I turn to follow when Mark takes me at the arm.

"What's up with the bag, dude?" He gestures to the large shopping bag Ray was able to quietly pass off to me once Rayna was making her way inside.

I follow his inquisitive gaze to the bag. "Ain't shit that concerns you."

"Holy fuck!" Mark yelps as he pulls out his phone and starts to type rapidly into it. "I'm telling Eric you're going to try for a little romp with Rayna tonight here in the club, you freaky motherfucker! That's why you've paid nearly double than I would've made on an ordinary night for privacy!" he lowers his phone when, I presume, he's done. "Why didn't you do it at *Cobalt* or your new jazz club on the beach?

"First of all, you goddamn prick, I have no plans to fuck my wife in a public place," I bite out, lying through my damn teeth. I've had Rayna in quite a few public places. "And secondly, this place has some sentimental value for her. Remember your re-opening? I scored points from the ambiance."

Adjusting his glasses, he sings, "*Ahhhhh*... So, that's when you first got a taste, huhn?" he wiggles his brows. *Fucking cornball.* "So, I, Mark Richardson, assisted the great A.D. Jacobs with getting ass that he eventually marries, aye! I like that." His phone apparently vibrates in his hand. He reads it and then laughs. "Eric says he bets you your *Lakers* season tickets that Rayna will not let your black ass lay a finger on her in here tonight. I'll lower my bet for two trips on your cabin cruiser with my new dame."

I shake my head and walk off. *These clowns always want to call a fucking bet.*

"Hey!" Mark calls from behind me. "It's clear I have more faith in you with my smaller wager!"

As I make my way to her at the booth, I can still see Rayna is a bit absorbed. A smile lifts from her face as she looks up and finds me advancing towards her.

"What's in the bag?" she finally inquires.

"A surprise."

"You really bought out the place for us?"

"For you," I answer as the waiter approaches the table.

He doesn't take our order because I've already arranged it, but he does ask for our drink order and informs us the show will start momentarily.

When he leaves for the kitchen, Rayna asks, "Why would you pay for an exclusive show when we can't even see the stage?"

"We don't have to see to experience the music. I only want to see you and have you see me. How are you?"

Rayna sighs, "Okay, I guess...actually great...I hope."

"Are you feeling some kind of way about me barbarically dragging you away from the twins' party tonight?"

I flew in this morning, just hours before their graduation, cohosted the party, and now I've snatched her up...to be alone. I've grown to be very demanding of her time.

"No," she breathes out. "You're the one who planned that ridiculously over-the-top affair for a pair of five-year-olds. Once again, they've outdone their friends, Azmir."

I shrug unapologetically. My kids have and will always have the very best in life. I busted my ass even when they weren't in the cards for me. Just like Rayna, I will give them the world I've abound.

"It is what it is," is all I offer. "Hey, you see Akeem getting down with the tots on the dance floor?" I chuckled.

"Yes!" Rayna joins in, and I've successfully navigated the conversation. "According to Kennedy, he's the best uncle ever!" she laughs. "I'm glad you're mentoring him, Azmir. I can only imagine where his spirits would be in if you hadn't been here, offering him opportunities."

Akeem was released two years ago. Integrating him into our lives was met cautiously by me. Learning of his pending release months in advance conjured bittersweet feelings. I knew Rayna had been emotionally tied to him all these years and would do anything she could to assist him in the next phase of his life. However, I didn't know shit about him and couldn't gauge if I wanted him to have said access to my wife. So, I had to dive in headfirst and introduce myself before his release.

I met with him several times while he was finishing up his bid. I didn't know the young dude and almost expected him to have been institutionalized from being locked up for so long. The first thing that struck me was he was gang-free. I couldn't have that shit around my family. Akeem was angry however, but not senseless. He's certainly been amenable to my pushing of him becoming an entrepreneur. He's had to. Akeem has a criminal record which would be hard to explain to potential employers.

So, I had him enroll in a GED program then business school immediately after being released. I then had him rotate a few of my businesses as an employee to find his niche. Once he decided on something I don't exactly have the corner market on, which is fashion retail, I had him draw up a business plan and we are now at the stage of opening his first boutique in Miami. He loves it down there; the energy, the contrast in climate and the women, of course. He flew in for the twins' graduation today.

"Indeed," I nod. The waiter returns with our drinks; *Mauve* for me and Riesling I ordered for Rayna. "Akeem has been a wonderful addition to our fold. This boutique is going to be a good look for the homey."

"Erin had me cracking up tonight, playing big sister. Did you see her orchestrate the soul train line like she really knows about it!" Rayna laughs and I chuckle myself. Erin's very fond of the twins. She takes joy in bossing them around as if she's so much older. It's cute to watch.

"Chyna seems to be doing well. I think she's going to start her graduate program this fall. I hope." Rayna says before taking a sip of her water.

Huhn...

"She'll find her way," I murmur before going for my *Mauve*.

I hear the staccato of the high-hat and realize the show is starting. The entertainer introduces himself and transitions into his first cut, *Desire*. Rayna's face lights up.

"This is nice, Mr. Jacobs."

I nod. Our first course is brought out and we go into our usual banter about the twins, work, and friends. Rayna has developed a tight relationship with April and Britni. So tight, it came to a point where Britni had to end her relationship with Lady Spin. Rayna never asked her to, but apparently, it was becoming a conflict of interest for Britni, and she decided to make a call. Britni along with April, Gerald, and their children attended the party earlier. All of my crew was in attendance as well. Petey, Kim, and Chanell spoil Dasu and Kennedy. I'm not all that in touch with Syn, though she's a shift manager at my new jazz club and seems to be doing much better. She's even laying off the bottle. Wop has his own car repair business and seems to be content with that aside from his hustle.

"Our world has truly come together, huhn?" I ask.

"What do you mean?" Rayna asks after swallowing her water.

"Remember right after you had the twins and we were still living at the marina, you fired Ruby Mae and Louise, saying you didn't need the luxury of a nanny and housekeeper? You said you and Akeem are only eleven months apart and Samantha managed you just fine without a nanny, housekeeper and chef?"

Rayna rolls her eyes embarrassingly. "Yeah, and that lasted all of four days. I thought I was going to lose my mind. The feedings, diaper changes, burping, soothing—"

"...times three," I interject.

"Yup," she slowly nods her head, with a roguish grin. "Can't forget how demanding you are. I still can't believe the way you made a big deal about wanting to taste my breast milk, Azmir. Who knew you were competitive of my time and body, even with *your* kids," she chides.

Yup! I was and still am. I could never share with my goons how I threw a hissy fit each time I saw my wife breasting feeding our helpless newborns, all because they were experiencing something from her body, I never had...until I pushed for it. I glance across the table to see Rayna shaking her head exasperatingly, obviously reminiscing about it internally just as I am.

"Anyway, I don't know what I'd do without the help we have, including our mothers. They've been so great. I know they're getting up there in age..." Rayna sounds like she's about to cry.

"Hey," I reach over for her hand. "They have the energy for their grandchildren. Samantha's health is holding out, and you can't tell Yazmine she isn't just six years older than she was when she went in the pen. They're having the time of their lives with the twins."

Rayna fights down a cry as she nods her head convincingly. Her nose has even turned red.

"I know," she whispers. She's been very sensitive lately.

We continue our meal with more lighthearted conversations over the romantic crooning. The music is great. My buzz sets in as Rayna chats animatedly about everything and nothing at all. This is exactly the place I was aiming for when I coordinated this evening—well, *almost*.

I'm over the forty-year-old hill now, still in shape, still working hard in all my businesses, including *Global Fusion*. I'm now co-owner of *Mauve*. After just a year of my well-strategized endorsement, sales of the product went through the roof, as I predicted. Therefore, I successfully purchased enough shares to have a seat at the table. And before other investors could catch the trend, I purchased enough shares, buying them out to have a majority over the Moreau brothers.

Big D is still in prison. He was sentenced to eighteen years. I heard from him a few times, just after his arrest, but he eventually got the memo that I'm no longer a part of his life. Tara's doing well from what I hear. She's dating a music producer. The first year after her father's incarceration and her daughter's father's death was hard on her. She would text me from time to time, venting. Rayna would see the texts, but never flexed.

Once Rayna texted back, letting Tara know it was her who was messaging her and invited Tara to reach out if she needed a listening ear. Crazy, right? I thought so myself. But it came as no surprise to me. Rayna has come such a long way since entering my boardroom. She's far more secure in my world and with herself. Tara took her up on her offer. They did two playdates with the kids before mutually deciding it was best they left the children out of their association. Apparently, Tara couldn't get past seeing my children by another woman. Rayna didn't trip, she's never had desires to be friends with Tara, just an associate if she needed a shoulder to cry on—a shoulder that isn't mine.

Not much in my life has changed over the past five years, especially my incredibly magnetic draw to this woman. Rayna has been much more than I propositioned her for in a wife. She's strong, loving, consistent, nurturing, and sexy as hell. And I can't forget stubborn as hell. Though only part-time, Rayna still works. She took off a year after having the twins. When she decided to return, she quickly realized full-time employment was a hefty load for a woman with twin children and a demanding husband who travels heavily. She eventually recommended Amber to assume the role of assistant supervisor in the LBC branch of their practice. Crazy, too, right? *Yup.* But that's my new and improved Rayna. Her bosses bought it so long as she stayed on as the supervisor to offset Amber's lack of experience, *as if Rayna had so much when she started as supervisor*. Rayna does more administrative work than attending. She's worked out a three-day work schedule with two administration days and one attending day. She's content with that and I've...*learned to live with it.*

As our table is cleared from our dessert course, we talk, and I observe my wife's glowing caramel skin. When she dips her head back in laughter, my groin tingles.

"You remember the first orgasm I gave you?" I ask abruptly.

Rayna quickly draws in a breath. I'm happy out my ass I still have this effect on my wife. It does a lot for my ego which seems to incline to her more the older I get.

"The one you gave while you touched me or when I was alone?"

"You masturbate without me?"

Rayna giggles bashfully, still shying at conversations of sexual nature. "No...well, once when we were in Mexico the first time."

Shit. My cock twitches beneath the table.

"For real?" I'm intrigued.

She nods as she tries to suppress the mirth in her embarrassment.

"Ain't that some shit," I muse.

Things get quiet as Raheem belts out notes about the "Four Letter Word" *L-o-v-e*. I take in the romantic atmosphere during the bridge he repeats. Rayna leans back and sighs contently. Her gaze eventually rotates the alcove of the booth to meet mine across the table, which is almost bare, but for our drinks. We find ourselves caught up in each other's gaze. Rayna's mood isn't so ruminative anymore. She's now someplace else.

"Show me."

"*H*-huhn?" she sputters.

I incline in my seat, take a swig of brandy, and instruct. "Show me how you touched yourself in Puerto Vallarta. And if you're good, I'll show you what I really wanted to do to you here, the night of the re-opening."

Rayna's eyes bounce between mine, trying to process my suggestion. Then she observes the table and large partition surrounding our well-nestled booth.

Her eyes go dark, and I see her chest rise. "You planned this," she deduces rather than questions, in a husky tone.

Again, I don't answer verbally. I stared into her beautiful face, challenging her obedience. There's a tentative pause, but soon after, Rayna's head tilts to observe her dress and then she slowly boards the table, positioning herself before me. She lies down with her legs slightly parted and her toes inches away from my abdomen.

"Open and show me," I hear the groan in my order.

Slowly and nervously, Rayna parts her legs and I see her treasure, neatly manicured and partially hidden behind thongs. I reach up and rip them in two to remove the obstruction of my view. Rayna's breathing increases. I glance up to her face and see her bottom lip between her teeth.

"Show me!"

She drags her right hand between her legs, pushing through her labia. My eyes collapse at the sight of her arousal. *Fucking beautiful.* Rayna's hands rove purposefully between her lips and eventually exclusively on her tight bud. When her hips start to gyrate, I rise up, reach over to the top of her dress, at her cleavage, and pull down the zipper. Rayna's eyes pop open and so does her globes. They sit perky and I can see they're pebbled at the apex. I see her lick her lips.

"Keep going," I growl.

And she does.

I lick her breasts around her bra, not wanting to release them just yet. I stroke my tongue down to her flat abdomen and moan at her belly button when I get the first whiff of her feminine aroma. Things are getting hectic. There is one too many people tending to her pussy; namely her. Gently, I swipe her hand away as I take back to my seat and bury my face between her thighs. Rayna's moans are not that quiet, but unsuccessfully rival the music.

This is exactly where I had planned to be when I organized this date with my wife. I'm growing to hate my travel. At first, it served as a healthy break for the two of us, at the very least. However, now that I have a full family and life has changed for Rayna and me, I feel like I need her even more if that's possible. Since having the twins, she regularly surprises me with pop up visits when their schedule permits. She throws the kids and nanny on a plane and surprises me, sometimes lying in my hotel bed naked...or the dining room table of the suite, coincidentally, this is how she was able to easily assume the position tonight. My desire for Rayna still burns wickedly.

"Ahhhhh! Azmiiiii—"

And when she moans my name in ecstasy like this as she claws the back of my head, I have no doubt that this woman is mine and I made the right decision chasing her each time I did all those years ago. Rayna detonates deliciously in my face and trembles in a fit, reminding me there is no better place for me to be. I slow my lapping while she comes down. When I pull back, I look over to her and find her chest still rising and falling viciously. Her face is flushed and it's clear to me she's in her zone. I know it'll only be seconds before she's ready.

Rayna leaps upward, grabs the sides of my face and throws her tongue into my mouth, devouring me. I let her take her time tasting herself on me. She eventually reaches down to undo my belt and pants without removing her lips. *My little minx.* I assist her, preparing to give her what she's asking for. I manage my pants down, just enough for my cock to spring out, and before I know it, Rayna sinks down on me. I stifle my groan, her not so much.

Quickly, I glimpse over to her glass of wine which is untouched. She starts with cautioned plunges to acclimate herself to me. Eventually her grinding turns wild and so does her tongue, lashing through my mouth. I feel her thighs clamp around me, her breathing growing desperate, her cries are feverish. I'm caught up immediately, pushing my pelvis into her, giving her all I have. I grip her ass to being sure to fill her to the hilt.

Goddamn, we have to do this live music thing again!

Rayna's walls constrict around me and I piston into her frame like a lunatic, I can't stop if I wanted to. I feel my heart about to beat out of my chest. I feel my orgasm tip well before I'm used to. *Fuck!* This is the crazy spin she puts me into, only tonight drives me into more of an intense whirl.

My mind literally dizzies as I sputter, *"I—I... I'm—"*

"I'm coming!" she pushes directly into my ear as my ass lifts and dips on the bench.

I feel my orgasm all the way in my ass, which has only happened a number of times. Very rarely. Rayna is still gyrating on top of me, though at a much slower rate, dragging out the last of her release as she clutches my head with her breasts buried into my face.

My head is trying to slow its spin, but before it's able to, I blurt, "You're fuckin' pregnant, Rayna?"

Her clutch onto me intensifies. Within seconds, I feel her neck nod against my head.

If I could slow my breathing, I'd let out a long sigh. It all makes sense now; her pensiveness over the past couple of weeks—even over the phone, her elusiveness, her not touching her drink. She's pregnant, and something deep down believes she wanted me to figure it out, taking the easy route. This concerns me.

"Why couldn't you just tell me?"

I can hear the whining in my delivery. I don't want her regressing to not verbally communicating and me having to use her body to tell me things her mouth can't. I peel her off my head and shoulders so I can see her face. She's sulking as if she's going to cry.

"Answer me!" my words shoot out harsher than I intend for them to.

"I—I was. I just couldn't decide when would be the best time," she murmurs apologetically.

"Wouldn't that have been when you found out? What's the big deal with just telling me that you're expecting?" I'm growing frustrated. "Did you miss a pill?

She shakes her head as bites her bottom lip.

"Well, what the hell happened, baby?"

Rayna's eyes go all around, but don't seem to want to focus on me.

"Rayna!"

"I didn't miss a pill!" she nearly shouts impatiently.

"Well, what the *fu*—"

"I stopped taking them. Okay!"

"Why would you do something like that? I thought you didn't want more kids."

I'm so lost right now. When the twins turned two, I expressed I wanted more children and Rayna protested and adamantly. I dropped the issue, seeing that she'd put such effort into getting her body back.

"That was before...when I didn't want more..." her voice trails off and she buries her face in my neck.

"More what?"

"More of you."

Okay, now I'm really confused.

"You have all of me. Always."

"No, but this is different. When we got pregnant before, it was an accident. I wanted the experience of trying to conceive as your wife. I feel like that strengthens our bond...like it makes us closer, you know? I *want* a baby now, not just to accept being pregnant at an awkward time. I like you as a daddy. I want more of it, and Dasu and Kennedy are getting so big so fast. I don't want this phase of our partnership to fly by so quickly. I want more. With you."

My chest tightens. I hate to see her so emotional. If she wanted another baby, I wouldn't have had a problem giving it to her.

"Are you happy?" I ask.

"About the baby? I'm ecstatic. About your reception, I don't know," she answers.

"I'm happy if this is what you want."

She lifts her head to gaze into my eyes. "Well, why did you react so harshly moments ago?" It's Rayna's turn to whine now.

"Because it's hard to learn of some crazy woman stealing your seeds for her own agenda. That has to be illegal," I mock.

Rayna laughs, one of her lighthearted laughs I love supplying.

"Seriously, I wouldn't have fucked you in public, in a booth had

I known. I wouldn't have put you in an easy access dress and killer heels either."

Rayna's eyes are smoldering in an instant. "I like the way you set me up tonight. It makes me feel like a M.I.L.F.," she groans.

"Yeah, you're the only mother I like to fuck, and I will be the *only* in the reverse as well, little girl."

Rayna laughs again. I reach over into the shopping back to get a few cloths to clean us up. Rayna is softly snoring before I'm done. *How could I have missed this for a second time?* I wrap her up in the big housecoat I brought along and then zip myself back up. Within seconds, I'm lifting Rayna in the air.

"I'm sorry, orgasms make me sleepy when I'm pregnant," Rayna mumbles on a yawn.

"Well, maybe I can arrange another one in the back of the car that will ensure you'll sleep through the night," I murmur as we're exiting through the rear of the club.

"I don't think so, Jacobs. We didn't bring the limo tonight."

"My car. My pussy."

"Indeed," she says and is out again before we're inside the car. *Cute.*

The end.
XXX

~LOVE ACKNOWLEDGES

Love's Betas - My first official audience. Kelly Anderson, Tondalaya DeShields, Shantel Hansford, Angela Jennings, Yorubia Ardell Belvin, and Juaquanna Gaines-Sams, thanks for being one of the first steps in pursuing my dream. Wanna sign up for the next project? Get in now before I blow! LOL!! (*I'm not entirely kidding here*)

Love's Promoters: Thank you to all of my family and friends for your assistance in promoting the L.I.P. series. Juaquanna, Angela, Karmen, Tondi, Zakiya, and other #TeamLB members, I alone couldn't do it. Special thanks to Brandy of ***Momma's Books*** for your tireless resources! You've schooled me on so much in this #IndieFictionalWorld! Can't wait to return the love! Thanks to all the bloggers who have assisted in sharing L.I.P.!

And my fellow-L.I.P.'ers... OMGee!! You guys have increased over the past few months and remind me that the trips to the recesses of my mind aren't only for my entertainment; I'm connecting with others, too! As of today (April 17th, 2014) your number isn't so great that I don't know who you are individually. I will never forget the notes, the pushes to continue, the requests for release dates, the emails, tweets, inboxes and love on IG. You guys have made my dreams come true already. I hope to continue to connect with you on future projects.

Marcus Broom of DPI Designs: Thanks for your talented artistry on the L.I.P. covers. Can't wait for the next cover!

Tanya Keetch - The Word Maid: Thank you for being such a warm spirit! And my best to you in all your endeavors. ~wink~

In-house editor: Zakiya Walden of **I've Got Something to Say Incorporated**. I can't say enough how my first published project would not have been as smooth a ride without your commitment. You have been so awesome throughout this entire process. You're definitely the brain behind my big my massive mess of a canvass. Thanks for your dedication.

Tina V. Young: Thanks so much for helping me comb through this baby for a good cleaning. I'm sure we'll do it again. LOL!!

Juaquanna: (THANKS!) Girl, I've lost some and gained others. If you stay put, I'll be good to you. That is all (*read between the lines*)!

MDT: First project down, God willing, countless more to go. Thanks for being **everything**! "*And we March...*"

To my **Master**, my *Jireh*, my **Rohi**, Amen (*It is well with my soul*).

~FYI

Intrigued by Azmir's friend, Jackson?
Find out more about him in **Love's Inconvenient Truth**!

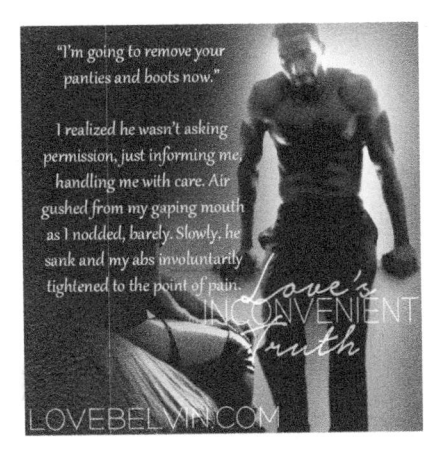

> "I'm going to remove your panties and boots now."
>
> I realized he wasn't asking permission, just informing me, handling me with care. Air gushed from my gaping mouth as I nodded, barely. Slowly, he sank and my abs involuntarily tightened to the point of pain.
>
> *Love's Inconvenient Truth*
> LOVEBELVIN.COM

#PenningWithoutParameters
#ImGonnaMakeYouLoveMe

~OTHER BOOKS BY LOVE BELVIN

Love's Improbable Possibility series:
Love Lost, Love UnExpected, Love UnCharted & **Love Redeemed**

The Letter (from Michelle to Azmir)

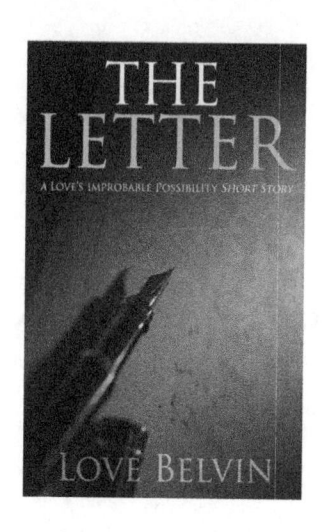

Waiting to Breathe series:
Love Delayed & **Love Delivered**

Love's Inconvenient Truth (Standalone)

Love Unaccounted series:
In Covenant with Ezra, In Love with Ezra & **Bonded with Ezra**

The Connecticut Kings series:
Love in the Red Zone, *Love on the Highlight Reel, *Determining Possession, End Zone Love, Love's Ineligible Receiver, *Pass Interference, Love's Encroachment, *Offensive Formations (*by Christina C. Jones), and Love's Neutral Zone.

Wayward Love series:
The Left of Love, The Low of Love _& The Right of Love_

Love in Rhythm & Blues series
*The Rhythm of Blues **&** The Rhyme of Love*

The Sadik series:
He Who Is a Friend, He Who Is a Lover & He Who Is a Protector

The Muted Hopelessness series:
My Muted Love, Our Muted Recklessness, & Our Reckless Hope

The Prism series:
<u>Mercy</u>, Grace, & The Promise

<u>Low Love, Low Fidelity</u> (Standalone)

LOVE BELVIN
low
love
low
fidelity
LOVE BELVIN
low
love
low
fidelity

~EXTRA

You can find Love Belvin at www.LoveBelvin.com
Facebook @ Author - Love Belvin
Twitter @LoveBelvin
Goodreads: Love Belvin
and on Instagram @LoveBelvin

Join the #TeamLove mailing list to keep up with the happenings of Love Belvin here!

Made in the USA
Middletown, DE
12 May 2025